Olga Bardel by Stacy Aumonier

Stacy Aumonier was born at Hampstead Road near Regent's Park, London on 31st March 1877.

He came from a family with a strong and sustained tradition in the visual arts; sculptors and painters.

On leaving school it seemed the family tradition would also be his career path. In particular his early talents were that of a landscape painter. He exhibited paintings at the Royal Academy in the early years of the twentieth century.

In 1907 he married the international concert pianist, Gertrude Peppercorn, at West Horsley in Surrey. A year later Aumonier began a career in a second branch of the arts at which he enjoyed a short but outstanding success—as a stage performer writing and performing his own sketches.

The Observer newspaper commented that "...the stage lost in him a real and rare genius, he could walk out alone before any audience, from the simplest to the most sophisticated, and make it laugh or cry at will."

In 1915, Aumonier published a short story 'The Friends' which was well received (and was subsequently voted one of the 15 best stories of 1915 by the Boston Magazine, Transcript).

Despite his age in 1917 at age 40 he was called up for service in World War I. He began as a private in the Army Pay Corps, and then transferred as a draughtsman in the Ministry of National Service.

By now he had four books published—two novels and two books of short stories—and his occupation is recorded with the Army Medical Board as 'author.'

In the mid-1920s, Aumonier received the shattering diagnosis that he had contracted tuberculosis. In the last few years of his life, he would spend long spells in various sanatoria, some better than others.

Shortly before his death, Stacy Aumonier sought treatment in Switzerland, but died of the disease in Clinique La Prairie at Clarens beside Lake Geneva on 21st December 1928. He was 55.

Index of Contents

OLGA BARDEL

BOOK I

PROLOGUE

BRAILLE'S PORTRAIT

It was delightful meeting Braille again after so many years. For some reason or other I had been to a smoking concert in connection with a hospital, and afterwards had adjourned with several doctors to a very gloomy club in St. James's. Now doctors are the dearest chaps in the world; but when they get together, and have one or two drinks and start talking shop, they are apt to make one feel uncomfortable. I had made some excuse and quitted their society, and I must say that I felt very relieved to get out into the air. As I was going round the corner of Jermyn Street I ran into Braille.

I had not seen Braille since we were at the Beaux Arts together, which was remarkable inasmuch as at that time we were inseparable. I forget the exact questions that had caused a final estrangement between us, but I believe that a series of differences in connection with housework may have brought matters to a head.

As far as I can remember Braille did not show up very well at that time. Of course it may have been a little ambitious on my part to attempt a bouillabaisse

with the limited accessories for cooking that we had at the Rue Quatre Septembre, but he certainly took a very exaggerated view of its failure, and the damage that was done to a folio of his water colors, that had in any case no right to have been on the east side of the stove. We had definitely arranged that they were not to be put on the east side of the stove, and he knew it. And at the same time his eternal omelettes—without seasoning of any sort—were not so superlatively wonderful as to give any sort of justification for the supercilious attitude that he adopted towards my bouillabaisse. Moreover, he was so ridiculously fastidious about certain matters in connection with washing up that I sometimes despaired of him ever becoming an artist at all; and it may also be a fact that his sudden and rapid leap to success whilst I remained somewhere near the starting post, may have helped to shatter that world of splendid intimacies which we shared for all too brief a period.

But whatever the reason—and you must please remember that at that time we were both very young, at an age when the affair of the bouillabaisse assumed portentous dimensions—it was a breach that personally I instantly deplored and for the rest of my life up to that period had profoundly regretted. It was one of those cases in which we were both too proud to take the first step at reconciliation, and then we left it too long.

But of late I had been thinking very intently of Braille on account of that remarkable painting of his called "The Mother," which of course you know, and which had just been exhibited for the first time in London. You may imagine then the feeling of elation that possessed me when I gripped his hand, a feeling that was further accentuated when I realized that Braille was by no means unmoved at meeting me.

"You look just the same," he said, and I felt his keen eyes searching ray face and seeing it "in terms of paint."

The hair on Braille's temples had turned quite gray, but otherwise he, too, looked remarkably the same. I remember that McCartney one day remarked, "Braille has an old-fashioned face. You expect him to quote Latin tags." I never heard him quote Latin tags, but he certainly had an old-fashioned face to the extent that his features were molded on classic lines. They were clean cut and strong and had something of that Puritanic cast that characterized the old Colonial pioneers. He was tall and straight, and on the surface very English. I remember another remark that McCartney made concerning him. Braille was standing one day, verj- erect, looking out of our window across a vista of roofs, and McCartney was sitting by me sketching feverishly with a pencil—he was one of those people who could not keep his hands still—he looked at Braille and muttered,

"Dreaming of his well-groomed lawns."

And somehow that phrase always stuck to me in thinking of Braille. "Well-groomed lawns" seemed to give a lively keynote to his character, as it does I fancy to many another Englishman in distant lands who dreams of his "brumous isle." It suggests centuries of a cultivated faith in certain things— Cold baths, dumb-bells, marmalade, conformity and well-ordered sport. The expression seemed peculiarly apposite to Braille—in any case to the surface of Braille—because his people had a lovely old manor house in Somerset, and they used to hunt and shoot, and do all those things which a real Englishman should do. He had a certain frigidity of manner with strangers, and enjoyed a reputation for aloofness and austerity. But those of us who knew him well, knew that, as a matter of fact, he was a man of very keen sympathies and sensibilities, although he had that infinite capacity for never betraying emotion before strangers which is an established tradition of our race. When one got him alone the edifice of this austere bearing would suddenly come crashing to the ground, and he would break into a delightful boyish manner. He loved to talk of intimate things, and he did so in a naive, unselfconscious manner.

His father had been an admiral who had died when Braille was twelve. His veneration for his father had an enormous influence on his life. It was difficult to get him to speak of him. He would only do so to people of whom he was fond, and only then on rare occasions and in a changed tone of voice. After a time he would shrug his shoulders and look contemptuously round the studio, as though embracing in his glance the whole fabric of human society, and mutter, "All these other things seem such—piffle!"

I know very little about Admiral Braille, but he must have been a man of unique character. He certainly handed down to his son great qualities of heart and brain, virility and resource, a fierce hatred of cruelty and uncleanliness, and a certain splendid chivalry. Neither do I know anything of his mother or of that mystic influence that lured him from the sea.

As a painter he painted with insolent cleverness from the first, and has since, as you know, become famous as one of the world's most dexterous portrait painters.

I 'm not sure that even now I admire his work to the extent that so many experts appear to. He loved to lay bare the shallow side of human nature, its glitter and appanage. Fat society women surrounded by greedy, expensive little dogs; anaemic princes standing under the protection of massive porticos that emphasized their insignificance; brainless, flaccid daughters of ancient families lying on gorgeous settees in rooms of magnificent proportions and appointments; all these things jumped at you from the canvas, and gripped your attention by their amazing cleverness of portrayal. You were dazzled by the virility of the thing.

I always found Braille a much more lovable person than the impression of his work might suggest. I remember that one day when I railed him on his outlook, he replied, "Perhaps if they would let me paint the poor I would paint with more reverence."

This of course was nonsense, for there was nothing to prevent him from painting the poor, except that the rich clamored to be painted by Braille and paid for it, and the poor did n't. My own impression is that Braille was capable of painting the poor and painting with more reverence, only that at that time the other thing excited his executive ability more, and it also satisfied a certain cynical—one might almost say "evangelical"—streak in his own nature.

That he was capable of painting with reverence and dignity has since been amply demonstrated. But I think it was his painting of "The Mother" that marked the first change in this direction.

"The Mother," as I have said, had just appeared in London a few weeks previous to the occasion of my meeting Braille in Jermyn Street, and it had created a stir. You remember the beautifully painted interior, very low in tone and very sober. It had none of that insolence that characterized so many of his portraits. A woman in a gray frock is leaning on the black frame of a grand piano, and looking at her son. He is a handsome young rascal in khaki. He is silhouetted against the window reading a letter. He is grinning—just in the way that any young rascal will grin when he reads any letter from any girl. And the mother's face is grave and thoughtful and very beautiful. It is a superbly balanced work. But what interested me most particularly was the fact that the lady in the gray dress was— Olga Bardel!

I can hardly tell you how amazed I was when I recognized this fact. In what way had Braille come in touch with Olga Bardel? And why had he broken his tradition to the extent of painting this singularly emotional picture? For as one gazed at the face of this "Mother" looking at her son, one seemed to read much of the mystery and beauty of her life. It could only have been painted by some one supremely conscious of these qualities. . . .

Braille took my arm quite automatically as he used to in the old days, and pulled me along in a panting endeavor to keep in step with his long strides.

"I have a little place over in Gyves Court," he said.

As we turned a corner an action of his brought old memories flooding back and sealed our sense of intimacy. He suddenly pulled my arm and peered down a passage, then he cocked his head at a slight tilt, and swept his stick round in a circle, thus defining the ambit of a picture. He was always doing this in Paris. When anything paintable struck him he just held it and defined it and we looked at it together in silence. I used to call them his "little visions." It wasn't necessary to speak at all, but sometimes I would say, "Yes, jolly! isn't it?" and occasionally Braille would amplify his selection by muttering, "Van Dyck!" or "Pieter de Hoogh!" or else, "Wants a figure to give it scale," or some other remark emphasized to give a workmanlike flavor to the enjoyment of this mutual vision.

We walked through a courtyard in silence, and up the steps of an eighteenth-century building, where a solemn Georgian-looking man ushered us into Braille's capacious apartments. They were furnished with a traditional and robust dignity that one would expect of Braille. We went into a dining-room where well-modulated lights revealed eighteenth-century paneling and fireplace. The walls were an egg-shell green with white moldings and cornice. Some Grinling Gibbons carving over the fireplace left in the original lime tree and going gray. A magnificent Chinese lacquer cabinet between the windows, and only one painting on the walls, a tempera by some early Siennese master of whom I had not heard.

The Georgian-looking gentleman placed a tray of glasses and a tantalus on the center table and drew up two easy chairs to the fire and then left us. Braille lighted his pipe and grinned at me.

"Now tell me all your news," he said.

My news was essentially of a prosaic order and we soon came to discussing abstract things.

Now it is a deplorable fact that, generally speaking, when we meet people who were our friends ten years or more ago and whom we have since dropped, we usually find them drab. We always imagine that we have gone on, whilst they have stood still. They probably have the same impression of us. In any case it is seldom that a great friendship dropped for any length of time is re-established with any degree of success. Perhaps it proves that we are all social cannibals! We batten on each other 's sympathies and thoughts. We exhaust each other, and when we find insufficient mental and moral nourishment we throw each other aside and seek fresh pastures.

It was very gratifying therefore to us to find that we seemed to go on from the point where we left off years ago. Braille always had the faculty of exciting me, and making me find surprising things within myself, and the years seemed to have given him an increased buoyancy. We had a wild orgy of talk that night about the people we used to know, about "shop," about ideas, and every conceivable thing. But still Braille seemed to avoid the subject that was uppermost in my mind, the subject of "The Mother." It must have been some unearthly hour of the night when he suddenly exclaimed, "I 'm just beginning, Tony—just beginning to learn something about painting. I 'm going to start all over again. I 've been too objective."

"Good heavens!" I answered. "What nonsense! Every year a Braille becomes more definitely a Braille. Why only yesterday I was in at the Grosvenor. I was looking at your portrait of the Due de Barre Sinisterre. I stood by it for quite a time and heard the remarks of the people. Eighty per cent, of them said, 'Why, that 's a Braille!'; as far as I can remember no one said, 'Why, that's the Due de Barre Sinisterre!' Isn't this evidence of subjectivity with a vengeance?"

"It is 'n't exactly what I mean," answered Braille. "Tell me, what did they say after remarking that it was a Braille?"

"Well," I replied, "some said, 'Deucid clever, isn't it?'; others said, 'What an old blackguard the man looks!'; and others, 'By Jove! the Buhl cabinet is cleverly painted!' I even heard some one say, 'Is it true that Braille gets five thousand pounds for a portrait?'"

"One might almost call that objectivity with a vengeance," he remarked.

"What would you like them to say?" I asked.

Braille thought for a moment and took up the poker. He threatened the fire with it and then put it down again. Then he said:

"I should like them to look at the portrait for a long time without speaking. Then I should like them to mutter, 'My God!' and then walk straight out of the gallery and never be the same again."

I laughed and answered, "Well, I can tell you that your demands were fulfilled in my case in respect of another painting of yours. I think that I may say that I gazed at 'The Mother' for a long time. I believe I muttered 'My God!' and I know I have been—not quite the same since."

Braille looked up at me quickly and there was a strange silence between us. I felt a little bit like a trespasser on sacred soil and I made a bold attempt to justify myself.

"I think I might go further," I said. "The picture appealed to something fundamental in me. At that time I did walk out of the gallery. I went to an aerated bread shop and drank quantities of hot weak tea. I was very excited. Then I went back to the gallery and looked at it again. I felt curiously stirred by the portrait—for I like to think of it as a portrait—I assure you it had the effect on me precisely as you prescribed. I was and am still under its spell. It has the stimulus of great art. As you know, I was a wretched painter at my best. And I see no reason to think that I should write any better. But 'The Mother' brought to a head a certain slumbering ambition that I had had for a long time."

"What is that?" asked Braille.

"To set down to the best of my ability the story of—Olga Bardel!"

I watched the queer look of surprise creep over Braille's face. Then he suddenly laughed and stood up. He stretched himself and looked at his long firm hands.

"It's a ridiculous profession," he said at last; "the profession of writing." Then he shrugged his shoulders and added, "I Mould help you if I could."

"I shall want the stimulus of your 'little visions,'" I answered.

I felt Braille looking at me pityingly, and then with a sudden boyishness he said, "I'm glad you feel like that, though! Perhaps after all, Tony, it's the only thing worth doing! You met her at the Guildefords', did n't you? One met every one at the Guildefords'. Doesn't it seem rum, you and I sitting here to-night after all these years—and after all that has happened, and the thing that appeals to us is that we want to 'set it down!'

You in your silly tablets, and I in paint. And it moves us more than anything. Do you remember in the old days when we used to talk about the 'fun' of paint? I overdid it, I think. It has always been the 'fun' of paint to me. I'm tired of saying that rich and vulgar people are rich and vulgar. It's so obvious and silly. There's something else I want to say, something of more permanent value. It's strange that you should have had—the same call, for I've thought of you a lot during these years. . . . May I have some of your John Cotton?

"Yes," he repeated, "writing is a poor business. You may say a face is 'beautiful,' and some one with imagination conceives a beautiful face, but you can't make a beautiful face in words. You can say the eyes are like a gazelle's, or the head like a Leonardo da Vinci, or the nose is retroussé or some silly expression like that, but you can't arrest some supreme moment or expression of life and fix it. You can ramble on and spend half your life setting something down, as you call it, but when it 's done it takes people a month to read it. And they road it in various moods, and go to sleep and forget most of it, and lose the shape, or jibe at it on account of some sentence that offends them. Painting does its work like a knife. You spend a month on a work, and the result is achieved in a coup d'ail. You see it all at once and can't pretend not to. Did I ever tell you of my old friend. Dr. Paes?"

I shook my head and Braille continued,

"I met him at an hotel in Alexandria. He was a most amazing old chap. I think he was of Portuguese stock. He was extraordinarily ugly. He had largo protruding eyes that looked perfectly fantastic through his thick glasses. He was narrow chested and went about in the hottest weather with a thick white muffler round his neck. I think lie suffered with chronic asthma. He talked to me at great length. He talked more freely and intimately about love than any one I have ever met. He had a theory of what he called 'apotheose.' He said that all life was a dormant condition except for certain supreme moments. He took the marriage of the queen bee as a basis. How on a certain fine day in the summer the queen will leave the hive and fly up into the vault of heaven, and all the males will follow her. She goes up and up and it is consequently the strongest bee that catches her. They have one wild, mad embrace up in the blue and then he falls to the earth—dead! He drew human analogies from this. Man is sustained up to the age of maturity, he contended, by the subconscious warning that this moment is approaching.

"And then it arrives. Youth meets youth—there is the contact. Nothing else in life is of consequence. Time ceases to exist; place and the whole paraphernalia of social progress have no significance. Gradually this love-phase passes, passion stales, and the consciousness of time reveals the fact that it is over, and then man calms down and prepares for—what do you think? The next reincarnation! He believed implicitly in reincarnation. He described minutely his own feelings and sensations during three weeks of his honeymoon with his wife, a remarkably ugly Dutch woman staying in the hotel. They seemed devoted. But he told me that after this impassioned period everything else is a cunning device of Nature to sustain the ego in a state of resignation until such time as he or she shall again enjoy the unconsciousness of time. Time he described as a convention of mind, and philosophy and religion as very little above alcohol, merely sops to the yearning heart! 'What is it you feel,' he said to me one day, 'when you are alone walking on a heath in your old age and the wan wind beats on your temples? A sudden confidence! Is it not that the normal attitude of the world is that of resignation? Truly! It is resignation born of the knowledge that one will one day again feel the mystic embrace and that time will lose its meaning.' I asked him if he thought that in his next reincarnation he would have the same wife. He said it was possible but not probable. The matter did not seem to interest him very much. 'Besides,' he added, 'one may be born male in one reincarnation and female in the next!' By some occult method he worked out the fact that he himself would be reborn in two hundred and thirty years ' time. You will not believe it! He was calmly looking forward to the occasion and to the impassioned three weeks that would occur two hundred and fifty years hence!

"I do not pretend to believe in old Paes' theory," continued Braille. "But I do believe, the older I grow, in apotheosis; that is, that one must learn resignation and then grasp supreme moments, especially in one's work. It is only by its great endurance and its great passions that life presents anything worth expressing."

Suddenly he went to the window and pulled back the curtain, and sat on the sill. He opened the window a little way, for the night was warm for February. The drone of sleepy London reached us. Vague lights flickered here and there, trying to penetrate her thousand mysteries, whilst overhead a few pale stars were dimly discernible as though holding an uncertain watch over this grim city that they did not understand.

Suddenly he said,

"It 's a lovely game!"

He did not attempt to explain this cryptic utterance. But as one who knew him very well I believe I might say that the thoughts that came to his mind at that moment, if expressed in his own language, were:

"It 's a lovely game—thinking and talking about people. It 's a specially lovely game painting the silly blighters! "What are they all doing mooning about? eating, sleeping, fighting, making money, making love, getting into trouble, weaving silly romances! None of them with any very set purposes, mostly doing things from mixed motives, good motives and bad motives, but they all come into our net in the long run—to be talked about, and 'set down,' and painted and given subjectivity! I love them all, even the bad ones. In fact I think I love the bad ones best, they 're so brave and so unhappy. So you need n't look so superior, you silly pale stars! It 's a lovely game!"

CHAPTER I

MECHANICAL ACTIONS

In the corner of a meager room in Canning Town a child was banging on a piece of iron. The action gave the child no satisfaction, for it gave forth a hard unmelodious sound, but the day was close and the atmosphere encouraged perversity. It was past the time when she was in the habit of having a thick piece of bread given her, covered with a thin layer of dripping—an operation called by the others "dinner." But this had not so far taken place. She felt restless and unhappy, and the banging on iron seemed in some way to fit in with her mood. She was conscious that she disliked the sound, but she enjoyed the agony of discord. She repeated the performance, and then a harsh voice called out, "Stop that row, you little beast!" She knew that this voice came from a very tall person who was called her sister, and whom the others called "Irene." She shared this room with Irene. It was their bedroom, and their sitting-room, their eating-room, Irene's workroom, and on very unique occasions—everybody's bathroom. In fact it was apparently the only room in the world. Other people came into it and made it hotter and more uncomfortable and then went out, apparently unable to stand it any longer. There were two people in particular who came in every night when she was very tired, and made a tremendous noise and ate food near her bed and were in every way most objectionable. These were called her "brothers," "Karl and Montague." They obviously did not like her, and sometimes were very cruel. They always referred to her as "that something little brat." Karl was the worst. He was the eldest, and the noisiest, and the most domineering, although he certainly did wear most lovely rings on his fingers. Sometimes he would come in in the night and behave in a most peculiar way, and she heard Irene accuse him of "being drunk." Montague was a little quieter in that respect, but he used to make most unpleasant noises eating his food. There were times, however, when Montague had been almost kind. She remembered one day last winter when she had a very bad toothache, and Montague had come and looked at her and said, "Poor little devil!" She felt that that was very kind of Montague, and somehow it reminded her of her father. She could remember her father quite well. He did not seem so large as the others, and he used to bend over her and fondle her, and she always remembered his kind watery eyes and the queer way he shuffled about the room. Then one day he went into another room and "died"; that is, they said he would never come back again. She could not bear to dwell on this. It seemed so terrible, and so unlike her father. She knew he would want to come back, then what was this "death" that prevented it? And since then there had been nothing to replace those weak watery eyes of her father's, and there were moments when she felt the world bursting, and she could not stand it. This was one of those days, and after a very brief interval she banged on the iron again. There was a quick movement and Irene's hand came crashing on to the side of her cheek, in three rapid slaps. "Haven't I told you to stop it, you little swine?" The blows stung, but the child did not cry out. She just stared at her sister as though surprised. She certainly was a queer child to look at. She had a squat chubby face with a small nose and a broad chin and square cheeks. Her hair, very black and frizzy, stuck out in peculiar square masses overhanging her shoulders. The neighbors said she was "weird." She had gray eyes with unusual depths. Most unexpected things would frighten her and make her cry, whilst chastisement, such as that just inflicted by Irene, or some fateful calamity like the loss of a doll or a dinner, would merely leave her with that strained expression of the face, as though she could not understand.

There was a somber silence, whilst the elder girl resumed her work at the table. She was ironing a tattered sheet. Olga could never understand why her sister wanted to stop in the room always, and do things of this nature, and to-day it particularly irritated her. She watched her for some time, and then she banged on the n-on again.

"Look here," said Irene, jumping up. "if you do that again, I 'll take you up to Uncle Grubhofer, and tell him."

This threat had the desired effect. Olga left her implements of torture, and slunk into the corner of the room. This "Uncle Grubhofer" was the terror of Olga 's life. The mention of him reminded her that there were other rooms, and that Uncle Grubhofer had a room. This room was surely the most terrible room in the world.

It was full of great spaces and shadows and boxes and things no one could understand. It was where bad people went, and Uncle Grubhofer just looked at them with those queer dark eyes of his, and they quailed and shrunk to nothingness. Irene and Karl and Montague were large, but Uncle Grubhofer was vast. He had besides the peculiar faculty of expanding at will. Sometimes he would seem to shrink away into being quite an ordinary size as he sat on his chair; in fact he became even smaller for his face was thin and hollow and his arms were very long and his fingers thin and bony, and then he would suddenly unpack himself! There seemed to be endless folds of him as he rose up, long lines of pendulous clothes draping from unexpected projections. One portion of his anatomy seemed incredibly enormous. She heard some one say one day that Uncle Grubhofer looked like a boa-constrictor who had swallowed a goat. She did not know what a boa-constrictor was, but she suspected that Uncle Grubhofer must have swallowed something tremendous; and she was sure he could not digest it, and that was why his face looked so sad, so sallow and so terrifying.

He wore a little round black cap, perched on the dank gray hairs on the top of his head which she took to be some insignia of power. For she knew that he was powerful, perhaps the most powerful person in the world, for the others would whisper about him, and when there was any dispute, Irene would say, "Well, I shall speak to Uncle Grubhofer." She knew that Karl and Montague were both frightened of him, and when there was no food and no money, as often seemed to be the case, one of them would go up to his room, and they always took Olga with them for some reason or other, and they cringed and crawled to him. And then Uncle Grubhofer seemed vaster than ever. He seemed to loom up and fill the awful room. He would shout and be very angry, and in the end would give them a small piece of silver, for which they had to write on a piece of paper a sort of confession. And then he would talk to Olga in a terrifying and incomprehensible way. He somehow gave her to understand that she was in the world on sufferance. That she enjoyed all its delights and benefits solely through his kindness, that her father had been a "shiftless wastrel" and that one day she would have to atone. He made her feel very, very wicked, and she would wake up in the night in a fever of terror, believing that her uncle had become so enormous that he had filled the whole world and there was no air.

Consequently on this day she had no desire to be taken up to Uncle Grubhofer 's room, and she sat stolidly in the corner without playing or moving. After a time Irene went to a cupboard and cut two slices of bread. She put a scrape of dripping on one and gave Olga the other,

"You won't get no dripping to-day," she said in explanation, "We got to the end of it,"

Olga munched her bread in silence for she was hungry, and she watched Irene eating hers with dripping, and she wondered vaguely why if there was enough dripping for one piece of bread Irene should have it and not she. It occurred to her to make some protest, but the impulse passed, as the bread gradually took the edge off her appetite.

She was so tired of this eternal food struggle. For up to that point, food had been the dominating thought of her life. She was practically always hungry, consequently her mentality was bounded by the desire for food. She knew it was the same with Irene and Karl and Montague. They fought and schemed for food. They suspected each other of getting food on the quiet, they begrudged the morsels on each other's plates, and she had seen Karl and Montague fight like dogs over a piece of fish one morning at breakfast time. It never occurred to her to wonder about this. She accepted it as the normal course of things. She presumed that it was the same with everybody except perhaps Uncle Grubhofer, and he, she knew, had lots of food. She had heard the others talking about it. They even said that he sometimes had hot meat for supper! It was rumored that he kept enormous quantities of food locked away in his cupboard upstairs, but he had never, never on any occasion asked any one to share it with him. She knew as a matter of fact that very often when he was out— and he would sometimes be out for days at a time—Irene would steal upstairs and creep into his room and poke about. Olga did not know whether she found any food there, but she certainly never brought any down. One day Olga followed her on tiptoe and tried to see, but Irene had shut the door. She came out rather suddenly, and Olga had the idea that she was eating. She looked very scared and angry at seeing Olga, and slapped her and called her "a prying little brat" and worse things. Other people lived in the house too, but they were all entirely under the rule of Uncle Grubhofer, and he could turn them out if he liked, and tell them never to return.

There was a brass plate outside the door that told you all about it. On it was written, "Julius Grubhofer, agent for Ochs, Boellman & Co., wire springs and mechanical actions." Of course she could not read, and no one had ever read this out to her, but she believed it was a proclamation that drew the attention of the world to the fact that Uncle Grubhofer was a person of tremendous importance. Sometimes other important people would come, and they would go up to Uncle Grubhofer 's room and stop there a long time, and most peculiar noises came from there, noises that excited her and made her want to brave the terrors of the room and go in and see what it was that caused it. But this she knew would be courting unspeakable terrors. And then Uncle Grubhofer would go out with the other important people, and sometimes he would not come back for days. And then more large cases would arrive. She believed he went out and collected food and it was brought up in the cases and stored away for him. But what was it that made the peculiar noises?

She sat in the gloomy corner of the room and pondered over these things, and then she suddenly remembered a fact that Irene had probably forgotten. Uncle Grubhofer had gone out that morning, and she had heard Irene say that he was not coming back till to-night. A sudden idea occurred to Olga. She watched her sister for some time in silence, and then she got up and casually left the room. She listened outside and assured herself that Irene was still at work, and then she crept upstairs. Her heart was beating very fast, and she felt that she was on the eve of some tremendous adventure. She arrived outside Uncle Grubhofer 's room.

There was no sound. Uncle Grubhofer had all that floor to himself, whilst on the floor above lived a very kind lady they called "Miss Merson." She was out all day, and they said that she was a "school teacher." Whenever she passed Olga she always smiled kindly and had once given her a biscuit, and patted her head and called her "You poor queer little thing," She would be out now, so there would be no one at all in this part of the house. She put her hand on Uncle Grubhofer's door handle. She felt terribly frightened but she thought to herself, "It won't look so terrible now. It 's daylight."

She turned the handle and the door gave. She peeped in, trembling in every limb. She quite expected to see Uncle Grubhofer there after all, looking larger than ever with his huge devouring eyes on her. But the room was apparently empty. She left the door open so that she had the means of a rapid exit at hand in case it were needed. She crept into the room and peered round. She went on tiptoe and looked carefully behind all the boxes and cases. No! there was not the slightest sign of life. She went back and shut the door very quietly and then stood by it. And then a fearful dread came to her. She was all alone in the most terrible room in the world. It was true it was daylight, but there were so many cupboards and boxes and most of them locked, supposing some one sprang out! She stood for a long time by the door, afraid to move. And then she began wondering where he kept the food. The restless spirit of adventure, born of the torrid day, gave her a new impulse. She tiptoed across the floor once more. There was a large sort of cupboard with a lot of small drawers.

She tried them. They were all locked. She tried other boxes. They too seemed nailed up or in other ways inaccessible. At last she found one box lying on the floor with a lid that had been apparently wrenched open and was lying loose. She eagerly looked inside. There was no food there, but there were most peculiar looking things. Very long coils of bright wire on different metals twisted about in most remarkable ways. She looked at them and thought they were very pretty but somehow dangerous looking. Then she touched them. She found that certain parts of them made sounds, the sounds varied according to where she touched them. It was a glorious discovery!

She sat on the floor and groped among the straw, pulling at the wires. Some of the sounds were most melodious and pleasant, and others less so. She did it very quietly, for she was afraid that Irene might hear her, and she waited for some time after her first attempt. But there was no interruption. Then she resumed. She forgot all about her search for food. She became absorbed in her hunt for satisfying sounds. She soon found that it was not only where she touched the wires, but the way in which she touched them that made the different sounds. In a short time she became entirely engrossed. It was an entrancing experience. She never thought the world contained such joys. She discovered that she liked plucking some of the wires in combination, and tried to find out which they were that gave her so much satisfaction. She lost all consciousness of time, when suddenly the world came crashing about her ears. A door slammed. She looked up and realized where she was, and there stood Irene, her eyes blazing!

"You little devil!" she shrieked. "What do you mean?" A heavy hand was laid on her shoulder, and the other proceeded to deliver chastisement all over her body. She was dragged from the floor, and bundled out of the- room. "I 'll teach you, you little swine!" cried her sister. "Playing with Uncle Grubhofer's things! If he 'd come in and caught you, it would have been a nice thing, would n 't it?"

Olga went to bed that night sore and bruised and hungry, but something within her arose, some conscious force struggling to soothe her, to palliate the gods of warring oppression, as though she had found something that the others could not take from her. She was dimly conscious at some strange hour of the night of seeing Karl reel into the room. He looked very ugly by the dim light of the gas flare. He moved about in a spasmodic, jerky fashion and breathed heavily, and ate a piece of cheese that he found in the cupboard. He sat on her bed with a jerk, and took his boots off and flung them with great violence and excess of noise on the bare boards. Irene woke up and roared at him. She heard him telling Irene in a thick voice "to go to the devil!" and then he banged out of the room and went downstairs; for he and Montague slept in a room that Olga had occasionally visited in the basement. She heard Irene muttering to herself and then another door banging downstairs. And then things quieted down, and Olga became conscious of the astounding beauty of silence. All day long her nerves were jarred by unpleasant sounds and voices, but now she could be quite quiet, and it was very nice to be conscious of being quiet. "It is a pity," she thought, "that people make unpleasant noises." And then through her mind kept running some of the nice sounds she had made with the strings. On the morrow Irene seemed peculiarly bad tempered, and food was grudgingly administered to her. She played in the corner and on the stairs with a piece of box, and the colored advertisement of lamp shades that served as toys. But they did not amuse her. She felt discontented and restless. About mid-day she heard a door bang, and footsteps descending. She knew that it was Uncle Grubhofer going out. She darted into the room, for she knew that Uncle Grubhofer disapproved of "dirty little brats playing on the stairs." She peeped out of the door and saw him go down. He had on a long black coat that reached to his knees, and a hard round black hat, and in his hand carried a small square bag. He was probably going to visit some one with one of those nice wire things, and going to make the pleasant sounds to them. She wondered profoundly why he should do this, for she could not conceive Uncle Grubhofer willingly doing anything pleasant to any one. Her experience of the world prompted her to imagine that there must be some sort of reciprocal arrangement. Perhaps they gave him food in exchange for his making the pleasant noises. She knew that Uncle Grubhofer had talked to her several times in a manner that somehow instilled this idea into her mind. People did things for people because those other people did things for them. This was universal. It applied to every one except Olga, who did nothing and was entirely useless and unwanted. In this way she was very wicked, and her defection could only be atoned for by one day making it up by doing a lot of things for other people without them doing anything for her. She was always to keep that in mind.

The day was again sultry and she followed him downstairs and stood on the pavement. She was allowed sometimes to play down there by the iron paling that railed off a deep stone area. This area was partially covered in by a broken wire netting on which were dirty pieces of paper and scraps of wood and empty match boxes. Nevertheless she could see through it sufficiently well to observe two very dark windows covered with dust. One of them was open a little way at the bottom, and she could see the corner of an iron bed in a state of dishevelment, and the corner of a packing case on which stood a broken wash basin half filled with water that some one had washed in. By the side lay a piece of yellow soap on which the lather had set. She had often looked into this room before; it was the room where Karl and Montague slept. She glanced up the street. As far as she could see either way were houses exactly like the one she lived in. She wondered whether they all belonged to Uncle Grubhofer. She looked with a certain pride at the brass plate, and she knew it caused a good deal of envy among the swarms of children who passed up and down. She did not like these children, and she knew that they did not like her. Many of them knew her by name, and the bigger ones used to tease her, and call her "monkey face." That was one reason why nearly all her time was spent in the room instead of on the pavement. These children terrified her.

Three of them came up at that moment, one large girl and two small ones. One of the small ones had a sore place on her upper lip that extended to her nostril, and she was eating a piece of sausage. They all three were extremely dirty and the eldest had a mouth organ. As they passed, this girl thrust her chin forward and blew a wild cacophony into Olga's ear. The sound seemed to go right through her. She said, "Don't!" and thrust her arm out. At this successful manifestation of having caused serious annoyance, the elder girl followed it up. She put her face close to Olga's and blew for all she was worth, and the two smaller ones chortled with delight at the sport. Olga ran away but the elder girl followed her, catching hold of her arm and blowing louder and louder. Olga saw red. She suddenly kicked the elder girl on the shin, and at the same moment made a wild thrust at her face, and managed to scratch it. The girl screamed and rushed at her, but Olga got to the door in time and slammed it. She heard her oppressor banging on the door and screaming, and Olga huddled on the stairs. She had never done anything of that sort before, and she was very shaken and frightened. The elder girl soon gave up her assault, but Olga thought perhaps she might still be waiting for her. "I shall never be able to go out again," she thought. She sat on the stairs for a long time and no one came down or went up. She felt a dread of going back to the room, and she dare not go out into the street. Then suddenly she remembered that Uncle Grubhofer had gone out again. She felt the call of that silent room upstairs, and those wonderful things that made nice sounds. She debated the pros and cons, but it did not take her long to decide; and somehow Irene's thrashings never seemed to hurt her very much. A certain innate cunning prompted her to revisit Irene casually, to satisfy herself that all was in order, and then she crept upstairs again. This time the room did not terrify her so much. She shut the door and made for the box. It was still there. In a few minutes she was indulging in the delights of yesterday. But alas! they were shorter lived. Irene heard her, and in less than half an hour she was receiving another buffeting. "I 'll skin you alive," shrieked her sister. "How dare you! after what I told you yesterday!"

Olga bore her punishment with a stoic indifference. She had allowed for it, when setting out on her adventure.

At five o'clock that same afternoon, Irene found her there again! The matter became incomprehensible. What could she do beyond thrashing the child? She discussed the matter with Karl and Montague that evening. Karl took the matter in hand. He told Olga that if she did it again, he would deal with her. Did she realize that by playing the fool with Uncle Grubhofer's property she ran the risk of getting the whole family turned out? or in any case of having to buy a key for the room which would cost a shilling? Did she understand that? He supposed she thought they were all millionaires to go buying keys. And if a key had to be bought, he knew who would have to pay for it. So just let her look out!

The next morning at half-past ten Irene found Olga again playing with Uncle Grubhofer's "wire springs and mechanical actions."

Karl came home very late that night and had been drinking, and when Irene reported the matter to him he thrashed the little girl with such frenzied spite that even Irene had to interfere.

The next afternoon Irene was at work when suddenly she heard a now familiar sound of wires twanging. She was frightened. She could not understand. She could not remember any previous occasion when the little ogre had positively ignored beatings and commands. In some curious way she had always felt a little frightened of this small sister. She had such a curious way of looking at one. She seemed to belong to some other world, and Irene had never got over her resentment at Olga's arrival, bringing with it a further division of already much-divided food. She was nine when Olga was born, and the mothering instinct had been starved out of her, while the disparity in their ages put out of court any communion of interests in common. When she heard these insistent twangings repeated in spite of many thrashings and threats, she had a sudden instinct that the little girl had brought some inevitable and uncomfortable element into her life that would never be checked except by death. And in that surmise she was not entirely incorrect. She jumped up and went to the door and listened. And then she thought, "I will let Uncle Grubhofer deal with this, come what may!"

And so it came about that Olga had a free and glorious afternoon and evening. She found another case that was open and even more wonderful things and wires and metals. She forgot all about Irene and Karl and the milk which she usually had at six o'clock. The room was getting quite dark, and she had found a more wonderful thing than ever that had deep vibrant tones when struck with a piece of wood. It gave her a curious thrill to do this, and to listen for the sound as it came and to hear it die away. She had a curious desire to see the sound. She wondered what became of it after it traveled across the bare floor of the room. Once she struck the wire louder than usual, and put her eye close to it and peered after the vibration. Her eye wandered across the room and suddenly looked full into the eyes of Uncle Grubhofer. She screamed and jumping up, rushed towards the door. Uncle Grubhofer did not move or speak. She gripped the handle and turned it. The door would not open, and the key was gone! She was locked in alone in the awful room with Uncle Grubhofer. She instinctively turned to him. His small eyes glittered at her with hard malevolence, but he said nothing. The little girl was terribly frightened. "Let me go! Let me go!" she shrieked as though he were holding her and crushing her. She tried rapidly to imagine what he would do. In the riot of dread that followed she remembered one thing, that was, that Uncle Grubhofer had so far never struck her. He was the only one of them all who hadn't, and yet she was a thousand times more frightened of him than of all the others put together. Suddenly he said, "Come here!" She had no power to resist. She remembered the remark about the boa-constrictor and she was sure that if Uncle Grubhofer had told her to jump into his mouth, she would have done so. He pointed to the spot on the floor where she was to stand, and then he rose up till his head nearly reached the ceiling. He started talking and walking. He was like some huge animal in a cage. He waved his tremendously long arms and slouched cumbrously across the floor. When he came to the wall he pulled himself up with a curious jerky movement, as though he had hurt himself, and then he slouched back. As he passed her, he thrust his face forward towards her, and showed his yellow teeth, which his small loose mouth seemed hardly able to control. His eyes rolled with anger and hatred. He talked wildly and incomprehensibly. He talked about "property." These beautiful things it seemed were "property." Property was the most sacred thing in the world. To touch the property of others was to scorch your soul. One day she would die. It might be to-day or to-morrow, and then she would go to a place called "Hell." In the dull room fast becoming dark, Uncle Grubhofer gave her a vivid word picture of Hell. It seemed to be a place specially designed by some accommodating Destiny for little girls such as she. It was a place of swamps and darkness, much worse than the basement where Karl and Montague slept, where black crawling things wriggled over you and bit you, whilst hairy monsters with luminous eyes hung above you in branches, and jeered at you. This went on for ever and ever and ever.

In the meantime he produced the key. For the rest of her time on earth, the awful room with the things that made beautiful sounds was bolted and barred to her. That night Irene heard sobbing at intermittent intervals coming from Olga's corner. It was the first time she had ever heard such a thing. She felt an increased respect for Uncle Grubhofer, but it did not entirely dissipate her uncomfortable sense of fear of her small sister.

CHAPTER II

Irene's antipathy towards her sister seemed to increase. She made the room almost intolerable. At the same time the child was afraid to go on to the pavement in case she met the big girl with the mouth organ. The days were drawing in and becoming colder, so the staircase with its drafts and darkness was not a pleasant playground. Uncle Grubhofer's chamber of magic was locked to her, and over it all hovered the terrible vision of that land of eternal torments, where "black things crawled and bit, and hairy monsters jeered." She had known so little of affection that she was hardly conscious of an innate desire for it, but she felt very wretched. In addition, the food seemed scarcer and more irregular. She would sometimes get to such a low state that she would think of nothing but food. Once she stole some from the cupboard while Irene was out of the room, but this led to more violent punishment than even her misdemeanor with regard to Uncle Grubhofer's "property." Months went by, and she became phlegmatic and indifferent, and she had periods of giddiness. One day she was standing in the passage down-stairs. It was past her bedtime, but she had been "naughty," and Irene in a fit of temper had gone out and left her, telling her she "could shift for herself." She sat on the bottom stair, and shivered for a long time. She never remembered having been up so late. She felt tired and faint. She heard some one fumbling at the front door with a key. An awful dread came to her that it might be Uncle Grubhofer. She stood up ready to scurry up-stairs. As she clutched the banisters, a strange feeling came over her that the wall and the ceiling were going up and up and up. She was just conscious that the door opened, and little Miss Merson—who lived on the top floor—came in. She heard her say: "Oh, you poor mite!" and then she knew no more.

When she came to herself again she was lying on a sofa in front of a warm fire, and Miss Merson was giving her something hot to drink, that sent a glow through her. She felt very comfortable and sleepy. She wondered what had happened. It all seemed very strange. Miss Merson stooped over her, and combed her hair. When she saw Olga looking about, she said,

"Well, you little thing, do you feel better?" Olga looked at the kind, gray eyes, and nodded. "That 's right," said the little lady. "You stop here a little while and rest. Don't you bother about anything."

This arrangement suited Olga admirably. She lay there blinking at the firelight. Miss Merson went to a writing desk, lighted a lamp that had a shade, and sat down and wrote. She noted how quietly Miss Merson did this, and how silently she moved about the room. She thought—"How different this is to Irene! Why do people always make a noise? Why don't they move like Miss Merson?" The silence was delicious. This was evidently the room they called "the attic," at the top of the house where Miss Merson lived. How nice it must be to live up here amidst the splendid silence! She heard the rhythmic movement of Miss Merson's pen, and occasionally the dropping of a cinder. She fell asleep. She had a troubled dream in which black moving objects in waves were moving towards her, but some one was thrusting them back, and saying—"It 's all right, it 's all right!" At last the same voice seemed to say a little louder: "Now, you poor mite, I 'm afraid I must take you back to your own people or they will wonder what has become of you! Stay here; I 'll go down and see if your sister is there. She was n 't half an hour ago!" She went out quietly. When the door had shut Olga burst into tears. She did not know why, and she struggled to get them under control before Miss Merson's return. She heard talking on the stairs below, and the unmistakable voice of Irene in a harsh crescendo. The door opened, and the two women came in.

"What 's been the matter with yer?" said Irene in a tone suggesting annoyance.

"I think she 's quite run down," answered Miss Merson for her. "I 've been giving her some hot gruel!"

"Run down!" exclaimed Irene. "I don 't see why she need be! She never does nothing but play. "The little basin of hot gruel still stood on the hob. Irene noticed it, and added: "If she had to work like I do, she might be run down!" She sniffed and Miss Merson said:

"Do you think perhaps she had better stop here to-night?"

Irene realized that she was not going to be offered any of the gruel, so she answered:

"No; I think she 'd better come with me. We can look after her all right, thank you. "This was said with a certain acerbity that was not lost on Miss Merson, who quickly rejoined:

"Of course! Of course! I only thought it might be more convenient for you, and more restful for her, not to be disturbed."

"We can look after her all right," repeated Irene in a sullen voice. She pulled Olga into a sitting posture and said, "Come on."

Olga stood up. She still felt very shaky, but she followed her sister to the door. She did not speak or look at Miss Merson again, but she was conscious that that good lady was helping her out and patting her arm. They went down the cold staircase, and re-entered the room. Montague was there, and asking for his supper. She stumbled across the room and quickly got into her bed. She shivered, and lay awake listening to the unpleasant noise Montague and Irene made eating their food, and they had no sooner finished than Karl came in, and it all started over again. Karl seemed in a good temper, and very talkative, and laughed in a series of mirthless barks, and then both the men smoked cigarettes and made the room very choky. Olga thought they would never finish making noises and smells, but at last the men went downstairs, and she fell into fitful slumber.

The next day food had no attraction for her, and she was feverish. Miss Merson came in in the evening to ask how she was. On finding out how the land lay, she brought down a white powder and a little milk, and by exercising great tact managed to get Irene to allow her to administer it. That night Olga slept well, in spite of everything, and spent the next day thinking of her new friend and the silent room. A great temptation came to her. Miss Merson was out all day. Why should she not steal up and sit in her room? But somehow it seemed different doing anything like that to Miss Merson. She was bundled to bed before the little schoolmistress came home, and she did not see her for several days.

And then a great and eventful day arrived. It was a day called Sunday, a day that she always dreaded and loathed, because it meant that Karl and Montague were in and out all day with their horrible smoke and noise, and Irene didn't do any work, and seemed in consequence to be more cantankerous. It is true that sometimes on these days food seemed to be more plentiful—there was sometimes meat in the middle of the day—and on one or two occasions Montague had taken her for a stroll round the streets. But these dubious benefits were more than counteracted by the noise and general irritability of the people in the room, and the peculiar strained atmosphere of the streets. It was as though on the week days the people were all doing things and forgot their wretchedness, but on Sunday they stopped, stared at each other, and brooded over the patent misery of their lives. They seemed conscious of their clothes, their houses, their friends, and their baser desires. Olga did not analyze these feelings if she went out for a walk with Montague, but she felt that she disliked Sundays, and all that appertained thereto.

On this particular Sunday, Karl and Montague had gone out together after a late and clamorous breakfast, leaving a trail of tobacco and kipper smell, and Irene was washing up with a tremendous clatter, and singing in a harsh and dreary voice, when there was a tap at the door. Irene went to it, and Olga heard Miss Merson's voice. Irene went outside, and a conversation which she could not hear went on for some minutes. At last Irene returned, continued washing up, and then turning to Olga, she said: "Here, you 're going to have your dinner upstairs!" She caught hold of her, and made a tentative effort at washing her neck. Her hair was hastily brushed, and she was pushed outside and told to go up to Miss Merson's attic, and, "Mind yer don't fall down the stairs and break yer neck."

Olga pulled herself together in the passage, and the news seemed too good to be true. She could hardly bring herself to set forth on such a dazzling adventure. She went up the first flight of stairs very gingerly, and then a sudden dread that Irene or Uncle Grubhofer might appear to drag her back caused her to hurry on. She reached the top, and never having been instructed in the convention of knocking on a door she just opened it and walked in. Miss Merson was writing at her desk. "Ah, there you are!" was her greeting, and she got up and came over and kissed her, then shut the door. Olga said nothing, but gladness shone from her face.

"Now come and sit down and tell me all about it." Miss Merson made her comfortable on the couch in front of the fire and gave her an apple. It was an entrancing morning. Miss Merson read her a book, showed her pictures, and opened out a new world to her. It was a world of fairies and sunshine and princesses, where people all moved quietly, and did things quietly, just like Miss Merson did. She was sure of that. Then she asked her questions about herself, which she could not answer. She did not know how old she was. She could not remember her mother. She did not know what her brothers did in the daytime. No one had ever taught her anything. She did not know her alphabet. To most of Miss Merson's questions she just shook her head. But she tried to say something about her father. This matter obviously upset her, so Miss Merson quickly changed the subject. And then after a time Miss Merson spread a cloth on a small table, and they sat down and had most wonderful things to eat. She felt too excited to eat much, but Miss Merson, instead of being pleased at this, as the others would have been, seemed quite upset, and insisted on her having everything there was. After this they sat cozily by the fire again and talked, and had another story. But the most amazing and fascinating event was yet to occur. After a time Miss Merson went to a curious-looking piece of furniture and opened a lid on it, and revealed a long row of flat, yellow-white things, with black things raised up at different intervals between them. She struck these black and white things with her hands, and most wonderful sounds came forth. She looked round, and caught the intent, eager expression on the child's face, and laughed.

"Oh! you quaint thing!" she said. She went to a box and got some music, and put it on the piano. And then she put on some spectacles.

"I don't know whether I can play this," she said. "I 'm no performer, but I 'll try." Then Miss Merson sat down. She certainly was no pianist, but she loved music, and she managed to give performances of some of the easier pieces of Schumann and Chopin in a manner that gave pleasure to herself in any ease. She played for about half an hour, almost forgetting the little girl. Then she looked round. Olga was sitting on the edge of the sofa, leaning forward, her large gray eyes sunk in the hollow of her chubby pale face, reflecting the riot of emotion that flooded her small soul through this new world of melody. "Oh, you queer little thing!" exclaimed Miss Merson, and she jumped up and kissed her. And then Olga broke forth into a torrent of weeping. She did not know why. She simply felt that she must hang on to the kind lady and cry and cry.

"Oh, you poor mite! What is it then?" Miss Merson pressed the little girl to her bosom. She felt strange emotions stirring within herself. She asked her why she cried, but she already knew, and the knowledge seemed to her pregnant with significance. She looked at the little girl in a new light. It was certainly remarkable. She said she would not play any more, and she made Olga lie on the couch again, and made her some tea. It was a very nice tea. They had bread and butter and jam and a cake, and they laughed and talked about all sorts of things. Miss Merson did not refer to the piano again, and after tea she took her back to her family. She wanted to think a little by herself.

On the following evening Miss Merson gave Irene some apples that she said had been sent her from the country, and also a cheese. Irene was very surprised, but she took the things, her greed dominating her suspicions. She did not like the schoolmistress and was jealous of her attentions to Olga, but food was another matter. Miss Merson insisted on being friendly, in spite of indifference and insult, and she soon realized Irene's weak point. She flattered her, and gave her food. She even endured having her in to tea one day, and at the end of a week was almost in her good books. She got possession of Olga for the following Sunday, and in a matter of fact way showed the little girl how to strike the notes of the piano in rotation, and then how to play a little scale, by turning her thumb under. She noticed how quick she was to do as she was told, and how well she remembered. She wanted to play all day long, but Miss Merson insisted on the fairy story, and on meals, and talk. Before she went that evening Miss Merson said casually: "You may come up here any time you like, dear, when I am out. You might like to play your little scales."

When she got down-stairs Irene asked her what she had had to eat. She seemed rather vague about it, and Irene's jealousy was once more aroused, until Miss Merson arrived later and brought her a small pie.

"It 's very curious," thought Irene. She wondered what the game was. People of her acquaintance did not give each other food without getting anything in exchange. Olga disappeared early the next morning, and Irene traced her up to the attic playing on Miss Merson 's piano. The child put up her defense that Miss Merson had told her she might. Irene was angry, and then realized that after all it kept the little brat out of her way, so she allowed her to remain.

Visions of glorious days floated before Olga. She climbed on to the stool and struggled with the notes. She had been there about an hour, when the door burst open and Uncle Grubhofer appeared. He was in one of his most devouring moods. What was she doing there making that confounded row—she must clear out at once! If Miss Merson encouraged her in this fooling she would be thrown out on to the pavement, piano and all. The world came crashing about Olga's ears. She knew that resistance was useless. She shut the piano lid, climbed down from the stool, and went silently out of the room. She spent the rest of the morning down by the front door, heaving with remorse and the sense of outrage. She felt like going out of the front door and running away—anywhere, never to return. It is more than likely that she would have put some such action into force had it not been for the restraining knowledge that Miss Merson would be back in the evening, and also a sudden recollection that Uncle Grubhofer went out sometimes for days together. She would watch, and wait for him to go. She kept up her ceaseless vigil for three days, and at length one morning she saw him going off with his little square bag. The front door had hardly slammed before she darted up, and clambered to her stool. She waited for some time in fear lest he should return, and then she lifted the piano lid. But she felt distracted, the pall of Uncle Grubhofer was over everything, nowhere seemed sacred from him. She felt the heavy gloom of his disapproval frowning across the keys. She knew she was being very wicked, and that one day she would have to atone for it. The stolen fruits from this mystic box would have a terrible reaction. She made attempts to practise, and then kept on leaving off, and listening. At last she felt too frightened to continue, and went and sat on the sofa. She became conscious of another quality in this attic. It was so clean. There was very little furniture, but it all seemed so different from the room down-stairs. It smelt differently, looked different, and felt different. She wondered whether there were other rooms like this and other people like Miss Merson; whether, in fact, there was a world beyond these dismal walls.

After a time a new courage came to her, and she went back to the piano. The nature of her environment gradually bred in Olga certain mild forms of cunning. It was as though some race instinct were fighting to assert itself, and we must remember that she came, however remotely, from Jewish stock—that stock which has proved itself to have the life instinct more keenly developed than any other. She showed this cunning in various subconscious methods of preserving her health in spite of malnutrition and bad air, in being able to put on a sort of armour of stoic indifference when swayed by some emotion that threatened to overwhelm her. But in no way did this instinct of cunning assert itself more forcibly than that by which she managed to make use of Miss Merson 's piano in spite of all obstacles. She developed an almost psychic sense of when Uncle Grubhofer would go out and return. She overcame Irene by sheer importunity and indifference to punishment, and she even sometimes feigned amusement at the preposterous antics of her brother Karl, In the meantime she played scales and exercises, and Miss Merson helped her. Nearly every Sunday she devoted at least part of the day to her, and occasionally in the week-time she would arrive home a little earlier, and she knew that the little girl would be on the look-out.

She was amazed at the rapidity with which Olga grasped the first principles, and the intense way she concentrated on whatever she undertook. In a few months' time she was playing little pieces on Miss Merson 's tinkley piano, and was giving that good lady much food for thought. One Sunday she played a tiny piece of Scarlatti, which she had learnt from memory. It was so musical and good that after she had gone, Miss Merson thought for a long time, and then she sat down and wrote a letter. It was addressed to a Miss Kenway at an address in Kensington. The letter was as follows:

My dear Miss Kenway:

I want to ask your advice. There is a little girl living in this house whom I suspect of having talent. She is the quaintest thing you ever saw, but her family are deplorable. The father and mother are both dead. I understand that the mother drank, and the father was a small jobbing tailor. I believe there were nine or ten children, but they all died except four, two appalling brothers, a dreadful sister, and this little girl. They are, of course, desperately poor, and there is a sort of Bluebeard of an uncle—the mother's brother, I think—who helps to support them.

I cannot find a gleam of talent, intelligence, or common decency in any of them except this child. I should be awfully glad if you could meet her. I think she would interest you. Might I bring her? or would it be asking you too much to ask you to visit this slum on Sunday afternoon? I might find it difficult to bring her to you, as, if the family heard of it, they would probably try and stop my bringing her, out of sheer devilry. Will you drop me a card?

Yours affectionately,

Eleanor Merson.

On the following Sunday Olga peeped into another world of romantic visions. She had played her exercises and her Scarlatti to Miss Merson, and they had had a nice talk about kings and cities and peoples, when there was a knock at the door. Miss Merson jumped up and opened it, and in floated a most radiant vision. She was tall, taller than Miss Merson, and she was radiant with health and nice clothes and cleanliness. Olga had never seen two people behave like that when they met. They kissed and called each other "dear" and asked how each other was in a way that showed that they really wanted to know. Then they turned to her, and Miss Merson said, "This is Olga." And the beautiful vision smiled at her, and said, "Well, Olga, how are you?" Olga was too dazzled to answer, but she tried to smile back some sort of response. Then the two women sat down and talked about her in a nice, kindly frank way, and the vision asked her questions without expecting any answer. It was all done in such a way that she did not feel uncomfortable. Then Miss Merson asked her to play her little Scarlatti. It seemed a very natural thing to do, so she went to the piano and played it as well as she could. In the meantime the two women carried on a telepathic conversation. They smiled at the frail little figure with the fat podgy arms frowning with intense earnestness at the keys. Now and then when the rhythm was particularly good, Miss Kenway would raise her eyebrows with approval, and Miss Merson would nod at her. When she played a finger passage with unusual brilliance, their eyes would meet again, and both women would laugh. When she had finished Miss Kenway said, "Thank you, Olga, that's very nice indeed." They made her sit between them and had another long talk. The conversation was mysterious, but seemed full of portentous promises. She felt a new world dawning for her.

There was a lot of talk about "Mr. Casewell" and other names, and constant references to "Levitch himself." There seemed to be a thing called a "method" that required a lot of discussion, also veiled and guarded references to her family. Olga could not follow much of it, so she sat looking from one to the other, feeling very elated. She realized for the first time that Miss Merson must be very old. She had almost white hair. She had not noticed it till then. But the contrast was very striking. The other lady had lovely, golden-brown hair, tucked away under a hat the like of which she had never seen. And then she had the most lovely complexion, clear and pink. Everything about her seemed to exude an atmosphere of "cleanliness" and exuberant health. She smelt different from anything she had come against before. After a time she rose and kissed Miss Merson. She patted Olga's hands, but Olga noticed that she did not kiss her. There was another long talk at the door, and at last she went.

The room down-stairs seemed more than usually unpleasant that evening, and it was not improved by the advent of two young men friends of Karl who played cards with her brothers and smoked innumerable cigarettes. Irene had gone out for the evening. One of the young men tried to be amused with her, and called her "monkey," and pulled her hair. She did not like him, and made herself as quiet and inconspicuous as possible. She went to bed without undressing, and later on Irene came home with another young man. This led to an incredible amount of noise and laughter. They all seemed to be there all night. She dozed, but was constantly awakened by the bark of Karl, and a snuffling guffaw of another of the young men, mingled with a sort of wheezy giggle that Irene developed. She could not recollect having heard Irene giggle before, and she wondered why she should do so to-night. In a half-conscious state she wondered whether the beautiful lady she had seen that afternoon was only a dream, or whether these people were all a dream. ... It seemed impossible that they could all be real people in the same world. . . .

A few days later she had the most impressive experience that her small life had so far undergone. She was fetched in a thing called a "hansom-cab." She knew there was something in the wind. For Miss Merson had had several interviews with Irene, during which she had been sent out of the room. And then Irene seemed to have a sufficiency of food, and to be fairly good tempered. In addition to this. Miss Merson made her a clean, cotton frock. And by a superhuman effort she had had Olga's face and neck washed, on that particular morning. Miss Merson was not there when the great event happened, but the beautiful person of the previous Sunday herself appeared. There was a few minutes' conversation with Irene, and then they went down-stairs. Quite a crowd of children had collected to see the cab, for it was a unique sight in that neighborhood. As she was being put in, she heard one girl ask, "Is she being taken to the 'orspital?"—for that indeed was the only purpose to which such luxuries seemed applicable. Olga glanced at the crowd, and hoped for the first time in her life to see the girl with the mouth organ. But to her disappointment she was not there. The general consternation, however, was in some way gratifying.

They dashed forth at a furious speed, scattering the jeering children right and left. In less than five minutes she had reached neighborhoods hitherto unsuspected. She was rather frightened at the way they dashed round the corners, and in and out of the traffic, but Miss Kenway talked to her calmly as though it were quite an ordinary experience.

They reached a broad river at last, alive with ships and barges. She had hardly time to glance at it before they rattled across it over an iron bridge. Then the world seemed to assume a different character. There were thousands of bright shops, and people seemed gayer and better looking. They wound in and out along dazzling streets and open spaces, and passed endless other cabs and carriages of incredible size and variety. At last they pulled up suddenly at a tall house in a quiet street. They got out and rang a bell, and immediately a boy in buttons opened the door. They went in and were shown up-stairs. She heard a piano being played by some one with tremendous brilliance whilst they waited for some time in a bright, clean room. After a time a girl came out of the room with a leather case, followed by a youngish, good-looking man with gold glasses. On seeing Miss Kenway he said, "Ah, good morning, Anna!" and Miss Kenway said, "How are you, John? This is the little girl I spoke of—Olga Bardel."

The young man smiled at her kindly, and shook her hand and said. "How are you, Olga?" What a wonderful world this was! Everybody seemed so nice to everybody else. They went into the next room which was almost bare except that it had a most peculiar looking piano, low and flat and very large, not at all like Miss Merson's.

"Now, what will you play to me?" said the young man in a brisk tone. She only had her one piece, and she sat down and solemnly played it. When she had finished the young man threw back his head and laughed loudly, and slapped his leg. "Well! well! well!" was his only comment. She did not know why the young man laughed, but he seemed so kind she was sure he did not mean to be rude. He turned to Miss Kenway, and another conversation went on very similar to that which had taken place between Miss Kenway and Miss Merson. There was the same discussion about "methods" and innumerable references to "Levitch himself." One fact seemed to be established, and that was that it was no good "Levitch himself" hearing her just yet. They then retired to a corner and whispered together, and Olga thought she heard Miss Kenway say, "Her people, my dear, are simply hopeless." After a time they went, the young man again shaking her hand, and saying, "Well, good-bye, Olga; we shall meet again." Then they got into another cab and drove to a wonderful house in a square overlooking a garden. Miss Kenway opened the door with her own key and they went into a brilliant hall. Miss Kenway seemed to expect her to wash again, though, as she had already washed that morning, it was rather surprising. The washing here seemed to take on something of the nature of a religious ceremony. There was a room full of marble basins with silver taps and lots of different soaps and rows of quite clean towels.

After all this they went into a gorgeous room where an old lady in gold glasses was reading a book. Miss Kenway introduced her and the old lady looked at her and said, "My goodness gracious, Anna! What will you do next?" Miss Kenway laughed, and they went into another room and sat at a table where two ladies in clean white aprons handed them most incredibly lovely things to eat. It was all rather overpowering, the smell of "cleanness" and the things you had to use to eat the food with, and the two ladies hovering at your elbow, and then the old lady constantly looking at her and muttering, "My goodness gracious!"

Olga was hungry, but too bewildered and excited by the pageant going on around her. It was true then! There was a world where people moved quietly and spoke kindly, and where Uncle Grubhofer did not hold sway, and this world was holding out infinite possibilities to her. These people had invited her into it, and been kind to her. After the meal, Miss Kenway made her lie down on a couch up-stairs, for two hours. But when they left her she was too excited to rest. She kept on getting up and looking out of the window, and touching the objects in the room. She felt an irresistible desire to sing and talk.

At length one of the ladies who had waited at table tapped on the door and came in. She called her "miss" and said Miss Kenway had had to go out, but she (the lady herself) was to take her in a cab back to her home. She was very tall and stiff and not apparently much of a talker, but when they got into the cab, Olga broke forth into a torrent of eloquence, the like of which she had never indulged in before in her life. She chatted interminably, and was quite satisfied for the tall lady to say occasionally, "Yes, miss." The brilliant shops and gay traffic flashed by, and Olga kept saying "Look! look!" This was the dominant instinct that possessed her—to see this great world, or rather to convince herself that she was seeing it, and that it was real. She felt that in a flash she had peered through the veil of dreary circumstance that had always enveloped her, and she wanted to engrave this vision deeply on her memory.

When the cab turned a sudden corner and she recognized a vista of gray unloveliness wherein her home was set, she struggled against the waves of moribund depression that seemed to come sweeping through the wretched lives of sorrow, threatening to destroy the reality of her vision. There were the same swarms of dirty children gathered on the roadways and playing on the pavements. As the cab drew up she noticed that there was a large crowd outside her own house and strange things were being shouted and said.

These children too had had their excitement on this mad day, though it was perhaps of a different nature. While Olga had been away Karl had been arrested for stealing money from a till.

As she went through the front door she saw the girl with the mouth organ grinning at her.

CHAPTER III

A FESTIVAL OF DEPRAVITY

The immediate purport of this tragic denouement in the Bardel family was somewhat obscure to Olga. But that it was an affair of great moment was apparent directly she burst into the room in her new cotton frock. Uncle Grubhofer was there standing like some immobile destiny with his back to the fireplace. Montague was seated in a corner feverishly biting his nails, while Irene was walking up and down the room crying and mopping her eyes with a ball of wet rag. Olga went to her corner and sat on her bed. Not a word was spoken. As she had passed through the front door the girl with the mouth organ had asked with a jubilant voice "if she knew that her brother was a dirty thief and had been locked up?" She had but a vague idea of what a thief was, but she had heard the children talk in excited whispers about prisons. She gathered that they were romantic editions of Uncle Grubhofer's hell, places of torment for the dangerous and vile, affairs of heavy doors and clanking chains. She was unstrung by the events of the day, and the sudden vision of Karl lying in some dark cell without food and perhaps being attacked by animals and other crawling things, sent a spasm of pity through her. She had never loved Karl, but now when she thought of him she could only think of his wretchedness, of the pathos of his face expressing unspeakable anguish. She looked at the faces of her three relations—all of whom had ignored her—and she suddenly burst into tears. They all looked at her with surprise, and a curious feeling of uneasiness seemed to creep over them. Irene stopped her crying, Montague stood up and looked self-conscious, and Uncle Grubhofer lighted a cigar. Irene had up to that point felt important in her grief; in addition she was tremendously moved by the whole dramatic situation, and excited by the publicity which the affair caused, and would cause. But here was a sob coming right from the bottom of a heart. She felt that that wretched little "scrub" was being in some way superior. And the reflection made Irene furious. She went up to her younger sister and struck her with the back of her hand. "What the hell are you sniveling about? You take off that dress and go to bed," she shrieked.

The blow seemed to steady the little girl and she did as she was bidden. But in the night the vision of her new world faded, and she thought only of Karl with his pale face pressed against the prison bars.

During the next few days she was left very much alone. The rest were away at Karl's trial. She soothed the turmoil of her soul on Miss Merson's piano, but she did not hear from any of her friends. Then on one tragic afternoon Irene and Montague came in. They were in a great state of perturbation. It seemed that Karl was to stop in prison for three months; but what seemed to cause them the greatest disquiet was that Uncle Grubhofer had refused to give them money, and now there was no money to come from Karl's salary and they were debating where the food was to come from. While this gloomy discussion was going on, there was a knock at the door and she heard a gruff voice talking, and distinctly heard her own name mentioned. Waves of fear passed over her. She at once thought of a policeman and expected to see him put his head round the corner and come in and carry her off. She tried to think what she had done. There were many things. She was very wicked, she knew. She had played with Uncle Grubhofer's "property." She had been for that wonderful ride in the hansom-cab. She had once stolen some food out of the cupboard—just like Karl! That was evidently it. She steeled herself for the coming blow. But at last the door was shut and she heard the heavy footsteps going down-stairs. Irene came in and turned to her and said, "You've got to go to school, my girl," and then she sniffed, and turning to Montague continued her discussion of ways and means.

Olga turned this information over in her mind and tried to think what it meant. She knew that those other children went to school. Would it be pleasant or unpleasant? Would she be taught to play the piano? would Miss Merson herself teach her? or Miss Kenway? That evening she hung about very late and managed to catch Miss Merson and tell her her news.

"Ah!" said her friend, "I was expecting that, my dear. I expect they will send you to Murford Street. I teach at the Collingwood schools. What a pity! I should have liked to have had you. Now what can we do about the music? Mr. Casewell was quite willing to give you lessons, but it is so far. I must talk to your sister."

But the talk with Irene was in every way unsatisfactory. Irene was in no mood to go out of her way to pander to silly whims of that sort. Besides, she was jealous of the interest these people had taken in her younger sister. She insisted on Olga attending the Murford Street School, and to every suggestion of Miss Merson's that might make music lessons possible she brought forward some objection. Miss Merson thought it advisable to bide her time.

So, on the following Monday, Olga was duly bundled off to attend the Murford Street National School, and the experience was more horrible than any she could have conceived. In the first place her introduction was unfortunate, for almost the first girl she met there was the big girl with the mouth organ, and her greeting was, "Hullo! dirty thief!" and it is a regrettable comment on the standard of education instilled at our elementary schools that as long as she remained there she was known as "dirty thief," except to a few of the more charitable minded who called her "monkey face."

The horror of these school days she was never able to eradicate entirely from her memory. She was the sport and plaything of all those dirty and objectionable children whom she had always avoided in the streets. She could not get away from them for a moment. They teased her in the playground and played terrifying tricks on her in the classroom. Their greatest enjoyment seemed to be to try and make her lose her temper and cry. She was packed into a class of about forty noisy, quarrelsome, embryonic, female hooligans. A thin wan elderly woman made desperate attempts to impart unattractive knowledge by means of blackboards and slates, and by a system of chanting in unison. They would all stand up and drone together, "Yorkshire—York—Leeds—Halifax—Sheffield—Huddersfield," or, "Seven—eights—are—fifty-six," and one statement seemed as unconvincing and incomprehensible as the other.

Perhaps this thin wan woman—whose name was Miss McQuire—was not sure of herself on her knowledge. She sometimes spoke in a tired voice as though she were not really sure that seven eights were fifty -six, but the redundant repetition of the statement by forty young voices gave her a comforting assurance. Perhaps she only arranged this chanting as a means of defense, a method of drowning the restless din with which she was otherwise incapable of coping. Olga could not understand why the same toneless sounds should apply to everything. Why not have different tones and different notes for different knowledge? "Things keep running through one's head," she thought, "but they've all same things." Then the children would be asked questions in rotation, and upon their ability to give the correct answer, their intelligence, character, and general proficiency was measured.

When she returned home in the afternoon she felt completely overwrought and wretched. A listless apathy seized her and she felt no desire to work or play. She would go up to Miss Merson's room and open the piano, but after playing a few scales she would burst into tears. Then she would sit in the dark and wait for Miss Merson to come home. That good lady was in every way sympathetic, but she realized that she was in a very difficult position. She discussed the matter with Miss Kenway, who discussed it with Mr. Casewell. Olga was now eight years old and of course they could not take her away from school. The question was—how to help her, and keep up her interest in music, for they were all agreed that the child showed promise. At length an arrangement was made. There was a poor but talented pupil of Mr. Casewell's who lived only a penny tram ride journey from the Bardels. It was arranged that she should go to Miss Merson's on Saturday afternoons and give Olga a lesson for a small fee which would be paid for by Miss Kenway, or rather by Miss Kenway's mother, who said "My goodness gracious!"

Miss Merson broke the news to Olga at the end of her first trying week, and her eyes glowed with the anticipation of new joy. This pupil turned up as agreed. Her name was Rebecca Cohen. She was a nice girl, very dark, with a pale fat face. She was not a good teacher, not having the faculty of lucid explanation, but she was patient and very encouraging. This new force in any ease tended to give Olga a renewed interest in existence. She felt that Rebecca Cohen was a link to that splendid world to which she had paid so brief a visit.

Since the departure of Karl it was true that the home seemed quieter, but the food was even worse and scarcer. Had it not been for Miss Merson she would not have had the strength to get through the day. And when she went up to her room to practise in the afternoon she always found a slice of cake on a plate on the piano keys. Poor Miss Merson! she earned the sum of eighty pounds a year out of which she contributed forty pounds towards the keep of a paralytic brother in Sheffield, and yet she always managed to give Olga the impression of being a lady of unlimited means.

At this time another character appeared on the scene in the person of Alfred Weekes, who apparently came courting Irene. Sometimes he came and spent the evening in their room, in which case Olga was sent up to Miss Merson's, or out on to the staircase, or else he and Irene went out together. He was a reedy youth, an assistant in a tobacconist shop near by.

Olga did not understand the idea of courtship, and she used to wonder why this strange young man was invited in and given food, when there was already not enough for the others. He would stay unconscionably late, and she would go to sleep in the corner to the sound of Irene 's special giggle that she reserved for these occasions and to an irritating "pat-pat-pat!" She could not understand this noise at first, but she found it was the result of a curious action on the part of both of them. They would stand facing each other and then Irene would give the young man three rapid pats on his back, and in a moment or two he would say something and then return them. They would keep up this reciprocal patting arrangement all the evening, and when it became time for him to go the patting would become more frequent and more violent, ending in other sounds by the door and on the staircase. It seemed surprising that Irene should derive pleasure from kissing this unattractive young tobacconist, but such seemed to be the case, for when she returned to the room Olga through her half closed eyes noticed the face of her elder sister looking flushed and happy, and she would stretch herself and look at herself in the broken mirror in a manner that Olga had never seen before.

It cannot be said, however, that Irene seemed in any way better disposed towards her. She seemed more irritable and unreasonable than ever. In spite of the penury of the family she appeared in new gay blouses and hair combs, and added to the general melange of odors that characterized the room by introducing a sweet and penetrating scent with which she saturated her clothes. Olga saw very little of Miss Merson during the week—she had secured some evening work that kept her out till late at night.

She lived through the agony of the week, buoyed up by the knowledge that Saturday and Sunday would come. But the days seemed interminable and exhausting. She began to see life as a cruel and terrible business. Her visit to Miss Kenway and Mr, Casewell had given her some sense of proportion. She vainly yearned for them to come again and take her away among people who moved softly and spoke kindly, and she could not understand why they did not.

The three months of that first term were the longest and most trying months she ever passed through. At the end of that time, the Murford Street National School teachers appraised her the fifth dullest pupil in a class of forty dull children. And then to her joy she was informed that there was to be a holiday for two weeks. The respite seemed too good to be true, and she lay awake at night dreaming of the splendid hours she would spend with Miss Merson's piano.

The next morning before she was up Karl returned home from prison.

If the idea of the prison system be to act as a corrective in any way, it certainly did not succeed in the case of Karl. Olga did not recognize him for some minutes. His face seemed to have shrunk and to look pinched and quite yellow, and his eyes looked more shifty than ever. His hair was quite cropped and he looked ten years older. Irene shrieked and kissed him, but he hardly acknowledged her, and he looked wildly round the room. "He is hungry," thought Olga. Such seemed to be the case. He ate some bread and dripping greedily and Irene made him some tea. Montague came upstairs a few moments later and a curiously self-conscious greeting took place between the brothers. Karl ignored Olga. He seemed tremendously anxious to get hold of some money. He said Irene had six shillings of his. This she denied, and a very unpleasant scene followed. Eventually he borrowed a shilling from Montague and three pence from Irene, and pulling his cloth cap right down round his ears he went out.

This sudden arrival upset Olga. She felt no desire to work, and that all her vague plans were in jeopardy, and so indeed they were. Karl did not come back till very late that night, and then he was very drunk. He behaved like a madman. Mr, Alfred Weekes was there looking very scared, and also Montague. Karl said that everybody was conspiring to do him down. He accused Irene of stealing his money while he was away, and on Weekes mildly seconding Irene's denial, Karl struck him on the mouth and made his lip bleed. He said his whole family could go to the devil. Even if he had taken a few shillings from the till, why had he done it? Simply to keep them. They ate up his salary and rounded on him when his back was turned. Pie called Irene names, and at one moment turned to Olga and said "he wasn't going to keep that greedy little either." Olga cried and he pushed her violently across the bed. Montague said "Steady! Steady! don't be a sanguinary fool!" And then Karl flew at Montague and the brothers fought all over the room, with Irene and Olga shrieking in the background, and the young man Weekes trying to get out of the way of the blows.

Suddenly in the midst of this turmoil, the door opened and there stood Uncle Grubhofer. The effect of the presence of this ponderous relation was electrical. The brothers fell panting apart, while the screams of Irene and Olga subsided into stifled sobs. Uncle Grubhofer never seemed so enormous as he did at that moment. He stood there, looking round without speaking. Curiously enough the person who seemed to attract Ms eye more than any other was the unfortunate Weekes. Uncle Grubhofer looked at him with a melancholy amazement, and suddenly said, "What the devil are you doing here?"

His voice boomed with a kind of sepulchral timbre. It seemed to convey the idea to the wretched Weekes that the Bardel family was quite capable of conducting its own festival of depravity without his assistance. He fumbled for his hat, and holding a handkerchief to his bleeding lip he slunk out of the room without a word. Uncle Grubhofer moved a portion of his person a foot or two one way, just to give him room to pass, and then the space closed up again like the damming of a river. In the case of the Weekes it may be said that it closed up again forever, for he was never seen in the Bardels' house again.

After he had gone there was a somber silence. Karl, looking sick and faint, huddled against the mantelpiece, whilst the others hovered tremblingly in the dim recesses of the room. The whole thing seemed unreal to Olga, unreal but unforgettable. She had dreaded the return of Karl, but had the idea that three months was a much longer period of time. She had never known affection from her family, and they had never tried to show her that it had a meaning. They had always seemed just to happen together like a lot of dogs eating out of a plate. After her glimpse of splendid things she had even dreamed of escaping from them all. But somehow on this evening they seemed to hem her in. They were all round her, with the immobile mass of Uncle Grubhofer blocking the door. In after years she vividly recalled that moment, for in her immature mind there suddenly flashed some premonition that it would always be thus. Wherever she went there would always be Karl and Montague, and Irene hovering in the other dark corners, and Uncle Grubhofer, sphinx-like and terrible, controlling their movements. But what impressed her in after years was the consciousness that at that moment the child knew that in her inmost heart there was a force more compelling even than the power this old man exerted. It was a certain call of the blood, a sort of ingrained sympathy with the abject figures of her relations. She knew that she could never eradicate this, try as she might. Uncle Grubhofer was speaking. His voice boomed round the room, and his small eyes glittered at them each in turn. He talked of their vices with a lingering satisfaction, as though the consideration of them gratified some inner lust. He might have been the arch-priest of some gray underworld reviewing an army of pallid sins. He mentioned names that Olga had not heard before,

Oscar, Jacob, Ferdinand, Walter, Emmeline, and Wanda. With a sudden shock it came home to her that these names were the names of brothers and sisters of hers who had died! They too, it seemed, were the victims of evil vices. They were born in sin, lived in sin, and died in sin. The devil's hoofs trod them under, as he would tread under and crush these four unfortunate remnants. They could never escape it.

A shriek interrupted this peroration and it came from Olga. She had suddenly noticed Montague turn very white and slip on to the floor. She thought he was dead. She imagined that Uncle Grubhofer had cast a spell on him, as he would on all the others and destroy them in turn.

"Don't!" she shrieked. "Don't! Don't!" Montague had fainted, and it was an action that came as a pleasant relief. Uncle Grubhofer disappeared and left Irene to bring her brother to. This she did by sprinkling him with some of her cheap scent, and then Karl had to be got to bed. It was a night in which every member of that family suffered an individual night of anguish, rocking with their own terrors. Olga was very silent and she tried to help Irene get the brothers to bed. When she retired herself she lay there wide-eyed all night going over again and again all that had taken place, and had been said. Then she thought of those other brothers and sisters and wondered what they were like. She sobbed pitifully and silently. She recalled each of the names. Were the boys like Karl and Montague? And Emmeline and Wanda, were they like Irene or like her? She thought Wanda was a pretty name. She wondered whether she would have liked Wanda.

But she was dead; she died in sin, and perhaps even now she was in that awful place that Uncle Grubhofer had so vividly described to her.

She thought of Miss Merson, and almost decided to creep out of bed and go up-stairs and find comfort in her arms. But the knowledge that she would have to pass Uncle Grubhofer 's door lay like a leaden weight upon her chest and kept her inert. At last the interminable night was broken by pale gleams of light through the tattered blind. Soon after came the rattle of milk carts and all the other inevitable sounds heralding the dubious industries of the day.

She remembered that she was not to go to school, and the satisfaction of this knowledge was somewhat marred by the fact of Karl's return and the nerve-racking effect of the previous night's events. Everything seemed late that morning and it must have been ten o'clock before she escaped to Miss Merson's room. The sounds of the familiar runs and chords seemed soothing to her tired frame. She ran her fingers up and down the piano with a sensuous thoughtlessness. She was just beginning to consider what it was that Rebecca Cohen had told her to practise, when the door burst open and Irene's head appeared, and her strident voice called out:

"You 've got to stop that row. Karl 's got a bad 'ead. You can come down and 'elp me wash up."

The door slammed to, and Olga rose and shut the piano quietly. Some fatalistic sense had prepared her for this and she went through the day's drudgery resignedly. For she was now reaching an age when Irene began to find her useful about the house, and all the most uncongenial tasks were allotted to her. It is true that great cleanliness was not insisted upon, but it was part of the contract that they had to keep two of Uncle Grubhofer's rooms in order and to make up his bed and to collect the cigar ends and in other ways rectify the irruptions of his domestic life. They also had to sweep down the stairs, and make some sort of order out of the chaos in the basement where Karl and Montague slept. And then the front door step was occasionally cleaned, and perhaps the most essential work of the day was to see that Uncle Grubhofer's brass plate reflected its eternal splendors to the admiring gaze of the local children.

All these duties devolved more and more on Olga as she became older and stronger. Nor indeed did she resent them. She derived satisfaction out of the physical sense of doing things that were wanted. Her only objection was that they came violently and at unreasonable moments. Her practising would be interrupted at any moment at the urgent command to perform some menial task.

Nevertheless she persevered and that innate sense of cunning in this matter did not desert her. For three days after Karl's return she was not allowed to go near the piano. For Karl stopped indoors and was very unwell and truculent. And then he started going out a little while at a time. Olga had to dovetail her practising into the moments when Karl was out and Uncle Grubhofer was out and when she was not required for housework. Sometimes this desirable combination of circumstances happened, but during the two weeks' respite from the agonies of school, it is doubtful if she put in eight hours' complete practice. And yet Miss Rebecca Cohen was able to report that the little girl, Olga Bardel, was getting on "very well indeed." And then the dreaded day arrived when she had to return to school, and all its monotonous horrors were repeated.

In the meantime Karl got another job through the influence of Uncle Grubhofer. It was to travel in trinkets and cheap jewelry. He carried a small black case and called in at shops, and private houses, and eating houses and saloons, and flashed his seductive wares in the eyes of all-too-human mortals. It seemed quite surprising that a man who had just come out of prison for stealing should be entrusted with a case of jewelry, but perhaps it only emphasized the amazing power of Uncle Grubhofer, flavored with a certain cynical enjoyment of the sense of the constant jars of temptation that this profession must entail.

Then followed a period of dismal monotony for Olga, broken by a few pale gleams of relief. The din and clatter of the school was always in her ears even in bed. She found one or two of the girls rather nicer and more friendly than the others, but they never became intimate. She was always terrified by the tricks they played on her, and amazed by their cruelty and roughness. She learnt a few facts mechanically like mnemonic tricks, but they bore no relation to other facts and did not help her to cope with the tribulations of her life. After school the home, housework, and the eternal struggle for food and petty comforts. She practised in spasmodic intervals, and Miss Cohen still continued to come on Saturdays. Even her lessons were interrupted and interfered with by household demands.

Irene had a period of hysterical depression following on the tragic evening when Mr. Alfred Weekes broke off his engagement and "patted" no more. And then Montague became very ill and was taken away to a hospital. He was not expected to recover, but he eventually did and returned after many months, looking paler and more phlegmatic than ever. Karl prospered in his trinket profession and became more noisy and domineering, and alas! indulged in more orgies of drink. There were nights when she would lie awake and the room seemed to become the playground of evil spirits. In the shallow shafts of light she could not disengage realities from hallucinations. There seemed to be a wild dance of frenzied passions, and at the door the impenetrable mask of Uncle Grubhofer with his lips upon a reed.

CHAPTER IV

ROLLY'S AQUARIUM

There came a great day in her life when she was taken by Mr. Casewell to play to "Levitch himself."

She could tell by the way her friends spoke of this visit that it signified an event of tremendous importance. Perhaps she was a little disappointed by her first impression of "Levitch himself"; she certainly did not imagine that the little bald-headed man with the short neck and the dark eyes, who bustled forward and took both her hands in his, was going to have the influence on her life that he did.

She noticed, indeed, that his eyes were very keen and kind, and that they twinkled with a certain humorous warmth, and that he moved with little jerky actions, but there was something too unusual and foreign about him to make an instant appeal.

"He 's like a bird," she thought.

He led her to the piano with a queer display of courtesy that she had not observed in any one before, and made her comfortable.

When she had played the piece that Mr. Casewell had instructed her to, "Levitch himself" threw his small head right back and laughed uproariously. She had never heard any one laugh quite so loudly or so freely.

It was a splendid laugh. It did not surprise her, because she knew that Mr. Casewell and all these nice people always laughed when they first heard her. It meant that they were pleased. She grinned herself with satisfaction to think that Levitch laughed. And then he came and stroked her hair and cried out:

"Brava! Brava! Very nice! Play me again."

And so she played again. She played everything she knew, and "Levitch himself" kept on calling out "Brava! Brava!" and laughing.

When she had finished he spoke to Mr. Casewell in a foreign language and seemed very excited.

As they were going he said:

"Olga, you shall be a gr-r-eat pee-an-eeste, isn't it? Now tell me, do you like apples?"

She smiled and said, "Yes."

He took one out of a bag and handed it to her.

"Apples," he said, "are goot, very goot indeed. You must always eat apples, and then you vill one day be a gr-r-eat arteeste!"

He took a bite out of one himself, and continued:

"Ven you are nairvous or troubled you shall eat an apple. You shall eat the skin too, for that is goot. But you must not eat the core, for the core will steek in your t'roat, and then there will be no more little pee-an-eeste." He spoke again to Mr. Casewell in the foreign tongue, and then he turned and patted her hands and said:

"So! you shall vork hart, and come and see me again already!"

It was so kind the way he did this, that Olga could find nothing to say. She was conscious of smiling through her tears.

In after-life she often recalled that first advice that "Levitch himself" gave her about the apples, and when she remembered to follow it, she found it in every way beneficial.

She returned to Canning Town in a very elated state. She felt that she was on the eve of some great and fortunate change in her affairs. She could not restrain her desire to talk, and she told Irene about the kindness of the great professor who had said "Brava! brava!" and given her an apple.

She was conscious after that that conflicting forces were at work behind her back: letters passed, and people called and talked in the passage outside, and one day, in Miss Merson's room, she was aware of Uncle Grubhofer listening furtively outside the door when she was practising.

A week passed, and then one day he suddenly summoned her to the awful room. He was cleaning his nails with a piece of wire filing. He glanced at her and said:

"I shall want you to go out with me this afternoon to see a gentleman; so get yourself ready by three o'clock, and you may have to play the piano, so take your pieces with you."

She protested mildly that she had her appointment for a lesson with Casewell that afternoon, but Uncle Grubhofer repeated very distinctly:

"Irene will get you ready. Be here at a quarter to three."

At a quarter to three, therefore, she reappeared in Uncle Grubhofer's room, having undergone a tentative operation of cleaning up at the hands of Irene. Uncle Grubhofer donned a square bowler hat with his long-tail coat, and a muffler, and lighting a cigar he led the way into the street. They walked a considerable distance, and then took a tram. The tram put them down at a bright corner, which seemed a junction for other trams. It was very noisy and gay. There were brilliant public houses and shops and a fried-fish shop, built apparently in blue tiles, which announced "SMITH'S FISH SNACKS," and then in smaller letters, "Say this quickly, and then come inside and order some." Next to this was a large red-brick building with columns and rounded arches, and in black letters on a mosaic ground was the inscription, ROLLY'S AQUARIUM. Outside which a very tall, military-looking gentleman in gold and blue was bawling, "Now showing! The Murder of Mrs. Quilles! Step inside!"

They went past this aristocratic person, and down a dark passage, and then knocked at a door. Some one said, "Come in!" and Olga found herself in a long, low stuffy room full of cases and canvas stacks of printed advertisements. At one end was a large roll-top desk next to a fire, where a fat man with oily fair hair sat smoking a cigar. He looked up and said, "Oh, is that you, Grubhofer? Just a minute!" He took up a pen and wrote something down in a small note-book, and then, turning towards them, he said, "Oh, is this the little girl? How old is she?"

"Fourteen," said Uncle Grubhofer, much to Olga's surprise. She was about to protest that she was not yet twelve, but Uncle Grubhofer put his hand on her shoulder, and continued:

"She 's very strong, though—strong as a girl of sixteen. You must hear her play."

The fat gentleman grunted as though somewhat skeptical of these pronouncements, and then said suddenly to her:

"Can she play coon music?"

She had not the faintest idea what coon music was, but before she had had time to answer Uncle Grubhofer interpolated:

"My dear sir, she can play anything. She can play anything."

The fat man got up and, removing some boxes from another corner, revealed an old upright piano.

"Let 's hear what she can do," he said.

The business now began to assume some meaning in the eyes of the little girl. There was a piano, and she was asked to play. She did not know what the significance of the demand implied, but she could play, and she would. She sat down and played a prelude by Chopin, putting all she knew into it. It was the same prelude that she had first played to "Levitch himself," the performance of which had made him throw back his head and laugh. As she lifted her fingers from the piano after the last chord, she instinctively turned to see what effect it had had on the fat man. Apparently he had not been listening. His shiny red face, with the cigar stuck in the corner of his mouth, was gazing blankly at a book in which he was busily writing. After a few seconds he glanced up, implying that he knew she had finished because she had left off, and then he rummaged in a waste-paper basket, at the same time saying:

"Yes. Can she play anything a bit brighter?"

She thought for a moment, and then started playing a Chopin waltz. She had only played a few passages before the telephone bell went. The fat man took off the receiver and bawled through in a loud voice, "'Ullo! 'Ullo! is that you, Carter? Oh, well, now look 'ere, I want you to find out what date Humphries and Plumbwell sent off that cast of the Duchess of Pleads, eh?" There was a pause, during which the fat man was apparently waiting information; his small eyes wandered round the room and suddenly lighted on Olga.

She had naturally left off at the first crash of the telephone-bell. He looked at her as though seeing her for the first time, and then something seemed to jog his memory, and he said in a matter-of-fact way, "Er—go on, Miss—er—Grubhofer. We won 't be long. "She sat there feeling furious and unhappy. She wanted to cry, but was restrained by the presence of Uncle Grubhofer, who, she knew, was hovering behind her. She stared hopelessly at the piano, wondering whether she had better make another desperate effort to begin all over again. She was rescued from her indecision by the action of the fat man, who had evidently got the information he wanted and entered it in a book. He cleared his throat and swung round on his chair and addressed himself to Uncle Grubhofer.

"Yes, well, you know, Grubhofer," he said, "this sort of thing 's all right, I expect, but it won't do for here. She must work up some coon-music, and—" He paused and then, turning suddenly to Olga, he said, "Can she play 'As Once in May,' or, 'Thy Lily Lips'?"

Olga felt her heart beating fast with outraged disappointment, as though something had gone entirely wrong with the world. She said weakly, "No."

"Um!" said the fat man, and then he ferreted about under his desk and produced some music. He rolled the cigar from one side of his mouth to another, and then said, "Let her take these, and work 'em up. And then perhaps we can talk business."

On the way home, Uncle Grubhofer seemed meditative, and the next morning he told her she need not go to school; she could stop at home and "work up the pieces Mr. Albu gave her."

These instructions rather excited her. In any ease, anything was better than going to school, and perhaps she would like the music. But what would Mr. Casewell think? And Levitch himself? She eagerly unfolded the printed matter and scampered through it. She could read very well, and yet she could make little of the coon-songs, though she thought "As Once in May" was rather pretty, and there were several other simple, sentimental little pieces. She played them through several times, and then got tired of them the same morning. She would not analyze her feelings, but she became more and more convinced that Mr. Casewell would not approve of her playing these pieces; it was as though some inner finer feeling were being outraged. Moreover, Uncle Grubhofer was hovering behind the door, and once when she threw the music down in disgust, and started practising her Chopin, she heard his heavy breathing, and she knew that he was in the room. She was almost afraid to look round. During the rest of that week, for the first time of her life, she almost wished she were at school.

When Saturday came round she was quite surprised to find that she was to be allowed to go to Mr. Casewell's. Her surprise would perhaps not have been so great had she been allowed to read the note that she was given and told to present to Mr. Casewell, together with a bundle of music. It ran as follows:

Mr. Grubhofer presents his compliments to Mr. Casewell and will be obliged if he will give his niece, Miss Olga Bardel, lessons on the enclosed pieces, and also if he will kindly teach her how to play coon music without delay and oblige.

When Mr. Casewell read this note his nostrils trembled with a grim defiance. He recognized it as a challenge, though he could not have guessed that it was to be the prelude to a long and bitter struggle between two forces that were to control ultimately what one must call—for lack of a less pretentious term—the artistic soul of Olga Bardel. He said nothing to Olga, but he seemed abstracted during her lesson, and afterwards he prompted her to find out what had happened. When she told him the whole story of her visit to Mr. Albu, he looked grave. Then he sat down and wrote a note, which he gave her to take back,

Mr. Casewell regrets that he cannot accede to Mr. Grubhofer's request His lessons to Miss Bardel are, of course, quite gratuitous, the outcome of his recognition of the very real talent and promise of this little girl. He cannot believe that any useful purpose would be achieved by teaching her the accompanying pieces or instructing her in coon music, and in both cases it would be entirely contrary to his own method of teaching, which he must be allowed to prosecute in his own way.

Mr. Casewell stopped. He was about to sign it, but a further idea prompted him to add:

He fully recognizes that Miss Bardel's talents, as they are, may be turned to some small commercial advantage, but he strongly urges that she may be allowed to continue in her present course of study for the present, in the conviction that in a short time they will be of a lucrative value out of all proportion to any temporary rewards.

After the exchange of these notes there was a lull in the proceedings for three days. And then she was taken by Uncle Grubhofer to visit a young man in the neighborhood whose name was Christopher Tilley. He was a bright and gladsome young creature, and he called Olga "Kiddy." It seemed that the idea was that he should teach Olga how to play coon music.

This he did with a sort of joyous abandon, singing and laughing and talking, at the same time. He was very impressed with Olga's pianistic abilities, and said, "You ll soon fix it all right, kiddy. It 's quite easy, you know—syncopated time. Look here, let 's do this 'Moonlight Darkies.' Rum-tum-tura-tum, rum-tum-tum-tura. Bang it out, you know. This is where you get the beat." And then he howled to his accompaniment:

"I 'm waiting for her,
The little Yoonah gal,

"Yum-tum-tum-tum—it 's just the rhythm you have to remember. You know what rhythm is, of course. Let it go, you know, what?"

She had three lessons from Mr. Christopher Tilley, and played coon music quite nicely. And then she was taken to Mr. Albu again, to show what progress she had made. That gentleman was obviously satisfied. He even went so far as to leave off writing in his book while she was playing "Moonlight Darkies," and to beat an accompaniment with his pencil on the roll-top desk.

After that there was a long and keen discussion between Mr. Albu and Uncle Grubhofer with regard to terms. It was at length agreed that Olga was to attend the aquarium for one week on trial. After that she was to receive ten shillings a week—or rather, Uncle Grubhofer was to receive ten shillings a week, payable on Friday nights. Her hours were to be from one to six one week, with half-an-hour's interval for tea, and from six to ten-thirty, the alternate week.

When they arrived home, Uncle Grubhofer took her to his room and gave her a long dissertation on morality and life. He drew a terrifying picture of the Bardel family, and emphasized all the vices and disabilities of each individual member. He spoke of their ingratitude to him, and expatiated on what he had done for all of them. But on none of them, apparently, had he showered such favors and tokens of affection as on Olga. He lingered on the question of the expense she had always been to him, but now it seemed there was just a small chance of her beginning to show just ever so little a return for all his kindnesses. She must work hard and stick to it, and try and demonstrate that one member of the family had a grain of moral decency.

All of which impressed Olga very much. She had no standard of relative values to go by. She believed that what he said must be the truth, and she felt crushed and unhappy. And the thought weighed upon her that she had perhaps no right to go to Mr. Casewell and visit these other people.

When the news reached Miss Merson, that lady did a thing she was not in the habit of doing—she lost her temper. She went down-stairs and bearded Uncle Grubhofer in his den. Nothing is known of what took place at that interview, but the next morning she received a week's notice to quit the house, "as her room was required for the extension of the business of Julius Grubhofer."

Poor Miss Merson! She was very upset, and she went to see Miss Kenway, but the philanthropist had no workable solution to suggest. Mr. Casewell and Rebecca Cohen were also consulted, but on the following Monday Miss Merson had to pack her meager belongings into a greengrocer's cart, and move further down the street; and Olga commenced her engagement with Mr. Albu at the aquarium.

Roily 's Aquarium was a characteristic landmark of South London at that time. Its principal attraction was its wax works. It had a large central hall with recesses all round. Some of these recesses—those for instance where a lifelike representation of the very latest and most piquant murder was displayed—were accessible only on an extra payment of twopence or threepence. The charge for admission varied according to what was considered the standard of public interest. In this connection it is perhaps to be regretted, that members of the Royal Family were free and in prodigal numbers. They even stood in the hall and on the staircase—the Queen and the Princesses having deplorably dirty necks, and their frocks having lost a good deal of their early splendor. Famous generals and politicians were also free of access to any one, whereas Ben Leatham, whose claim to public notice lay in the fact that he had strangled Mrs. Quilles in bed, had a recess to himself, and was visible only on the payment of sixpence. It is true that one saw not only Ben Leatham himself, but what was claimed to be the actual bed and the actual rope. There was also the terrifying figure of Mrs. Quilles lying huddled under the sheets. It was in any case a popular recess and fully justified the management's business judgment in making it the most expensive. There was also a recess where sat the figure of the Countess of Fyshe-Slayce resplendent in diamonds and a faded maroon dress. She had been convicted ten years previously of putting poison in her husband's tea, but the glamour of the romantic episode had somewhat waned, and one might gaze at her penciled eyebrows for a humble twopence.

From the body of the hall two iron staircases led to an upper gallery, where were booths and stalls and a place where people shot at moving targets, rabbits and lions chasing each other over hillocks.

This combination of attractions, living and wax, seemed to require the chastening influence of melody to bind it together, and Olga discovered that her duty bound her to sit behind two screens next to the shooting gallery and play the piano for five hours on end with a few short intervals. The Aquarium was open from ten in the morning till ten-thirty at night, but music was not considered necessary till one o'clock. She started on the following Monday at one o'clock accordingly, feeling rather important and excited. Very few people came in till two or three, and then it seemed to become noisy and tiring. People would occasionally come up and peer at her through the screen and say, "It 's a little girl!" and then go away.

She soon discovered that her most trying difficulty was to be the shooting gallery next door, and for the life of her she could not think why the piano had been placed in the noisiest spot in the whole building. She would get fairly interested in the slow melody of some sentimental song when suddenly would come the sharp "pop! pop! pop!"

She felt at times that it was a distraction she might have got accustomed to if it had been regular and rhythmic but it was the horrible uncertainty of when the sound was coming, that in a few days produced in her the sensation of being struck by a whip every time she heard that penetrating toneless snap.

It was very hot up in the gallery and the time seemed interminable, nevertheless she struggled through the week with credit, and at the end of that time Mr. Albu said that he thought "she would do all right. She must get a bit more snap into the bright things, and play 'Thy Lily Hands' much slower."

On the following week she started in earnest, but her interest and enthusiasm had somewhat abated. She would start the day well, but after an hour she would feel tired and irritable. About four o 'clock an attendant would bring her a cup of tea with a thin slice of bread and butter poised on the saucer. This revived her for half an hour, and she had to flog her energies to get through till six o'clock. When it was over she felt dazed and weak, and her head throbbed.

When she arrived home at night, she noticed that she was given something definite to eat, some soup or stewed potatoes, with occasionally a small piece of meat.

She was not allowed to visit Miss Merson on Sunday, and spent most of the day lying on the bed.

On the following Monday she had to play in the evening, and this she found more exhausting still, although the hours were a little shorter. She relieved an elderly woman whom she found playing there at six o'clock and then she had to keep going till ten. The air seemed much fouler in the evening and there were many more people. There was quite a long queue waiting to get in to "the Murder of Mrs. Quilles." Once during an interval an attendant had allowed her to go in. It had been very terrible. She wanted to scream. She had never seen anything more awful than the face of Ben Leatham stealthily creeping away from the bed with a small black bag in his hands, presumably containing Mrs. Quilles's jewels. She did not meditate upon the tragic co-relation of jewels and that meager room, she was consumed with a violent horror, the thing huddled beneath the sheets! and more with a sort of intensive, pity. She wanted to rush forward to help, to throw her arms around it.

"The Murder of Mrs. Quilles" did not amuse her, and when she got back to the gallery she could not play "Thy Lily Hands"; it seemed incongruous and profane. She felt very upset, and she scampered over the keys feverishly, striking wrong notes. In the evening crowds of young men came, and the "snap, snap, snap" from the shooting gallery went on all the time.

After two hours of it her temples would begin to throb with pain.

On the third evening Mr. Albu came and looked at her meditatively, and then he touched her on the shoulder and said:

"Come round and see me at my office at eight o'clock."

A wave of hope that she was to be dismissed for incompetence passed over her, merged with the dread of the effect of such a circumstance upon Uncle Grubhofer. But her fears were set at rest on entering Mr. Albu's office. He said:

"You 're looking peeky. We 'll go and have some fish."

He nodded to her to follow him, and they went out through the corridor and entered the resplendent edifice consecrated to "Smith's Fish Snacks."

This was the first intimation that she had that Mr. Albu was a person not altogether without a heart. As a matter of fact, he was just a type of whom she was to meet hundreds in after life; that is to say, he was just purely and exclusively commercial, with a preference for compromise over any form of tyranny. He was a manager of an Aquarium appointed by a syndicate, and he managed it to the best of his commercial ability, regardless of all other considerations. He paid Olga what he considered a fair wage as regulated by supply and demand, but it was not to his interest or to the interest of the syndicate that she should crock up. He looked at her in the same way that an engineer looks at a machine. If he thinks the machine looks creaky and dry, he injects a little oil. In the same way, if the pianist is getting run down, he fills her up with "fish snacks." And so these fish suppers became quite an institution with this strangely assorted pair.

What impressed her was that during the meal he never spoke to her at all. He strode into the gorgeous establishment with a splendidly proprietary air, looking neither to the right nor to the left. He selected a table and sat down, motioning where she was to sit. He would order the fish, and a large cup of cocoa for Olga, and coffee for himself, and then bury his red face in voluminous newspapers and trade magazines. When the fish was brought, he would stretch out his arm and take up her plate and press his large flat nose against her fish with a ponderous solemnity, as though he were the sacristan at some high altar, harboring suspicions that the sacerdotal offering had been tampered with by the minions of a rival faith. After a few mouthfuls of his own fish his red face would again emerge from behind the papers, and he would say:

"Fish all right?"

Olga would nod and say, "Yes, thank you, "and there the conversation for the meal ended. They would be out about fifteen or twenty minutes; and then Mr. Albu would look at his watch and say, "We 'll be getting back now."

Olga found these suppers a great help for getting through the evening, and the fish was extraordinarily good. It was always fresh and browned over with amazing uniformity. And it was a great relief that Mr. Albu did not speak. Nevertheless the work became more and more of a strain, and she found that when she did get home she would fall into a dead sleep for a couple of hours, and then wake up and hear the buzz of talking and the snapping of air guns, and the tunes she had been playing would keep running through her head with maddening reiteration.

She struggled with the torment of this life for nearly two months, against the strain of giddiness, and the burning temples, and then one afternoon, after starting at the usual time and playing for nearly half-an-hour, she suddenly threw herself on the keys in the middle of a passage and burst into tears. She sobbed and sobbed and sobbed and nothing could assuage her. They gave her water and biscuits and tea and even brandy, but the torrent of anguish could not be stayed. Mr. Albu rubbed her hands and coaxed her and tried speaking sharply to her, but it was all of no avail. At last they sent a boy on a bicycle for Uncle Grubhofer. The appearance of this relation had an even more torrential effect upon her than anything else. She screamed at the sight of him, and burst into louder and louder sobs. Mr. Albu said to Uncle Grubhofer, in a tone of annoyance:

"I told you she was too young. You can't rely on 'em at that age—hysterical! You 'd better take her home. Here, Dixon, just ring up Miss Foster, and tell her to come on at once."

And so Olga was taken home, still shaking with tears. The speech which Uncle Grubhofer thought out on the way, epitomizing his sense of the Bardel family's base ingratitude, and the lack of character of Olga herself, seemed indefinitely deferred, for she sobbed all the evening, and, it is believed, nearly all the night. And on the morrow an inspector called from the school to know how it was that "Olga Bardel" had missed nearly the whole term.

Uncle Grubhofer had been expecting this, but he had a shrewd suspicion that the matter had been precipitated by "that Merson-Casewell set."

CHAPTER V

CHESSLE TERRACE

Every one in the musical world knows Concert Director John Goldman Pensiver. Assisted by an elegant son with manners as irresistible as his father's, he occupies the upper part of a large house in Gainsborough Square, where he conducts what is—to a layman—a very mysterious business. He is sometimes described as a "musical-miracle-monger." He speaks French, German, and Italian fluently, and English with a slight lisp. He is a large, fair-haired man with a suave, ingratiating voice, and during the whole thirty five years of his career as a concert-director, there is no record of his ever having lost his temper. He accepts a very low commission on engagements and he tells every one that the musical profession is "in a very bad way," nevertheless he manages to keep up the establishment in Gainsborough Square furnished like an ancestral home, and also a florid red-brick house, surrounded by five acres of land, at Hindhead.

To penetrate the inner sanctum of Mr. Pensiver 's private office without a proper appointment is as difficult as the proverbial difficulty of interviewing the Emperor of China.

Nevertheless, in this inner sanctum Olga found herself one day, in company with Uncle Grubhofer. Not being aware of the importance of Mr. Pensiver, she was not so impressed by this successful intrusion as she was by the spaciousness of the apartment and by the overpowering magnificence of the clothes of a crowd of people who seemed to have collected. The "crowd," in effect—not including Olga and her uncle—only amounted to four people, but they were people of so much assertion and apparent wealth and importance that they gave the effect of a crowd. There were Mr. Pensiver and his elegant son, both beautifully dressed and both voluble and declamatory, and two other people, a lady and a gentleman called Mr. and Mrs. Du Casson. This garrulous couple were also gorgeously appareled, and Mrs. Du Casson rustled as she moved, and Mr. Du Casson creaked with stiff shirts and new patent-leather boots. Olga became aware of another fact concerning them, and that was that they both smelt of scent, and of the same scent. She often wondered in after life why it was that this fact seemed peculiarly repelling to her. She felt it would have been in some way more tolerable if they had each had their own scent, but Mr. and Mrs. Du Casson both exuded a strong aroma of lily-of-the-valley and an undeniable atmosphere of material prosperity.

Mrs. Du Casson was large, larger than her husband, and she had an unnaturally pink-and-white complexion and a wealth of gold-brown hair. She was embellished with quantities of small jewelry that glittered from most surprising parts of her person. She had small diamond ear-rings, and small diamonds and emeralds nestling under folds of chiffon and lace on her chest, and glittering things at her waist and even on her shoes. Olga was fascinated by the interminable revelation of fresh wonders. She called Olga "dear," and Olga detested her from the start.

Mr. Du Casson was rotund, with curly black hair turning gray, and a very black mustache. He wore a perpetual, self-satisfied grin revealing most resplendent teeth.

All of these people seemed to be in a high state of excitement, and they all talked at once and tried to shout each other down, with the exception of Uncle Grubhofer, who stood moodily in the background and puffed at a cigar.

Suddenly Mr. Pensiver junior opened the lid of a grand piano, and amidst the din of conversation she understood that she was to play. She took off her gloves and obeyed. She played as well as she could, although she found the atmosphere extremely disconcerting. Mr. Du Casson kept humming snatches of the phrase she was playing, while Mrs. Du Casson kept up a running fire of superlatives. Mr. Pensiver rustled papers and Uncle Grubhofer had an unfortunate habit of clearing his throat during a soft passage. Nevertheless when she had finished, the company seemed extremely satisfied. They all talked at once as before, and Mr. Du Casson came over and fondled her in a way she resented. She could not follow the gist of the conversation that then took place, but just as they were going Mrs. Du Casson said to her:

"Would you like to come and live with me, dear?"

The question was so unexpected that Olga could not bring herself to answer. She merely wriggled and blushed, and Mr. Du Casson stroked her hair and patted her once more, and she and Uncle Grubhofer returned to Canning Town.

And then the most surprising thing happened. A week later she was suddenly bundled into a four-wheeled cab, with a large brown paper parcel that contained all her belongings, and sent over to an address near Regent 's Park.

Here she was received by Mr. and Mrs. Du Casson and was given a small bedroom at the top of the house, and another room underneath where she was allowed to practise. She was given an entirely new outfit of clothes and most beautiful things to eat. She went to bed at night brooding over this amazing change in her fortunes, and vainly trying to analyze the motives of Uncle Grubhofer who should have consented to it.

The material satisfaction that she derived from these changed conditions was somewhat tempered the next day by the discovery of the fact that Mr. Du Casson proposed to give her music lessons. She had taken an instinctive dislike to Mrs. Du Casson, but Mr. Du Casson was to her—anathema. She hated the patronizing and endearing way he spoke to her, and in the course of a few days she was convinced that his method of teaching her was somehow wrong. She could not argue with him, but she felt a fundamental contempt for the man and his character, and she was astute enough to know that if his character was contemptible, his ideas of music would probably be not much better. She took her meals—with the exception of dinner—with Mr. and Mrs. Du Casson, and she practised six hours a day. In the afternoon she would be sent for a walk in Regent's Park with one of the maids, and usually accompanied by a swarm of expensive little dogs that were Mrs. Du Casson's pets. The house was tall and gaily decorated, and seemed to be the center of a good deal of social life. Noisy dinner parties frequently took place in the evening and occasionally she would be sent for, and made to play to people. Most of the guests seemed to be musicians of varying degrees of celebrity, or people of position or patronage in the musical world. Some of them were occasionally sympathetic and kind to her, but the majority seemed entirely insincere and treated her like a toy. At first the comfort and cleanliness of this new life excited her, and in spite of the importunate lessons from Mr. Du Casson she went through the day in a spirit of elation. But gradually this sense of excitement cooled, and when she became tired at night a feeling of dejection and loneliness would come over her. She would wonder about Irene and Karl and Montague, and would suffer a strange nostalgia for the mean streets. She saw nothing of her brothers and sisters, nor even of Uncle Grubhofer, and she felt surprised at this. Once she ventured to speak to Mrs. Du Casson about them, but that lady seemed very reticent and did not encourage her enquiries. As the months went by the atmosphere of the house in Chessle Terrace became to the child more and more insupportable. On a certain day she felt that she could not bear it any longer. She found out that the Du Cassons were going to be out all the afternoon, so soon after lunch she slipped out and started to walk to Canning Town. She had a few coppers, but she had not the courage to face the ordeal of taking buses or trains. It took her two hours to reach her old neighborhood, and at the sight and smell of the dreary streets an unaccountable excitement possessed her. She walked rapidly past the groups of noisy children and found the old house. The front door was open and she crept in. She went stealthily up the stairs and then paused and peeped into the Bardels' sitting-room. Irene was ironing, leaning over a table, and her face was perspiring, and some linen was hanging over a line across the room; some plates and saucers unwashed-up from the midday meal were piled up on the bed.

She could not account for the sudden wave of emotion that swept over her. Irene looked tired and hot and unhappy, and so very, very poor. And she was her sister! Why was she bedecked in nice clothes and enjoying comfort and good food, while her sister was wearing out her life bending over that steaming board?

She suddenly burst into the room and threw her arms round Irene. Irene screamed and dropped her iron. She was very frightened.

"What is it?" she cried out. "'Ave they given you the bird?"

Olga did not answer. She clung to her sister and cried.

Irene was alarmed. She pushed her away and said excitedly:

"What is it? What 's the matter? What 'ave you come for?"

But the little girl could not control her violent emotion, and after a time Irene sniffed and said in a lower voice:

"Oh, chuck it, for Gawd's sake!"

Then they sat there silently, Olga shivering, and Irene looking at her furtively. At last Irene made some tea, and they drank it in big gulps, and Olga observed the hungry way that Irene ate her thick bread-and-butter. But Irene was not satisfied. It was all very suspicious, and when the first cup of tea was consumed, she said again:

"'Ave they given you the bird?"

Olga shook her head and her lips were still quivering.

"What 'ave you come for, then?"

Olga looked down, and at last she said:

"I wanted to come."

Irene looked at her quickly. She gulped some more tea and then asked:

"'Ow do you get on there? Do they give you plenty of grub?"

Olga nodded again, and looked round the room. Suddenly she said:

"I wish you could go back instead of me," and then unreasonably she cried. The whole thing was entirely incomprehensible to Irene. She still harbored a suspicion that Olga really had "got the bird." Otherwise what was she blubbering about? Hadn't she plenty of grub and warmth and clothing? Was there anything in this room in Sendrake Road that she was envious of? What was the child 's game?

"You 'd better go before Uncle Grubhofer cops yer," she said at last. She took up her ironing, and was conscious that Olga's eyes were on her. Nevertheless the little girl prepared to go, but when she reached the door she suddenly turned and came back, and said in a quivering voice:

"I hope you 're getting on all right, you, and Karl, and Montague."

And then she sobbed very violently. Irene felt a curious contraction within herself; it was inexplicable, but no one could stand up against the flood of this emotionalism. She snuffled and turned her back. Suddenly she felt Olga's arms round her neck and her lips on her cheek. She gave a little whimper and tried to say, "Oh, chuck it!" but the words would not come. She pecked her sister's cheek in turn and pressed her in a mild embrace, and then broke away and busied herself at the fireplace. Olga dashed the tears from her eyes and hurried from the room.

She was thoroughly exhausted and footsore when she got back to Chessle Terrace, but when she lay her head upon the pillow that night, she felt strangely comforted.

CHAPTER VI

"THE ARMENIAN FROCK"

The debut of the Child-Wonder, Olga Barjelski, at the Queen's Hall was surely one of the most incredible things within the memory of music-lovers. The public had been forewarned of it three months ahead by the following paragraph appearing in all the daily papers:

WONDERFUL CHILD PIANIST

A Romantic Story

The famous Professor of Music, Louis du Casson, is to be congratulated on a remarkable and romantic discovery. Visiting the East End of London a short time ago on philanthropic work, he happened to hear a little girl strumming on an old upright piano. The performance of one phrase was sufficient to inform the experienced ear of the professor that here was a genius. He made inquiries and discovered that the little girl was named Olga Barjelski. She is nine years old and the daughter of Polish parents who had settled in Turkey. The whole family were massacred in a pogrom, being taken for Armenians, except this little girl who was smuggled out of the country at night in a basket labeled "vegetable produce," and convoyed across the border into Greece by an old Magyar woman. This old woman—who has since died—was a mystic, and sincerely believed that the child was a reincarnation of Chopin, the great Polish composer. She brought the child to London and gave her into the care of a distant relation, in whose house the famous professor heard her.

The story, of course, with regard to the reincarnation may or may not be accepted by those who believe in these things, but there is no doubt but that the child is a very remarkable pianist. Professor Du Casson declares that she plays with an almost uncanny sense of EXPERIENCE, which in a child of nine is unaccountable. She will have a few finishing lessons with Professor Du Casson and will make her debut at the Queen's Hall in October.

Up to the day she was kept hard at work. She had devoted practically the whole year to that one program, till she knew everything so slickly that she had hardly to think about it. She had broad long fingers capable of any pianistic demands, and Mr. Du Casson certainly initiated her into the mystery of thrills and effects. The paragraphs had appeared in the newspapers at intervals, becoming more and more frequent as the day approached, working up to a crescendo of large bills, advertisements, and lithographs of her portrait, whilst two dozen hungry-looking sandwich men paraded the West End for a week beforehand, bearing the insistent posters.

People who were present at that debut are not likely to forget it. The hall was packed from floor to ceiling, and though it would be invidious to say that the majority of people had paid for their seats, there was a surprising number of people of influence in the social and musical world. When she came on to the platform there was a roar of welcome, mingled with a buzz of exclamatory conversation and laughter, which subsided into a dead stillness of anticipation as she took her seat at the piano. She was not nervous. She loved playing to people and she knew she could do it. If the Queen's Hall had been three times the size, it would have affected her little more than if she had been playing in a room, providing that the people could hear and wanted to hear. And in her platform manner she had been perfectly schooled by Mr. Du Casson. She was dressed in a somber but dramatic fashion as became one who had nearly been massacred by the Turks. She had on a broad black and white check frock, and her long legs were in black stockings. Her hair, parted in the middle and brushed right back, hung in two huge plaits right to her waist and were tied at the ends with scarlet bows. She walked quickly on to the platform—some people thought that her legs were rather long for nine!—looking neither to the right nor left till she reached the piano, then she gave the people two solemn nods, and sat down. There was still a violent buzz of comment going on, and the noise of people who could not find their seats, and other people hushing each other up. But Olga was in no hurry. She took out a handkerchief and wiped her hands and looked at the piano. Then she looked solemnly round the hall again and waited. She waited until there was a dead silence and even then she did not seem in a hurry.

At last as though the music had already commenced in her mind, she lifted her arms above her head and held them there, and then crashed down upon the keys. From that first chord she never lost her grip upon the audience. She sat there, the quaint little figure with her intent, strained face unconscious of anything except the music, and her fat podgy little arms pounding out most amazing passages and runs. She seemed to be juggling with emotions she could not possibly understand, and sending vibrant thrills through people at most unexpected moments. Sometimes she would play a passage so brilliantly that a lot of them would laugh in the same way that "Levitch himself" laughed. Her technique was indeed remarkable, and Du Casson had chosen just those pieces that showed it to advantage. At the end of each piece she rose solemnly and bowed, and she almost ran off the platform between the groups. She did not give them a smile till nearly the end, when a large bouquet of carnations was handed up. When it was all over the applause was tremendous, and she played two encores (as arranged beforehand with Mr. Du Casson), and even then the people recalled her again and again.

At last she escaped to the artists' room, panting, flushed, and wildly excited, and people poured in and kissed her and flattered her. Mr. and Mrs. Du Casson were in the highest spirits and both kissed her, and introduced her to a lot of people whose names she did not catch. Mr. John Goldman Pensiver cried "Bravo! Bravo!" and warmly shook her hand.

Olga did not sleep that night at all. Everything she had played kept racing through her mind. She went over her whole program again and again, including two slips she had made in the sonata, and a smudge in one of the studies. And then the applause! It thrilled her. It was very thrilling to have people applauding and flattering you. She tried to think of all the things they had said. She wondered whether Miss Merson was there, and Irene and Karl and Montague. None of them had appeared, not even Uncle Grubhofer, though she believed he had been there, for she heard some one say that he was by the box-office (wherever that was). She wanted to talk to some one, but all the time passages from the sonata kept racing through her mind. Life had become very violent, and she was not sure whether she was glad or sorry.

When she came down in the morning the breakfast room seemed full of newspapers and Mr. and Mrs. Du Casson were vociferously shouting quotations from the various critiques to one another.

They both seemed rather disturbed and disappointed about the press, and were less effusive to Olga than they had been the night previously.

"Oh, well, we shall see what Pensiver can do with this," seemed to be Mrs. Du Casson 's verdict. That gentleman arrived about eleven o'clock, also with a collection of papers, and it was largely in the manner with which he dealt with these same criticisms that he revealed that Napoleonic quality, which gave him a unique position among concert-directors of the time. In the first place he railed the Du Cassons and heartened them by saying that the critiques were excellent, "couldn't be better." He then proceeded to draw up his advertisement for the next day.

Some of the papers of course were entirely enthusiastic, as enthusiastic as the audience, and from these he extracted the most enthusiastic sentences. Others were milder and had to be considerably curtailed, whilst some were extremely bad, and it was in dealing with these that Pensiver showed his genius. One of the soberest journals whose judgment carried considerable weight devoted a paragraph to deploring the practice of foisting immature artists on the public in the guise of infant prodigies, of passing talented children through a hothouse training for breeding an artificial technique which when it is acquired can have nothing to express. It contended that in this present instance of the little girl Olga Barjelski—as an exhibition of finger talent and precocity it was indeed remarkable, but as an exposition of the art of the piano it was—simply ridiculous! Mr. John Goldman Pensiver ran his pencil through this and quoted, "As an exposition of finger talent and precocity it was indeed remarkable"—The Temple; another journal had a notice in the same strain, only ending up with references to her frock and appearance, and said that "certain platform manners cleverly manipulated and an engaging personality undoubtedly combined to account for the tumultuous applause that the friendly audience seemed to consider that the performance merited."

From this he quoted, "Engaging personality ... tumultuous applause"—The Meteor. The next morning he had half a column of advertisements of press cuttings of a like nature in every London daily paper and the leading provincial ones. And the advertisement was headed, "Phenomenal Success of the Child Wonder." And then followed an announcement that owing to the colossal success of Miss Olga Barjelski's debut, Mr. John Goldman Pensiver had the pleasure to announce a series of three further recitals in December, February, and March.

There was a certain amount of trouble about this, because Pensiver wanted to give the recitals at once, but Du Casson knew that it was impossible to produce another program so soon, so December, February, and March were announced, but in the meantime the good Pensiver did not mean to be idle or to allow his client's protegee to be idle either. He flooded the London and provincial press with further paragraphs and advertisements. He then approached the secretary of a very old musical society whose funds were not in too good an order and offered to buy fifty pounds' worth of tickets for one of their next season's concerts if they would engage Olga Barjelski. We blush to say that this offer was accepted. He practically bought another important orchestral engagement in London, and one in the North. He then drew up an advertisement contract with most of the leading London papers to cover a period of six months. He interviewed the advertisement managers personally, and when possible took them out to lunch. When they arrived at the coffee and cigar stage

Mr. Pensiver would say, "By the way, Mr.—, if we give you this contract, you might ask your editor to let us down a little lightly, you know, eh? Last time the tone of your paper was not too friendly if I remember rightly." And the advertisement editor, with the bouquet of an expensive port wine still in his nostrils, would say, "All right, my dear chap, I 'll say a word about it at the office." Every daily paper earns its bread and cheese on advertisements, and it is to be deplored that the suave suggestion of Mr. Pensiver had its effect on the majority of cases. At her next recital a great number of the papers noted a marked improvement, and generally took her performance more seriously. And then people—who in the ordinary way took no interest in music whatever—began to say in drawing-rooms, "By the way, my dear, have you heard that little girl, Olga Barjelski? She 's perfectly sweet!" and the friend would answer, "Oh, yes; she 's an Armenian or something, isn't she? Nearly murdered! I must go and hear her." And then the conversation would drift to the terrible age we live in, but the friend would not forget, and would eventually have to go and pay half a crown to hear Olga Barjelski because everybody was talking about her. And then the question of the reincarnation of Chopin was discussed and it was definitely established in an occult review that one could be male in one reincarnation and female in the next.

Mr. Pensiver did his work thoroughly but did not escape trouble, and the trouble originated in this way. Uncle Grubhofer had invested £333-6-8 in the syndicate to run Olga, but he did not mention to the syndicate that he had floated his own share in a separate concern.

He persuaded a gentleman named Gregory Bausch, who ran an agency for dealing in motor accessories, to invest a hundred pounds in the scheme, and another man named Ben. Carter, who was a pawnbroker and moneylender, to invest fifty pounds, whilst two other gentlemen whom he met "in the course of business" put up thirty pounds each, and also Karl, who had been surprisingly successful in his sales of trinkets during the last year. It is difficult to know what means of persuasion Uncle Grubhofer employed to get these various gentlemen to risk money which they valued more than human life, or what papers or securities they held over him in the matter, but they certainly took the shares.

Now when Olga began to be a popular success and was seen to be playing everywhere, they began to want to know what returns were coming in, and Uncle Grubhofer himself began to be suspicious. It was difficult for Mr. Pensiver to explain that one can be a great success and yet not make much money. "We must wait," said Mr. Pensiver expansively. "This next year will show." But after a few months Uncle Grubhofer's syndicate became restless, and Uncle Grubhofer himself became restless, and there were stormy scenes in Pensiver's office. Members of the syndicate followed Olga about, and danced attendance at box-offices. They were dissatisfied with the hold that Uncle Grubhofer had over Mr. Pensiver, whom they suspected of robbing them, as so indeed he may have been. Moreover, the Du Cassons began to object to these friends of Mr. Grubhofer's always being in evidence and asking questions.

Olga herself was only partially aware of these things. She had to work tremendously hard on new programs, and also on learning concertos. When she was not working she felt bewildered and unhappy. Sometimes she would go and hear other musicians play and then she was conscious of something lacking in herself. One day she heard Harold Bauer at the Queen's Hall, and his playing revealed a new world to her. It made her feel that she wanted to go away somewhere all alone, and think things over.

At the end of the first year Mr. Pensiver revealed to the syndicate that the expenditure had so far been £1135 and the net takings from engagements and recitals £475. He stated that he considered this entirely satisfactory, and an extended provincial tour had now been booked, from which he expected great things.

The tour started at Wimbledon, and was to last three months, Olga giving a recital practically every night. Enormous bills were sent ahead announcing that Olga Barjelski, the child marvel, the reincarnation of Chopin, who made the sensation of the London season, would positively appear on such and such a date. The story of the Armenian massacre was embellished with more lurid details, and her own portrait, brooding despondingly at the piano, was perpetrated in color. Moreover, for this tour she wore on the platform a scarlet dress with white embroidery, and a sort of bead head-dress. It was Mrs. Du Casson's idea of an Armenian costume, "anyway near enough for the provinces." It was difficult to know why a little Polish girl should wear an Armenian dress when she was trying to escape from Turkey, but it was mentioned on the program that it was the identical frock she had on when she crossed the border in a basket labeled "vegetable produce."

On the first night of the tour there was an unfortunate scene. Karl turned up with Mr. Bausch and another gentleman of Uncle Grubhofer's syndicate. Karl was drunk, and they demanded access to the box-office, which Mr. Pensiver refused. They squabbled and called each other names in the foyer and in the corridors, and ended up with a regrettable incident in Olga's dressing room just before she was due to go on. The child was so upset that the recital had to be delayed nearly an hour. The police were called in to turn Karl and his friends out, and Mrs. Du Casson had to drink a large quantity of brandy to steady herself, whilst Mr. Du Casson hid till it was all over. Olga was hysterical, and it seemed at one time that she would not be able to play at all. When the other men had disappeared Mr. Du Casson turned up and started coaxing her, and then, when she seemed obdurate, his dark eyes blazed with anger, Mr. Pensiver came in and fumed, and fussed, and patted her hands, and at last Mrs. Du Casson insisted on her having a little brandy. It burnt her throat, but it seemed to give her courage of a sort, and Mrs. Du Casson powdered her face and pushed her on to the platform. It was a wretched evening, and she forgot once or twice in pieces that she knew quite well.

She derived no pleasure from this triumphal tour. Mr. or Mrs. Du Casson—and occasionally both—accompanied her everywhere, and a young man from Mr. Pensiver's office, and sometimes Mr. Pensiver himself. She got thoroughly sick of the train journeys and the hotels, and hated the sight of her poster in the streets and of her Armenian dress. She lost interest in her program, and played mechanically. Nevertheless the tour was in some respects a success. The halls were nearly always full, and the audience enthusiastic. The Du Cassons seemed pleased with her and had noisy supper parties, and Mrs. Du Casson occasionally gave her money to buy anything she wanted. One day she received a letter from Irene which ran:

Dear Olga:

I here you are doing fine in the country can you send us a bit things are very bad and Montague has got the bird Uncle Grubhofer has moved out let his rooms to some people and too childrun he has taking a shop in the Wallace road

Your affectionat sister

IRENE.

Olga's first instinct on reading this letter was to go straight back home and take everything she had. It was her first recollection of Irene making any sort of advance to her, and the thought gave her a little thrill of satisfaction. On maturer consideration, however, she collected all the money she had, which she found amounted to seventeen shillings, and decided to send it to Irene. She laboriously addressed an envelope and wrote a note as follows:

Dear Irene

I was so please to here from you I was sorry to here things bad what a pity about Montague getting the bird I hope he will soon get in again It is very nice travellin about I enclose the munney I send my love to Montague and to Karl and to you with my love

Your lovin sister

OLGA.

This letter was written on the notepaper of the King's Palace Hotel, Hull.

A week later Olga received another letter from Irene. It was to thank her for the postal orders and to say that things were very bad still, and whenever Olga had any money would she send it. And so it came about that any money that Mrs. Du Casson handed to her was converted into postal orders, and sent to Irene.

And then one day she had a letter from Montague to say that he heard she was doing well in the provinces. He was out of a job himself, and could she lend him three pounds which he would pay directly he got a job?

This letter distressed Olga very much, for when it came she had not a penny in the world, having just sent her last shilling to Irene; Mrs. Du Casson was not there, and Mr. Du Casson having the matter explained to him vaguely waved his arras, and said he couldn't do anything in the matter; she had better speak to his wife. This was at Leicester and she noticed that the hall was very full that night, and she knew that people paid money as they went in at the door. An idea occurred to her. She waited till after the performance and then she spoke to the young man of Mr. Pensiver's. She asked him confidentially if he could n't give her some of the money which he had taken at the door, as she wanted some to send to a friend. The young man looked puzzled, and then laughed, and said he was afraid he could n 't do that. He then said that if it was only a small amount she wanted of course he would be very pleased to oblige her out of his own pocket. She would not accept this arrangement, and lay awake that night puzzling over the problem of economics. It seemed strange that if money were handed in by people who only came to hear her play that she could not have some of it to do with what she liked. Her musings on this theme were further disturbed by another letter that came two days later. It was from Karl.

Dear Olga

I expect Uncle G— has told you I invested money in your career. This quite apart from what I have spent on your keep cloths ect. Since investing this money I have had no return whatever. I shall be glad therefor if you will make inquiries about this as I hear you are making a lot of money and I am very hard up. Uncle G has left here. If you cannot make that swine Pensiver give proper account perhaps you can spring me a bit on your own as I have to meet a bill this week.

Yr affec: bros.

KARL.

This letter seemed to make things more difficult and incomprehensible than ever. What did Karl mean by "investing money in your career" and "making Pensiver give a proper account"? It occurred to her on the face of it that there was a conspiracy to rob her brothers and sister, and the smug Mr. Pensiver was at the bottom of it. It stood to reason that if people came to hear her play and paid for it that the money should go rather to Karl and Montague and Irene, than to Mr. Pensiver.

It was strange that all three should have written to her the same week. She dreamed that night they were unhappy and that they wanted her. She thought she heard Montague crying—it was the most heartrending sound she had ever heard. She thought she saw Irene bending over the fire and stirring an empty saucepan, and groping on the dusty shelves of the old cupboard. She felt there was something unjust and terrible about this whilst she was living in hotels with everything she could desire. The next night she was to play at a place called Epsom, and the following night Croydon. She knew that they were towns not far from London, and that Mr. Pensiver was coming to Croydon. She brooded over this the whole of the next day and night, and on the day after when they arrived at Croydon she felt she could not stand it any longer. During the two days she had been smuggling rolls and olives and fruit and any small portable food she could lay her hands on out of the hotel and concealing it in the small brown bag of her own. They arrived at Croydon at four o'clock, and her recital was to be at eight. They passed the usual display of bills heralding the child marvel, and on one hoarding she counted fourteen full size colored posters of herself. It was a dull day with a fine driving rain. They drove to a hotel, and Mr. Du Casson went to his room to rest. Mr. Pensiver 's young man had a good deal to attend to, especially in view of the visit of his chief. Olga watched him go to a quiet corner of the lounge with a bundle of bills and papers and sit down, and then she followed him. Her heart was beating very fast, but she controlled herself with surprising success. She said almost casually,

"Oh, Mr. Leighton, could you give me some money like you said you would the other day?"

The young man looked up.

"Why, yes, Miss Barjelski; how much do you want?"

This was a difficult question. She wanted to ask for a huge sum, two or three pounds at least, enough to keep Karl and Montague and Irene in comfort for months and months. She hesitated, and to her joy the young man said,

"Would three pounds be any good?"

She could not control the exclamation of delight, and thanked him profusely. Mr. Leighton asked her to sign a paper acknowledging the receipt of the sum, and then buried his head in the accounts. Olga gripped the sovereigns in her hand, and went to her room. She put on her Armenian dress. She had a very vague idea of time, and thought that as it was only afternoon she would get back in time for her concert in the evening. She covered herself up with a long wrapper and crept downstairs. There were two or three people in the lounge, but they did not take any particular notice of her. The young man was still bending over his papers. She fixed her eyes on his back, and then glided to the door. When she got into the street she ran. She asked a policeman for the station. It was only five minutes' walk. When she got there she had to wait twenty minutes for a train. She sat in a dark corner of the waiting-room. As she was going out to her train she nearly ran into Mr. Pensiver and Mrs. Du Casson. They were laughing and talking, and a porter was getting them a cab. She shrank out of sight and watched them go, and then she boarded her train. It seemed a very long journey to London and she began to think she would not get back in time for the concert. But to her mind the business she had in hand seemed more urgent.

When the train drew up at Charing Cross it was five minutes past seven. She had begun to have some experience by this time in traveling and she had changed one of the sovereigns at Croydon. She boarded the right bus, and then the tram. By the time she reached Canning Town it was nearly half-past eight. It was very dark, and she began to be frightened by her adventure. She arrived in the Bardels' street. There were very few children about—it was too late for them—and she looked at the numbers on the dim doorways. At last she found the house. The door was shut. She was disappointed about this. She would have liked to have crept up, and found them all as she saw them in her dream, and then to have gone in and put the sovereigns down on the table, then have had them fall upon her, and kiss her and welcome her back to them. However, there was nothing to do but ring, and this she did. She rang and waited, but there was no answer. She rang again, and still she could not hear a sound. She felt frightened, and wondered whether they had all gone away. She tried a third time. Then she thought she heard some movement on the stairs. After a time the door opened. In the dim light she could see a pale face. It was Montague's. He peered at her, and said hoarsely, "Who is it? What is it?" and then he came nearer, and recognized who she was. He did not seem tremendously surprised to see her. He seemed under the stress of some more terrifying emotion. He was trembling, and could hardly speak. He clutched her arm at last and said, "My God!" He pulled her into the doorway, and stepped past her, and then he turned and said, "You can go up, if you like. I can't stand it. My God! My God!" He vanished into the night and left her there. Sick with fear, Olga groped for the stairs. What could n't Montague stand? What was happening upstairs? She clutched the handrail and the wall, which seemed damp. As she reached the first landing she heard shrieks coming from the floor above. She dashed up and forced her way into the old room. A paraffin lamp on the side table revealed the figure of a woman bending over a bed. For a second she thought the woman was murdering some one in the bed. She shrieked herself and dashed forward, when a hand gripped her by the shoulders. She struggled to get free and her cloak slipped from her and she stood there in her scarlet Armenian dress paralyzed with fear. Suddenly something of the true position of affairs began to dawn on her. The woman at the bed turned sharply for a second, and Olga realized that she was a nurse, the hand that was gripping her was the hand of Uncle Grubhofer, and on the bed lay her sister Irene. In the struggle the sovereigns dropped from her hand to the floor with a clatter, and the nurse said, "Silence, child!" as though she were desecrating a temple with the crash of jocund cymbals. She sank back to a chair and watched her sister's agony. At eleven o'clock that night Irene gave birth to a child. The father was a baker named Hazell, a married man with five legitimate children of his own. When the agony was over and Irene had fallen into a restless slumber, and the nurse had soothed the querulous infant, Uncle Grubhofer stooped and solemnly picked up the sovereigns from the floor. He looked at them meditatively as though they held the secret of the world's most unforgivable sins. He held them on his palm, and then looked at Olga. She dare not turn her face in his direction. She was conscious of the parafin lamp flickering and revealing Uncle Grubhofer in spasmodic glints, sometimes he almost vanished altogether and then he would suddenly loom up, holding the incriminating evidence almost under her nose. She fancied at moments that he was smiling as though the vision of these two sisters exposed in their individual vileness satisfied some bizarre kink in his own nature. At last he frowned, and put the coins in his pocket and went slowly out of the room.

CHAPTER VII

"REVOLT"

The next day Uncle Grubhofer accompanied her to Guildford, and he did not leave her for the rest of the tour. To her surprise, nothing was said to her about her defection. The only difference in the arrangements was that Mr. and Mrs. Du Casson returned to town and Uncle Grubhofer took their place. The tour trailed northwards again, and they visited gaunt manufacturing towns. Uncle Grubhofer kept close to her. He engaged her room at the hotel and occupied one close by. During the day he sat about the lounge so that he could see her if she attempted to go out. He accompanied her to the concert hall, and was always in the artists' room apparently asleep when she came off the platform, and then he took her silently back to the hotel. He sat for hours over Gargantuan meals, breathing heavily, and reading a newspaper, and occasionally glancing furtively at her. She had never seen any one eat quite like Uncle Grubhofer. He would gaze at the dish set before him by the waiter for a long time, and then he would push it with his fork, and a pained expression would come over his face. Then he would call the waiter, and talk to him about the dish in a low voice, and in the majority of cases send it back with some precise but cabalistic instructions. When it was brought for the second time he would go for it quickly as though he wished to catch it at its most supreme moment. He would fill his mouth with food and hold his face close over his plate, with his napkin tucked into his neck, and his small eyes would roll suspiciously round the table. He looked dangerous at such moments. Sometimes he surprised her by his attention. She would be conscious that he was gazing at her furtively with a melancholy expression as though the sight of her stirred some quick but dubious memories. "When she looked up at him he turned away. He drank copiously but only in proportion to his meal, and never to excess. He would drink a whole bottle of hock with his dinner, but hardly ever touched spirits.

Olga seemed to spend months sitting opposite Uncle Grubhofer and watching these lugubrious exhibitions, and then afterwards would follow tedious train journeys in smoking carriages, and another smoky town hemmed in by fantastic chimneys and flares. The same posters, the child-wonder, the Armenian frock, the same concert halls, and apparently the same people. They went through Lancashire, Yorkshire, Newcastle, and Scotland, and it was eight weeks before they returned to town. Olga had received no further letters from Irene or Karl or Montague, and whether they had written and the letters been intercepted she could not tell, but when she began to see the gray outskirts of the big city in the early morning light, a fierce excitement seized her, and various perverse resolutions filled her small heart. During all this latter part of the tour she had not been allowed to have any money, and she had none now. She had been held in a sort of soporific trance by Uncle Grubhofer, her volition paralyzed by the fear of him. But the sense of London gave her courage, she recognized its various landmarks as the train lumbered through, and the recognition inspired her with dim desires and half-formed determinations. In London she knew her way about. It was the city of freedom. At the station Uncle Grubhofer delayed progress by ordering a prodigious breakfast which occupied a full hour, and then he ordered a four-wheel cab and delivered her at the door of the Du Cassons' house in Chessle Terrace.

So this was to be her home again! She waited in the morning-room. The Du Cassons were not yet up. She heard all the usual sounds that characterized the prebreakfast hour in Chessle Terrace. The rushing of water in the bathroom, the singing of a maid in the kitchen and of a brass kettle on a tripod on the table, and Mr. Du Casson's voice shouting to his wife through the lather on his mouth and chin, and then the banging of a breakfast gong answered by the loud and strident yapping of the little dogs as they darted about the hall increasing in volume as they heard Mrs. Du Casson's metallic voice on the stairs: "Ah, my darlings, did 'um want 'ums little breakums then?"

Mrs. Du Casson kissed her effusively, and said she was so pleased to see her back, and to know that the tour had been a success. Mr. Du Casson followed, and indulged in many antics of mock veneration and affection. They tried to persuade her to have some breakfast but she refused, and sat there watching them eat and play with the dogs.

When they had finished she followed Mrs. Du Casson up-stairs and said to her abruptly, "Mrs. Du Casson, will you give me some money?"

Mrs. Du Casson started. "Money! my dear, whatever for?"

"I want some. I want to go and see my sister. She has a little baby."

"Oh!" said Mrs. Du Casson with an expression of relief. "Why, of course, dear. But you mustn't forget that Mr. Pensiver has booked you for the Royal Tonic Society's concert on Saturday. You will have to practise, you know!"

"Yes," said Olga, watching Mrs. Du Casson 's movements.

That lady went to a drawer in her escritoire, and opened a cash box. Olga noticed that in one section was a whole heap of sovereigns and in the other a little silver. She took half a crown and gave it to Olga and said, "There, dear! Will you be back to lunch?"

Olga was a little disappointed at the amount, but she said, "Thank you. I 'll try and be back to lunch." She then went to her room and changed her frock, and washed herself. Within an hour of entering the house she was out again in the street. She hurried along and jumped on to a 'bus. The day was dull but fine, and she enjoyed the journey across London, When she arrived at her old home, she rang the bell as before. After waiting some time a strange woman opened the door, and stared at her.

"What d ' yer want?" she said.

"Oh," said Olga, trying to pass in, "I want my sister, Miss Bardel."

The woman looked at her bad-temperedly. "They gorn awy! Gorn awy months ago!"

"Gone away!" said Olga. "Where to?"

"I don't know, 'ow should I know? They 've gorn awy, I tell yer. Fetchin' me down with all yer silly nonsense! Why don't yer find aht before you go callin' on people!" And she banged the door in Olga's face.

Olga's heart sank. She stared at the door and couldn't believe the story. She looked down in the basement, and observed that the room that was formerly Karl's and Montague's bedroom was no longer occupied. And then her eye wandered back to the door, and she observed that Uncle Grubhofer's magnificent brass plate was missing. She remembered that Irene had said in her letter that Uncle Grubhofer had taken a shop in some street. Then she remembered the name, Wallace Street! She moved off, and walked to the corner. She asked a policeman if he knew Wallace Street. After mature consideration he directed her to the other end of the neighborhood. It proved easier to find than the policeman's directions had led her to expect. It was a fairly respectable street off a main thoroughfare. She walked the length of it and at last recognized Uncle Grubhofer's brass plate. The plate glass window of the shop was painted brown up to a certain height, and had gold lettering on it, identical with that on the brass plate. There was a swing door and the evidences of a moderately high-class business. She walked in and a young man came forward.

"Can I see Mr. Grubhofer?" she said.

"What name, miss?" said the young man.

"I 'm his niece," said Olga.

The young man went into an inner room, and presently Uncle Grubhofer appeared looking like a ruffled elephant. He came out and stared at her.

"I want to speak to you," she said. It was the most aggressive remark she had ever made to him, and he looked at her curiously. Then he turned and told the young man to go out on some errand, and retired to his inner room, thus non-committingly ordering her to follow him. When they arrived there, he sat down and she said:

"Where is Irene?"

There was an attitude of revolt about the child that was new to her.

Uncle Grubhofer took up a piece of metal-turning that was on his desk. He held it up to his eye and looked along it, as though to see if it were true. Then he put it down and rolled ponderously on his swivel chair. Tears of anger darted to the girl's eyes, and she rose at him as she had never done before.

"What have you done with Irene and the baby? Where is Karl and Montague? I want some money; you must give me some money. I want to go to them."

Uncle Grubhofer said "Oh!" in a deep sonorous voice, and then he added in a lighter but more melancholy key, "So you want some money, eh?"

Olga saw that he meant if possible to evade her question, and she rushed and struck the desk in front of him in a blaze of fury. "Where is Irene? ... if you don't tell me I shall go and tell people . . . and then I shall go away."

It was a strange duel, the small child like an angry sparrow darting about the room, consumed with emotions she had no power to express, conscious of an outraged sense of justice which she could not focus; and the man, secure in his own bulk but slightly disturbed and surprised, revolving meditatively the means of action within the ambit of his dubious desires, using his conscious power of brooding silence to strike terror and to gain time, hoping that from the turgid depths of his own being some inspiration might spring to adapt this new development to his own ends.

"You are not fair to me. . . . You frighten me . . . but you can't do this! You shan't! you shan't!"

The storm reached a climax in a fit of sobbing, and Uncle Grubhofer thought it well to temporize.

He spoke in sorrow. He said that Irene had been ill. She was away in the country. If Olga did not behave so extravagantly there was no reason why she should not go to see her sister. It was very nice to see sisters loving each other so much! "With regard to money, he had none. She had cost him a lot of money, thousands of pounds which he never expected to recover. If she wanted money she had better go to Mr. Pensiver or to Mrs. Du Casson; they had any amount.

"The people paid money to come and hear me play," said Olga with sudden inspiration. "Who has that?"

Uncle Grubhofer shrugged his shoulders. "You had better ask dear Mrs. Du Casson or Mr. Pensiver," and he laughed with a queer malignity.

Olga thought for a moment, and then she said, "I shall ask them. And now you must tell me where Irene is."

Uncle Grubhofer rose and walked to a small paraffin stove and held his hands over it. He stood there for some time with his back to her, and then he turned and looked at his watch. At last he said very deliberately, "You may meet me at—Gower Street Station at five o'clock, and then I will take you to see Irene; but it is on a condition."

"What is it?" said Olga breathlessly.

"You shall not say anything to Mrs. Du Casson. You shall not say where you are going, or that you are to meet me."

Olga was surprised at the simplicity of this condition, and she agreed. Uncle Grubhofer turned again to the paraffin, stove and she was struck by the inadequacy of this tiny fountain of warmth for the overpowering proportions of the man. There seemed nothing further to say, and she went out of the shop while his back was turned.

She returned to Chessle Terrace, surging with varied emotions. There was a note for her from Mr. Du Casson to say that he and his wife would be out all day. They would be back to dinner at 7:30. He then reminded her that she had to play at the Royal Tonic Society's concert on Saturday, and she had better start practising. But Olga did not practise that afternoon. She felt too perturbed by her experience of the morning, and too excited by the prospect of adventure for the evening. She lay on her bed revolving many thoughts, and watching the clock. Would Irene be glad to see her? She wondered what the baby would be like, and where Karl and Montague were. Would they be angry that she had not sent them the money? How lovely it would be if she could take them some now—lots of money and good things. Then she suddenly remembered that she had not even any money for her fare. Supposing Uncle Grubhofer refused to buy her ticket, or still contended that he hadn't any. She remembered what he had said, "You had better ask dear Mrs. Du Casson. She has any amount. "Of course Mrs. Du Casson had; she kept lots in her escritoire in her boudoir. It suddenly occurred to her that she would see if it were open, and if so, she would take a little, just enough to pay her fare, and perhaps a few shillings for Irene.

It was getting late and she would have to start soon. She washed herself and brushed her hair. She wanted to look nice. Then she put on her hat and coat and went quietly down to Mrs. Du Casson 's boudoir. She felt rather frightened, for she knew that this was tampering with property. And her moral teaching had instilled the fact into her that if you are discovered tampering with property you are very severely punished. But this was essentially a day of revolt. She crept into the room. It smelt strongly with the scent she always associated with the Du Cassons. It was a very pretty room, all pink and with shiny yellowish furniture. She went to the escritoire, and to her relief saw that there was a small bunch of keys on a ring, and one of them was in the lock. Mrs. Du Casson had evidently gone off and forgotten them! She opened the escritoire and found the cash box, but it was locked. She tried all the keys on the ring, but none of them fitted. She looked in all the drawers, and at last found a small key in a nib box. To her delight it was the right one. She opened the cash box. There was all the money, as she had seen it that morning. She grabbed four shillings and then her eye lighted on the pile of gold.

In a flash the thought came to her of her demand of Uncle Grubhofer: "The people paid money to come and bear me play. Who was it?" and then she remembered bis significant grin, "You bad better ask Mrs. Du Casson?" Good Heavens! this was it! She bad a moment of poignant revelation. She knew why these people were so kind to her. They took the money which rightfully belonged to her. It must belong to her. She played alone at the concerts, there was no other attraction—people came in their hundreds and paid money to hear her. She rolled the sovereigns over in her hand. She thought of Karl and Montague and Irene, and the baby perhaps without proper food. And she had sent them nothing, had nothing, and here was all the money that she rightfully should be allowed to give them lying in this box. She counted it out on the green baize top of the desk, her ears alert for any disturbance from below. There were nine sovereigns and five half sovereigns. It was a fortune! She would go away and take Irene and the others to somewhere in the country, and never come back. She put the coins stealthily in a handkerchief and tucked them away in her small reticule. Then she closed the desk and went out of the room.

When she met Uncle Grubhofer at Gower Street she was quite calm.

He said, "You have not spoken?" and she shook her head.

They took a train to Waterloo, where be bought two more tickets. It was dark by this time and they boarded a slow train and sat in the corner of a smoking carriage without speaking. The train stopped at all the stations and people passed in and out like phantoms. They trundled through the country for about an hour till the train arrived at a station at which porters were declaiming a title that sounded something like "Larrsham!" Uncle Grubhofer peered out of the window, and then got out, Olga following him. The station seemed bleak and deserted, but outside were two cabs of a sort. Uncle Grubhofer motioned to her to get into one of them, and then he gave some directions to the driver. They rattled off into the dark country, and passed through a village. About a mile further on they pulled up, and Uncle Grubhofer told the driver to wait. They got out and clambered over a stile, and crossed a field. In a hollow on the other side a dimly lit cottage was discernible. Uncle Grubhofer led his charge towards it. He listened for a minute or two outside the gate, and then went through and tapped on the door. They heard some one moving inside, and then the bolt was slipped back and the door opened an inch or two, and Irene's voice said: "Who is it?"

Uncle Grubhofer said, "It 's me. Let me in quickly," and he pushed his way into the passage.

"Who is this?" said Irene, peering at Olga; then suddenly recognizing her she said, "Oh, Christ!"

They trooped into the room where the lamp was burning, and a few dull cinders lay shivering in a small grate. Uncle Grubhofer did not remove his hat. He went to the fireplace and placed one of his feet on the bars of the grate. Olga wanted to greet Irene in some way, but the impulse of affection seemed atrophied in! her. She felt tense and strained, and was conscious that; the silence was oppressing her and Irene in different ways. Neither of the girls moved or looked at each other. They were staring at Uncle Grubhofer 's back.

At last the silence snapped in the chilling percussion of his voice.

"Well, well," he said, "are you alone here? Quite alone—still? None of the tradespeople here, eh? Not the butcher, or the milkman? or even—the baker?"

Olga noticed the top of his head moving as though he were shaking with the vibrations of some fountain of secret enjoyment. Irene did not answer. She shrunk against the wall, and he continued:

"So! Your dear little sister has come to see you. She wants to stop with you—she loves you so! You see—you have so much in common—thieving and harlotry!" he chuckled to himself. "She wants to have a nice loving chat. She will like to hear all about Karl. You can't tell her much about Montague, can you? and then—who else is there? Who else? How sad that Nathan didn't have more children! robbing the prisons and brothels of their hard-earned fodder, eh? You can put her up, can't you? I expect she has money. Look in that little black bag she carries. I expect she 's brought you something. You see she lives among rich people. She 's used to having everything. And when they don't give it to her she takes it. Oh, yes, don't worry. She 's a Bardel all right. She 's one of Nathan's children—the apple of his eye! I remember he devoted special care to this one...." At that he turned and looked sharply at Olga, and at her small black bag. Her hand trembled, and she knew that if he chose to snatch it from her, she would not have the power to resist. It was horrible, the way he rambled on about her father. She felt at one moment that she would be glad to throw the bag to him, if only he would leave them, but the desultory flow of anathema pursued the even tenor of its course. Much of it was incomprehensible to Olga, and he referred to names and incidents that conveyed nothing to her; the terrifying conviction came home to her that he was glad that she and Irene and the others were vile. He knew it and wanted them to be and rejoiced in his power to gloat over them. She tried to reason this out but she could not. It was horrible. The next time he mentioned her father, she suddenly cried out:

"Don't! Don't! I won't stand it! You shan't say these things of my father!"

And then he did a most surprising thing. He looked quickly at Olga and then suddenly started as though he had been struck with a whip. He gave a sort of whimper. She really thought for the moment that he was going to cry. He fumbled with the lapels of his coat, and the expression of jeering satisfaction gave way to one of dejection. He took off his soft hat and crumpled it in his hand and then put it back on his head. He kicked the grate peevishly and then walked to the door. There he stopped as though about to continue his diatribe but changed his mind. He gazed at Olga with an expression of melancholy anguish and then gave a snigger that carried no conviction of mirth, and walked right out of the cottage.

The gate snapped, and they heard the heavy thud of his footsteps on the field path. The sisters stood there in silence, each listening to the tramp, tramp, tramp, across the field, almost unconscious of each other. Minutes passed and then they heard the crack of a whip, and the crunching of wheels on the road. They hardly breathed till they heard the wheels die away in the distance, and then they turned and looked at each other simultaneously. It was a strange encounter; for the first time in their lives they seemed to be looking at each other as equals. Olga had become taller and had acquired elements of assurance. She carried herself well; Irene looked at her for a moment, and then sat by the table and buried her face in her hands and cried. Olga went to her and kissed the top of her head and said, breathing rapidly, "Don't cry."

But Irene enjoyed her cry—she was quite unstrung. It was some minutes before she could speak. Then she said:

"Why did you come?"

Olga was dreading this question, particularly as she knew she had no answer ready that Irene would understand. At last she said, "I wanted to come. I wanted to see—the baby."

A drawn expression came over Irene's face, but she answered in a low voice, "You shouldn't have done that. The baby 's dead. He died two months ago."

"Oh, dear, I 'm sorry. I 'm so sorry," Olga tried to say, but her words were lost in the renewed sobbing that shook Irene. At last she said:

"Oh, it don't matter. It was lovely having him. I didn't know—what anything was till he came . . . and went."

This seemed a most surprising statement to Olga. "It was lovely having him"—What did she mean? Would she rather have had him and lost him? He was a boy then. What he had brought to her had been dashed away! But no, not quite. What was it about Irene? Olga recognized that her sister had some quality— she could not define it. Something that came out to meet one, she had never had it before. She could not have cried like this. "I didn't know what anything was till he came—and went." It was the most tremendous statement Irene had ever made to her. It was the first time in her life a message had come direct from some other heart to hers, as though valuing its intimacy. She did not speak, but she felt glad that she had come. At last Irene looked up and said, "What was that he said about you? Have you brought me something?"

Olga nodded and opened her bag. She untied the handkerchief, and put the pile of gold on the table. Irene started and trembled. She ran to the window and pulled the curtains closer, and stood listening as though she expected to hear the footsteps of Uncle Grubhofer returning. Then she came breathlessly to the table, her eyes glistening.

"My God!" she kept repeating. At last she said in a whisper, "Where did you get this? Did you pinch it?"

"It's mine," answered Olga simply; "the people paid to hear me play."

Irene stared at her suspiciously, and she stroked the coins and sniffed.

"Did they give it to yer?" she asked suddenly.

"No," said Olga placidly, "I took it. It 's mine. They paid this to hear me play."

"My God!" whispered Irene, and she went on tiptoe to the window again. She seemed afraid to return.

She stood there and said in a husky voice, "I thought so! I thought so! It's no good. We 're all alike! The old devil 's right. Did you bring it for me?"

"Yes," said Olga, "but I would like Montague to have some and Karl."

"'Ave n't you 'eard then?" said Irene without moving. "Karl 's in quod again—forging this time—got eighteen mouths. Montague 's gone off—America, I think, or Australia—some foreign parts. You brought it for me, eh?"

Her eyes transfixed the coins greedily. She seemed drawn between two fears. At last she came to the table and counted them.

"Eleven pounds ten!" she said meditatively as though trying to visualize the potentialities of such a sum. At last she said, "Where did you get this from?"

"Mrs. Du Casson had it," said Olga. "I took it while she was out."

Irene stared at her sister and trembled. She noticed her small square chin and the curious placid determination written on her brow. She looked different from Karl when he had pinched things. She felt frightened of her, even as she had felt frightened on that day when Olga persisted in playing with Uncle Grubhofer's "property."

"Did you know what this means?" she said quickly. "It means that if they cop you they will put you in quod like Karl!"

"It's mine," said Olga doggedly; "the people paid to hear me play."

"You 'd 'ave to prove it. Oh, my God!"

The sisters sat there arguing about the first principles of economics and justice in a scratchy, elementary way, but they could make no progress. Olga could not persuade Irene that the money rightfully belonged to her. And Irene could not convince Olga that she had done a criminal act.

Olga lay on the couch in the sitting-room that night. In the middle of the night Irene came down and she found that Olga was awake.

"It 's no good," she said; "you 'll have to go away. I 've been thinking about it. Uncle Grubhofer will come in the morning with policemen and all that, and I can't stand it. I 've been ill. I was in the 'orspital, you know—the baby died there. They said I was to go to a 'ome, or I 'd go off my nut. And then Uncle Grubhofer sent me down 'ere. He had this cottage, it seemed. I believe he thinks I 'll go off my nut anyway. I believe he wants me to. He comes sometimes like he did last night. Stops ten minutes and looks at me as though I was some animal. I 'm allowed to order five bobs' worth of food a week from the shop 'ere, and I can take things out of the garden. Any shock will send me off my nut, the doctor said, and if the policemen come in the morning—Oh, my God! ..."

Olga sat up and rubbed her brow. "Yes, yes," she said, "I 'll go. I 'll go at once."

Then Irene cried and kissed Olga. "You didn't ought to have done it—to have stolen the money—I somehow thought you 'd be the only one. ... I 'm glad you come though. ..."

The sisters lay in each other's arms in a sort of intimacy for the first time in their lives.

When a pale light began to filter through the blind, Olga rose and bathed her face.

She accepted one of the half sovereigns to pay her expenses to London, and leaving the rest with Irene, she started out across the fields.

CHAPTER VIII

"THE BOARD MEETING"

It would be idle to pretend that the syndicate had at any time been a united body. The Du Cassons and Mr. Pensiver distrusted and disliked each other, but in any case they understood each other. They were of the same class, and had the same standard of ethical values. But Uncle Grubhofer introduced an alien and in every way objectionable element into their councils. Of course they were bound to have him as he had control of the child, but they were always ashamed of being seen with him, and they were also a little afraid of him. This fear became accentuated when Uncle Grubhofer began to show open discontent with the financial results of the scheme, and to demonstrate to Mr. Pensiver that he distrusted the statements in his books. He had harbored a grudge against Mr. Pensiver from their very first interview, because he knew that Mr. Pensiver had taken advantage of his lack of knowledge of business as conducted in the musical profession. But Uncle Grubhofer was beginning to understand the ropes a little himself, and was resenting the large profits that might ultimately go into the pockets of his fellow directors. The tour had been a fair success, making net profit of over eight hundred pounds, and out of his share of it Uncle Grubhofer tried to buy out Mr. Bausch and the other members of his own syndicate, but these gentlemen—with the exception of Karl who was in prison, and one of the men who had invested thirty pounds—having heard of the fame and reputation of Olga Barjelski, stood out for a larger sum than Uncle Grubhofer was disposed to pay.

On the night when Olga paid her visit to Irene, the Du Cassons had invited Mr. Pensiver to dinner with the idea of having a little business chat, the prime motive of this being a desire on the part of the Du Cassons to buy Uncle Grubhofer out. The Du Cassons had social as well as commercial aims, and they were tired of "explaining" Uncle Grubhofer to their many friends, and they were particularly tired of the unsavory parasites who were always in his train, and were apt to be objectionable and not always particularly sober. For the coming year Mr, Pensiver had booked a lot of good engagements for Olga and they were to be of a more paying nature. That fact of course would have to be suppressed, or in any case considerably modified when discussing terms. It would have to be suggested that musical business was at a deadlock, but that out of the kindness of their hearts the Du Cassons would look after Olga for the rest of the time and would give Mr. Grubhofer— say a hundred pounds to relinquish any further claim on the syndicate. They arrived home at seven o'clock and hurried up to their rooms to dress for dinner. As the maid was spreading out Mrs. Du Casson's frock, that lady remarked,

"By the way, Laura, where is Miss Olga? has she been practising?"

"I haven't heard her, madame," replied the maid. "I don't think she has."

"Oh!" exclaimed Mrs. Du Casson petulantly. "Just go and tell her to come and speak to me, Laura."

Laura retired, but returned in a few minutes to say she wasn't in her room. They called all over the house but there was no answer. Mrs. Du Casson was angry. She called to her husband.

"Louis, what 's happened to Olga? She 's not in the house!"

Mr. Du Casson came in in his shirt sleeves.

"Eh?" he said, "not in? Oh, I expect she 's somewhere about. Where is she, Laura?"

"I don't know, sir. I haven't seen her since—lunch time."

"Well, that 's a nice thing," exclaimed Mr. Du Casson, sitting on the bed. "I told her she was to practise. She 's got to play the Grieg concerto on Saturday. She ought to have practised all the afternoon. I don't believe she knows the slow movement at all. I wonder whether we 'd better— What is it? What 's the matter, Eva?"

These latter queries were addressed to Mrs. Du Casson, who had suddenly started in the middle of her dressing and rushed to her escritoire. She made violent movements of opening and shutting drawers and then shrieked and burst into tears.

"What is it? what 's up?" ejaculated her husband.

"Do you know what it is?" screamed Mrs. Du Casson. "The little devil 's stolen my money and bolted!"

"What!" gasped the world famous professor. "I tell you she 's bolted!" cried the lady hysterically.

"You fool! you might have known what would happen, having slum children in the house! She 's just stolen everything and gone. I knew something like that would happen! After all I 've done for her! I 've been like a mother, I 've given her everything she wanted! Everything! and then she turns on me like this!" Poor Mrs. Du Casson broke down, and her husband tried to soothe her.

"But, I say, you know, Eva, we don't know. Perhaps there is some mistake. She wouldn't—why, it wouldn't be worth it, it 's ridiculous! How much had you?"

"Eleven pounds in gold, and some silver," sobbed Mrs. Du Casson; "of course she 's taken it. She asked me for money this morning. She watched me taking it out of here. I noticed her greedy, cunning look at the time, as though I hadn't given her enough! They 're all criminals, all the family—I 've heard about them—one of the brothers is in prison now for stealing. And I expect that horrible uncle is in it. He 's probably put her up to it. Oh, it 's awful!"

Mr. Du Casson was incredulous. He poked about in the escritoire and asked a series of pointless questions. He went up-stairs to Olga's room and routed amongst her things.

"She can't have bolted," he shouted down, "she's left some of her clothes and so on."

In the midst of this confusion the bell rang and Mr. Pensiver was announced. Olga's patron and patroness hurriedly finished their dressing and went down to him. Mr. Pensiver took the news magnificently, as became a person who gambled in big things. He listened attentively to all they had to say, and then started immediately to consider the wisest course to pursue. Dinner was announced before he had time to formulate any plan and the three of them adjourned to the dining room. Two maids waited at table, so that the discussion was deferred till the dessert stage. In spite of their misgivings and Mrs. Du Casson's broken, maternal heart, they all managed to negotiate a very excellent dinner. When the maids had retired and a bottle of Benedictine had been passed round and the men had lighted their cigars, Mrs. Du Casson said,

"Well now—what are we to do?"

"Do you think there might have been a street accident?" said Mr. Du Casson suddenly. "You know she 's rather an—er, abstracted child. Taxis coming round the corner and so on." He illustrated the line of his pessimistic foreboding by a sweep of a dessert knife, but neither of the others evinced a serious interest in this theory.

Mrs. Du Casson said, "Do you think the man Grubhofer is at the back of this, Sir. Pensiver?"

Pensiver held his Benedictine up to the light and said,

"We must be prepared for this, dear lady. But there is one point I want to make quite clear. Nothing must be said about this money that she has—that has disappeared. You will understand—there are considerable sums at stake during the next few years—so we will write this amount off—how much did you say it was—ten pounds? We will consider it one of the aberrations of genius," and Mr. Pensiver laughed pleasantly. "Good heavens! I 've known nearly every artist in Europe personally and intimately. I don't think there 's one who hasn't got some wayward kink in his or her composition. Many of them are criminals. We make allowances for them." Mr. Pensiver tossed the contents of the small glass of yellow liquid into his mouth as though the aggravating stuff had tantalized him long enough and then continued, "So if this young lady shows a certain—light-fingered proclivity, the only thing for us to do is to—er—keep temptation out of her way and protect her." He smiled expansively, and Mrs, Du Casson nodded and said,

"Yes. You 're right, of course. You 're quite right, Mr. Pensiver, but you can't think how upset and disappointed I am. I had looked upon her almost as my own child. It seems so horrible! Stealing! There's something so—unclean about it." And the good lady selected a salted almond from a silver jardiniere and crunched it despondingly between her teeth.

"Please accept my sincere sympathy," said Mr. Pensiver earnestly. "It must be indeed terrible for you. Now what I think is this. I do not believe that Grubhofer is at the back of this. I think the eleven pounds settles that. He would not have encouraged her to steal eleven pounds when he has so much more at stake. It would be ridiculous, and Grubhofer is no fool. I 'm inclined to think the child has gone off on some wayward business of her own, to visit some of these choice members of her family perhaps. I hope this may be so. In that case Grubhofer is the only person who will be able to get in touch with her. In any case I think no time should be lost in getting in touch with him. We shall in any case know the worst. "

"He 's not on the telephone," ventured Mr. Du Casson.

"No, and I don't think that would be the best way to approach him either," said the impresario.

"What shall we do?" said Mrs. Du Casson.

"I think one of us ought to go in a ear over to his place in Canning Town. If there is no sign of the girl there, we should persuade him to come back there, to hold a meeting, as the matter is urgent. I should say nothing to him about the stolen money."

"Good!" said Mr. Du Casson. "That's right and you 're the one to go!"

"I bow to the decision of the majority," said Mr. Pensiver magnanimously as Mrs. Du Casson nodded an agreement with her husband. Within twenty minutes the impresario's cab was at the door, and the great man, with his half-smoked cigar rolling between his teeth, stepped across the pavement and gave the driver instructions in an apologetic voice as to how to approach the mephitic neighborhood of Canning Town. It took the cab rather less than half an hour to arrive at Uncle Grubhofer's shop. Mr. Pensiver got out and walked quickly up to the door and rang a bell. Everything was in darkness, but presently Mr. Pensiver thought he heard a window open. He looked up. A shadowy head was peering at him.

"Ah!" called Mr, Pensiver in a loud and genial voice. "Is that you, Mr. Grubhofer?"

"Who is it?" said the face.

"I 'm John Pensiver. May I speak to you for a moment, Mr. Grubhofer?"

The window shut deliberately and there was a long interval. At last a bolt creaked behind the door, and Uncle Grubhofer appeared in a dressing gown, holding a lamp. "Come in," he said. Mr. Pensiver followed him into the shop.

"Your niece has disappeared from Mrs. Du Casson's," he said, and he looked Uncle Grubhofer very searchingly in the eye.

Uncle Grubhofer started and blinked. "She has disappeared?" he repeated.

"It is very urgent," continued Mr. Pensiver. "We presume you know nothing of her whereabouts?"

Uncle Grubhofer seemed dumbfounded. "What do you mean?" he said. "She 's disappeared! When did she disappear? I took her there this morning!"

"She went out this afternoon and has not returned. She is engaged to play at the Royal Tonic Society's concert on Saturday at a good fee. She should be practising. It is a serious thing!"

"Dear, dear!" said Uncle Grubhofer; "this is awful!"

"As I see you know nothing about her whereabouts—we think it would be a good thing if you would come back with me to the Du Cassons ' so that we may discuss the best thing to do. I have my car here."

"Oh, dear! I do hope there hasn't been an accident. Have you informed the police?"

"No," said Mr. Pensiver, and then after a pause he added, "Not yet."

The men stood staring at each other, each trying to read the other's thoughts. At last Uncle Grubhofer said, "Yes, I will come."

He left Mr. Pensiver to wait in the shop. While he was robing himself in more appropriate garments, Mr. Pensiver devoted his time in listening keenly for any sound that might give him a clue that the little girl was on the premises. In this he was unsuccessful, and at last Uncle Grubhofer appeared and they entered the car together. This important board meeting of the syndicate took place nearly at midnight, in a small room on the ground floor passage which they called the smoke room. They held it there because Mrs. Du Casson gave her decision that "she would not under any circumstances ask that dirty old blackguard into her drawing room."

The four partners were all nervous, and not sure of each other, and consequently the meeting promised to be entirely formal. Mr. Pensiver began by saying that, although it was a board meeting, they could do nothing. They could make no decisions. Mrs. Du Casson said that the thing they could decide was—whether to inform the police, and if so, when.

Mr. Du Casson said, "Surely, Pensiver, there 's a good ad. here! 'Disappearance of infant Prodigy!' What?"

Mr, Pensiver said it might or might not be a good advertisement. It all depended on how the girl was discovered and the reason for her disappearance. If they were certain of producing her for the concert on Saturday and some romantic reason for her disappearance were forthcoming—that she had been kidnapped or had wandered into the country in search of flowers—of course it would be excellent. "But if, on the other hand," he said, "we are not able to produce her and the reason of her disappearance is a—shall we say—discreditable reason, it would act in a contrary fashion.

Managers, you know, do not like an artist they cannot rely on."

"I have a feeling she 'll turn up," said Mr. Du Casson. "You 're sure she 's not with any of her family, Mr. Grubhofer?"

"I have seen her sister only this evening," said that gentleman. "And her brothers are—er—abroad," and he shook his head doubtfully.

"I should suggest," said Mrs. Du Casson, who had her original project always in her mind's eye, "that we discuss future arrangements on the assumption that she will turn up," and she looked at Mr. Pensiver.

The impresario caught her eye and produced some papers from his pocket and turned them over on the table. He cleared his throat and put down the stump of his cigar.

"It would, of course," he said, "be idle to pretend that the little girl has been the—er—commercial success that we hoped. And the bookings for the coming season are fairly numerous but unfortunately not very remunerative, and after that, speaking as one who has had a very considerable experience in the profession, I 'm afraid the outlook is not encouraging and for this reason. We shall soon no longer be able to produce her as a prodigy or even as an infant phenomenon, and then of course the value of the attraction sinks to zero. Now our contract holds good for seven years and I am sure that none of us will be desirous of burking our obligations. But there is, of course, no reason why any member of the syndicate should not—with the consent of the other members—sell his or her shares to an}- other member, I am naturally speaking hypothetically—"

"On the assumption that the child is found, of course," interrupted Mrs. Du Casson.

"On the assumption that the child is found before Saturday" said Mr. Pensiver.

"Oh!" exclaimed the lady.

"I attribute great importance to her appearance at the Royal Tonic Society's concert. It will strengthen my hand in the provinces enormously."

"But if not?" she said; "if the child is not found?"

Mr. Pensiver shrugged his shoulders. "I think in any case we will have covered our expenses," and he bowed slightly to Mrs. Du Casson as though he had rendered some signal and gallant service in a chivalrous cause.

"It 's a pretty dreadful outlook," said Mrs. Du Casson at last, scratching with a pen on a blotting pad. "I 'm afraid you will feel this very much, Mr. Grubhofer." There was a pause, and then Uncle Grubhofer said,

"I believe that the God who divided the waters for the children of Israel will deliver our little lamb back into the fold."

This sentence murmured in a thin melancholy voice seemed to stab the air like some obscene blasphemy. The other three gasped and sat back, and small beads of perspiration gathered on the brow of Mr, Pensiver and he laughed unpleasantly. And then he said,

"Come now—I will be a sportsman. Would any one like to sell me their share in the syndicate? Mrs. Du Casson?"

It is difficult to know how much of the little scene that followed had been rehearsed beforehand by the Du Cassons and Mr. Pensiver. But the upshot was that Mrs. Du Casson said that from a purely commercial point of view she would be willing to sell her interests in the concern for a hundred pounds, but as she had promised to look after the child she felt she could not back out of it. Besides she had developed a very sincere affection for her and she should stick to her as long as she could. Fortunately she and Mr. Du Casson were not entirely without means, so that the prospect of Olga not paying her way did not disturb her in the least. It seemed dreadful to be exploiting a little girl like that, and she was sure they all felt the same.

Uncle Grubhofer was licking the wet end of a cigar and dabbing it with his finger, but he said nothing. He might have been nursing his inconsolable grief at the loss of the lamb from the fold.

Mrs. Du Casson continued in level tones: "Of course with Mr. Grubhofer I'm afraid it's different. He has already had all the—bother and responsibility of bringing up a child, who, after all, is not his own. We can hardly expect him to—persevere. Besides he has his business to attend to in such a—in a part of London which makes it difficult for him to get in touch with—musical matters. And he is launching out, I understand, in new premises. That must take up all his time and any capital he has to spare." She waited as though expecting an interruption, but it did not come, and she continued: "I think one of us who have a more working interest in the child should take the responsibility out of his hands. If you agree, Mr. Grubhofer, I will pay you a hundred pounds for your share in the arrangement."

They all looked at Grubhofer. He still patted his disheveled cigar and then he said,

"And what will you pay me, Mrs. Du Casson, for my broken heart? or for my lonely life without my little niece to cheer me?"

Mrs. Du Casson bit her lip. She was a little annoyed. She said, "Oh, well, of course, Mr. Grubhofer, you would always have access to the child. She would be able to come and see you on Sundays and so on. "

And then Uncle Grubhofer made a surprising statement.

"It is strange you should have made this proposal," he murmured in a doleful voice, "because I proposed to make a similar offer to you, only for a different amount. I will give you five hundred pounds for your share in the syndicate, Mrs. Du Casson."

The three of them started as though a bombshell had fallen in the room, and Mr. Pensiver said in a hard voice,

"Does your offer still hold good?"

"I make it in all faith to you, Mrs. Du Casson, and to you, Mr. Pensiver. If you will both forego your interests in the child, I will pay you five hundred pounds each to-night." The three looked at each other as though trying to read how much the others considered this bluff and how much genuine. And then Mr. Pensiver laughed uneasily and said,

"But of course we are all talking a little wildly. The child has disappeared. For all we know she may—we may never be able to complete."

Uncle Grubhofer produced a grubby check book and a fountain pen, that he tried by languidly jerking it on the tablecloth. And then he said'

"I am willing to take my chance. Will you both agree to accept five hundred pounds to forego your claims whether the child turns up or not?"

"Ah!" a chilling gasp escaped Mrs. Du Casson and Mr. Pensiver.

"You seem very confident," said the impresario deliberately, "that the child will turn up." And then he shivered with a dread that Uncle Grubhofer would make some reference to the "lamb returning to the fold." But he did not. He seemed to be waiting indifferently for the decision of the others.

It was Mrs. Du Casson who had the instinct to act. Her eyes looked strained and hard, as though she had become aware of some unpleasant fact, and meant to deal with it at all costs. She looked across the table and fixed her eyes very intently on Mr. Grubhofer and said, "If the child turns up by twelve o'clock to-morrow, I will pay you seven hundred and fifty pounds for your interests in the concern."

"Oh, dear! Oh, dear!" said Uncle Grubhofer. "Don't let us talk as though the dear child may not turn up."

"Let us say then—if you promise that the child will turn up!"

"I say, Eva!" It was Mr. Du Casson who exclaimed this. He began to feel that the atmosphere was unpleasant and he had a dread that his wife was going to make a fool of herself. But she turned on him angrily and gave him an expression that dried up all his instincts of interference for the rest of the evening.

Mr. Pensiver rustled his papers about and pressed his hair back.

"I hope you have given your offer consideration, Mrs. Du Casson. It appears to me a surprisingly generous one, and of course if Mr. Grubhofer accepts it, it is a tacit admission that he knows where the child is and can produce her. It practically amounts—"

He did not finish the sentence, for Mrs. Du Casson, who had never taken her eyes off Grubhofer, said in a high, detached voice:

"I have a curious faith that if Mr. Grubhofer says that the child will turn up to-morrow, she will turn up. I am prepared to back my opinion to the extent of seven hundred and fifty pounds."

Uncle Grubhofer never raised his eyes from the blotting paper in front of him. He had made a little pile of cigar ash and he kept pushing it with his fingers. His appearance was in every way disconsolate. At last he said:

"This arrangement would break my heart. Think of it! all my dear brother-in-law 's children are now scattered. There is no one to soothe their uncle's last years. This little girl,—" there was a catch in his voice—"she is the last. For seven years she might be my guardian angel, brightening my lonely home, attending to my meager wants. How tragic is this genius! what a trail of sadness it always leaves. One cannot encompass it, or understand it. At the end of seven years what may she not be?

She may have forgotten her uncle entirely, or he may be dead. It is terrible. I appreciate what you say, Mrs. Du Casson, and it is nice in this hard world to find such a woman as you, with your pure, maternal, disinterested heart"—just for a second he glanced up and his smile was one of the most horrible episodes of the evening, and then he continued, ruminating in the pile of tobacco ash—"She will never forget you. You will always be the bright maternal figure to her, taking the place of—every one else. She will learn to love you more and more, and in after life she will repay your old age. Ah!" he sighed lugubriously, "I know it is probably my duty to accept, and yet—well, Mrs. Du Casson, only God can judge these things. For a thousand pounds I will do what you say, only from Mr. Pensiver I shall also want a hundred pounds a year while the contract lasts!"

"I 'll see you damned—" commenced Mr. Pensiver, but Mrs. Du Casson jumped up and exclaimed:

"Wait a moment! Mr. Pensiver, Louis, come into the next room. I want to have a word with you before anything further is said." Mrs. Du Casson was a little hysterical and not to be denied. The three others trouped out and left Uncle Grubhofer to his pile of tobacco ash. They were out of the room less than five minutes. "When they returned Mr. Pensiver said:

"We 've thought this matter over, Grubhofer, and we accept the terms. On this condition, that during this time you make no claim at all upon us or the child. That you do not attempt to see her or us and that you sign a contract to that effect, and also that the child returns to-morrow morning by twelve o'clock. Mrs. Du Casson will give you a check for a thousand pounds now dated the day after to-morrow, so of course if the child does not appear, the check is stopped. Do you agree? "

Uncle Grubhofer was too upset to answer. He merely nodded his head, as though agreeing to his own execution. The check and contract changed hands.

And then the large man rose up and walked to the door. He seemed dazed. He was apparently too heartbroken to indulge in any valediction. He rolled heavily through the hall, with his eyes on the ground, and out into the street.

When the door slammed, the other three looked at each other and Mrs. Du Casson gave a sigh of relief. No one spoke for a few moments and then Mr. Du Casson said,

"I say, Eva, you know, it 's all very well, but that blackguard has blackmailed us!"

"I know! I know! but. Good God, it was worth it!" and she gave a little hysterical sob.

"Of course he 's got the girl at home all the time!" said Mr. Du Casson, as though expecting some credit for his perspicacity and restraint. "He just came bouncing in and blackmailed you both."

"It is the first time in my professional career that I have been blackmailed," said Mr. Pensiver, "but I think it was worth it. You were right, Mrs. Du Casson. After all I 've booked nearly a thousand pounds' worth of engagements for the coming season, and then I think we can start on America. A successful American tour will soon take the taste of this out of our mouths."

"Oh, the relief of feeling that we 've done with that— nightmare forever!"

"Do you know it's a quarter to three!" exclaimed Mr. Du Casson. Mr. Pensiver 's car was still waiting and he took his departure.

The Du Cassons had had a disturbing evening and when it was over they could not sleep. They lay awake for hours discussing the situation, indulging in recriminations and doubts and hopes. It must have been nearly daylight before they went to sleep.

At half-past ten the next morning they were still sleeping, then Mr. Du Casson half wakened. He was wondering why a certain air kept running through his head and it seemed more and more insistent. At last he sat up doubtfully and listened and rubbed his eyes. Then he awakened his wife.

"Eva, Eva," he said. "Listen!"

Mrs. Du Casson yawned and said peevishly, "What is it?"

Then she looked at her husband and the truth flashed through both of them.

The "lamb had returned to the fold" and was hard at work practising the slow movement of the Grieg concerto!

CHAPTER IX

THE TWO METHODS

Olga's mind worked with peculiar transcendence on her return journey from her visit to Irene. The railway carriage was very cold and she shivered in one of the corners, but her spirits were buoyant. She saw things at oblique and interesting angles, and felt for the first time a desire to put them in their place. She looked out of the window and saw the green country bathed in a gray dew. She left the window open and the air felt damp, but sweet and good. Impulses within her moved towards a greater sense of independence. Life had so far played the unholy jest upon her of giving her a great heart, and then depriving her of any great object of affection. She was like a splendid, untuned instrument lying forgotten in a drawer. The only affection she had ever enjoyed had been for Miss Merson, and this she realized was because Miss Merson had been kind and good to her. There was nothing fundamental about it. She had a fundamental affection for Irene and Karl and Montague, but it had been cabined and confined by their indifference to her. The rest of the people were but shadows acting in incomprehensible ways. The dominant thing that life had so far given her had been—moods. Moods of terror, of fear, of unexplainable passion, of longing; moods of pity too deep for expression; moods of sorrow that could not be assuaged, and yet that left her tranquil; moods of little jealousies and uncontrollable dislikes. Life had also given her most wonderful hands, and an inborn sense of rhythm. There also came to her at moments a certainty that she had experienced all this before.

Sometimes on the tour and in artists' rooms in London people had come to her and spoken kindly to her. She had looked into their steady eyes, and felt a desire to know them. But they came and touched her hand and vanished. People seemed to be always coming and going—like that—passing by her like a pageant. But often they left her something—just a word—a look, something that helped to quicken her sensibilities.

Often she longed for Mr. Casewell again, and "Levitch himself," who gave her the apple. She felt somehow that she would get on with these people. Behind the dark half-humorous eyes of "Levitch himself" lurked unexplored worlds, where things would be better balanced, saner, more beautiful . . . There must be others like Levitch.

The train rumbled through Clapham Junction, where some workmen got in on their way to work. She felt important and independent traveling into London with workmen. She never lost that feeling all her life, the feeling of mental stimulus when approaching London in a train and of mixing with people on their way to work. The rows of houses with their gray faces each expressed something different, and then here and there some great church or factory rose with insolent assertion above the general level of domesticity.

"Do you mind having the window up, miss?"

She was being appealed to by a man. He may have been a stonemason or a carpenter. It was very kind of him to ask her like that, an acknowledgment of her civic rights in this great and illimitable city.

"Not at all," she said and yawned with a pleasant sense of ease.

As the train was crossing the river, Irene's remark occurred to her about the police and taking the money. Perhaps when she arrived at the Du Cassons' she would be arrested and taken away to prison. She felt curiously indifferent about this. It would be interesting to go to prison, to see what it was like. Perhaps she would see Karl. And then one day they would let her out again; they never kept people in prison forever, and then she would see the great river again and the fields in their morning dew. . . .

It was in any case much better for Irene to have all that gold than Mrs. Du Casson. Irene was very, very poor, and Mrs. Du Casson was very rich.

She arrived at the Du Cassons' very early, again before they were up. She surprised the maid by ordering some breakfast for herself. She was cold and hungry. They took a long time making the tea, but at last it came. She had an egg and lots of marmalade and bread and three cups of tea, and then sat in front of the fire. She felt well and buoyant and the desire to create came to her. She went up to her room and took off her hat, and in a few minutes was immersed in the intricacies of the slow movement of the Grieg concerto. She found it absorbing. She was convinced that Mr. Du Casson was wrong about the reading of certain passages. She worked on for nearly two hours, when suddenly the door opened and Mr. Du Casson's head appeared. He was smiling as usual, his dark mustache lifted with an irritating regularity above his perfect teeth.

"Well," he cried out breezily, "so we 're back again, are we? Well, well, how are we getting on?"

He made no further reference to her disappearance or to the loss of the money. He talked only about the music. It was very difficult. She knew she could not play it as it should be played, and yet she felt even surer than ever that Mr. Du Casson's way was not the right way. She argued with him on certain points, and she hated the patronizing way he spoke to her. When the lunch gong went, she went down to the drawing-room. Mrs. Du Casson was there surrounded by her yapping dogs. She kissed her, but Olga was instantly aware of the slight chilling difference in manner. She believed Mrs. Du Casson said: "When you want to go and spend the night with friends, Olga, you must let us know. It 's very worrying not knowing where you are."

She believed she said this, but the dogs made such a noise it was impossible to be certain. They went into the dining-room and got through a rather self-conscious meal, Mr. and Mrs. Du Casson seeming at a loss to know what to say to her, and so keeping up a loud, vapid conversation between themselves shouting above the din of the dogs. After lunch she went back to her room. She worked hard at the Grieg concerto but did not feel happy about it. She had a rehearsal with the orchestra on the Friday and was introduced to the great Emil Maunlyas, the world-famous conductor. He was a large, distinguished-looking man with a pointed beard, and a keen reflective face. He shook hands with her amiably. They played the first movement. It was not a success. The great man kept stopping the orchestra and looking at her askance. She asked him a question once, and he shrugged his shoulders and said: "It is for you to lead, Miss—er—"

She knew he was displeased with her, and she did not know what to do. She could not play the concerto any better, the time was all wrong in places, and there was no one to help her. She felt like crying and then she thought, "I must do the best I can," and she went through with it. She felt ashamed of meeting M. Maunlyas afterwards and she avoided him.

On the Saturday for the first time she felt very nervous. It required great will power to force herself to go on the platform. When she did, she was received with the usual applause. She started well, but soon got into difficulties. Her runs came off splendidly, but she was conscious that it was all wrong somehow, wrong and meaningless. At the end of the first movement the people applauded vociferously, and she stood up and bowed, but as she turned again to the piano, her eye caught the grave meditative look of M, Maunlyas. She bit her lips and started on the second movement. x\t the end of the concerto the applause was tremendous. She bowed again and again to the house and the orchestra. M. Maunlyas was clapping too, but she could tell by the way he did it that it was done out of courtesy. She went off the platform, but was recalled four times. And then M. Maunlyas lead her on himself and bowed stiffly to her, and the people applauded this act even more.

At last she got back to the artists' room. She was very unstrung and struggled to keep back the tears. There were several people there, and M. Maunlyas was talking to a man by the door. Mr. Du Casson was dancing about like a wild cat, and Mr. Pensiver was looking smugly satisfied. M. Maunlyas moved towards the door. He would have to go on in three minutes' time and conduct another piece. Olga jumped up and touched him on the arm. He looked round.

"Oh! I'm so sorry," she said, and her face was racked with anguish. "I 'm so sorry I played so badly! I couldn't—I wanted it to be different—I—" her voice stopped, choked with tears.

The great man looked at her surprised. He patted her hands kindly and said, "My dear young lady!" He bowed stiffly. Some one was calling him, and he went out and she did not see him again.

There was a great deal of noise and confusion. In the distance she heard the droning of the 'cellos and fiddles tuning up. She shut her eyes and tried to steady herself. Suddenly a voice said, "Do you remember me, Olga?"

She looked up quickly and found herself looking into the keen, intelligent face of Mr. Casewell. She gave a little gasp and put out both her hands and he took them and pressed them.

"You seem to be becoming a great lady," he said. "I felt I must come round and see you. How are you, Olga?"

She glanced quickly round the room. It seemed providential, this sudden advent of Mr. Casewell. Mr. Du Casson had danced off somewhere else, and Mr. Pensiver had no doubt returned to the box-office. Mrs. Du Casson was in front. There was no one in the room who knew her. She clutched his forearm.

"Take me away, will you? Take me out of this!"

"Why, of course," said Mr. Casewell kindly but a little surprised. "Put on your cloak and we 'll go and have some chocolate at Coutis'."

She did as he said. She pulled on her cloak rapidly, and changed her shoes and then darted out of the room. He followed her through a dimly lighted basement and up some stone steps into the street and noted her fearful eagerness to get away. When they were in the street she did not speak but hurried along at his side. When they were quite clear of all that appertained to the concert hall, she said, "Mr. Casewell, is there anywhere we could go? Do you know, I don't want to go to a public restaurant. I want to talk to you. May I?"

"Quite," said Mr. Casewell. "Will you come to my rooms? You don't think your guardians will mind?"

"Oh, I don't care," she said suddenly.

He laughed and called a cab. In less than five minutes they were sitting in front of a fire in Mr. Casewell's bachelor chambers, and he was making her some cocoa.

"Now!" he said as he poured some direct from a saucepan into her cup, "tell me."

Olga took a sip of the hot drink and looked into the fire, and then she said, "Tell me, Mr. Casewell, how did you think I played?"

"Brilliantly," he answered, "brilliantly!"

"No," she said firmly, "tell me what you really, really think."

He laughed, and after a pause said, "Well, of course, I—it may sound like professional jealousy or interference."

"No, no," she said eagerly, "go on! That 's just it, that 's what I want."

"Well, my dear, I thought, of course, your technique was remarkable, but honestly I didn't think you grasped the shape of the music a bit. I don't think you understood it."

"Ah!" exclaimed Olga, and she took vicious little sips at the boiling cocoa.

"Of course I take it that this is Du Casson's reading. Anything I say may—"

She interrupted him by stretching out her hand and holding his.

"Oh, Mr. Casewell," she said, "I 'm so unhappy!"

Richard Casewell suddenly felt himself on dangerous ground. He had always liked and admired this strange little girl, and had great hopes of her and wanted to be her friend. But the sudden appearance of this rival faction of guardianship over her made it very difficult. It was obvious that any approaches that he made to regain her either as a pupil or a friend would be subject to serious misunderstanding. He had a hardly won reputation as a serious professor, and it was a reputation he was a little jealous of. He also had responsibilities, a mother and a sister who were dependent on him. He had been round to see Olga to-night because it seemed a reasonable and kindly thing to do. but he had had no intentions of acting in any way that suggested that he was trying to regain her. He saw now that the situation was going to be complicated by some confession, and he could not make up his mind how to act. He looked at her face and noticed that it had developed since the day when she first came to him. The chin seemed squarer and she held herself with a certain looseness and independence. Her eyes were deeper and more reflective, as though they had already suffered the pangs of introspective sorrow, as apart from the sorrows of beatings and bad food that she suffered in the earlier days. She brooded tensely as she leaned forward on the tuffet that he had drawn up for her in front of the fire.

"Good God!" he thought to himself, "what a woman this will be." He wanted to gain time and so he said, "Unhappy! Oh, come! You who have been the success of two seasons! You who have sat at rich men's feasts!"

"Don't!" she said and tears started to her eyes. "You know, Mr. Casewell, that all this is nothing! or at least not everything."

Mr. Casewell stared at her and wondered.

She continued. "I don't know how it is. I sometimes think I would rather go back to Canning Town. There is no one—nothing here. Do you know what I mean? I feel sometimes at the Du Cassons' as though I shall go mad. I hate everything about them. They seem to choke me. Of course they 're kind—in a way. It 's just that, as though I was choking all the time. And I want to play—differently somehow—and he, Mr. Du Casson keeps on pushing me round and round in a circle. Do you know what I mean, Mr. Casewell?"

Mr, Casewell knew too well what she meant, and the knowledge did not make his position easier. He put her cup down for her and lighted his pipe.

"I would like to do anything I could," he said after a time; "of course, you will see, Olga, it is a little difficult for me, won't you? I cannot take you away from Du Casson. You are no longer a waif of the streets. You are a person of note. You make money. You are independent. Of course, I don 't see why you should n 't come and see me sometimes—as a friend. It would make me very happy if you would do so, and if you let me help you in any way I can."

"Will you help me with my work?"

Mr. Casewell looked at her meditatively.

"That of course is rather the difficulty. While you are with Du Casson I can hardly—"

"I won't let him know," said Olga quickly, with a sudden change of countenance.

Mr. Casewell looked solemnly into the fire, and readjusted his glasses.

"Say yes, yes." Her round, eager young face was very close to his, and her deep eyes were pleading. Some instinct made him stoop down and kiss her cheek.

"All right, you little schemer," he said, "we 'll do it. And now I must take you back!"

"So soon?" she said, and as she lay curled on the tuffet it struck him that there was something feline and sinuous about the lines of her. She smiled and was very much a child again, "Tell me, have you any news? Have you seen Miss Merson?" she asked.

"No," he answered, smiling in turn, "I believe she has gone to Birmingham—to a school there. I see Miss Kenway sometimes. We often talk about you and read about you. What a trying time you must have had among the Armenians!" He added this last sentence suddenly with a sly smile.

Olga blushed and said, "Isn't it dreadful! It makes me so wretched— that sort of thing. And 'Levitch himself? Where is he?"

"He's in Prague," said Mr. Casewell. "He lives there, you know. He only comes over for three months every year. He will be here in May. Come! I shall get into dreadful trouble if you do not come back now. Come and see me on Wednesday afternoon at four o'clock, if you are free."

They walked back to the concert hall and Mr. Casewell said good-by to her outside. When she got back to the artists' room Mrs. Du Casson was there.

"Hullo, child," she exclaimed. "Where have you been? We 've been looking for you."

"I had to go out and get some air. It was so close. I felt I couldn't breathe."

"But not by yourself, my dear child, surely?" "Why not?" said Olga, and thus saved herself the ignominy of telling the lie she was prepared to tell. The concert was nearly over, and the orchestra was playing the last item on the program. Mrs. Du Casson said they had better wait so as to have a talk with Monsieur Maunlyas and anybody else of importance who came round.

The idea of this seemed repulsive to Olga, so while Mrs. Du Casson 's back was turned she slipped out of the artists' room and went out into the street. She found the Du Cassons' car and got into it and waited for them. They did not come for about twenty minutes and when they did there was a real row for the first time between the Du Cassons and their charge. Olga would give no other explanation of her disappearance than that she was tired and did n't want to see any one. Mrs, Du Casson got really angry and said that while she was in their charge she was to do as she was told. It was disgraceful conduct on her part to go off like that, and very bad business. She, Mrs. Du Casson, had given up all her time and energy to making her a success and it was extremely ungrateful. One of the first things she had to learn was to be gracious to every one, and when it came to the conductors she must simply do anything to try and please them and get in their favor. They—the Du Cassons—had spent an enormous sum of money making her a popular success and they hoped to make her an even greater success, but if she was going to behave like that, well, Mrs. Du Casson didn't know what she should do, she should have to reconsider everything.

"I played badly," said Olga.

"Badly!" exclaimed Mr. Du Casson. "Why, you were a great success! Everybody was delighted!"

"They don't know," persisted Olga. "I played disgracefully."

"What on earth is the child talking about?" A horrible thought struck Mrs. Du Casson. Was that appalling uncle of hers, Grubhofer, at the back of this? Was he trying some secret game to make her discontented? to get her away from them? She leaned forward in the car and looking at Olga very searchingly she said, "Have you seen your Uncle Grubhofer to-night?"

The mention of that name seemed to send the vibrating passions of the three of them off into more chilling channels. Olga said, "No," and she shivered slightly. She had been forgetting about Uncle

Grubhofer during the last few days, and the thought of him brought back a thousand dreads. She did not fear the Du Cassons. She disliked them and despised them, the experiences of the evening had bred in her a virulence toward them. Certain things were rankling, and one was that the great Maunlyas despised her, despised her because of these people and their mode of thought, and the way they trained her. She could not picture Maunlyas in Mrs. Du Casson's drawing-room, talking vapid things among the little dogs. He was one of them, like Mr. Casewell and "Levitch himself." He knew. He was one of the great people, people who did n 't fuss and say things they did n 't mean. She was excited at meeting Mr. Casewell. It opened glorious prospects to her. She didn't care about the Du Cassons. They could do what they liked, turn her out in the street. She would go to Mr. Casewell in spite of them. But somehow she felt afraid of Uncle Grubhofer. The very mention of his name cast portentous shadows across the fair prospect. And the mention of his name dulled the spirits of the loquacious Du Cassons. They arrived home, and Olga, refusing any refreshment, went straight to bed. The Du Cassons sat up some time and discussed the situation and were peevish with each other.

"I don't like it," said Mr. Du Casson. "I believe the old devil has put her up to it. She 's been like it ever since she came back—argues with me about readings, if you please! Seems to think she knows. She 's sullen and obstinate, and to-night she was rude to you in the car, Eva, By God! she flew out like a little cat! Makes one feel one would like to chuck her!"

"Yes," said Mrs. Du Casson bitingly, "and chuck away the thousand pounds we gave for her last week! That would be very clever."

"I never wanted to go in on it," said Mr. Du Casson.

"No," said his wife savagely, "I know you didn't. In the first place you haven't got a thousand pounds and in the second place you haven't any enterprise. I tell you there 's a thousand a year clear to be made out of this arrangement while it lasts. What sort of turnover on one's money is that, do you think? Oh, no, I 'm going to stick to it. And I 'm going to have her watched. We have our contract. If I find that old swine has been seeing her and getting at her, I 'll have him sued."

Nevertheless Mrs. Du Casson did not put her threat into immediate execution. On the next morning Mr. Pensiver rang up. The Royal Tonic Society concert had been a great success. The press was eulogistic and booking and enquiries were coming in from all over the country. Moreover, a New York agent was in town, staying at the Savoy, and had written to Mr. Pensiver for an appointment to discuss business in connection with "Barjelski." Mrs. Du Casson decided to see how things went and in the meantime to keep a sharp lookout on Olga herself. All her movements were checked and when she went out for a walk, she was always accompanied by a maid in addition to the little dogs. Olga was instantly aware of this change of attitude, and she determined to deal with the matter in her own way.

On the following Wednesday she started out with the maid and the little dogs, and when they got to the corner of Great Portland Street she suddenly said,

"I have to go down to Conduit Street to order some music, Emma, so I shall have to leave you. I shall be back about five," and without giving the maid any opportunity of repeating any instructions she may have received she jumped into a 'bus and disappeared.

She found Mr. Casewell awaiting her and a tea had been prepared. They grinned at each other and he said, "Well?"

"Isn't it a ripping day!" said Olga. "Now tell me how I ought to have played the slow movement."

She was in a great hurry and devoured everything he told her. It was only with the greatest difficulty he could get her to take any interest in the tea that he had taken such elaborate pains to prepare. He enjoyed talking to her and teaching her. She grasped ideas in a flash. Her mental virility excited him. They became conscious of nothing but the lofty claims of the muse they worshiped. Suddenly Mr. Casewell glanced at the clock. It was half-past five.

"You must go, my dear," he said in a low voice.

When Olga realized the time, she started.

"It 's been awfully good of you," she said and there were tears in her eyes.

"It 's been a delightful pleasure to me," said Mr. Casewell. "Come again next Wednesday, or when you can—Only let me know—I 'll always arrange it."

When she returned to Chessle Terrace, Mrs. Du Casson was walking up and down the hall. She looked at Olga suspiciously.

"Oh!" she said. "It seems to take some time to walk down to Conduit Street."

"Yes," answered Olga nonchalantly; "I went for a stroll afterwards down Regent Street and Piccadilly. It 's a perfect day, is n 't it?"

"Lying as well as stealing!" thought Mrs. Du Casson. "What can you expect from a slum child? I hope to goodness the American tour comes off. After that she can go to the devil!" Out loud she said—"Well, you had better change your shoes, dear. Mr. Du Casson is expecting you up-stairs. The appointment for your lesson was five, you know!"

As a matter of fact Olga had forgotten this, and she got out of it on this occasion by pleading a sudden and unaccountable headache. Mrs. Du Casson said it was undoubtedly due to strolling about looking in shop windows. In future she had better take her walks in the park.

During the next three months Olga, by all sorts of cunning tricks, managed to visit Mr. Casewell on an average once a week, not knowing that during a part of that time her visits were observed and noted by a private detective. The more often she visited Mr. Casewell, the more agonizing did her lessons become with Mr. Du Casson. She became more and more argumentative with him, and then reverted to a sort of sullen indifference in which she ignored what he said.

When the Du Cassons discovered what was happening—that she was visiting Mr. Casewell on the quiet and having lessons from him—they were at a loss to know what to do. The point that disturbed them was—Who was paying Mr. Casewell 's fees? Immediately they saw the hand of Uncle Grubhofer, The dark villain of the piece had some diabolical plot on in conjunction with the hireling of the Levitch school to get control of the child or claim the credit of her training. How the Levitch crowd would love to call her one of the "Levitch pupils!" There was nothing Mr. Du Casson so despised and condemned as the "Levitch method," partly because he had been instructed in a different and more old-fashioned method, and principally because he found that people were asking for and insisting on the "Levitch method," and all the most promising pupils and young artists were disciples of the Levitch school.

Mr. Du Casson was intensely angry. "The girl 's a little devil!" he shouted to his wife one morning in the bathroom, "I 've taught her everything, everything! and now she turns on me, sneaks over to the Levitch crowd behind my back. Insults me when I talk to her. She can go to blazes! I 'm not going to do any more for her."

"Don't be a fool," said Mrs. Du Casson. "What does it matter what they teach her? You 've had the credit of her bringing out. They can't call her a 'Levitch pupil' after she 's been playing for a year as a 'pupil of Du Casson.' I don't see that this matters. The thing is to keep a hold over her till after the American tour. Thank heaven it comes off in the autumn! Pensiver 's booked her from September 29th. We mustn't have a row now, whatever happens, especially after having to just fork out five hundred pounds guarantee to Johanson in New York."

And so the Du Cassons winked at Olga's secret visits to Mr. Casewell, and Mr. Du Casson attempted no more with her than formal lessons, just listening to her play, and at times nursing an ironic resentment that in spite of his passivity she was improving wonderfully!

Olga led a very busy and disturbing life. Two or three days a week on an average she had to travel to various towns in the country to play at concerts or to give recitals. On these occasions she was always accompanied by either Mr, or Mrs. Du Casson or a maid. In the meantime she had to practise. The meetings with Mr. Casewell made a tremendous difference to her and spurred her with new hopes and ambitions. She was surprised that during this time nothing was seen or heard of Uncle Grubbofer, and consequently she could not get to hear anything of Irene. She even got Mr. Casewell to go on a wild goose chase to the village of "Larn-shan" one Sunday, but he returned to say that the cottage she described was shut up, and he heard from a local general shop that the "young lady had left there some months ago." This was very disturbing, and she determined to make another visit to her uncle at the first opportunity. It was some time before she found such an opportunity and when she did, to her surprise, she discovered that Uncle Grubbofer 's new shop was occupied by a ham and beef merchant, who could give her no information of the former tenant's whereabouts. She wont back to the old street, but on this occasion was nearly assaulted by the same woman who had opened the door before.

CHAPTER X

THE LANTERN

In the spring Levitch came to London, and on a certain afternoon Mr. Casewell took Olga to play to him. It was an entrancing experience. The little man had not forgotten her, and he was astounded at the progress she had made; nevertheless he was disturbed by some of her tricks, and the stiffness she had acquired under the Du Casson tuition. Mr. Casewell explained the situation as well as he could. Levitch nodded his bald head in rapid little jerks, and ejaculated, "Ah! yes . . . yes . . . ah!" He looked at Olga meditatively and then he suddenly stroked her hair and said:

"Ah! Come now, what is it they do to you?" He took her forearm. She had just played a passage from a Beethoven minuet with remarkable brilliance, and an even more remarkable flourish. "Now! Gif me bote your arms. . . . Now, vat is it you call eet? R-re-lax! No! See, you are pulling me! Re-re-lax! Now! I vant you to fall trough de zeat, so!" He took hold of one of her knees. "No, here you see, you vas all tight! Fall, fall, be nozing, so! Ah! now, dat is better—tranquil, isn't it? Forget all dees,"—he waved his short arms at the keys—"they vas nozing. Tink! I am Olga! Olga! Olga! What eet ees I vant to do? Tink dat. Begin all again. Forget all dees tings. Tink. Now it is the music. Tink! It ees ver' beautiful, ees n't eet? dees passages. Eet ees Beethoven, echt Beethoven! Tink! I vill play de beautiful passages just tranquil, just as I know. Neffer mind dese!" And he swept his arm round the room as though indicating an audience. "Now, Olga, play me again!"

Olga played the passage again. She found it difficult to understand his language, she had never heard any one else speak like that, but the meaning was clear, and a curious sense of repose stole over her. With little gestures and exclamations Levitch helped her to see the sense of a phrase, and to keep the balance of the whole. It was very absorbing. She had never met any one before like Levitch, with just that strange, magnetic power. Mr. Casewell, she believed in; she was conscious of his sanity and equipoise and a certain intellectual fervor, but with Levitch it was somehow different. She was at once transplanted to a higher sphere, and for the first time tasted the alluring sweets of hero-worship. The little man became to her a god, a person who held all the secrets that she would ever want to know. She thought of him day and night and hung on every word he said. He was, too, so surprising, so full of strange directions, a mixture of mysticism and sound, material common sense, and his dark eyes had that faculty of mellowing his stern discussion with a most engaging smile. Before she went he asked her questions about her digestion, even examined the quality of her dress material. At one moment he solemnly patted her forearm, and said, "Nice fat arm! that ees goot!" She could tell by the way ho nodded his head and said this that, although it was said a little facetiously, he was really pleased that she had a nice fat arm, and he considered it a valuable asset to her career.

To her joy Levitch agreed with Mr. Casewell that he would hear her once a fortnight while he was in town. That was a glorious summer to Olga. She still had to travel about and play where she was told, but she felt more confident of herself and the advent of Levitch had opened up a new world to her. She was still haunted by the idea that Uncle Grubhofer would appear at some terrible moment and snatch this new-born joy from her, and she was worried about Irene. Once she asked Mrs. Du Casson if she could find out anything about her sister, but that lady replied that she hadn't the faintest idea where any of the family were, and she did not seem disposed to exert herself in the matter. Olga was young, and had that enviable quality of being able constantly to renew herself. Her affection for Irene did not absorb her life, it only impressed her in little waves, and then in the form of a wondering pity. She pictured Irene in all sorts of trouble and distress, and also Karl and Montague. But these visions usually came to her when she was tired or when things had gone wrong. Half an hour later she would be walking in the sunshine, inhaling new impressions, conscious of the vibrant life in her. There was a little girl, a pupil of Mr. Casewell 's, who also visited Levitch, and whom she often met, and made a friend of. She was a slight little thing, surprisingly fair, with very clear skin and gray-blue eyes. Her name was Emma Fittleworth. She seemed to take a great fancy to Olga, and could not take her eyes from her when they were in the room together. She always came to the lessons in a large motor car, attended by a maid or by her mother.

Mrs. Fittleworth was a plump, middle-aged American woman who had married a young Englishman. The marriage had not been a success, she had divorced her husband, who had since died. She had two little girls—of whom Emma was the elder—and she lavished on these children an adoring affection, tempered by a sort of mild surprise that they were so unlike herself. They were both very slight and fair, and almost ethereal, whilst Mrs. Fittleworth was a broad, solid woman with a kind but capable face, upon which the traces of unhappiness had set their seal. She had brown, pensive eyes, and she spoke in a deep, purring voice that was only relieved from monotony by a pleasant burr, and an occasional upward inflection that gave it a peculiar attraction. It was her voice that first attracted Olga, and then afterwards she found everything about her attractive. She felt "comfortable" in her presence, and she noticed that Mrs. Fittleworth had the faculty of imparting this sense of comfort and security to others. She was very rich and they lived in a house in one of the large squares, but it was not this that made one feel comfortable. It was just some inner power that Mrs. Fittleworth possessed. Olga could not conceive her being any different. She was a woman who would know exactly how to act under any circumstances, and she would not be disturbed or exasperated. She invited Olga to lunch, and on the strength of her new sense of independence she accepted. The Du Cassons had ceased to check her movements, and were only satisfied that she did not fail to keep her engagements.

It was a very pleasant lunch party, just the four of them, Mrs. Fittleworth, Olga, Emma, and the younger sister, Mollie, who was only eight. After lunch they went into a sort of schoolroom and talked, and Olga found herself telling Mrs. Fittleworth all sorts of things about herself, things that she had never broached to any one. She told her about her family and Uncle Grubhofer and the Du Cassons and her experiences as an infant prodigy. She told it quite simply, and Mrs. Fittleworth listened attentively without surprise or horror, but with the magic light of understanding.

She found in the society of Emma and Mollie an element she had not encountered before—fun. They played and exchanged confidences, and Mollie, in spite of her delicate appearance and her innumerable toys, was a regular tomboy, and a joy to be with. The friendship soon ripened between these girls, and they hated the days when they were apart. They also shared in common the mutual worship of "Levitch himself." As the summer wore on, and the aspect of approaching separation became a reality to them, it hung like the doom of all things above their heads.

Olga's American tour was to start in September, and at about the same time the Fittleworths were going to Prague, so that Emma could continue her studies with Levitch, and both the girls study German. They would remain there till the following summer; that is to say, from their point of view, forever.

There came a day in July when "Levitch himself" went back to Prague. At her last lesson he said: "You must gom vif me to Prague, yes?" and he pinched her cheek.

In broken accents, Olga explained to him about her American tour. The little man shrugged his shoulders and said, "Ah, zis is bat! tch! tch! no, no, eet ees bat! . . . one day—yes! but now—ah, no, no!" He seemed very distressed about the matter and said he must speak to Mr. Casewell, This gave her great hope. It seemed impossible that any opinion that Levitch expressed should not be obeyed. But when she next saw Mr. Casewell, he dashed her hopes to the ground.

"My dear child, I 'm afraid it 's inevitable. I know as a fact that they have billed and booked you all over the States." And he showed her a New York musical journal with a front page photo of her in the Armenian dress, and three columns inside which purported to be an interview! During the interview she apparently had again given a description, even more breathless, of her wonderful escape from Turkey in the basket of "vegetable produce."There was also a column of press cuttings and a photograph of Professor Du Casson!

The Fittleworths left London at the end of July, for Mrs. Fittleworth wanted to take the children for a month to a manor house that she had taken on the Sussex Downs. She invited Olga to come and stay with them, but this of course was practically impossible. The Du Cassons did not even know of Mrs. Fittleworth, or that Olga had any friends outside their circle. Olga explained this to Mrs. Fittleworth, and that good lady gave the matter consideration, and then boldly drove up to Chessle Terrace in her carriage, and called on Mrs. Du Casson. It was an imposing equipage, and Mrs. Fittleworth was not a woman to be put off or ignored. Mrs. Du Casson happened to see it from her window, and she liked to make the acquaintance of people with carriages like that.

Mrs. Fittleworth apologized for calling, and she said she was afraid Mrs. Du Casson would think the reason of her visit a little strange. She understood that Mrs. Du Casson was the guardian of that remarkable little pianist, Miss Olga Barjelski. Well, she had two little girls who were musical, and they were tremendous admirers of Olga's. They always went to hear her play when possible, and on several occasions they had been round to the artists' room, and spoken to her. They had taken such a fancy to her that Mrs. Fittleworth ventured to ask if she might possibly go so far as to ask permission for her to come and stay with them at Rollminster Manor, near Kailhurst on the downs—for a little while? It would be so extremely kind of Mrs. Du Casson!

Mrs. Du Casson was surprised and unprepared. She had admired the car, and her eye wandered over Mrs. Fittleworth 's costume. It was amazingly well cut. Everything about her was unobtrusive, but undeniably the best and the most expensive. This was not a woman to be snubbed. Mrs. Du Casson prevaricated. She said it was very kind of Mrs. Fittleworth; of course she could do nothing without consulting the professor. lie was out. Olga would have to practise hard for the American tour. As a matter of fact they—she and Mr. Du Cason—had thought of going to Bournemouth, and of course they would take Olga, but she would see and write Mrs. Fittleworth later. She thanked her and shook hands. Two days later, however, she wrote to say that "the Professor thought it would not be advisable to interrupt Olga's studies, and the child would go to Bournemouth with them and prepare for her great undertaking."

"When the Fittleworths had taken their departure, and Olga realized that she was not to see them again, a great depression came over her. It was a very hot August and she was suffering from a nervous reaction from the excitement of the previous months. Moreover, Bournemouth did not agree with her. She felt phlegmatic and disinclined to work. They stayed at a fashionable hotel among some pine trees, and she was given a small room with a piano in it where she was to work "in any case in the afternoon and till dinner time." It was a wretched hotel, full of rich disagreeable-looking people. She felt suddenly imprisoned. Everything of value seemed to have gone in that hotel. She saw the hideous perspective of her future epitomized in its cabined walls and customs. The arbitrary arrangement of its set meals, the tyranny of its servants, its conventional flower beds and promenades, the hopeless dullness of its guests casting furtive glances at each other, and droning in self-conscious reiteration safe sayings for each other's ears. She sat opposite the smug Du Cassons still surrounded by the horrid little dogs. This was their element. This was where they wanted her to stop—in this world, to be a success in it, the wonderful child pianist! There would follow an endless amount of this, more hotels, trains, concerts, and the inevitable reclame, posters, advertisements, puffs, more success, more hotels, newspaper interviews, steamships, agents, managers, and then again hotels, hotels, hotels!

She lost her appetite and went for walks by herself.

But she could not get away from the town. She walked for miles till she was footsore, but nothing relieved the pines but the interminable new houses, the pensions, the asphalt promenades. Everything about Olga was premature. At the age of fifteen she had encompassed many of the experiences of a woman twice her age. Her mind was quite untrained except musically, but she had keen intuitions and an unnerring sense that was almost psychic. She lay awake in bed one night and heard the drone of the electric lift. It filled her with a strange repugnance. Moreover, the sound kept converging into a musical phrase repeated over and over again. It suddenly seemed to cleave the forces that acted on her life into two bold groups. On the one hand stood the Du Cassons and Mr. Pensiver and the people they represented who wanted just that, the drone of that phrase repeated and repeated and repeated. On the other hand, somewhere out there beyond the pines, the wind was blowing across the downs making unfinished symphonies, breaking free like the laughter of those children; somewhere out there beyond the seas Levitch was striving "to think all over again."

He too was like a child. He had that attitude of amazed delight at the never-ending discovery of new joys. She wanted to be like that. It seemed a thing more worth fighting for than anything in the world. She was annoyed that she could not define it to herself more clearly. She could only feel it. It was something that they represented—these others—freedom perhaps and a sense that some things counted more than success.

For the rest of that week she was so moody and apathetic that the Du Cassons were a little alarmed.

They took her for motor rides, and eventually consulted a doctor. The doctor said she was "a little run down" and prescribed her a tonic, and she was given the tip that she had better not practise for a few days. On the Saturday week following Mr. Pensiver came do\vii for the week-end. He seemed in good spirits. After dinner that evening at an hour when she should have been in bed she snuggled in a corner of the veranda where none of the hotel people would be likely to see her. After a time the Du Cassons and Mr. Pensiver came out and sat at a table in the dark and talked and smoked. They had dined well, and were a little garrulous. She overheard some interesting information. It appears that the tour was to last five months through the States and Canada, that the bookings already totalled over eight thousand pounds, that business had been so brisk that they had to advance Johanson of New York another five hundred pounds on advertising "and it was worth it." That Mrs. Du Casson had had six of the Armenian frocks made, as traveling over there "was so disastrous to one's clothes." That they were all coming to New York, and would visit some of the principal cities, but that a "very reliable person named Miss McHarness would act as cicerone and maid to the child for the tour." That they were all returning to London on Tuesday, and would sail for New York on the following Saturday.

All of which information did not tend to raise her spirits. She felt a steel ring closing round her. In spite of the doctor's tonic she became paler and she slept badly. The Du Cassons noted this, but they said, "The voyage will put her right."

On the return to town they were all very busy shopping and packing. Special iron-bound trunks arrived on which appeared in white letters "Olga Barjelski," and gaudy labels bedecked the sides. In the midst of the commotion Miss McHarness appeared. She was a Scotch-American woman with a hard, monotonous, penetrating voice. She had come through from Paris, and immediately took charge of all Olga's property and person. She was undoubtedly a very capable and energetic cicerone, honest and keen, probably kind and sensible, but, thought Olga, "I shall have to listen to that voice all day every day for five months."

It was a remarkable voice; it had the faculty of crashing above the din of the little dogs; one could imagine it in a noisy station or on a windy steamer making insistent demands. It would not be denied. It seemed a special by-product of the telephone age. By the Wednesday evening Olga felt that it would be the most terrifying adjunct of the terrifying tour. She felt that she could no longer stand it. Her nerves were on edge before it arrived, and it seemed to bring all her half-formed resolutions to a head. "I won't go," she said to herself as she retired to her room that night. She had not the vaguest idea of how she was to accomplish her perverse decision. She presumed that if she refused they would fetch policemen, and she would be dragged off to the steamer. She moved feverishly in her bed all night, hugging rebellious impulses. In the morning she seemed steadier. Her face had a set, resigned expression. She assisted in the packing, and much to Mrs. Du Casson's surprise she offered to go and get some small purchases for her early in the afternoon.

Mrs. Du Casson was quite disarmed, and thanked her for offering. She wrote down one or two precise instructions, and gave her a sovereign. Olga put on her hat and taking a small black reticule she walked out of the house. Mrs. Du Casson would not perhaps have been quite so delighted with her protegee's change of front if she had known that she never intended to return! She took a 'bus to Victoria Station and went into the booking-office.

"I want a ticket to Kailhurst on the Sussex Downs," she said.

The booking clerk looked at her. "There 's no such station," he said; then noting the expression of chagrin on her face, some sympathetic chord in him was stirred, and he added, "Wait a minute." He examined a map.

"You had better book to Cloton," he said; "it 's nine miles from there."

She thanked him and bought the ticket. She had to wait forty minutes for a train and it was six o'clock when she arrived at Cloton. She was tired and hungry when she got there, but it was with a strange feeling of exhilaration that she gave up her ticket and passed through the barrier into a free world. Cloton was a sleepy old market town, and the people of whom she asked the way to Kailhurst seemed to think it was an incredible distance, like an expedition to some remote and unexplored land.

"You might get old George Har-r-way to drive 'e," one suggested rather skeptically. But "George Harrway" shook his head and said he might manage it tomorrow, but he would want "fourteen shillun." As Olga had only eleven shillings and some coppers she started to do what she had secretly hoped she would have to do all the time—walk there. She got the direction verified by several of the inhabitants and started out.

When she was quite free of the town she felt tremendously excited. The rhythmic action of walking and the sea-laden air soothed her spirits. The white road looked like a ribbon binding the sinuous lines of the downs. She walked past isolated houses and then out to the open country, past chalk pits and groups of friendly trees which nodded to her as though approving of her action. Here and there smoke from some dreamy hamlet revealed its hiding place in the gray seclusion of the hills. Sheep bells tinkled pleasantly in her ears, and birds sang overhead. She walked on and on. It was certainly going to be a long way, and she rather wished she were not so tired, but it was very beautiful, very beautiful and soothing. A flock of rooks rising from a clover field struck a plaintive note. They made her sigh a little and think, and she did not want to think too much. She knew she was doing something terrible and punishable, but the impulses which drove her along seemed apart from right or wrong, something tremendous that she could not comprehend. She felt very tired. She wished she had thought to have some tea somewhere—perhaps she would get some in the next village. She wondered what time it got dark. She must get there before dark, or she might not find her way and she would be frightened. She walked faster.

At the next village a woman in a shop told her she had come out of her way. She ought to have "taken the road by Bayes farm and kept along the valley way over at Paseby-Coudhurst." She bought some buns, and retraced her steps. The sun set as she passed the bend in the downs that led from Paseby-Coudhurst towards Milcester. They told her that Kailhurst was "five mile from there, six maybe or six a ha-a-af mile," some said. Her legs ached and her shoes were not constructed for country walks. They were intended for promenading the deck of an ocean liner. She began to walk more slowly, and to pause and rest against stiles. A wind got up and blew thin white clouds that melted into gray distances. She felt warm with walking, and yet sometimes she shivered slightly when she stopped. Things began to lose their form somewhat and there seemed little left but the white road in a dim setting, and the hurrying sky above. Past Milcester the road led up and up. She went by a disused chalk pit that looked very solemn in the dull light. The road became little more than a track after that and she seemed right up in the clouds. Their moist density obscured the sheep, but she knew they were all around her by their bells which tinkled in a variety of keys. A little way off the track she saw a figure dimly silhouetted against the sky. She made a sudden resolution, and walked over to it. He was a shepherd in a smock exactly as she had seen in a story book at Miss Merson's.

"Will you kindly tell me if I am on the right road for Kailhurst, sir," she asked.

He looked up at her with a detached, far-away expression. He seemed an incredibly old man; his face was cracked and lined, as though battered by life-long struggle with the wind and sun, and his small eyes were glistening but unresponsive. He spoke in a high reedy voice like a call coming to her through the centuries. He was like a man to whom anything that could happen had happened long ago and passed beyond, but he still haunted the husk of his body and shouted into the wind, because Nature wanted him there, in that obscure corner of the downs, for the reason that she could not find a substitute.

She repeated her request, and he peered obliquely down the road, leaning on his staff. After a long silence he said in his thin voice, "Ay . . . th' be beyond . . . do 'e know ole Dave Tar-r-by, leddy, way over t' down yan Nan Car-r-sway's far-rm?"

She could not understand what he said, but she realized that he was asking her a question, and so she shook her head and tried to smile.

The old shepherd leaned forward on his stick and gave a long call that sounded like, "Coom . . . by . . ." There was a movement among the sheep, as though this conveyed some definite message. After a pause he said, "Ay, oil t' ole sheep know me, young leddy. I karls 'un and they com' to 'e. I moind t' time when me an' ole Dave Tar-r-by, way over a' Cou'rst, drive 'un tew score yews o' Squire Garfey roight along o' lees where be now Mel'ster. Ay . . ." He sighed as though meditating on the ravages of time that had in the course of threescore years converted a pleasant meadow into a thriving village. Then he continued:

"I moind the toime when 'is b'ys growed. Tom Tarr-by 'e were away at t' great war . . . 'e was for foightin' against t' Roosians. Ay, 'e were killed out there, 'e were shot . . . that were nigh sixty year. . . . Old Dave still dra'es breath. The Lard preserves 'un agenst 's good toime. . . . Ay." He looked at Olga with his clear abstract eye, and added, "T' Lard giveth and t' Lard taketh away."

It was impressive the sense of unlimited time and space that the old man seemed to convey as he sat there among salt-bitten slabs of rock, and the bleating sheep, and it occurred to her that he was the first person she had ever met who talked of God.

"Have you tended sheep here for sixty years?" she asked at last. A considerable time elapsed while this question apparently sank in, and then the voice called out across the mists of time.

"I h'arded fowerscore long o' John Ma-a-son when 'e 'eld t' ole far-r-m by Nan Car-r-sways. Ay, but 'e did n' bide there—'e were af t' be'yond St'enham." He waved his hand contemptuously as though any one who went beyond the ridge of the downs showed a lack of moral stability. It was getting dark, and Olga repeated her request for the direction to Kailhurst.

"Ay," he answered, nodding his head, "I be tcllin' 'e. Ef a tek t' track yonder, by yon ellums, a meks t' road under t' lea of Scuddy's cuttin'. Tha' meks beyon' there the len b' ole Dave Tar-r-by's cottage. 'T' nowt mowr beyon' nor an hour's steppin' to Laffy's mill-stream. Ole Jane Hale ef she be by 'll p'int ye t' way by Chane."

"I see," said Olga faintly. "Thank you very much. It 's a manor house I want called Rollminster. A Mrs. Fittleworth lives there."

But the old shepherd who apparently looked upon this last statement as a sort of frivolous digression, unworthy of the attention of one who gives his life to permanent things, merely nodded and said "Ay."

Olga had been able to make out very little of what he had said, but she got a sense of direction from his gestures, and she gathered that somewhere at any rate was "an hour's steppin'" to somewhere else and even that was not Kailhurst! Her heart sank within her as she stumbled along the track. A fine rain began to drive in cold gusts, and penetrated her stockings. She set her teeth, and kept her eyes on the lookout for lighted buildings. She would not let herself be afraid of the darkness, but she wished she were not so tired, and that the strange shivering did not keep assailing her. It was nearly an hour before she reached a village, and then she was told that it was two miles farther on to Kailhurst. She forced back the desire to cry and once more set out into the darkness. It was very dark now, and she was wet through to the skin. Between an avenue of trees she could see nothing. She groped her way, trying to keep to the middle of the road by looking up at the tree tops, but even then she slipped and stumbled, and once fell into something soft and slushy. "When she got through this avenue, and the road became a little lighter, she was trembling all over. "I mustn't faint," she kept saying to herself, and made a desperate effort to hurry. But at times the road seemed to be behaving in a peculiar way, twisting about, and going sideways, and rocking. She went on and on till she became hardly conscious of her legs. "I will get there! I will get there!" she repeated on an occasion when the road seemed to be rising up, and striking her knees. At last she reached a dimly lighted cottage near the road. She entered the garden to it, and heard a dog bark; the noise went through her like a knife, but she reached the door and knocked. A woman opened it and peered out.

"Can you tell me where Rollminster Manor is?" she gasped and the light from the room blinded her to dizziness. She heard the woman talking to some one inside. She could not hear what they said. She was too busy keeping herself from falling. At last a man came out with a lantern.

"Do you want to go up to the Manor to-night, miss?" he asked.

She said, "Yes! Yes!" And there was more talking. Then the man came out and said, "I 'll show ye the way." She could not thank him, and she crawled behind the lantern, and fixed her eyes on it. She did not know how long this walk lasted. She believed the man talked to her, but she could not hear him. She was so much engaged watching the lantern, and going on, and on, and on, to where it led. Things seemed light and irresponsible, nothing mattered but that, that the lantern should be followed. She remembered clutching herself once or twice, and bumping into the man, and once she thought she heard her voice sobbing curiously. Then the lantern stopped. It was awful. She felt at the crisis of her trials. Then a black object seemed to give way and there was a square block of light—people were talking. She could not look up, the light was too strong and blinding, but down in the square of light there was a frock—there was some one standing in a frock not far from her—a voice she seemed to know sent a vibrant passion through her frame, and something snapped within her, as she fell forward and threw her arms round Mrs. Fittleworth 's knees.

BOOK II

CHAPTER I

Maybe I don't look at women in quite that way. I was coeducated. Were you coeducated?"

"I wasn't educated at all."

The man and the girl laughed as they strode side by side up the hill. It was a glorious day, and between the silver stems of the larch trees they could see far away beneath the blue waters of the Moldau.

Among the numerous students who came to Prague—English, American, German, French, and Russian—Olga found none more companionable than this curious, heavy-framed American boy-man.

His name was Irwin Cullum and he was looked upon as a crank. Emma objected to him because she said that his skin and hair and eyes were all the same color. They were indeed of a negative hue, but they expressed warmth, and his face seemed in some way an index of self-reliant power.

He had a mildly Napoleonic countenance and enormous hands. His fingers were so large that it surprised people that he could manage to strike only one note on the piano at a time. There was a certain heavy sanity about him, from the serviceable, badly cut clothes to the gold-stopping in his teeth. He spoke slowly and with a drawl, and belied the general urbanity of his appearance by making surprising statements, and expressing—what seemed to Olga—unique ideas.

During the three years that she had lived with the Fittleworths at Prague she had tasted for the first time the joys of the "things of the mind." She became slowly conscious of her own mind and its power. She knew she had been very ill for a long time, and then Mrs. Fittleworth had brought her over here to Prague. She believed there had been a lot of trouble and a law case, but Mrs. Fittleworth would not speak of these things.

As the memory of the terror of those days of insistent material demand began to recede, she seemed to suddenly awaken in a new world. She gradually began to coordinate certain ideas and impulses; morality, of which no one had ever spoken except in terms of what is punishable and what is not punishable; beauty, which puzzled her by its elusiveness; and sex, which puzzled her most of all. And though she formed within herself certain conceptions of what her mental attitude would be towards these things, she did not hope to understand them. She was always searching the bounds of her conscience for rigid precepts but always there were doubts.

"I am conscious," she had said to Mr. Cullum one day, "of being more susceptible to the influence of people than of principles. I sometimes come up against something in which I feel I no longer have the power to know how to act, and then I just think of some person—like Mrs, Fittleworth—and try and act as I imagine that she would under the circumstances."

"Mrs. Fittleworth's all right," Mr. Cullum had answered; "but it won 't do. What you 've got to do is to get a conception of yourself—not a rigid conception but a fluid one working on definite lines—and live up to that. You 've got a big push in front of you. Don't always be justifying yourself. Play the Liszt rhapsody like you did this afternoon. My! I wish I had your temperament."

And then one day a most inspiring thing had happened. She had been to a students' dance in the town with Emma. During a mad dance she had suddenly felt a glowing interest in a young Hungarian officer. He was a tall, delicate young man with exquisite manners and dreamy eyes. She had followed the impulse set by the dance, and treated him with a certain railing abandon. Emma told her afterwards that she had flirted with the young man, but she did not gage the significance of this at the time. She only knew that finding herself alone with him upon the terrace afterwards, he had suddenly seized her hands and made violent love to her. It was very entrancing but bewildering. It seemed suddenly to shatter the spectrum of that moral vision that she had been so laboriously constructing and split into a hundred vari-colored lights. And it was of this experience that she was telling her "comfortable" American friend as they strode together up the hill.

"What surprises me," she said, "as I look back upon this experience—for you must remember it was last spring, and of course I was very young then—is that I felt a curious pride about the whole thing. I was tremendously flattered. I believe I tried to make myself fall in love with him, but something seemed always missing when it came to the point. I know that on that night when he called for the last time, and threatened to throw himself into the Moldau if I refused him, I felt that there was something ridiculous about it. And yet, after he had gone I looked out of my window; the moon was shining on the river, and I felt a strange and unholy joy in it. I peered down at the water and tried to visualize a white, upturned face. Of course, as you know, he went away. I believe he went back to Vienna and rejoined his regiment. It is three months ago, and he has probably forgotten me by now."

She sighed, and the American boy grinned expansively.

"It 's fine," he said, "that you can take your first encounter in such a 'decorative' manner. It hasn't got through to you—that 's clear. You just see yourself playing a part, while poor Paul Kolnyay's heart is probably broken. You 're beginning to be a person with ideas. Do you know what I mean by ideas? "

"I 've heard the expression."

"It 's very important. You must think about the real meaning of 'ideas.' You 'll gradually get to understand, as you grow up, that everything is illusion except ideas. It is inconsequential whether people fail or succeed as people, but it is essential that ideas prevail. I 've found this a very comforting thought myself. Do you know what has been my greatest enemy?"

"Tell me," said the girl.

"My own sentimentality." The boy hunched his large frame together, and struck at a stone on the path with his stick. Then he thrust his head forward and said:

"My people raised me on sentimentality. You wouldn't believe it. I recall that when I was a kid of six I used to sob in bed at night with thinking of my love of my mother. There was no call for it. My mother was quite well and happy, but I used to think of her face and cry."

"I know what you mean," said Olga quickly. "I 've done the same sort of thing."

He looked at her and nodded, and then continued:

"It 's a very destroying thing, this sentimentality. If it could be eradicated from the race there would be no unhappiness at all. My sisters were terrible. They used to harbor little things—mementoes and anecdotes and so on. They used to keep certain days sacred in memory of certain events. I was younger than they, and I think I was worst of all. It was not till I started thinking about this question of 'ideas' that I was able to combat it at all. Sentimentality is essentially a question of looking back, and there is—so much to push on to."

He flung out his arras in a wide gesture, and they sat side by side on a fallen trunk of a tree. Three sparrows flew over their heads and darted behind a gorse bush, where they quarreled insistently. It was a splendid view across the river, with the hills beyond, and the sun was flooding the valley with a glow of amber light.

"The other night," said Olga, "I was thinking of Levitch in somewhat the same way you mention. You know I am very fond of him. I think of him heaps. In the morning I was in his dining-room. Over the mantelpiece is a painting of his wife. You know they were married for a year, and then she died. She looks very wistful and sweet, and she has on a blue pelisse—a dear old-fashioned thing. The portrait is set around with candles like a shrine. Well, on this day I suddenly saw Levitch look at the portrait, and an expression came to his face I had never seen before. He said nothing, but all night I kept thinking of his face and of his—loneliness. I suppose it was very sentimental of me, Mr. Cullum? I sometimes think of Mrs. Fittleworth in that way, and other people of whom I get fond."

"Death is an idea and love is an idea," he answered. "They are both normal and rational and evolutionary: it is only the sentimental contact of these two ideas that makes for unhappiness and remorse. Say, you once told of a little lady who helped you when you were a kid—"

"Miss Merson! I 'd almost forgotten her."

"Ah! And once I guess you thought of her like that. Listen, Olga, you 've got something big in you. You 're one of the rare ones. Don't fiddle about with friendships."

"What do you mean by that?"

"I mean that we 're all hemmed in by material demands, by animal demands, by sentimental demands. We have to fight our way out. Some of us never fight our way out. We get crushed and die. But you have already 'hitched your wagon to the star,' as we say. My! the way you played that Liszt rhapsody was simply—" He blinked at the sun-bathed landscape as though searching for a suitable epithet, and then suddenly affirmed in a deep voice, "bully!"

Olga blushed with pleasure, and took a rose she had been wearing at her breast, and buried her nose in its petals.

"It 's nice of you to talk like this," she said, "but I don't altogether understand you. You seem to think that because I can play a little I 'm necessarily a high moral type of person, and then you don't seem to want me to have friends!"

The grave-faced boy thought for some moments, and then he looked down into the valley, and said:

"As I see you and your life, it 's like this. An artist is always hampered by the chimera of ambitions he does n 't attempt to qualify. They usually take the form of material success. On the other hand, he is handicapped by a too-sympathetic heart. You remember telling me the story of how you followed the lantern up the hill? You must have believed in that lantern very implicitly. Why? Because it embodied to you a desperate craving for spiritual development. You have the right stuff in you. Material claims lose their appeal, friends die and are forgotten, and in the end nothing is left but— the instinct of worship!"

"Worship?"

"It is perhaps the same thing as your friend calls 'looking at life like a child.' As I see it, yours will not be a life of great friendship—for friendship has no place in 'ideas'—but it should be a life of great passions." He paused and fumbled with the lapel of his coat, and then continued: "I envy you that. It is only the elect who are capable of great passions, and they hew their way to realms where we cannot follow them." As he said this, a young peasant came slowly round the bend, leading a horse and cart laden with ferns.

He was young and strong, with queer dark eyes, and he looked at her with a lazy insolence. The sun was beginning to set, and the lines of the bracken were broken by the long shadows from the larch trees. As the cart bumped over the slope she heard the musical tones of the peasant's voice speaking to the horse, and through the shadows cast from the trees she saw square patches of sunlight on his bronzed body. At that moment a curious feeling of exhilaration came to her. In a flash she seemed to see her life like the golden panorama in front of her, series of splendid actions and fine episodes of which she would be the guiding figure. She turned to her companion, and his grim strong gaze was fixed in a dreamy contemplation of the scene.

She suddenly thought, "One day perhaps some one will come down from the mountains like that . . . some one who will understand, who will see things with my eyes, some one to whom everything will matter tremendously."

For some reason she felt afraid to pursue the tenor of these thoughts, and she said to her fellow-wanderer:

"We must be going."

They walked in silence down the hill. As they neared the outskirts of the town, she said:

"Next week we are going back to England."

And he answered:

"And I will be going back to Los Angeles."

"We must be friends still—in spite of my illusions, Mr. Cullum. You must write to me."

He strode along in silence, and then he said:

"One of the greatest illusions of humanity is—topography. A man leaves a town in England and goes to live in a town in British Columbia, and by this means believes that he is 'seeing the world' or 'broadening his outlook.' Place can make no difference. My friendship would only hamper you. I will like to think of you going on, leading a big life. Let yourself alone. You 've got the right stuff, and I don't see ambition destroying you like it does some others. I have ambitions too, and I expect I have illusions, but I have no illusions about my own abilities and I have no illusions about topography. I 'll be going back to San Martino—it 's just a bunch of wooden shacks nestling in a valley. Don't you think I can be ambitious there? If you don 't think I can, you 're wrong! It 's 'ideas' that make a man's ambitions. But, Gee! the way you played that rhapsody!"

They neared an inn, by the door of which a man with a dark mustache was playing a mandolin. He smiled at them and showed his splendid teeth. Inside the inn four peasants were having an impromptu dance, their bodies swaying to the rhythm of the wild Bohemian music.

Olga caught her breath, and she felt her heart beating rapidly. Then they passed on. The sun had nearly set, and the sky was flooded livid color.

She suddenly said:

"Nature is very violent."

Her companion seemed to be thinking, and he looked at her queerly, but did not answer. She felt the need of trying to express something stirring within her. She walked closer to him and said rather breathlessly:

"Even in my time I have seen lives and people destroyed by passion and violence. ... It seems terrible that what we desire most brings us the greatest pain. We want to be loved, to be understood, and then the thing destroys us."

He took her arm and led her towards the gate of the house where the Fittleworths lived. He seemed for the moment on the point of saying something, and then he changed his mind. He strode forward, his eyes fixed on the ground. When they arrived at the gate, he smiled and took her hand, and, looking at her, he said:

"Sometimes it 's worth it, though, I guess!"

She felt that this remark somehow crystallized the thought she wanted to express, and yet the significance of which she could not at the moment determine. She felt a curious little stab of pride, like she had felt on that night when the young Hungarian officer made love to her, and she smiled uncertainly at her fellow-traveler, and went quickly through the gate.

And Irwin Cullum passed on down the road and out of her life; and she did not know that in his large hand he held the crumpled petals of the rose that she had thrown away.

CHAPTER II

"THE GUILDEFORD SET"

It is perhaps only consistent with the general precocity of our heroine that within two months of her twentieth year she was married and the mother of a son.

But before chronicling the events that led up to this desirable attainment, it may be advisable to give some description of what was known in those days as "The Guildeford Set."

Walter Guildeford and his wife Marion, with their two sons, Edward and Giles, and their two daughters, Agnes and Christobel, lived in a medium-sized house in St. John's Wood, with a studio and a large garden. Walter Guildeford was a publisher of works of reference. They were a very devoted, lovable family, and they kept a sort of open house for the waifs and strays of the artistic and musical professions in the neighborhood and elsewhere. It was an attractive garden, and contained an excellent tennis-court, where any afternoon in the summer one could be sure of getting a game, and of finding congenial people who were pleased to see one, and who were willing to talk, or play, and to give one tea. In the winter, or if the weather was wet in the summer, you would find them in the studio playing paper games. Some people said that the principal attraction was the tennis-court and the studio, for it was difficult to find about the Guildefords themselves any particular quality that would cause them to be the center of so many shining lights of the art world at that time.

They were a physically unattractive family, having badly proportioned figures, and very plain faces. They were all short-sighted and wore thick glasses, except the mother, and Christobel—whom people used to call "Robin" for some reason or other. Neither can it be said that their mentality was of a very high order. They never expressed particularly original or individual points of view, and they were quite devoid of any critical faculty, having an unqualified admiration for the work of any one who had the habit of visiting their tennis court. They were, however, very quick and intelligent, and one was immediately conscious of their innate kindness, and their loyalty to each other and their friends. Their dominant characteristic was their unselfishness. They were surely one of the most elaborately unselfish families that ever existed. They carried their principle of unselfishness to such a degree that it was always defeating its own ends. For instance, Mrs. Guildeford would get an idea from some stray remark of his that "Walter"— as the whole family called Mr. Guildeford— wanted to go to the East Coast for his summer holidays. She hated the East Coast herself, and she knew that if she suggested going they would see through her, because she never expressed any personal predilections about anything. So she would tell the girls on the quiet that their father wanted to go to the East Coast. Now the girls hated the East Coast also, but they would pretend that they wanted to go, so that Mrs. Guildeford could tell Walter that they did. Walter had never meant anything by his stray remark, and he detested the East Coast more than any of them, but understanding that his wife and the girls wanted to go there, he would fall in with the idea with alacrity. And the boys would give up an invitation to Devonshire—a county that they loved—for the dubious benefits of the east wind, for the same reason. It is recorded that the Guildefords went to the East Coast for seven years running before they discovered that none of them really liked it! This system of secret scheming and planning to do what the others might want went through everything, and generally resulted in none of them getting what he or she really liked. They tried to forestall each other's wishes, and read each other's desires before they were expressed, and even when they were expressed they had to be suspected. It became terribly involved at times. They really could not trust each other. It was perhaps this quality of never expressing personal wishes or ideas, and never making remarks that might run counter to the feelings of the people they loved, that rather tended to give the Guildefords a negative character; and though their garden and studio became a headquarters of the "Guildeford set," the Guildefords themselves were not essentially the pivots of that set. It was remarkable the people who used to go there. There was a family of extremely pretty girls, called the Callabys, to whom in appearance the Guildefords acted as a kind of foil. They were very great friends. Two of them, Mildred and Cicely Callaby, were actresses by repute, though no one had ever heard of them having an engagement, except occasionally at some special matinee for some Society for the Advancement of the Higher Drama. But they brought there quite a lot of well-known actors and actresses, for whom they seemed to have endearing nicknames. Mildred Callaby was engaged to a rather dirty-looking sculptor named Rodney Chard. Glebes the 'cellist played quite a good game of tennis. Sir James Penn, the R.A., and both his sons were frequent visitors, and the great John Braille, who rode up on horseback, brought an atmosphere of aristocratic artistry into the place. Among others that one can remember offhand were McCartney the painter, and Eric Waynes, who wrote "Celtic twilight" verses in Chelsea, Boder the dramatic critic, and his sister, who edited a Women's Rights paper, Godfrey Beel the architect, who was the only one who really played tennis well, and a boy known as "Scallops."

In addition to this there were invariably people staying in the house, and a procession of girls who seemed to be Agnes and "Robin's" "best friends." There was also an American woman whom nobody could quite locate. Her name was Polly Jocelyn Mainwright Willard. The name alarmed you, but she was, as a matter of fact, a delightful person. She was elderly and very square and broad, and had deep gray-brown eyes. She may have been some sort of relative, in any case every one kissed her, including Mr. Guildeford, and any one else who felt in need of mothering, and every one called her just Polly. She was nearly always staying there, and was a tower of strength on many difficult occasions. She had an engaging way of saying right out things which the Guildefords would hesitate over for months. When the Fittleworths returned to London for good, they settled down again in the house in Mazeburgh Square; and it was arranged that Olga should give three recitals, with a month's interval between, and that she should play under her own name of Olga Bardel. Mrs. Fittleworth allowed the agent to advertise them well, but without any undue flourish. When the day of her first recital arrived, she discovered a new quality in herself that she had not experienced before, a feeling of intense nervousness. She could not account for this, but it was a condition she never afterwards got over, wherever or whenever she played. She was so nervous that she made three slips in the first piece she played, and got hopelessly involved in the turnings of a Schumann arabesque. After that she played desperately and gradually regained her composure. She knew that Mr. Casewell was in the audience, and she thought, "I will show him how much I have improved." She played the Liszt B minor sonata better than she had ever played anything in her life. She rose from the piano-stool with her face flushed and confident. She enjoyed the rest of the program and enraptured the audience with a performance of a Chopin group, charged with the glow of fine color. Her success was assured, but somehow different. She was more moved by it and yet more sobered. She could hardly speak when Mr. Casewell came and gripped her hand and said, "You have come into your own, Olga. It was grand!" Many people came and congratulated her, most of whom she did not know. She felt that she had really affected them in some way, something of herself had gone out. Mrs. Fittleworth kissed her and said, "I 'm so proud of you, dear," and the little girls were almost speechless.

They returned to Mazeburgh Square and had a merry supper-party, and Olga did not sleep till dawn, going over everything she had played again and again, and dreaming of the world at her feet.

The press the next day was encouraging, but there were no superlatives, and several papers spoke mostly about the slips she had made in the earlier pieces. Two of them mentioned that they believed Olga Bardel was the same person as the little girl Olga Barjelski, who had made some sensation a few years back as an infant prodigy. But the public has a short memory for prodigies, and the allusion did not arouse much interest.

Olga was disappointed to find that in spite of her success it did not seem likely that she was to have many engagements that summer, and the agent—a gentleman named Whitbread—said that the great thing was "to keep pegging away."

At her second recital, the hall was by no means full, and Mr. Casewell had sent out some tickets for her. Among other people he sent to were the Guildefords, whom she did not know. But afterwards Agnes and Christobel came round to see her, and brought a nice tall man named John Braille. She had never met people before who were so affectionate at sight as the Guildeford girls. They raved about her to her face, would hardly let her go, and ultimately invited her to come and see them, and asked if she played tennis. She had played tennis once or twice at Prague, and she accepted their invitation, "Any afternoon," said Agnes, as they were leaving. "Do come."

And so it came about that on a certain afternoon in June, Olga, wearing a wonderful frock of gray-blue, with a black hat, made her initial appearance at the Guildefords, little suspecting how her visit was to be fraught with fateful consequences to herself. She had never been among people like that before in her life. They all seemed so clever, and said such surprising things. She felt that every remark of hers was ordinary and unnecessary, so she remained very silent, watching them. There was something very charming about them all, in spite of their cleverness. They seemed so ingenuous and genuinely affectionate. She was surprised that both the girls kissed her, although they had only met her once before. It was curious, too, that she felt a slight repugnance at this action. They were lovable girls, but they were physically slightly repelling, and she thought that if she had been allowed to choose she would have liked to know them a little longer first. They introduced her brazenly to people as "Olga Bardel—that perfectly adorable pianist." They talked about her in a laughing, admiring manner, about her clothes, her hair, her deportment. They made her play tennis, and she was relieved to find how badly they all played, but in what good spirit. She was conscious of many undercurrents in certain games when it seemed to be desirable to let the other side win. As on occasions the other side also harbored desires of a like nature, the tennis did not reach a very high standard. But it all seemed amazingly free and interesting to her. She did not know who all the people were, and they were often introduced to her by their nicknames. But they were all people who had "jobs," she was sure of that—they talked of their jobs and each other's jobs in an easy-going, sympathetic manner. And the nice Mr. Braille—who they said was a very great painter—talked to her about her job, and seemed to have a peculiar insight into its intimacies for one who was not a musician.

It was on the occasion of her second visit that the thing happened.

Mrs. Fittleworth had gone over to Paris for a few days on business, and the weather had become duller. On a certain afternoon Olga had a strange fit of depression. She had had a slight tiff with Emma over some question in which their point of view in regard to a book they had been reading did not coincide. She was feeling a little discouraged about her work. Her second recital had apparently been another great success, but Mr. Whitbread did not seem to have booked her for more than two engagements, and they were in the autumn. The large house in Mazeburgh Square seemed lonely, and the streets did not entice her. She felt suddenly very much alone in the world. She thought she would practise, and then changed her mind. After a time she put on her hat and went out. She took a bus to St. John's Wood and went to the Guildefords. It seemed a ridiculous day to go. It was cold, and might rain at any minute, and no one would want to play tennis. When she arrived the garden was empty, but the studio door was open. She peeped in, and heard Agnes cry out delightedly, "Why, it 's Olga!" and arms were thrown round her neck.

Christobel was also there, and Giles, and Mildred Callaby, and Rodney Chard, and the boy they called McCartney. They were apparently all doing nothing, and Christobel exclaimed:

"Oh, you 're just the person, dear. Do play to us. We 're all so disagreeable."

Olga felt rather in the mood for this, and she sat down and played some old Bohemian folk-songs that Levitch had lent her copies of in the manuscript. The Guildefords loved it. They lay on ottomans and smoked cigarettes and adored her. She came to the conclusion some time after that they were not really a musical family. They were always more concerned with her appearance and atmosphere.

After she had played three of these folk-songs, she heard some one say, "Why, here 's Harry!"

She rose from the piano, feeling that the atmosphere was in some way disturbed, and walked away. As she did so, her eyes met those of a young man standing b}' the door. She started. It was very strange! And yet she could not think for the life of her what it was that was strange. She had felt the music very much, that restless disturbing throb that seemed to accompany all the music from the

Bohemian hills. In a flash she recalled that day when she returned from the walk and saw the peasant leading the cart, and he had looked at her "with a certain insolence." This music came to her so often when she was restless. It penetrated her with a bitter-sweet thrill. There were times when she was almost afraid to play it. She believed the others were speaking to her, asking her to go on, or raving about her frock. She did not know. She was very near the door, and those dark eyes were peering into hers, and a voice said in a deep musical cadence:

"Please go on."

She did not speak, but looked away from him. There was a skylight in the studio, and the branches of a plane-tree were visible on which some noisy sparrows were quarreling. She looked from them to her hands, and for some reason or other brought them together with a rapid little action of supplication, and then flung them apart. She looked back to where the piano stood almost invisible against the wall, and waited.

"Please go on. It was glorious."

The tones of the voice had a quality that was new to her, poignant and vibrating. She felt something within her stirring, as though the key of her mental and moral outlook were being suddenly transposed. She did not want to play again. Something told her it were better not to, better to go away, or laugh, or play some Bach, or do something that would establish a definite hold over her cosmic consciousness. And yet she went, by some irresistible impulse, back to the piano. She sat down and played the maddest thing, a wild Hungarian dance with a plaintive second theme that quivered in the background like the ghost of an outraged lover. It always disturbed her very much, this wild tune. It was so desperate, so passionate, so unutterably sad. She was glad when she had finished that it was almost dark. Her heart was beating very fast, and she breathed in little short stabs. They all moved away, and she went out into the garden. She wanted to be quite alone for a moment. She walked round by the studio and peered into an old timbered summer-house. It was a place no one ever went into, because it got so dirty. She heard the voices of the others laughing and talking by the door of the studio. She put her hand to her brow and waited. She knew it would happen, and she hardly looked up. lie was standing there two paces from her, and said in those furry tones:

"How gloriously you play!"

She did not answer for some moments. She was trying to control herself entirely. Then she said:

"They're fine, aren't they?—those old folk-songs."

She looked at his face. The eyes and hair were very dark. He was very young. She had seen a boy like that in some old Italian painting—she could never remember the names of painters. She believed in the painting he was nude, with small wings on his heels, and there were two very beautiful women in the picture and a cupid. She did not know what they were all doing, but they were obviously gods and goddesses, unreal people. One must be a god or be unreal to have such beautiful eyes, and a voice that—went through one like that . . .

"I came to-day because I thought you might be here ... I was at your recital. . . . What a ripping frock that is!"

She laughed. It was a relief that a god used such ordinary expressions. She strolled round the garden, and he followed her. It did not seem strange that they should not have been introduced, or that he should have spoken to her like that. They did not speak again, for the others strolled across the lawn and joined them, and Mr. Guildeford came home, and talked to the god about a sale he had been to at Sotheby's that afternoon. Olga was impressed by the knowledge the god seemed to display about old and rare books, and the deference and attention that Mr. Guildeford seemed to pay him. She noted the gleams of light that illumined his face when he smiled, and the gay brilliance of his remarks to the others when the conversation became more general and discursive. He said things that conveyed nothing to her, and the others laughed or flashed their approval. And she found herself feeling proud at this. It seemed only right that in a brilliant throng, the god should be the most brilliant, and he had said, "How gloriously you played!"

She slid away from this gathering without saying good-by. She felt a certain diffidence, as though she might not carry it off in the right way.

She made up her difference with Emma in the evening when she got back, but she was strangely abstracted and went to bed early. She had much to think about, but one thought obsessed her. She must educate herself. She must learn up all sorts of subjects so as to be able to talk to her god and the others. After a time she put on her dressing gown and went down to Mrs. Fittleworth's library. She routed amongst the books, and at last took a copy of a play by Mr. Bernard Shaw up to bed with her. She had heard them talk of Bernard Shaw. She rapidly read one act of "Mrs. Warren's Profession," and her eyes sparkled. Yes! this was it. She had heard them talk rather like this. These were the sort of things they said to each other. But it was horrible. She could not understand a lot of it. All the people seemed to talk in the same way. She wondered why they talked like that, and what they meant. Occasionally something would come to her, something reasonable and true, and then they seemed to fly off at a tangent.

"I shall never be able to talk like that," she thought. "One must be awfully clever. How does one begin?" She read part of the introduction, but it seemed more and more difficult. The feeling of loneliness came to her again, and on that oppressive night she cried, cried because the vision of her inability to talk like one of Bernard Shaw's heroines came between her and the eyes of the god.

It was strange how difficult the days became after that, difficult and disturbing, yet mellowed with a penetrating sweetness. She would not go again to the Guildefords for some time. It would look as though she went to meet him. She tried to work very hard, but that face was always coming between her eyes and the keys, and the mellow tones of the voice followed her about the room—"How gloriously you played!" This was specially so in the afternoons when the sun shone again, and she thought to herself, "I might be there now, talking to him." She pictured him walking on the Guildeford lawn, with the white scarf round his neck, his dark eyes flashing as he talked to the others, and all the while furtively watching for her. Would he be watching for her? This thought disturbed her more than anything. She had never had any one who watched for her hungrily like that. Ah! if it were true!

On the Saturday she went again. It was a warm bright day, and there were many people there. He was playing tennis when she arrived, in a four with the Callaby girls and the boy McCartney. She fought her way through the general effusion and sat on a deck chair on the slope above the tennis-court. The god glanced at her and smiled. The voice of Boder, the dramatic critic, was drawling in an insistent iteration:

"His construction is bad! His construction is bad! Now, a play that is based upon some moral propaganda, upon the conflict of social forces, requires to be treated in the grand manner. Much has to be sacrificed to the concentration on the main idea. Now, you will notice that when Lady Cheevil leaves Hemingway at the beginning of the second act, and he opens the telegram from Olive ..."

She did not know whether he was playing well, but did any one ever return a ball with such grace! She thought perhaps she liked him best when he was standing negligently at the net. She liked the easy pose of his body, and the alert way he swayed to crush a return from his partner's serve. His teeth gleamed and he gave a boyish whoop of glee at the successful execution of the stroke. A girl in a brown djibbah was saying:

"My dear, the color makes you squirm! Pinks, and greens, and orange, painted, I should think, with a nailbrush. It reminds me of those awful colored diagrams of diseases of people's insides. You know, you can see them at the College of Surgeons. Roony says ..."

The set was finished. He was putting on his coat and saying something amusing to Mildred Callaby, and she was shaking her racket at him. The four broke up, and scattered into the group, and "Robin" was trying to make up another four, but was experiencing the usual difficulty at the Guildefords, everybody apparently insisting that it was "their turn to sit out." Olga refused to play, and tried to talk to McCartney. He was a nice boy, round and fat, but very silent. lie had an unconquerable habit of scribbling on bits of paper, and making surreptitious sketches of people which he would never show. He could not keep his hands still. They called him "The Oracle," partly on account of his silence, and partly because he occasionally let drop some cryptic phrase that became historical and was quoted. He had a genius for giving people nicknames, and for summing them up in Attic metaphors. The Oracle, however, was in an unresponsive mood this afternoon, and it was another voice that suddenly vibrated near her,

"You ought to be able to play tennis well."

"Why?"

"From the way you play Bohemian dances."

"I 'm afraid it 's very different."

"Con fuoco! Tempestuoso!"

"I 'm afraid the balls might go out, or be hit into net, if I played tennis too much like that."

"They wouldn't if you wanted them not to."

It was a ridiculous conversation. Their eyes were searching each other's, and yearning to say other things, and they were hemmed in, with all these good people around them. Olga arose and strolled towards the corner of the lawn where tea was being prepared. He followed her. When they were just out of earshot of the others, he said in a low tone:

"Where have you been? Why didn't you come before? All this week I—"

She looked at him quickly. She was inexperienced in these affairs, but something told her that things were progressing too rapidly. It came to her mind that she ought to be in some way frigid, and yet— a lock of his hair shaken free by the exercise curled upon his temple, and his eyes were earnest, imploring.

"I have been working," she said.

"Ah! Will you let me come and see you? Will you play to me?"

The lawn seemed to end abruptly against a trellis. A white cloth was spread, and her eye lighted upon the contours of a large homemade cake. It had the genial, innocuous air that was characteristic of the Guildefords. This seemed a desperate adventure. Could she invite the young man to Mrs. Fittleworth's? What would that good lady say and think? She was to return tomorrow.

"Olga dear, will you sit here? Harry?" It was the placid voice of Mrs. Guildeford trying, as McCartney once remarked, to introduce a sort of collectivist spirit into a community of anarchists. She sat between Harry and Mr. Guildeford, who was in very good spirits, and indulged in a lot of mild fun regarding the death-dealing properties of the large cake. He warned Olga against it, and said that another famous pianist had had some of a similar description the previous summer, and had not been heard of since. Harry, on the contrary, contended that he had heard that the pianist had improved considerably since eating the cake, that his tone had become fuller and more resilient. Mrs. Guildeford kept saying:

"It 's too bad to laugh about my cake."

It was almost impossible to have any sort of intimate conversation at the Guildefords', they had so great a sense of this impersonal love of theirs that they never realized that two people might like to whisper in corners or say exclusive things to each other. After tea she was made to play tennis, and the god was not even in the same set. It was not till she was going that he made the opportunity he had been lying in wait for. He met her in the hall and said, "May I walk with you a little way?"

They crossed a bridge over the Regent's Park Canal, and took a turning into the Park. And there, on an unromantic seat facing the iron railings of the Zoo, he made love to her.

Could this be real? "Was this the dawn of that desperate gladness of which the poets never tired to sing? Would it really come to her? Now that they were alone they seemed more than ever afraid to speak of what was in their hearts. They juggled with the most absurd banalities, and only their eyes gave them significance. It surprised her, the clearness and the radiance of it all. She tore herself away, and all the evening she felt him by her, the memory of every little thing he had said and every action seemed vivid and poignant. When she went to bed his face seemed very near. She could see the sentient lines of his mouth and chin, the eyes adoring her, and hear that voice that touched some hidden chords.

From that day the world assumed a new radiance. It was as though all her vital interests became accelerated. She walked serenely and found new joys in little things. All the terrors of her young life vanished. The forms of Uncle Grubhofer and Irene and the Du Cassons were but dim memories behind the veil of time. She felt proud and virile. She could not analyze her pride, neither did she desire to do so. Life itself was sufficient. She was very gracious and affectionate to her foster-mother and the girls, and developed a surprising interest in her clothes. She practised hard, and found new and pregnant meaning in the music. She found she had to concentrate with greater force, or otherwise those eyes would appear between her and the keys.

On the Wednesday he called. Mrs. Fittleworth had been forewarned by a statement that "a clever composer, a friend of the Guildefords, named Mr. Streatham, wants to call and play me some of his compositions. I hope you won't mind, dear Mrs. Fittleworth?" Mrs. Fittleworth was very kind to him, and he was soon an established favorite with Emma and Mollie. But it seemed strange that it did not apparently occur to either of them that she might want to talk to the god alone. Even when she suggested showing him her room where she worked, the little girls must needs follow. They conversed with their eyes, and once he touched her elbow. He made her play, but would not play any of his own compositions to her. He said she must come and see his people.

This visit took place two days later, and it cannot be said that it was a success. He lived with his mother and three sisters, all of whom worshiped him, and were jealous of his friends. They seemed to Olga rich, conventional people, rather like refined editions of the Du Cassons. They treated her with a frigid courtesy, and did not leave her for a second with the god. He played some of his own compositions to her, and she felt a little puzzled and disappointed. They were very involved and clever, but somehow they were not quite what she expected of him. She told herself on the way home that she was not clever enough to understand them. They must be very wonderful. She would study more and more, and one day perhaps she would be able to appreciate them at their full worth.

They met again at the Guildefords, and it was surprising that the Guildefords did not see! Again he walked home with her through the Park, and touched her hands an unnecessary number of times.

It was in a punt up the river near Marlow, under the shade of young willows, that things at last took a definite turn. He had invited her with one of his sisters and a young man to whom the sister was engaged, and the couples became conveniently separated. He tied the punt to the branch of the willow and came and sat beside her. Unlike her vision in the Park, where everything seemed transcendentally clear, this day took on the nature of a dream. She lay on the cushions, and watched the glittering sunlight through the branches and bathed her hands in the little dark pools beneath the boat. Cattle were lowing in a meadow near by, and the lapping of the boat against the drift of the stream gave the illusion of movement, as though the whole thing, boat and river and tree, were drifting away into some new and glorious existence. She noticed how graceful his pose was as he leaned over the side of the boat, the sun bronzing a patch on his neck and shoulder. And then he moved toward her. She felt him touching her skirt, and the boat wobbled. He was very near to her, and she hardly dare look into his eyes. He took her hand, and she heard his voice lower than a whisper. "Olga!"

Why did he say it like that? She looked at his eyes and smiled, and then looked away and down into the water. Was it really moving? Was the whole thing drifting away out into some unknown sea?

"Olga dear, you know, don't you?"

She breathed quickly, feeling a little uncertain of herself, only very, very conscious of him, and the almost imperceptible sway of the boat. His face was nearer. It was so near, she shut her eyes, dazzled and not knowing how to act. She knew that he was all around her, and his lips were upon her eyes. A strange sense of repose possessed her. Ah! if she might never open them again, but drift away like this with this river, and the tree, and the eternal memory of that moment!

"Olga dear, look at me. Oh, my darling!"

The lips followed their burning course across her cheek and settled with a fiery ecstasy upon her lips. Then it was that something within her stirred. She felt a wild, conflicting tumult of emotions, as though some life force were battering at the gates of her soul. The impulse of desire stood naked before the mirror of its own too fervid expression. Whither? Whither? Whither was the river drifting, with all its little particles scurrying by the boat? She gave a cry and thrust out her arm, and stammered:

"Oh, I don't know. I don't know, dear."

In the silence that followed, she noticed the lines of chagrin on his face. Her bosom heaved, and she clutched his hands and stroked them feverishly. The tears stole down her cheeks. She murmured in little jerky sentences:

"I 'm so sorry. You see, I hardly know, Harry. Please don't misunderstand me, dear. My life has been very difficult ... all sorts of strange things. Some people have been very good to me, of course, but—I don 't know; I feel I want to talk to you lots first. And I want you to talk to me." She dabbed her eyes with her handkerchief, and he murmured:

"Olga darling, I know—I know. Only, tell me—I may love you, mayn't I? Don't kill me by saying no. It doesn't matter what we do or talk about, I shall always love you."

She pulled at his hands feverishly while he tried to kiss her cheeks.

She shut her eyes again and lay back on the cushions, and said almost inaudibly:

"Not like you did just now, dear ... it makes me frightened."

CHAPTER III

KARL'S VISIT

Mr. and Mrs. Harry Streatham were seated on a lounge in their private sitting-room in the Hotel du Soleil, Paris. He was smoking and they had been silent for some time. At last she said:

"Harry."

"My darling?"

"Harry, I want to talk to you. When we get back—home, it will be—different there, won't it? We shall have our work and—you want me to continue with my work, don't you, darling?"

"Of course, darling; anything you like."

"Yes, but—you see—I want to—we must work together, must n 't we? You must help me, and I must try and help you. Of course I know, dear, it 's no good pretending: you 're clever and all that sort of thing, and I 'm not. But we must try and see things—with each other 's eyes, must n 't we?"

"Why, of course, dear. You shall always do as you like. Of course, I suppose—"

"Yes?"

"Well, just this year, darling, your work may be a little—hampered, mayn't it?"

'Yes . . . yes ... I know," she said, and her lips were slightly pale. "But, oh, Harry, you won't want me to give up all I 've worked for, will you? You won 't expect always—"

Streatham rose and knocked his cigarette ash into the fireplace, and repeated:

"Of course, dear, it shall always be as you like. I think I 'll go for a stroll round before turning in."

She saw him yawn and glance at an oleograph of Zermatt that hung on the wall by the door, and then slowly pick up his hat that lay on the table. He came over and kissed her chin, and said, "Shan't be ten minutes, darling."

With a sudden clear transcendence she beheld her vision of him split as by a double refraction; the splendid ease and poise with which he graded these little actions, broken by the shafts of supple arrogance that underlay them. He was like a cat that gambled on his soft fur and the beauty of his lines, expecting from life as his traditional prerogative the right to be fed and clothed and loved, and allowed to wander at random. He had the cat's superb insistence, too—the right to mew for what he wanted till he got it, and then to blink and purr with satisfaction.

She noticed the lines of his well-cut clothes as he hesitated for a second by the door, and the delicate poise of his beautiful head as he leaned a little forward and gripped the handle. "With a quick movement he turned, and smiled at her, and was gone. She sat there, gazing at the door, trying to reconcile certain misgivings, certain matters that seemed to demand "thinking all over again," as Levitch would say. Of course it was all right, everything was all right, only—She could hear his voice talking in the hall, to the hall porter, no doubt—he liked talking to these people in French; he spoke French very well. What was it she was thinking about Levitch? Ah! yes, "to think all over again." She must n 't forget that. She must n 't lose that faculty. He had told her not to—under any circumstances. She must be able at all times to look at things like a child, to keep her perceptions and impressions fluid and unspoiled. Something like that he had said. What was that Harry was saying? He was not talking French at all, he was talking English, He was speaking in a strange key for him, and there was another voice she seemed to recognize, rising in a whining crescendo. She heard the drone of the traffic outside, and the pleasant tooting of horns, and then the door opened suddenly, and Harry stood there, looking somehow ashamed, with an expression on his face she had not seen before. He was saying:

"Do you know this person?"

She glanced from him to a figure that huddled by the door, a figure that was grinning at her and muttering:

"Olger, Olger!"

She peered at it, and it came closer. It was a man with a thin, cadaverous face and close-cropped hair. He stooped very much, and held a cloth cap in front of his mouth. He gave a furtive glance round the room, and it was this movement, accompanied by the tones of the voice, that brought home to her the fact that the figure was that of her brother Karl!

She had the instinct to cry out. She was very moved and upset. He was the most pitiable apparition. But something rose within her to cope with this feeling of weakness. It was a sort of hardening of her heart against her husband. She was conscious of his attitude of outrage, as though she had brought some dreadful and unpardonable infliction upon the comfort and security of his life. After all, she had told him about her family. It is true he had hardly seemed to listen, as though such things were outside the pale of his imagination, as though she were picturesquely exaggerating. And nothing could alter this: it was her brother, a poor broken creature, object for any one's pity rather than contempt. And he, he ought to have been sorry for her and for him, but instead of that he almost bullied her before her brother's face. She steadied herself and said very deliberately:

"It 's my brother— Karl."

She was conscious of her husband giving a sudden vicious tilt to his hat, and turning aside, and then lighting a cigarette, and of the voice of Karl in a thin, quavering key:

"I 'm sorry, Olger, to disturb yer, I 'm right down on me luck, old girl—I see you git out of a feeaker this evening and come into the hotel with this toff. I waited for yer—I thought yer might come out again. I 'ope you 're all right, Olger, I 'ope things are all right?"

She put out her hand, and shook Karl 's, and said very calmly:

"Yes, I 'm all right, thank you, Karl. "What are you doing in Paris?"

The derelict blew on his fingers and shuffled from one leg to the other, and then answered:

"I come over 'ere some time ago. I 'ad a job in some stables at Shanteely, I been doin' different things. I got a touch of the roomatiz in me shoulder some time back—I was in a 'orspital."

He blinked at the magnificence of the little salon, and repeated, "Yer doin' all right then?"

A sudden inspiration came to the wife of Harry Streatham, and she walked to the fireplace and rang the bell; at the same time she said:

"Come and sit down, Karl, and tell me all your news. You 'll have some supper, won't you?"

She noticed that, as the waiter entered, her husband shrugged his shoulders and went out. She ordered some cold chicken and salad, and a small bottle of red wine. It was a strange meal. Never at any time had she and Karl had anything in common except this mutual desire for food.

He looked at her furtively and self-consciously, nibbling his food like a rat. He did not seem very hungry, but he gulped the wine greedily. As he sat there, the vision of the old room in Canning Town came back to her. She could almost see the black wood of the chimneypiece, and the worn spot on the cupboard door where dirty hands—just above her reach—had rubbed it bare, she could see the lighting of it revealing the tattered blind, and Irene bending over the table, ironing.

"Are you married to this bloke?"

It was Karl 's voice that broke upon her dream. Was she married? She knew that in some circles such a question would rouse indignation, but, after all, why should Karl know? What chances had Karl ever had?

"Yes," she answered.

"Got money?" came the next question slick upon her answer. She knew that this was a natural corollary to the suggestion of happiness, from Karl's point of view. Had she got money? Honestly she did not know. Some, at any rate. She had heard people say that the Streathams were well off, and she knew that Harry had his remittance regularly. It was in any case ample, enough to be happy upon. It was Karl himself who eventually answered his own question.

"'E dresses yer all right—anyway."

Somehow this statement struck the first really objectionable note that Karl had so far indulged in. It emphasized the idea of possession so crudely. He dressed her all right! It was true; she was bedecked and splendid, and led about like a prize animal through Europe. Ah, no! Harry was not like that. He liked her to look well, but he would not harbor such a mean concept of her. He was too sensitive, too refined. Besides, was she not a free woman, and no man's property? Had she not played in all the towns of England, and "the people had paid to hear her"? Any time she could go away again, and earn enough money for all practical ideas of happiness. She thought she would shift the ground of this personal inquisition, and she said:

"Have you heard any news of the others, Irene or Montague?"

"No," said Karl. "Montague went to Orstralia, I believe. I never 'card from 'im. I see Irene two years ago. She was livin' in fine style in B'yswater. She was 'a keep,' I think—seemed to 'ave pots of money—never gave me none, though."

A sudden horrible dread came over Olga.

"What do you mean by 'a keep'?" she asked.

"Why, you know," chuckled Karl. "Being kept by some bloke!"

"Do you mean—" gasped his sister, and then she steadied herself, and asked quickly, "What sort of man was he, do you know? "

Karl swirled the claret round in his glass, and said:

"Seemed to have a bit of stuff. They was livin' all right, got a servant and that."

Was there no other standard by which Karl could judge these things? Was he entirely dead to any human feeling or sensibility? What could she ask him that he would understand? He did not seem to know the man's name, or to have kept a record of their address. His only concern in the whole business seemed to be that "they would n 't give him nothing." He spoke of Uncle Grubhofer, and she could tell by the tones of his voice that he still had an unconscionable dread of him. He believed he was running some business in Hammersmith, a sort of agency concerning which Karl was particularly mysterious and leery.

When these family matters were disposed of, there was an interminable pause. Olga racked her brains to think of something further to say, and Karl for his part stood picking his teeth, with his back to the fire, and occasionally looked at her out of his small greedy eyes and coughing nervously. At last he said:

"Well, yer doin' all right then, Olger?" He cleared his throat, and prepared the ground for the opportunity of the "scoop" which he felt too good to be lost.

"I s 'pose yer could n 't raise a bit for me? I got a good thing on at Shanteely—a deal over some 'orses a friend of mine could put me up to. There 's a French marquis wants to buy a brace of roan mares—I know just where to put me 'and on 'em. I could bring off a good scoop if I 'ad forty pounds—eh? D ' yer think the toff 'd—"

Olga resented the attitude with regard to the "toff" more than anything, and she felt a burning desire to assert herself, to prove to Karl that she was not a puppet dangled on a string. She cut the harangue short by saying:

"If you call here to-morrow at twelve o'clock, I will lend you forty pounds."

The face of Karl lighted with amazement mingled with regret. It was the easiest thing he had ever pulled off, and he was consumed with remorse that he had not asked for fifty, or even a hundred. However, he thought it wiser to go warily. After all, if forty pounds was so easy to raise in this quarter, it could be done again, and perhaps again and again. He was almost maudlin with gratitude, and a little uncertain whether it would not be advisable to try and get a little on account to-night. After all, it was only Olga who had said that he could have forty quid; perhaps when the toff came home—however, he did not want to spoil a good effect, and he took his departure.

"When he had gone, she took a book up to bed and made a ridiculously abortive effort to read. Harry returned just after eleven o'clock. Through half-closed eyes she saw him enter her room and peer at her. He looked a little ruffled and important, but he smiled at her and said, "Asleep, old girl?"

She said, "No."

He whistled under his breath, and said:

"The river looks awfully jolly to-night. I saw a regular Goya subject near the Tuileries, looking down into some gardens. There were booths lighted up, and figures in white caps, and a bonfire burning—"

He paused and examined some spot on his chin in the mirror, and then said, "Your brother went, then?"

Olga called him to her and held his face very close to hers, and whispered breathlessly:

"Harry darling, I want you to help me. My brother is in great trouble. I have promised to lend him forty pounds by twelve o'clock to-morrow."

He started from her and exclaimed, "Forty pounds!" and then he laughed uneasily and added:

"But, my dear girl, I have n't got forty pounds here."

She said, "No; I thought you might not have, but we can get it, can't we? I have promised, you see. If you can't get it, I can cable to Mrs. Fittleworth. I am sure she would lend me forty pounds."

Harry got up from the bed and walked up and down the room, a shadow passing over his face.

"I suppose this doesn't mean," he said at length, "that this—brother of yours will want to be always hanging about, and borrowing money. We don't want Mrs. Fittleworth wired to for money on our honeymoon. I suppose I could manage it somehow, but—"

He looked at her, and saw that she was crying. In a second his arms were round her and his lips were pressed against her cheek. But she was in one of her strangely emotional moods. He could not quite understand her. Why all these tears?

"I have told you of my people, dear," she gasped. "I can't help it—I know they 're different—not like the people you are used to—but, oh, my God! they are my people. I can't cast them off—entirely." She buried her face in the pillow. A feeling of splendid magnanimity pervaded Streatham, and he murmured:

"There, there, darling! It 's all right, of course. We must do what we can. We must try and help them, and so on. Come!"

He tried to kiss her lips, but she shrank from him, and shivered in somewhat the same way as she had that day upon the river at Marlow. The situation appeared to him very trying. He wanted to be magnanimous, but he detested this sort of situation. He shook himself free, and disrobed himself in a deliberate and mechanical manner. He felt that it was due to himself to exhibit certain traces of hardness and authority.

They had a horrible time after that, gaging the emotionalism of each other by opposing standards, misjudging, and misunderstanding. He went to sleep in her arms at last, and she noticed that his eyes were wet with tears also. In the still night she could see his face, by the pale reflection of the moon, sleeping and breathing heavily like a spoilt child. Had she been cruel to him? Why should she expect him more than any of the others to understand everything? It was only that when he came, she wanted him so. She had thrown around him such a glamour, such a halo. Was he not her god? the being who was to respond to all the calls of her slumbering restlessness? She somehow had imagined that such a being would understand, would dovetail with every little wish and thought. She had given him a divinity, and it was a cruel and perverse standard for her to have set up. To-morrow she would be kinder and more considerate, as became one who was to be the mother of his child.

Before they left for England, Karl had reaped his maximum "scoop." He set forth on a wild bacchanale through the cafes of Montmartre with notes for six hundred francs in his pocket, and an address in London where he expected that in a crisis he could get some more.

The Streathams returned from their protracted honeymoon, and occupied a small but distinguished-looking, modern Georgian house in Hampstead.

It was a proud day for Olga when, with everything in order, she dispensed tea in her own drawing-room to Mrs. Fittleworth and her girls, and the Guildefords, and many of their other friends. And it was with a thrill of pleasure that she once more started practising on her own grand piano, given her as a wedding present by Mrs. Fittleworth.

She found, however, that her practising was subject to very serious disruptions. She had the responsibility of three servants, and they seemed to vie with each other in causing dissensions and upsetting "the master." And they had a genius for leaving at the most inopportune moments, and for banging doors and making unseemly disturbances. Moreover, Harry had a great idea of sociability. At least two or three evenings a week he required to have people asked to dinner, and on the other evenings he liked to go out to dine with other people, or go to the theater or the Queen's Hall. All these things distracted her, and tended to eat into the valuable time and effort that still remained to her before she would have to retire for the while. It was only by great persuasion that she managed to get Harry to consent to her giving another recital in October. He seemed to think it rather a waste of time and money, as, "if she got engagements from it, she might not be able to fulfil them."

It grieved her to know that Levitch had decided not to come to London again. He would remain now always within his walled garden at Prague. He sent her a box of peaches, and told her that "a time arrives when it is better to say that one becomes old."

She did not feel happy with the people that Harry liked to have round them. They were mostly literary people, or people holding positions of direction or patronage in the artistic world. They liked to sit over their wine and beat about to find surprising theories. They drawled recondite phrases in comfortable, detached voices, as though they themselves were not a part of life, but a sort of coterie of languid thoughts that found in life a certain mild field for their expression. Their conversations left her nerveless and physically fatigued. The only people she liked were John Braille, who came but seldom, and a certain Sir Philip Ballater, who lived alone in a large house in Hampstead, near them. He was an Englishman who had lived so long abroad that he spoke English with a foreign accent. He was a middle-aged, distinguished-looking man, and she liked him because he had the faculty for silence. They said that he had been in the diplomatic service at Vienna, but what gave them a common ground of sympathy was that he knew and loved Prague, and had met Levitch. He was at the present time a director of the National Museum of Applied Art, and was considered one of the greatest authorities on armour and ceramics. His house was in itself a veritable storehouse of priceless works. He had extremely courtly manners and entertained with a silent magnificence.

She was conscious in his house of a sense of repose. They dined in a circular hall of black and white marble, and at a large circular table, where masses of fresh flowers (usually orchids) trailed from a central jardiniere up to the plates of the guests. Well modulated lights enhanced the beauty of gleaming silver, and were sufficient to make the faces of the diners discernible, but vague and interesting. An uncountable number of servants glided in and out between the marble columns, and silently brought and carried. They were the most unnoticeable servants she had ever encountered. The only sound audible during the dinner was the sound of a fountain that always played in a courtyard off this room. She liked the murmur of this running water. It seemed to make it not so necessary to force conversation, it filled up intervals, and had a message of its own. It was true that even here conversations would become extremely "precious," but they were less general, and one became more intimate with one 's next-door neighbor. And if one said something that was not entirely brilliant or important, it became lost in the large spaces of the room and mellowed by the eternal chant of the running water.

Sir Philip Ballater seemed to take to Olga. He followed her closely with his large pathetic eyes and talked at times quite volubly. He showed her all his paintings and his ceramics, over which he brooded with a maternal tenderness. The house had something of the nature of a show place. After dinner one wandered all over it, and sat and talked where one would, or with whom one would. It had no centers of attraction, no focus of social life. It was all equally beautiful, equally comfortable and equally heated—a passionless, cultivated atmosphere.

One evening after dinner, Sir Philip took her to see some Ming that he had just had brought to town from his place in the country. It was set on a black case in a small room decorated in a Japanese style. He puffed feverishly at his cigarette as he approached it, and put on his spectacles. He passed his hands over it and asked her to feel the glaze. She did so and duly approved.

"Ah," he said, "dear lady, you should approve if any one. There are not many who have the sensitiveness. What you call your color in music, my glaze is to me. It is very subtle, very difficult to define, isn't it? But it is there." He stroked each piece with a lingering caress.

"Do you mean, Sir Philip," said Olga, "that you can tell the different pieces by the touch?"

"My dear," he said, "it is all I can tell by. I sometimes come down here when it is quite dark, and talk to these children of mine. Is not the value of all life in that, the recognition of these finer sensibilities? One can never trust the outer semblance of anything. One may have a handsome face, or one may conduct the fifth symphony of Beethoven brilliantly and correctly, but it is only those of us who have the sense to know in the dark who can decide if the face is really beautiful, or if the performance is really worth doing."

He looked at her closely, and she was conscious of a sort of magnetic power about him. He sighed and closed one of the cases, and they passed through into another room and sat down. There was a Musabeh screen at the back of them and she heard two voices in conversation. One of them was Harry's and the other Boder's, the dramatic critic. Boder was saying:

"As far as that goes, my dear chap, I must acknowledge that the music of Wagner always has that effect on me—

'Each man kills the thing he loves'

sort of feeling. That is why I prefer Tchaikowsky. He is more definitely passionate—cleaner in a way. I am too old to have my emotions honeycombed by these abstruse desires—"

She heard the mellow tones of Harry's voice, perhaps made even a little more mellow by the excellent quality of Sir Philip's port.

"I am not contending that the music of Wagner is any more immoral than any other music. All music is immoral. It is one of the antennie of the senses. One of the gay appanages of the creative being, like flowers or the beauty of women, all a part of the cunning scheme of creation."

And then the booming voice of Boder:

"But, my dear chap, what is there immoral in creation? or the beauty of sexual attraction, as far as that goes? "

"Nothing at all," answered Harry's voice. "It is only that music appeals to the act and not to the idea. It is exclusively sexual. It inspires women with a sort of glamorous sense of surrender, and man with a dynamic sense of creation or destruction. The Puritans recognized this in the seventeenth century when they even abolished music from the churches, or allowed it to be performed only by unsexed boys. Have you noticed how many of the great creative people loathed music?—Darwin, Carlyle, Victor Hugo, Flaubert, and so on. Even your 'cleanest composer,' Tchaikowsky, destroyed himself. I said it was one of the antenna? of the senses, but I 'm not sure it 's not a diseased antenna, the legacy of some perverted god."

She heard Boder's ingratiating snigger, and his voice broken by a slight stammer that often accompanied it:

"My d-dear fellow, I 'm surprised that you have the courage to prosecute such a d-dangerous calling."

And Harry 's comfortable laugh:

"I? Oh, I love it!"

She caught the eye of Sir Philip and moved away, feeling strangely perturbed. Why did Harry talk like that? Was it talk? just the love of talk? or did he really mean what he said? If he meant what he said, why did he never speak to her in that strain? Was he afraid that she would not understand him? or was he afraid that she would understand him?

"Ah, my dear Mrs. Streatham, I must show you my Spode. You have not seen my black Spode, have you? It has a quality you will admire. "

He pulled aside a curtain, and bowed in a courtly manner. She was not sure whether he had heard the conversation and was trying to distract her from its possibly unpleasant effects, or whether his mind had never left the cloisters of his temple of earthenware. But she stepped gladly past the curtain, feeling that in the company of black Spode she would at least inhale the incense of tranquillity.

CHAPTER IV

THE DRONE OF LONDON

The day was close. A humidity hung over the Hampstead garden, where she lay in a hammock between the mulberry-tree and the wall. The little son was four mouths old, and it was only during the last week that she had been out. She had been very ill, very ill indeed; and at one time two doctors had despaired of her. But she was now able to walk again, and the child was sleeping up-stairs in charge of a nurse. Harry was out for the day, playing golf with some friends. The Fittleworths were in Paris. "Robin" Guildeford had called on her the previous day, but to-day she felt lonely and restless. She got up and went into the drawing-room, and struck a few chords on the piano, but her nerves were jaded, and her fingers seemed stiff and unresponsive. She went back to the hammock and meditated. It seemed very silent there, and in the distance she could hear the drone of London, a dim, muffled roar. It sounded very suggestive and remote. It seemed so wonderful that all these individual and desperate noises should merge into one sound. Seven million people all doing different things, struggling, creating, disputing, and then—one sound to express the whole. She looked at her watch. It was half-past five. Harry would not be back to dinner till eight. He had gone to Northwood, or Richmond, or somewhere. She suddenly got out of the hammock and went indoors. She went to the telephone and ordered a taxi, and then went up-stairs and put on her hat and a cloak.

When the cab came she told the man to drive to Oxford Street. It was pleasant rushing through the air, the only thing to do on a day like this. She had been out for drives before, but never on so adventurous a journey. She had a great desire to see people, all sorts of people, good and bad, rich and poor, to split up this insistent phrase of sound, as it were, and get in touch with its component parts. She was one of the parts herself. There must be millions like her, not entirely happy, and not entirely unhappy, helping to make this sound. It would be something just to glance into their eyes in passing. There must be many who were lonely like she was, calling restlessly into the void, trying to awake an echo.

The cab wound its way through Camden Town, amidst the squalling cacophony from coster stalls and smaller shops, and the smell of uncooked meat and fish. In a few years they would have all gone, all these component parts with their petty trials and tribulations of the heart; but still the one sound would go on, droning, droning, droning. What did it all mean? Or did it mean just nothing? A dull reiteration of the Will-to-live, as Harry would say?

She dismissed the cab at Portland Road Station and started to walk down Great Portland Street. She went past some shops, and then took a turning to the left. In a few minutes she was amongst mean streets, like those in which she had passed her youth. She saw the bedraggled children, pale and ill-nourished, but vaunting a sort of strident happiness just like they did in Canning Town, mostly by noise and by their unconquerable imagination. It struck her for the first time what a wealth of creative genius was always being born. With pieces of chalk and string and broken boxes, they invented games, and deeds, and images of the great world. What happened to all this inventiveness that was absorbed in the drone of the great city? She looked up, and found her answer in the repelling masonry of tenement blocks, and buff gray houses which frowned and absorbed the children and ultimately crushed them and flung them forth—mere atoms of the dreary iteration of the Will-to-live. She remembered what Levitch had said—"You must never lose that—the power to look at life with child-eyes."

She felt somehow soothed by the desperate fecundity of these children; it seemed like the assertion at least of some primal divine intention. She thought of her own son. He should always look at life "with child eyes." She would fight for that in him. No one should rob him of that. lie should keep all his impressions and intuitions fresh and unspoiled. Was she keeping her own? Was it possible? She steadied herself against an area railing. She saw a small girl, very dirty, trying to reach a bell. She was a strange, dark little thing. She must have been rather like that herself many years ago. She said:

"Which bell do you want, dear?"

The child said:

"Top one. Mrs, Osgrove."

She rang the bell for the child, and gave her sixpence. The little girl stared at it open-mouthed, and as the door opened, dashed in as though she dreaded that the money might be taken from her. As she did so, Olga turned and noticed an evil-looking man standing by her. He had seen the transaction, and he called out:

"'Ere!"

He pushed his way through the door and slammed it, and she heard a scuffle and a scream. She instinctively banged on the door, but there was no answer, and she felt rather as though she was going to faint. She stepped out into the road and walked slowly away. The action and the fresher air steadied her. She turned back into Great Portland Street. She met several girls walking furtively, some singly and some in couples.

"They have been crushed," she thought; "crushed and thrown out of the great buildings. Once, perhaps, they could build images, and now the world is dead to them."

She passed one fair little French girl. She seemed little older than Mollie Fittleworth. A wave of unspeakable pity came over her. She went up to her and suddenly said in a strained voice:

"May I help you?"

The girl looked at her quickly, and a bewildered expression came over her face—a mixture of doubt, sorrow, and a sort of desperate cunning. For a fraction of a second she hesitated, and then said:

"Oh, mon Dieu! no . . . no!"

She darted down a side street and left Olga staring into the face of a man. He grinned at her, and raised his hat. She felt rather frightened, and jumped on to a motor 'bus going west. What was this conspiracy of destruction? Was that the note of London, a dirge of destruction? Children, women, and men devouring each other, and buildings crushing them? Would nothing come out of all this? But were these people, in their animal vileness, any worse than others who sat at cultured tables and talked of the Sensuality of Music? who carved all aspirations into libertinous phrases?

Was the man who stopped her in the street any worse than the man who married her and showed a critical sense of esthetic values in the thing? It was only that he had cast a spell over her, had made her his bondwoman, a slave of her own sense of attraction to him. Good God! what was she thinking about? Were these thoughts true? or only some chimera of this humid day? She had never dared to give them shape before. She had thrust them away whenever they dared find entrance in her fears, but there was something about the freedom of the streets, the friction of the lives of these crude people that made her see the clearer. But she would not believe that. She loved her husband; she would set her teeth, and win out to the end.

She walked down Regent Street. The varied character and costumes of the people excited her. As she neared the lower end, she saw two women coming towards her. They were apparently of the same class as those she had met in Great Portland Street. One was rather stout, with fair fuzzy hair, the other was dark, with very bright coloring. She had almost passed them, when she noticed the dark one nudge the other, and she heard her exclaim:

"My Gawd! if it isn't my sister!"

Olga started. She was almost afraid to look. When she did, she gazed upon the most horrible sight she had ever beheld. A strange feeling of sickness came over her and a sense that the world was crashing about her ears. Irene's eyes were heavily penciled, her cheeks were red, and her mouth was large and loose. Her dark hair was cunningly twisted under her hat, and her clothes gave her figure a surprising but unconvincing development.

It was strange that in the first moment of that tragic meeting, some instinct for the conventions disturbed Olga. She wondered whether she ought to let Irene see that she understood, whether she ought to be affectionate or tragic; she wondered, in short, how she ought to behave. The moment seemed so fraught with horror and surprise, that it found her nerveless and quite unstrung. It was almost a relief that it had apparently no such effect on Irene, who seemed quite self-composed, and grinned at her with her broad slit of a mouth. All through the scene that followed Olga could not take her eyes from Irene's mouth. She could not remember her having a mouth like that. She could not quite remember what Irene's mouth was like, but this one was horrible.

"Well, 'ow are yer gettin' on? All right?" was Irene's greeting, and it occurred to Olga how remarkably identical it was with Karl's greeting. There was no need to analyze its meaning. It simply meant, "Have you got plenty of money, and enough to eat and drink?" She almost dreaded a reference to the "toff," and remarks that "he seemed to be dressing her all right." She instinctively made up her mind that she wouldn't mention her marriage. She managed at last to say:

"I 'm all right, Irene. How are you?"

The duologue was immediately interrupted by the third woman, who said:

"My Gawd! Chadsworth, you never told us you 'ad a lady for a sister. Let 's go and 'ave a drop of rum and milk."

Irene laughed in a peculiarly free but mirthless manner, and stepped to the outside, so that Olga was between the two women. They all started to walk slowly down a side street in the direction of Soho.

"Fancy meeting you!" repeated Irene. But it was said with no great sense of surprise, no regret, no moral misgiving, without conveying any feeling of intimacy or personal sympathy.

"She is crushed," thought Olga; "crushed. I can never get her back. She is dead. I must comfort myself by thinking that she is dead. Everything has gone out of her. . . . Oh, God! how horrible it is!"

It was strange how at that tragic hour the person of the third woman seemed more attractive and companionable to her. She said in a dreary, almost aggrieved voice:

"I 'm surprised at you, Chadsworth, never telling me you 'ad a lady for a sister."

Chadsworth? What did Chadsworth signify? What drab story might not be connected with this somewhat grandiloquent name! They turned suddenly to the left under a covered way, and Olga found herself being conducted through a dim cafe where some Italians were playing dominoes and drinking vermouth and beer. Two other women were sitting near the door, and one, a very large person with little earrings, caught hold of Irene and whispered. Olga could not hear what was said, but she thought she heard Irene say, "Of course I will, dear."

There was a curious atmosphere of freemasonry in this place. Men and women seemed under some loyal bond. They took very little notice of each other, but when they did they called each other by affectionate names, and exchanged understanding glances. They passed through into an inner room where there were several marble-top tables, and sat down. The air was very close, and had a quality of its own. Olga felt rather faint. A waiter with a fair beard came up, and she heard the third woman say, "I 'll have my usual. Tommy. What 'll your sister 'ave, Chaddy?" Irene was appealing to her, but she put her hand to her head and said:

"I don't think I 'll drink anything, thank you."

"Oh, go on! Bring 'er a drop of brandy."

She was relieved for the moment that Irene and the third woman seemed to ignore her. They started a conversation between themselves, about some one called "Lily," who had not been seen lately. When the drink was brought, Irene suddenly said:

"'Ere! 'Ave you seen Uncle Grubhofer?"

Olga said:

"No."

Irene gave forth a hard metallic laugh and said:

"Lord, you must go and see 'im. Only don't go if you 've got a split lip—'e 'll make you die!"

She laughed again wildly and tempestuously, as though the vision of Uncle Grubhofer in his present state were an object of mirth even to the damned.

"What is it?" asked Olga. "What is he like?"

Irene undid a small reticule she was carrying, and took out an envelope and wrote a name and address on it; then she said:

"You go and see him. Oh, my Gawd, it 's too funny! 'E 'll make you die!" and then she added, as though the priceless jest might not have penetrated, "Only don't go if you 've got a split lip."

An electric music-box started in the next room, and they had to raise their voices. Olga drank some of the brandy. She felt in need of it. It burnt her throat, but its fumes produced in her an elevated sense of her position. She wanted to talk to Irene, to try and find if there were anything left underneath, any glimmer of that intimacy they had shared on that last night they had spent together in the cottage in Surrey, when she had given her the eleven pounds, and Irene had said, "You didn't ought to have done it. I thought you were somehow—different—" Something real and lasting between them. But it had all vanished, everything, even the memory of it was dim. But what cruel jest of fate was this that had given her certain aspirations, had given her talent and understanding, had led her into smooth and sunlit spaces, and at the same time had crushed the soul of her sister?

Did she deserve one fate and her sister another? Were they not children of the same parents? "Was Irene responsible for her own weaknesses and defections? The organ in the next room was grinding out a gay Italian love-song with a lugubrious rhythm, occasionally broken by a scrunching, grinding noise, as though the pain of expressing these transcendent joys in this atmosphere were almost too much for it. The third woman had had several glasses of rum and milk, and she showed a disposition to be maudlin and confidential.

"Why don't you drink up your brandy, dear, and 'ave another?" she said to Olga, and then added, "Oh, Gawd! I s'pose you don't need it, do you? I never needed it at one time." Then she looked at her face, and said, "You 're a pretty thing, strike me blind if you 're not! I love to 'ear this music, love it and 'ate it at the same time. Do you know what I mean? . . . 'Ere, do you know why I come to this? Because I 'm too fond of it—you know, everything. That 's what I mean—too fond of everything. 'Ere. I 'ad a little boy, pretty as a flower, 'e was. While I 'ad 'im I run as straight as a die. . . . D'you know what 'appened? 'E was five years old. We was living in Willesden. My 'usband was a drunken swine. I went out one morning into Padds Lane—d'you know it? Suddenly I sees my little boy on the other side of the road, see? I calls out to 'im, 'Charlie!' I said. . . . And even now I can 'ear 'is voice. 'E says, ' 'Ullo, Mummy!' 'e says, and dashes across the road. Christ! 'E dashes clean into a van! I sees 'im crushed right in front of my eyes, in a flash! Oh, Gawd! do you hear? I 'd called 'im! I 'd called 'im! D ' you understand? . . . ' 'Ullo, Mummy!' 'e says, and runs to me into the van!"

The third woman was trembling, and shaking her rum and milk round in her glass; her eyes were fixed in a hard, terrified stare. Almost as though some one had struck her, Olga heard Irene's voice, saying:

"Oh, chuck it, Florrie! Don't make a fool of yerself."

The third woman did not heed this remark. She drained her glass and continued:

"When I got 'ome that evenin', and I told my 'usband, 'e says, 'Oh!' just like that. 'Oh!' 'E 'd been drinkin' at the time. If 'e 'ad n't, I think I 'd 'ave killed 'im. As it was, I just slogged 'im in the face, cut 'is eye open, and knocked 'im out, and then I walked out of the 'ouse and never went back."

"Oh la, la la la!
The gay Posada!"

With fitful starts and jerks the organ was endeavoring to recall to Olga memories of her honeymoon. It was the night of a serenata. She and Harry were lying huddled together in a gondola, clasped in each other's arms. The dim profile of the Santa Maria della Salute was silhouetted against the sky. Overhead the stars flashed their wireless glitter of sympathetic understanding, as they had to Troilus and Cressida in immemorial times. Troy had droned, as London droned, and Troy was no more. Perhaps a day would come when the whole drone of all the cities living and dead would be expressed in one note. What was it? An A? It could be divided and subdivided! Was all life dominated by this unanswerable phrase—the Will-to-live? She realized that it was an infinitesimal expression of that note, the words he breathed in her ear—"Darling, darling, darling, my darling!" Had he said anything else? She could not remember. It was his expression, the world's expression of the desire of propagation. The Will-to-Perpetuate. . . .

The third woman was talking again. She liked this woman, with her horrible and human story. Why had n't Irene anything to say like that? "Why did she sit there with that ghastly slit of a mouth of hers, and grin, and grin, and grin? and when the third woman said something lovable and understandable, why did Irene interrupt it with her raucous voice: "Oh, chuck it, Florrie!"? The third woman was worth a thousand of Irene. She was not yet dead. She had something in her, some spark of the divine efflatus, that could not be subdued, something of that quality that Olga was struggling to preserve in herself and that she had sworn to fight for in her son. She drank some more of the brandy, and then, turning suddenly to Irene, she said:

"Do you remember that night down in that cottage in Surrey? The night I brought you the eleven sovereigns? "

She could see by her face that Irene had honestly forgotten it. She drank some more of the port wine that was in front of her. Then she said, after a pause:

"Oh, my Gawd! yus, I remember. I can almost hear the thud of the old devil's footsteps as he went across the 'ill, can't you?" She took a cigarette out of a case and lighted it. The music from the organ increased in volume. Suddenly she turned, and said:

"Why, yes, it was you what give me that money, was n't it? D' you know what I did? I went off that same morning. I went to London."

She threw her head forward, and laughed hysterically. She grasped the sleeve of the waiter who was passing, and said:

"Tommy, bring me some more of this bloody poison, darling." Then she grinned at Olga and said:

"It was your eleven quid what give me the taste of this muck. I wasn't in no mood to be sentimental. There was a soldier I remember, I met him in the Euston Road. ..." Her eyes suddenly blazed with anger because a passer-by had brushed against her. She turned irritably on her sister and said:

"You 've always managed for yourself all right, 'aven't yer? Who 's keeping yer now?"

An instinctive desire came to Olga to say, "I 'm being kept by a man at Hampstead," but she restrained herself, and the third woman chimed in:

"You 're making a fool of yourself now, Chadsworth. What business is it of yours whose keep she is?"

But Olga leaned forward, and whispered to her sister:

"Irene, is that true? Was it the money I—took that first gave you a taste for—this sort of life?"

"The money you—what?" sniggered Irene. "The money you pinched, you mean, out of that lady's writing-table. Why, you told me of it. Oh, go on! what does it matter? You 're no better or worse than the rest of us. William, I ordered a port about an hour ago! For God's sake buck up with it, darling."

Other people were coming into the room. It seemed to get noisier and stuffier. Irene was saying, "If you want to go and see anything really amusing, you go and see Uncle Grubhofer!"

The third woman started talking about the disappearance of "Lily" again, and the feeling of faintness once more began to creep over Olga. She stood up and said she must go. It occurred to her afterwards that even at that moment it was remarkable that her departure seemed to affect the third woman more than it did Irene.

She felt attracted by this wayward, primitive creature; but Irene sat there grinning, remorseless, and expressionless. Olga knew that as far as she was concerned Irene was dead to her. Ah! if she had only given one flicker of understanding, some little inflection of the voice that showed that she remembered, that she realized, that she had any human tie; even if she had only listened to the third woman's story with a gleam of sympathy, instead of crashing upon it with that cruel, "Don't make a fool of yourself," Or was it that under the grinning mask of Irene's lay the greatest horror of all, the dread of her own self-pity, if the floodgates of human feeling were ever loosened in her? Was it possible to destroy—everything? . . .

It was a quarter to eight when she arrived home. The maid who let her in said that the master was back, and had brought two gentlemen home to dinner. They were in the drawing-room. She went up-stairs and changed her frock. When she had removed her bodice, she suddenly looked at her shoulders and arms in a mirror. The vision seemed to suspend her power of action. She gazed at herself for some moments in the half-light and muttered:

"Oh, God! is it possible?"

Then rapidly throwing a dressing-gown round her, she went into another room where the child was sleeping. The nurse had left him. He was lying curled up with one of his tiny arms hanging free. Her bosom heaved wildly as she held her face close to his, as though drawing strength from the smell of his warm firm flesh. She kissed the down on his head again and again, and then returned and finished her dressing.

When she entered the drawing-room, her husband was just walking toward the door. He said in his calm suave voice:

"Hullo, dear, you are late. I was just coming to look for you. You know Boder, don't you? This is Mr, Stave,"

A large, red-faced man, with curly hair and a tortoise-shell monocle in his right eye, came forward with rather a fierce expression, and said:

"Charmed to meet you, dear Mrs. Streatham."

She knew him by sight. He was the editor of a monthly review. A gong was going outside and she took the large man's arm, and they all passed through to the dining-room.

"It 's been a nice day," he remarked.

"Yes," she said; "it has—very nice. I 've been out, I 've been listening to the drone of London."

"Eh?" said the editor. "The drone of London! Oh! fancy that! That 's very interestin'. We 've been playing golf. Your husband is uncommonly good on the green."

CHAPTER V

AMBITION

Harry's mother and eldest sister had just driven away, after one of their periodical visits, and as usual had left the nerves of Harry 's wife all on edge. She stood by the French window looking on to the lawn, and her husband was glancing at a magazine and smoking. There had been a certain amount of criticism with regard to minor details of the child's bringing up, and one remark of the elder Mrs. Streatham's had rankled through her mind. "Of course, my dear, you can hardly be expected to have everything entirely satisfactory with your first." First! She looked at her husband, and it suddenly occurred to her that his face had filled out. It was rather too sleek and comfortable for the face of a god. She had a sudden vision of her life to come. This was her first child. There would be more, and perhaps more. She would be the eternal matron in the Hampstead drawing-room. She noticed the clean white paneling, and the satin-wood furniture, and the neat orderliness of the room with its dark-green hangings and the large silver tray whereon the things from tea still reposed, reminding her of her function as a hostess. There would be more of this, years and years of it, dispensing tea, bringing up children in the correct way, keeping things orderly, keeping orderly herself, listening to the refined talk of her dinner table, being "the mistress" of the servants and the master. Sometimes when the guests were well fed, and they were in the mood for it, she would be asked to play the piano to them. And then she could almost hear the euphuistic tones of their voices:

"Oh, dear Mrs. Streatham, how perfectly fascinating! is that Scriabine? I adore Russian music—so passionate! so elusive!"

She suddenly said:

"Harry!"

He looked up at her from the magazine. For the fraction of a second she thought she detected an expression of furtive suspicion on his face. She was conscious that ever since that night in Paris when Karl had paid his visit, there had come between them a certain something she could hardly divine. There had never been any quarrel, and nothing more had ever been said about Karl. She knew very definitely that Mrs. Streatham and the sisters held the view that Harry had married "out of his class." Was it some unexpressed feeling of this sort that was occasionally reflected in his face when he looked up at her like that? She went over to the settee, and put her arms round his neck from behind, and rested her cheek against the top of his head, and said:

"Harry, we mustn't stagnate, must we?"

She felt him laughing in an uncomfortable way as he replied:

"Stagnate! What on earth do you mean, darling?"

"I mean," she answered, "that we must always be doing things, going on. Do you know what I mean, dear? We mustn't get—satisfied, must we?"

He laughed again, and said:

"Good Heavens! Do you want to move into a bigger house?"

She rested her cheek against his.

"No, no," she said. "You know quite well I don't mean that. I should be contented with two rooms anywhere. It 's ourselves I mean. I sometimes think we do want to move into a bigger house in a sense. You haven't been working very hard lately, have you, Harry?"

"My dear girl," he answered, "what are you talking about? One can't compose every day from nine to six, like a clerk, can one?"

"No," she said; "but it 's not only that. But there comes a time—Levitch used to say to me that one must always be able to look at life like a child; you know—keep on re-creating, thinking over again, keeping oneself susceptible to impressions. After a time one loses that faculty if one is not careful. One becomes 'atrophied'—is that the word?"

"Do you feel," said Streatham, "that you don't get sufficient intellectual stimulus here?"

"Heavens! yes—too much of it, of a kind. But it 's not that. I wish I could make you understand more clearly what I mean. I 'm so bad at expressing myself. I want to play more—I want to get on. But it 's not only that, I think. It 's when one gets satisfied, one—goes down the sink, as it were. I 'm sure of that; more sure of that than anything."

Harry shook himself free and stood up.

"I 'm afraid, my dear," he said, "that your metaphysics are a little obscure. I really don't know what you want, except that you apparently want us to be both dissatisfied. Good Lord! it 's a rotten world. I suppose we all are dissatisfied at heart. But the whole idea of philosophy is to combat this. What is 'to be philosophic' if it isn't to be resigned to the ugliness and silliness of things?"

"But by being dissatisfied," she protested, "I don't mean cynical—like that—that is being dissatisfied with other people. I mean being dissatisfied with oneself—searching inside oneself for—finer things. I don 't think the world is rotten. I think it 's very beautiful. I find amongst all sorts of people, vile and vicious people some of them, qualities that I envy. They 're not rotten. There 's nothing rotten except—being satisfied."

And then the god performed a little act that was never forgotten, and which brought the whole edifice of his godhead crashing to the earth. lie stretched himself and examined the backs of his long white hands. For the moment he appeared to be going to reply, then he turned his hands over, and made a little noise that can only be expressed—

"'M—'m," the second "'m" being a tone higher than the first. It was a little action, but it distinctly conveyed this meaning:

"What on earth is the good of me talking to a child like you? I 've discussed all these elementary things years ago—when I was at Gueldstone's house at Winchester. I 've discussed them and gone beyond them. It would simply bore me to death to talk philosophy with you. I 've read Plato, and Aristotle, and every one up to Nietszche and Bergson. And you 've read— nothing. You know nothing. I feed you, and clothe you, and give you every comfort, and your business is to love me, and look after my children. If you knew a little more—well and good, but as you don't, you can't possibly expect me to teach you."

She did not say anything more after that, but her lips were a shade paler as she moved towards the door. There she stopped, and looked back at him, but his eyes were concentrated on the delicate modeling of his fingertips, and she went out.

From that day she started to build a world within a world. She worked hard at her piano, and went down to see her agent. Concert Director Whitbread was very desirous that she should give more recitals, and suggested a scheme of spending a large sum of money that savored of M. Pensiver.

"Of course, Miss Bardel, you 've lost ground," he said. "It's always bad to have to cancel engagements, and the public soon forgets. I should suggest giving three recitals and engaging the London Imperial Orchestra for an orchestral concert. I think they would guarantee in exchange to engage you for one of their series next season."

He said that with two hundred pounds he thought he could establish her once again and make her a popular favorite. She reported the matter to Harry, and that gentleman said:

"Of course, darling, it would be awfully jolly to do it. I wish we could."

But then it appeared that there were difficulties. The Streathams, it seemed, had been living above their income even before the child was born, and that event, with its concomitant demands from doctors, specialists, and nurses, had placed poor Harry in a very difficult financial position. It occurred to her to suggest drastic reforms in the home. To move to a smaller house, to reduce the number of servants, and to live more simply, but she knew that these changes would make her husband very unhappy. She thought of asking Mrs. Fittleworth to help her, but this she knew would be a stigma upon his family pride, an indignity he would never agree to. She gave up the idea of playing in public for the time, and contented herself with working for the joy in the thing itself.

Sometimes she would go down and visit Mr. Casewell, and play to him and talk "shop," and occasionally she went alone to Sir Philip Ballater's. He had a splendid music-room, which he had suggested that she should use at any time. If she wanted to work seriously, without interruption of any sort, she found that that was the best thing to do. In addition, the house had a curiously steadying effect on her. It was so silent and passionless. Sometimes Sir Philip himself would come and listen to her, and somehow she did not mind him being there. He seemed to reflect a placid orientation of the finely wrought earthenware, something toned by centuries of cultivated eclecticism, almost impersonal and universal.

Once or twice she went to see John Braille, and she was amazed to discover a fact concerning him. He had always shown a remarkable insight and a sympathetic knowledge of music, but to her surprise she found that he had been to every recital she had given in London, and he seemed to remember nearly everything she had played. She found a curious satisfaction in telling him little things about herself, and it was he more than any one who encouraged her to work. He had also that quality that stimulated the mind. He was tremendously virile, and she came away from her visits to him feeling buoyant and ambitious.

She had often thought of Irene's suggestion that she should go and see Uncle Grubhofer, but had so far been afraid. There was something about Irene's remark, "Don't go if you 've got a split lip; it will make you die!" that caused Olga to shiver. She could not bring herself to make this visit. She had one day thought of asking Harry to accompany her, but she knew that if it were in any way unpleasant, the breach between them would become wider. Moreover, Karl had turned up again with another pathetic story. The man with whom he was in partnership had robbed him and disappeared. Karl was starving in London. There was another very painful evening, Karl having pushed his way in while Harry's sisters were there, and he seemed inclined to make a scene. He was eventually got rid of with four pounds, which was all the available cash in the house. But the affair had had unpleasant consequences. Harry's family had taken the matter up, and were anxious to put the police on Karl's track. They thought it was "too bad that poor dear Harry should be troubled in this way." Olga had objected to the procedure, and an ice-cold enmity immediately sprang up between her and the family, an enmity that nothing would be ever likely to assuage.

From the day when she had spoken to Harry about being "satisfied," he seemed to keep a little more aloof from her, but she observed that he set to work in a rather furtive manner upon a "tone poem" that he had started the previous winter. He was always secretive about his compositions. He only discussed them and played them to Eric Shaughan and one or two other protagonists of a very advanced school. They spoke in terms of pitying contempt for all other schools. She knew that they had a mild admiration for "Wagner and found certain old-fashioned virtues in Beethoven, but she had heard Harry say that "Schumann bored him to tears"; neither did they take any great interest in the work of the other older composers. They discussed Strauss and other modern composers, and even then without enthusiasm. Moreover, they all held, she knew, a contempt for what they called merely "performance." She was fully aware that it did not really interest Harry to hear her play. He was only' interested in what she played, and when it happened to be something in his own rather neurotic line.

It was therefore an unfortunate fact that the thing which should have been their greatest bond of sympathy—music—was that which tended to alienate them.

One afternoon she was playing a chorale of Cesar Franck. It was a thing she had been working at for some time. She was conscious that she was playing it remarkably well. She got the full deep organ quality that the piece demanded. She listened for it coming and heard it die away against the four walls of the room.

A sudden feeling of depression came to her. What was the good of playing like that to four walls? "Would she never again feel the electric response of a listening crowd? Were these four walls to be the tomb of her ambitions? She wanted so much to give all that she felt with regard to this chorale to some one who would want to receive it, but the music died away against bricks and furniture. She got up from the piano and went to the window. It was a gray day and the wind was turning the leaves of the mulberry-tree. She thought she would go over to Sir Philip Ballater's and practise there. And then it occurred to her that even there the sound would only die away. It is true it would go further, and percolate among the limbo of centuries; it might even pass through Sir Philip himself, but it would eventually die against marble and inanimate things. And then suddenly she thought of John Braille. . . .

The large leaves of the mulberry-tree were slowly turning and flapping each other and occasionally revealing the unripe fruit. She would like to convey those large organ tones to John Braille. They would flood his soul and something would spring to life. She could almost see the sensitive, quivering nostril, the strong fine lines of the face, and the keen sympathetic eyes. He would understand. There would be little need to speak. He was so sure, so—wonderfully in tune.

The day was drawing in. He would be finishing his work now. It was almost too dark to paint already. She would go and see him. She went up-stairs and put on her hat, and got the maid to telephone for a cab.

In twenty minutes' time she was at the door of his studio near Portland Place. "When she entered the studio, she saw him in the half-light. He had on a very painty overall, and he was vigorously washing out some brushes at a sink. He looked up, and she thought he started, like one awakened from a dream. He smiled a welcome to her and just murmured "Ah!"

He wiped his hands on a towel. Then he pulled a chair up to the hearth, where a log fire was burning, and turned on an electric light standard on an oak table by the wall.

"Won't you sit down?" he said. He spoke as though he had expected her. On an easel in the middle of the studio was the freshly painted head of an elderly woman. He followed her eye fixed upon it.

"This is Lady Schuck," he said, "wife of the dealer! Please don't let it worry you. I 'm afraid it 's a shocking pot-boiler."

"It 's fine," she answered. "I envy you. Tell me, Mr. Braille, is it wicked to be ambitious?"

"I think it 's wicked not to be," he laughed.

"I 'm tired of playing to four walls," she said. "I don't think I 'm greedily ambitious. I don't want to be an infant prodigy again. But I want what I can do to get through to some one. Do you know what I mean?"

Braille looked at her with one of his keen glances. Then he drew up a stool and sat opposite her by the fireplace.

"Of course," he said, "you must play. It 's absurd. All art is a telepathic business; it 's just what we convey to others. One has to 'get through, ' as you say. I could certainly not paint a stroke if I thought that no one would ever see what I did."

"I 'm glad you think that," she said.

"Let 's think what it really is," continued Braille meditatively. "I suppose it 's a development of our primal love instinct. I walk along a country lane and I see a rick against a ploughed field, and I think to myself, 'By Jove, that 's jolly!' I hug the vision for some time, but it 's not enough. I think, 'By Jove, old Tony Saunders would like that.' I am filled with a desire to remind Tony Saunders how jolly a rick looks against a ploughed field, to share my vision with him. But not only Tony Saunders; there 's Jimmy Carthill—he 'd like it too—and a lot of other people. I am immediately obsessed with a crazy passion to get my vision down, to make a permanent thing of it, so that I may give it to others. Art is essentially a question of 'giving'—one must give all the time. It is the same with you. Some passage of Beethoven fills you with an uncontrollable desire to share the feeling it produces on you with others, to fill the world with it. To practise always within four walls, with no hope of 'getting through,' would send any one mad. It would be spiritual starvation. Too horrible to think of,"

"I think that too," said Olga eagerly. "It 's so nice of you to talk like this."

Braille laughed, and they looked at each other for some moments. Suddenly he said:

"Play me something now."

She smiled at him, although her eyes were moist.

"Would you really like it?" she asked.

He got up quickly and walked to the grand piano in the corner of the studio, and opened the lid. Then he came back, and took her cloak from her, and said in a low voice:

"You know I should love it."

She took oft' her gloves and sighed. Then, going to the piano, she sat down, and played the chorale of Cesar Franck. When she had finished she looked at him out of the corners of her eyes. He was standing very straight on the hearth-rug and gazing at the ground. There was something knightly about his pose, as though he were holding himself four-square against the tumult of a great remorse. She rose from the piano, and for some reason they could not speak to each other. It was as though something had happened of which they were afraid to speak. She came and stood by the fire, and rested her toes on the steel fender. At last she said:

"Mr. Braille, I have an old uncle I want to visit. I have not seen him for years. I 'm afraid he is a terrible old man, and he may be ill—I don't know. But honestly I am afraid to go by myself, and I do not think Harry would care to go with me. I wonder whether you would accompany me one day?"

Braille passed one hand over his brow, and then said:

"Of course. Where does he live?"

She took the envelope that Irene had written on, out of her bag. It was an address in Netting Hill. She came very close to him and showed him the envelope. He gripped it firmly and took it to the light.

"Notting Hill!" he said. "Why not go now?"

It was nearly six o'clock, and Olga had to be back for dinner at eight. They decided that it would be just possible, by taking cabs each way. As they drove along she told him all about this Uncle Grubhofer in little jerky sentences, and also about the rest of her family.

The cab drew up at a buff brick house that overlooked a canal. It was almost dark. A young hollow-cheeked woman opened the door, and peered at them.

"Could I see Mr. Grubhofer?" asked Olga faintly.

The woman stared at them vacantly, then she went to the foot of the staircase, and called out:

"Mrs. Mahoney!"

There was no answer, so she clattered up into the darkness, and left them at the door watching the flickering gas-jet, that threatened to be blown right out, and conscious of the comfort of each other's presence. They heard voices up-stairs, and then the woman returned and said:

"What might ye be wanting with Mr, Grubhofer at all?"

Olga answered:

"I am his niece, Olga Bardel. I would like to see him."

The woman stared at her again, and then once more mounted the stairs. There was more talking, and then the voice called down:

"Will you be coming up here then?"

They entered and Braille closed the front door. Olga went first, but he kept close behind. At the top of the landing, on the right, was a room lighted by a candle. There were two women there, and the one who had let them in came out and passed by them down the stairs. The other was an old woman with short gray hair, and an aquiline face, with dark eyes like a bird's. She was sitting on a rocking-chair by a meager grate, and she did not attempt to rise. She called out in a shrill voice:

"And who is this ye 'll be bringing with ye? Olga Bardel 'll visit y' old uncle, is it? And he dying and alone in 's old days. "

Olga did not know who the old woman was, but she said:

"Dying! Is it—really so—so bad as that? May I see him?"

"Ay," said the old woman. "Come and feast your eyes on the lovely sight—come and see the poor boy passing out to beyond. Who would be helping him now but Ellen Mahoney?" She stood up, and held the candle close to Olga 's face, and said:

"Ay, the spit and image ye be of that same troll. Ye have the same cow's eyes 'ud lure me boy from me in the old days and then leave him for that spavined spawn of Israel—Nathan Bardel—lure him and break him, would ye?"

She suddenly raised her voice, and led the way through a folding-door into another room.

"He 's lying here now, the pretty baby. Come and see the pretty sight, Olga Bardel—"

The three of them passed through the door. The inner room was larger, and was lighted by five large candles, that illumined a bed of massive proportions. On the pillow was the dark masque of a head, with the eyes opened watching them. Olga gasped, and for some reason remembered one of the last occasions she had seen Uncle Grubhofer very distinctly. It was when he was greedily eating off a plate in a palatial hotel in the Midlands. It seemed—not very long ago. How strange it was! How wonderfully serene and quiet he looked—almost majestic. His cheeks were hollow, and his gray hair and beard seemed darker, and lent to his face a patriarchal dignity. All the passion, and malice, and greed had passed out of him. He lay there watching and waiting, in an impenetrable repose. Something told her that he would never speak again, never move; he would lie there till the time came when he would glide away into the shadows. She suddenly thought with a shiver of Irene's remark, "He 'll make you die! Don't go if you 've got a split lip!" Was it possible to be more inhuman than that? Was every shred of hope in Irene crushed? or was this the last cynical cry of a soul that was afraid of itself?

She approached the bed, and touched one of the arms hanging straight and stiff outside the quilt. She murmured quietly:

"Uncle!"

The unseeing eyes blinked at her, and she was not terrified. It seemed that all terror was dead, all remorse, everything vile. Yet in the background there raged the dull reverberation of a spent storm. The voice of the old woman was saying, "Ay, you may call the pretty one. Call till your crow's throat rusts. He 'll never come back to ye. And the Blessed Saints 'll know it was Ellen Mahoney herself who nursed him when he was called, not the dark troll of the city of sin. Ay! and himself knows it, and his lips have prayed to the Mother of God of her."

Who was this old woman? What strange romance of the past was here being shouted across the years? She looked at John Braille, and she believed that in the sudden glance that they exchanged they shared a common vision. It was of her mother, "the dark troll of the city of sin."

What was she like, this mother of hers? In appearance—according to the old woman—the "spit and image" of Olga herself. What loves and passions had swayed her life? What was he to her, this figure dying on the bed? Was it possible that at one time he was young, and comely, and strong? Perhaps her lover? She remembered having seen in a drawer at Canning Town a faded photograph of Uncle Grubhofer, which Irene said was taken when he was forty. He wore a curious stock and peg-top trousers, and his face was firmer and fuller than it became in later years. He had Dundreary whiskers and there was the suggestion that he was by no means dissatisfied with his appearance, and that he lavished considerable thought upon it. Something must have happened that suddenly loosened all his moral fiber, made him desperate of himself, the plaything of some wilful passion. Was he really her uncle? She thought of her father, Nathan Bardel, with his mild, appealing eyes. She remembered how bitterly Uncle Grubhofer always spoke of him, bitterly and vindictively, as though the hate of him colored all his actions. As she looked back on those days it appeared as though Uncle Grubhofer pursued a deliberate policy of spite and hatred upon the children, as though he rejoiced at every evidence of vileness on their part, and laid cunning traps to keep them so, as though he were not merely satisfied with the wretchedness of their bodies, but as though he wanted to destroy their souls.

These thoughts flashed through Olga's mind, prompted by the ravings of the old woman with the candle.

Ah, God! what was this love that outlived all the stress of these tumultuous passions? The old woman too had felt the glow of youth; doubtless, in gay rooms she too had danced, with "dark carnations in her hair," her blood had stirred to the rhythm of the strings. She too had known the pangs of love, of jealousy, despair. They had left her worn, battered, like the husk of some dim passion. What was it that made her stand there, holding the candle like a fiery star above her, content that in the end, she—and she alone—found beauty in the ravages of death, content that it was she alone who had drawn from those lips the prayer "to the Mother of God of her"?

How fierce she looked! the animate eyes belying the tremulo of the quavering voice.

She could not understand a lot of what the old woman said, but she heard for the first time that it was her birth that caused her mother's death. Her mother, it seemed, was a faithless, irresponsible hussy who mixed in vile company, danced, sang, drank, and knew no master. She left behind her a trail of sorrow, sin, and broken hearts. It appeared that she had lured Uncle Grubhofer from the arms of his bride-elect, lured him away, destroyed him, and left him.

Olga could not stand to hear this story, and she could not believe it. She stood there dazed, and trying not to listen to the old woman. She was conscious after a time that the strong hands of John Braille were supporting her arm, and he was leading her downstairs. He had said or done something to quieten the old woman, for they passed down the stairs in silence, and at the door the younger woman curtsied and called John Braille "Your honor."

The cab was waiting, and when they entered it she was tremendously alive to the comforting virility of his contact. She felt very shaken by the experience, and she still clung to his arm. She kept feasting her eyes on the clean-cut sanity of his face, and drawing strength from it.

Was it possible that her mother was really like that? and if so, what of herself? She suddenly thought of Harry. What would he think if he knew? How would he have behaved if he had been there?

"I'm afraid you 'll be thundering late for your dinner," said Braille's clear voice.

She sighed and gave a little gasp of relief. This sudden appeal to material, every-day things steadied her. She tried to laugh, and said:

"Yes, I shall have to invent some excuse." And then she added:

"I don't think Harry likes me—visiting my relations,"

"I don't think your Uncle Grubhofer is any more a relation than I am," answered Braille, and he looked straight out of the cab,

"Ah! You think that too, do you?" They exchanged glances, and the cab turned the corner by the Park, Then she said:

"The last time I was late I said I had been listening to 'the drone of London,'"

She looked at him quizzically, and they both laughed, as though they had both found a sudden piquant delight in the adventure,

"I know," said Braille at last, "Why not say that you have been sitting for your portrait to the famous portrait painter—John Braille?"

"It would certainly be a very picturesque lie," she answered.

"As a matter of fact, it would be the truth," he said.

They both pondered over this statement. As the cab was passing along Oxford Street he suddenly said:

"I wanted to ask you, Mrs. Streatham, since the matter has come up. Will you sit for me? I would like to do a full-length of you, but if it would bore you too much, will you let me do a head?"

The cab spun along down Portland Place, and she did not answer. He thought for a moment she had not heard. Her brow contracted, and her eyes looked down at her muff. She seemed to breathe rather rapidly. It was not till they got to the outer circle of Regent's Park, and the streets were silent and deserted, that she said in a low voice:

"Yes, whenever you like."

She said this breathlessly, as though she had uttered some irrevocable edict, the significance of which she was a little uncertain how to determine.

CHAPTER VI

RETROSPECTION

The sun streamed through the long French windows, and gave to the chintz coverings of the drawing-room an almost garish appearance. It was too brilliant a day to allow any furniture, even rare antique, to have a semblance of appropriateness. It searched it out in the remotest corners of the room, and seemed to say:

"After all, you 're only sticks and stuffs. I made you, in my good time, many thousand years ago, in woods and forests, and on the backs of wild beasts. How ridiculous to deck yourself out like this!"

She went to the window and lowered the sun-blind. She was expecting Mollie Fittleworth, who had been on a visit to the States. The room looked better, more "together," in the modified light. It was indeed a very beautiful room, a real Georgian room now, not a modern Georgian room, and the furniture was old and costly. It was a certain satisfaction to her to know that this move into a larger house had been due rather to her than to the Streathams. It was, in fact, due to her dear friend Mrs. Fittleworth, who had died suddenly the year that Richard was born, and had left Olga quite a considerable sum of money, the bulk of which had been spent on old furniture and paying debts. This satisfaction was modified by searing regrets. As she looked back upon these six years she could not resist reflecting on all that she might have done. There was a time when the ball was at her feet. Everything tended to show that with just that little extra fillip she might have been one of the world's great musicians. Perhaps it was wicked to have wanted this, and yet she could not help it. She felt the power surging through her, and the phrase of John Braille would often recur, "spiritual starvation."

For three years after the marriage she and Harry had always been in what were called "financial straits." And then the money had come, with all its golden opportunities. She recalled the terrible conflict that its coming caused between her husband and herself. Terrible because so suppressed and so unreasonable, just two forces silently pulling in opposite directions. She with her ambitions, spiritual and evolutionary, yearning to help that which required helping, trying to grasp the elements of the social equation, and not being able to with any satisfaction, seeking to find her own niche within the ambit of her social life; he, cynical and reactionary, content to amble round in a circle, with no ambitions other than intellectual and social ones, fully satisfied with his material gloss, and the pleasant stimulus of mental calisthenics.

There were days when she had broken her fetters, and performed free and desperate actions. But she could not resist the call of him, or banish for one instant the straining of her heart when she pictured him unhappy. lie was such a baby, such a clamorous, spoilt darling. When the money had come, she had made a bold plan to further both their musical careers, but Harry had never finished the concerto that had been so much advertised and arranged for, and for herself, at the time when this second opportunity came, her other son arrived. Even then she had not lost hope, and when well enough again she started to work once more. But there were many delays: Harry 's insistence on moving into the new house, and all the work that this entailed, and then he had not been well, and a long holiday in the Pyrenees had followed. When once more they had settled down in Hampstead, she knew that for her it would be useless, for the time being, to make further arrangements, for four months later the third child was born. Then she was very ill, and the little girl had died.

Those indeed had been terrible days, and she shuddered to look back on them. She sometimes wondered whether there was in herself some faculty that banished friendship. People seemed to come, to touch some chord in her, and vanish. Had one no permanent hold over those fleeting visions? She remembered that on the day of Mrs. Fittleworth 's funeral, for some reason or other, she tried to recall the face and voice of little Miss Merson, and she found it difficult. Would the memory of Mrs. Fittleworth become as dim? Would all these people she had loved become shadows and pass away? It occurred to her that if Harry went away, if she did not see him for years and years, he would come back to her—a stranger. Irene and Karl and Montague she felt she could never forget in that way. They were more than a vision. They held a pitiless grasp over the roots of her being, but she had no love for them. She had no love for any one except the two boys and the headlong helter-skelter of passion that bound her to her husband.

Emma Fittleworth had married a government official stationed in Scotland, and Mollie had gone to America to stay with relations. But to neither of these girls was she tied by any unbreakable bond. She was aware that the somewhat restrained quality of this affection was due to some defect in herself. She had an affection for them that she shared with the rest of humanity. She often remembered the remark of the woman whom she met with Irene:

"Do you know why I come to this? Because I 'm too fond of it—you know, everything!"

Sometimes she felt that quality in herself. She was too fond—of everything. Sometimes the angle of a pale cheek that passed her in the street would send her quivering on her way; her heart would bleed with sorrow at the pinched face of a child. She would want to take them, all these people, take them and raise them up. No personal affection that she had ever experienced seemed greater or more vital than this impersonal love of the poor, and the down-trodden, and the wretched. On occasions when she had been alone there trailed across her dreams the vision of some compensating splendor, as though the restless anguish of the world could dovetail with some sympathetic image within herself and build a passion, but it would be a passion that should go crashing to the stars.

Perhaps it was some feeling of that sort that made her search deeper and deeper within herself, that made her turn again fiercely and desperately—like a cat that is being robbed of its food—to her only means of subjective expression—her music. Perhaps that was why, when it was so often taken from her, she raged within herself, beating her wings against the confines of this social cage. She was being stifled, smothered, crushed into a wayward, perverse creature. "Spiritual starvation!"

Ah! why, on this afternoon as she sat there waiting for Mollie Fittleworth, with the sun streaming into her drawing-room, must this phrase keep recurring to her and reviving bitter-sweet memories? Why to-day must she think so intently of John Braille? Why to-day were those memories concerning him so vivid?

Perhaps it was such a day as this, so brilliant that the sun had to be shut out. She was seated on "the throne"—as he called it—in his studio. She was dressed in a silver-gray frock, and she wore a black picture hat, such as was fashionable in that year. She sat there—occasionally standing, for it was a full-length. He wore a black screen on his temples to protect his eyes, and to aid the concentration of his gaze. It made him look very queer, like a magician. And surely he was something of a magician. She could not stand there without being aware of the concentrated fury of his gaze—like a frenzy it was, something that consumed her, and revealed her innermost thoughts. They spoke very little till the work was finished, when a man would bring in a tray of tea-things; but she could see his eyes and watch the nervous, sensitive poising of the hand, and then the sudden masterly movement of the brush. He was no courtier when she sat to him. He seemed sometimes almost as though he were unconscious of her, as though he were merely searching for something inside. He spoke at times quite bruskly: "Head a little more tilted!" "No, no; this way!" "Your left shoulder, please," as though he were some wild thing obeying some higher command. It interested her to notice how he worked, and to observe that the action of painting produced in him an elevated sense of excitement. His mind was on a different plane. It was quite noticeable how, when the sitting was over, he would gradually become more normal. She would go and stand by him, and they would look at the portrait, and discuss it. She was intensely ignorant about painting, but it did not seem ridiculous for her to say, "Don't you think, Mr. Braille, you have made my neck too long?"

He had taken all her remarks with the same eager intentness, and discussed them exhaustively. And then the mental process of "cooling down from the picture" would take place in him. He would keep darting back to it for a momentary glance. It became a sort of rallentando of movement till he left it altogether for the day.

Not till then would something of the courtier return to him. Then he would wait on her, and move about the room with big sweeping movements. During those days she worked hard, for John Braille always wanted to know what she was working at.

She had never met any one who seemed so broad and big as he, and yet who could be so gentle. He had a way of speaking to her like a wistful schoolboy thoughts that came spontaneously to him. He would lay them bare and look at them, and they would stand side by side and examine them, in the same way that they examined the picture. In spite of a certain autocracy of bearing, he was always the student, susceptible to impressions, and carrying with him a sort of reverence for mystical and unexplained things. He stood by the prescript of Levitch to fight for the power to renew himself, to "think all over again."

How splendid were those days! They stood apart—in her life—like gleams of gold that will suddenly flood the heavens after a day of rain. How little she realized at the time how much they were to be to her, that in after years the memory of them would be a sanctuary from distressing thoughts!

She had seen the tragedy of those days rise, reach its climax, and die away, and she heard the curtain fall with mathematical precision on its last words. In fact, there was something mathematical about the whole thing. For she had observed its inception in connection with the rallentando mentioned above. She knew that in the mind of John Braille, she and the picture were two very different things. He had the power of putting himself outside her personal contact. He expressed her in paint, or rather it was his own intense personal vision of her that he expressed. He came under the spell of it and it possessed him. When the painting was finished, he shook this vision off, and returned to her—Olga herself. It was as though the spell of her were contending with the spell of his personal vision of her. She would have been blind if she had not been conscious of this. He seemed quite abruptly to lose the power of painting her. She felt that intense gaze fading from his subjective view, and becoming lost in her. It was terrible, and she did not know how to act. She could see the struggle going on under the dark shutter. He gradually lost the naive bruskness with which he had originally ordered her to "hold her chin up." He became sympathetic, and personal, and would keep on saying in a low voice:

"I'm sure you must be tired, Mrs, Streatham."

She remembered the afternoon when she went—it was nearly the end of the summer, on a glorious day like this—and found him sitting deep in thought. He had not heard her come in. His face looked white and set, and he had jumped up and greeted her. And then he turned away. She thought he looked self-conscious, and in a moment he spoke, and she could tell that he did not find it easy to keep his voice so steady as it sounded. He had said:

"I 'm afraid the portrait is not being a success, Mrs. Streatham. I have scraped it down. See!"

And there indeed was the pale ghost of two months' work scraped to the canvas. She had said:

"Oh, what a bother I am to paint! Would you like to give it a rest, Mr. Braille, and take it up later?"

He had seemed very reticent at that, and framed his mouth as though he were about to speak, and then had stopped. He had walked up and down the studio once or twice, looking at her almost furtively, and then had looked at his depleted canvas. At last he had said quite calmly:

"Yes. That would be the best way. Perhaps—in the autumn we can—finish it."

He had seemed rather frigid and at a loss. He had tried to pass off his attitude as she was going, and had said:

"Please forgive me, Mrs. Streatham. I 'm afraid I 'm rather—run down. I want a change. I feel very culpable—wasting your time."

She had struggled to smile, but for the life of her she could not say what she wanted to say. She had said:

"I'm sure it's all my fault. I talked too much."

But she had not meant to say this. She was not quite sure what she wanted to say. Perhaps she had wanted to say:

"Oh, splendid person, please, please, please don't be unhappy. I know something worries you. I want to help you. It doesn't matter about the picture. I 'm only a little thing. If I cause you uneasiness, banish me! banish me forever, only let me always hold the memory of you standing there, looking so strong and splendid. Whatever happens to me in after years, you will always know that the memory of you has made life more possible for me."

But she had not been able to say this, she had only been able to smile through her tears and to shake his hand.

And then some months had passed. He had gone to the Austrian Tyrol, and she and Harry and the child went down to Devonshire. She had but a vague recollection of those days except that they all seemed the same, and the Streatham family was there, and they all did the usual things that one does at the seaside.

On the return to London she had telegraphed to him that she was back, and could continue the sittings, and he had replied asking her to come on the morrow.

He had seemed bronzed and well, and he had given her an eager smile of welcome. The old canvas was in its place and everything prepared. They resumed their silent intercourse, and she felt strangely happy sitting there listening to the occasional dropping of a cinder in the stove, and the stealthy movements of the brush on the canvas. She was watching and listening very intently, and once or twice she thought she heard him sigh. At the end of twenty minutes he had said:

"Won 't you have a rest, Mrs, Streatham?"

She had answered:

"No; please go on."

And then she thought he sighed again. He seemed to hover restlessly in front of the easel, and in a few minutes he had said:

"Tell me, what have you been working at?"

"Alas!" she had answered, "I have been very lazy. I have had a complete holiday. We did nothing in Devonshire. "

Then, after a pause, he had said:

"By Jove! you look awfully—well."

She had laughed and answered:

"Yes. I 'm afraid I 've upset all your coloring."

There was no rallentando of transition from the picture phase to the personal phase on that day. He suddenly dropped the picture altogether, and came over and talked to her. It was as though something had been freed in him. He spoke gaily and boyishly, and insisted on her not sitting for long at this first sitting. They suddenly became intimate again, and sat facing each other, exchanging mental experiences. They talked of Bohemia, and the effect of physical conditions on character. He spoke of his father—Admiral Braille—of whom he had not spoken before.

"His character was molded by the sea," he had said. "Sometimes when I am in doubt how to act, I try and visualize my father's eyes. He used to say, 'Man has chopped the precepts of his conscience into a thousand fragments, but the doctrine of the sea is never wrong.'

It is a great consolation that, something vast and incorruptible that may always be gone back to. I have read many books, sacred and profane, and they have given me many impulses, but they have taught me nothing of fundamental value that I could not read in my father's eyes." He had seemed volatile and discursive after that, and had brought her her parasol and chatelaine with an air of mock reverence. It was only just as she was going that something happened that shook the foundations of this engaging edifice of happy communion. Her shoe-lace came undone, and she put down her parasol, and went back to the throne. She put her foot up on the throne, and stooped and tied it. The action took perhaps two minutes, then, as she looked up, she saw him standing six paces from her. He was leaning forward, and his eyes were fixed upon her with a strained and tortured expression. Their eyes met and in that glance was born the indelible impress of an understanding. They were both strangely silent, breathing quickly. He hardly dared to look at her again, and he handed her her parasol once more and bowed with a curious, old-time courtesy.

Ah! why had she stooped like that? What was this conspiracy of nature that had used the curves of her body to send him cringing from her? How happy they might have been even now, with their fine occasional communion of thoughts! She had returned that day trembling with apprehension. She knew the catastrophe was coming. It was no surprise to her to receive his note that same evening:

It is no good. I cannot finish the portrait. I will call tomorrow to say good-bye. J. B.

And then, that day! Ah! how vivid and poignant every moment of it had been! She had waited for him here in this same room. She remembered that the nurse was going to take the child out, and she had hoped they would go before he came, but of course they didn't. Things never did happen like that. She brought the child in soon after he had arrived. But what had happened up till then? She was standing here, by the fireplace. The maid showed him in. He advanced rapidly and took her hand. She knew that her hands were cold. She could not speak. She put them both in his and he crushed them together in his strong grip. He drew her over there to the settee, and they sat down side by side. They did not like to look at each other, and like the weak fool she was, she could not keep back the tears that trickled down her cheek. He did not leave go of her hands, but she knew that his head was very close to hers, and he was devouring her whole soul with his glance. And then he said something so magic, the exact sound of it would ring through her ears forever: "Olga dear, you must not be unhappy!" It was the first time he had called her Olga! She "must not be unhappy!" Heavens! what was this madness? She could not keep him and she could not let him go. Forces suppressed within her all her life found their apotheosis at that moment and cried out in desperation. What had all this silly business of life to do with this? What did she care? The stars were calling, what did it matter if the satyrs piped, and the inane edifices of humanity crumpled to the dust? Happiness! Why should she not fight for that secret within herself, that surging desire to seek a compensation in some blinding passion that would raise the images within her to the heavens? Had the world been so glad a place for her, so understanding, so sane? Did she not feel within herself something greater than the life expressed around her? Should she not fight for this, tooth and nail, like a wild beast expressing its primitive virility? She put out her hand and touched the hair upon his temple.

"John," she had said, "you . . . you, tell me, are you happy?"

And then he had burned her with his eyes, the longing was so tense, so poignant. She had given a little cry and put her hand across his eyes, as though she dare not let them see how much she understood.

He had sat there then, immobile, like an image cast in bronze, looking down at his hands.

It was at this moment that the nurse brought the child in. In the constrained minutes that followed, in which they both sought to find the matter-of-fact things to say, she was conscious of him gazing at the child as though he were transcending the inner mysteries. Some impulse bade her dismiss the nurse, and she took the child herself and hugged it to her bosom. She did not know why she did this, for the child at once seemed a burden to her, and she wanted to send it away again. It awakened, too, and seemed conscious of its importunity. She rocked it on her knee, and in a little while the querulous sounds subsided. She smiled and beckoned him to her, and they sat together once more side by side. It was she who ultimately broke the silence.

"Perhaps," she said, "one day you will find it in your heart to finish the portrait."

He had looked at her with that wistful, boyish look, and said:

"Who knows? Perhaps one day the vision of you will not blind me . . . perhaps one day when the nails in my flesh have lost their power of transmitting agony, I may not be ashamed to come to you. Then I shall paint you as 'The Mother' looking down at her son. I shall be modest then, reverent— they often accuse me of insolence as a painter!—I shall have passed through the great fire. Strange, isn't it, that subject that all the greatest masters have painted, that they have excelled at painting— the subject of 'The Mother'? It is always that—the Mother looking at her Son. Perhaps it is because it is so symbolical of sacrifice. Fire and anguish, and lo! something indestructible is born!"

She leaned towards him, and her face was flushed.

"Oh, my dear," she had said. "My dear! My dear! You asked me if I were unhappy. Good God! I am! I am! There is nothing for me, no hope, no refuge, if you do not help me."

He had looked startled at her desperate appeal, and she had suddenly added, with the tears streaming down her cheeks:

"If you were to ask me, I would throw my child from me. I am alone. Do you understand?—alone in the great drab world."

She saw him tremble and go to the window. He stood there very erect, his nostrils quivering. His chin was set, and suddenly he turned and looked at her. She was conscious of some great change in him, and the knowledge came to her that in that tragic interval he had been gazing into the vision of his father 's eyes. She rose and went toward him, but lie put up his hand, and cried out:

"No, no! Let me look at you again like that."

She obeyed quite easily, as though she had no power to do otherwise. She could not remember how long she had sat there looking down at the child, but she knew that at length he had come and put his hands, one on either side of her head, and raised it gently, and looked at her. And then he had touched her hair, passing his hand over it as though forming an imaginary frame. And then, without looking back, he walked on tiptoe from the room.

How vividly the whole thing came back to her to-day as she sat there in the drawing-room, listening to the singing of the brass kettle on the tripod, waiting for Mollie Fittleworth. She rose and looked at herself in the mirror. She had not aged much during these years, and yet it struck her that she did not look an appropriate hostess for such a room. It seemed to demand some one gayer, of a different mould. As she turned once more to the table, the door opened, and a maid entered, followed by a vision of loveliness.

"Miss Fittleworth."

The maid's announcement was drowned by the cry of greeting from Mollie herself.

"My dear! how good it is to see you again!"

The women embraced, and then Olga held the younger one apart.

"My dear," she exclaimed, "how pretty you 've grown!"

The flush of pleasure that lighted Mollie's features at this remark did not tend to lessen the impression. She was indeed a very pretty girl. Her brilliant coloring and bright eyes and the mass of fair hair cunningly waved beneath her hat emphasized the vivacity of her engaging presence. There was still something of the rogue about her, and her eyes never ceased to sparkle with the joy of living.

"I 'm just dying to see the children and to hear all your news!" she exclaimed.

It occurred to Olga that as she sat there in the setting of chintz and satinwood and the glitter of little silver things, how well she took her place. John Braille would like to paint her sitting there. He would call it "The Hostess." He would find an amount of mordant "fun" in doing it.

"You must have tea first," she said. "And tell me all about 'God's country.'"

And then Harry came in. He was dressed in flannels—for they still went to the Guildefords to play tennis. He looked very handsome to-day. The years had affected him little, except for the slight increase of girth, and a certain inelasticity in the lines of his face. She saw him advance, and his eyes suddenly lighten with undisguised admiration when he beheld Mollie. There was considerable laughter in recalling old days, for Harry could hardly believe that this was the little fair child that he met at Mrs. Fittleworth 's so many years ago. She soon noticed that he assumed one of his gay, animated moods that he always put on when any one was present whom he wanted to please, and Mollie sparkled with pleasant Americanisms that she had gathered on the other side. Olga's task as a hostess soon became a negligible one, but after a time she said:

"I 'm going to America too, Mollie; so you must give me some introductions."

They both looked up at her, surprised, and she continued:

"Yes, I 'm tired of inactivity. I 've been talking to my agent, and he thinks that if I play here in the autumn he can arrange a tour for me in the States next year."

"My!" exclaimed Mollie. "But what will you do about the babies, dear?"

"I have an excellent nurse," said Olga; and then, after a pause, she smiled and added, "And you can come, and keep an eye on them sometimes, Mollie, if you 're here."

CHAPTER VII

"THE COMFORTABLE CRUCIFIXION"

She was lying on the couch in her hotel—the Chateau Barzac—at Quebec. On the morrow she was to return to England. The tour had been what is known in the musical profession as a "half-success." Her agent, a small, frog-faced man in New York called Johansen, of tremendous virility, had raged with promises and optimism. But these she found had only been fulfilled in a minor degree. She also suspected that a sum of money that had been advanced to him for advertising purposes had only partially been expended, and she had experienced the greatest difficulty in getting her fees from him. The worry of this, added to the discomfort of living continuously for three months in overheated trains and hotels, had brought about a slight nervous collapse. She had had to cancel the last three weeks of the tour and rest in this hotel in Quebec. The placid little American woman named Edith Yarrow, who had acted as companion and courier to her, had had to return to Boston that morning.

She rose and went to the window. It was a gorgeous view. She looked down on to the roofs of the old town. The whole country was buried in snow, except where the waters of the St. Lawrence, reflecting the blue vault of the winter sky, rode proudly seawards.

In spite of her illness and the unsatisfactory business arrangements, she had enjoyed the tour. She had felt that she was to an extent satisfying some fundamental purpose. She had again felt that "magic thrill of listening crowds," many people had been kind to her, and in some towns she had had a great success. Nevertheless her heart was yearning for the two children, and she was always thinking of Harry, and worrying about the little things concerning him, wondering whether he was being properly looked after, and whether he was wretched without her. He wrote her short affectionate notes, and when she was tired she yearned for the warm embraces of his arms and the pressure of his heart against hers.

The bright winter sun danced upon the snow. In ten days she would be back. She would feel the warm comfort of her home life once more around her. She would not give up her playing. She would work harder, and be more ambitious, but she would stifle something within herself, and be loyal to the conditions fate had imposed upon her.

She put on her furs and went out into the sun. It was entrancing, this town, with its tortuous streets, and its old-world associations, and its sturdy habitants, introducing a note of French vivacity into the stern business of living. It seemed peculiarly peaceful after the almost fantastic modernity of the American cities. She went to the post-office and sent a cable to Harry:

Passage booked Saturday Philomena love.

OLGA.

Then she wandered down towards the river. As she passed through a narrow street of dilapidated buildings, a tall man in tattered furs passed her. His face was wan and his black, unkempt beard gave him a wild, bizarre appearance. He looked at her abstractedly and passed on. When he had gone about ten paces, they both turned, and looked at each other simultaneously. She gave a cry, and ran towards him.

"Montague!" she called.

He stood there gazing at her, as though probing the depths of his memory, and then he said in a low voice:

"Olger!"

She put out her hands, and he held them tight. She was conscious that in spite of his disheveled appearance and his gaunt and hollow features, there was about him some wistful and humanizing quality. His eyes lighted with pleasure at seeing her, and he murmured:

"My! . . . Olger! It 's little Olger!"

"I 've been playing here," she said, "on a tour. I 'm going back to-morrow. Can 't we have a talk? "

He looked down, and said:

"I 'm working till seven o'clock—unloading timber. Could you—could I—see you this evening?"

"Will you come to my hotel?" she asked.

He looked at his clothes, and smiled, then shook his head.

"I can't do that," he said. "Will you come and see me, 337 Montcalm Avenue, just above Powel's saloon?"

She nodded and answered, "All right, Montague, I 'll come. 337 Montcalm Avenue," and she wrote it down.

He scratched his ear and grinned at her once more, then, taking off his cloth cap, he slouched away.

She thought it as well that evening, in view of the cold and her recent illness, to hire a sleigh, and she arrived at the address Montague had given her just after half-past eight. She told the driver to come back for her at half-past nine.

It was a poor but solidly built house, with double windows like nearly every other building in Quebec. She passed through a passage that skirted a saloon where men were playing a game something like skittles, and some one was singing to the accompaniment of an accordion, and went up the stairs. On the first landing there were several doors, and there seemed to be a good deal of noise and confusion, but Montague was standing there, waiting for her. He smiled a welcome and said:

"Come into my room."

She followed him into a square room where there was a bed and a table and a few other odds and ends of furniture. There was no stove, but it was apparently centrally heated; it seemed warm and was fairly decent. He gave Olga a chair and sat on the bed himself.

"This is one of the Skinner buildings," he explained, "laid out for mechanics. Three dollars a week I pay. Not bad, is it?—includes a hot bath any time. Great country this is. A man may live here and be free," and he made a sweeping movement with his hand and then said:

"Now tell us all about yourself, Olger."

He seemed to have lost the apathy that was so characteristic of him in the old days. He spoke roughly but eagerly, and was obviously anxious to hear her news. She told him as briefly as possible that she was happily married, and had two children—both boys—that she still played the piano, and had just had a successful tour through the States and Canada.

"Yer 'usband didn't come with yer, then?" Montague asked when she had finished.

She hesitated and said:

"No; you see it 's such a long way and so—expensive. Besides, you see, he is a composer—it would have wasted his time."

Montague said, "I see!" and he looked at her narrowly.

"Now tell me what you 've been doing," she asked quickly.

Montague passed his hand over his beard and looked down. He seemed to be trying to remember something, and at last he sighed, and said:

"Oh, I dunno—most everything. Trying to do and undo, trying to make and unmake. Doing things, and then wondering why I do 'em—going round in circles like."

"We all do that," said Olga.

"Yep," said Montague, looking up at her again. "And the happier you are the smaller the circle is likely to be."

The sound of the accordion reached them from below. The doleful sounds immediately reminded Olga of the last evening she had spent with Irene. She must not tell Montague the truth about Irene. It seemed strange, but she instinctively felt that it would probably upset him very much.

"He has improved," she thought, "beyond all recognition. Fancy him saying that about the circles! What has Montague been through that has raised him above the others?"

Montague fidgeted about, and then, without looking at her, he said in an altered voice:

"'Ave yer seen anything of Karl and Irene?"

She was prepared for this, and she answered:

"Not for a long time. Karl had some work in Paris, something to do with horses. Irene—I have not heard from for many years. She was living with a—lady then. Uncle Grubhofer died, you know."

Montague looked at her with a far-away expression, and then he said:

"Uncle Grubhofer, you still call 'im, eh? You don't know, then?"

Olga shivered slightly, and then said:

"No. I don't know. I was there just before he died. There was an old woman there. I had the idea— But what does it matter now, Montague? It 's all over!"

Montague lighted a cigarette, and his hands trembled.

"No one can never say that it don't matter, never!" he enunciated. "Lord! we 're all victims of it. Don't you see, we 're all the playthings of little things that 'appened long ago? 'Ow many of our aristocratic families are descended from the mistresses of kings what died thousands of years ago, eh? Think of that! That 's something to think about, ain't it? The sport of idle passions, eh? Each one of us at some mad time, eh? D' you know what I 'appen to know? When Uncle Grubhofer—as you call 'im—died, I was in Scotland. I saw it in the paper, and I made a bee-line for London, and went to a lawyer I know of. I was a bit late, 'cause Karl was there afore me. And then d ' you know what we found out? Uncle Grubhofer had left nine thousand pounds! And not a penny could we touch! 'E was no more our uncle than the King of China was! He left no will, and 'e 'ad n 't a relation in the world, and the 'ole bally lot went to the Crown! Nine thousand pounds! forty-five thousand dollars! Think of it!"

Montague opened and shut his hands, and looked at the wall, as though considering whether the amount seemed more attractive in pounds or dollars; then suddenly the tone of his voice changed.

"I don't care. I 'm not sure we 're not better without it. Karl and I quarreled like the devil at the time. I thought Karl would get D. T.'s. He drank and nearly went mad. The lawyer was a nice bloke, and we found out some things. I 'll show yer something. "

Montague went to a drawer and rummaged amongst some papers. At last he found a letter written on a faded mottled paper, which was in an envelope addressed to "Mr. Julius Grubhofer." The writing was in a quaint, formal hand, rather neatly written but giving the impression that the writer had been at great pains to complete it. It simply said:

My dear, this can't go on. I believe Nathan smells a rat, besides it is breaking my heart. H.

Olga's lips turned white when she read this, and she looked at Montague aghast.

"What does it mean?" she said.

"'H' stands for Hilda," he answered, with the pupils of his eyes distending. "D'you know who that is? It 's your mother."

No! . . . No!" Olga hissed her negation as though she had been struck with a whip.

"Oh, yes, yes, yes, it was," cried Montague excitedly. "It was your mother, yours and mine! I found out more than that—the whole pretty story. Oh, my God! the playthings of idle passions, eh? This Grubhofer was engaged to marry an Irish girl. They were both young. He left her in Liverpool because he heard your mother sing one day at a concert. He followed her to London. She was a singer, you know, quite a concert artist. He followed 'er about like a dog. I believe she led 'ira on, amused 'erself with 'im, then chucked 'im and ran away. It must 'ave bin a fine old game. Lord knows what 'appened precisely. The Irish girl turned up, and there was pretty good trouble, no doubt. Suddenly one day she runs off with Nathan Bardel; a tailor from Whitechapel,"

Montague feverishly licked the end of his cigarette and looked at his sister furtively. Then he continued:

"A lot of the rest of it is what you call 'conjecture,' eh? and things what the lawyer found out. 'E was a nice bloke to me. 'E knew Uncle Grubhofer in those days hisself. 'E says 'e was a good-looking bloke and used to attend church and all that. When this 'ere business 'appened, when she went off with the tailor, the lawyer says 'e collapsed like a pack o' cards. 'E lor.st 'is moral sense, says the lawyer. 'E went in for awful vices and spoilt 'is figure; then 'e became religious—you know, mad religious. Then 'e chucked that, as though it weren't no bally consolation, and went after 'er again. 'E followed 'er, and made 'er life a misery. 'E lent Bardel money, tied 'im up with contracts and got 'im in 'is power. Then 'e went to live with 'em, 'E terrorized their lives, d ' you understand? 'E was clever, and Bardel was a fool."

The air was tense and strained; the brother and sister gazed at each other. The accordion was droning on, and a voice kept ascending:

An' he left his little yaller gal
On the ole plantation.
Yalloloo! Yallaloo! he left his yaller gal.
You may hear her sighin',
You may hear her dyin'
On the ole plantation.

"Tell me," said Olga after a long pause, "why did—If Uncle was fond of—Mother, why did he—why did he treat her children—like he did?"

"The lawyer 'ad 'is theory about that," answered Montague. "It 's in some ways the only good point about the 'ole awful business. 'E believes that in spite of everything—Mother never—"

Montague's voice sank to a whisper and neither of them dared look at each other.

"You know what I mean, Olger—whatever might be said, we 're Nathan 's children! Don 't you know 'ow 'e liked to 'arp on that?—'Nathan's children,' 'e says! It was always that. 'E saw all 'is chances go, 'e became sort of withered, sour, desperit, cruel. 'E nurtured an 'atred against Nathan's children. 'E worked out 'is starved passions on 'em, d'you see? What was it the lawyer calls it? A sort of noorosis! Oh, ray God! D'you know why me and Karl quarreled in the end? It was all over the nine thousand quid we never got. I says to 'im one night, 'Well, thank God, Mother wasn't a harlot!' and 'e says, 'Harlot be damned! We might 'ave had nine thousand quid! ' D ' you 'ear that? 'E says, '"We might 'ave 'ad nine thousand quid!' D'you see what 'e meant? When 'e says that, I struck 'im over the mouf."

Olga jumped up, and the tears started from her strained eyes.

"Oh, Montague," she said, "I 'm glad you did that!"

A strange silence followed, each feeling a quivering sense of satisfaction in the communal understanding between them, but each shuddering under the shadow of these dubious passions that had clouded the past.

"What could she have meant," murmured Olga after a time, "by 'This can't go on'?"

"Women are different to men, Olger; you know that by now, don't you? I can't explain it. She likes the glamour of things, but man is more of an out-and-out—devil. 'E wants all 'is satisfaction or nothing. D'you know what I mean? I don't profess to know what 'appened in that 'ouse in Canning Town, only I look on the fact that Uncle Grubhofer was cruel to us as a satisfactory sign."

Olga looked at him quickly and said:

"Yes . . . yes, I see what you mean. I shall take it so too. I 'm glad you 've thought like this, Montague."

Montague got up and walked up and down the room.

"I 'ave n't always, God 'elp me! You only learn things by experience, by suffering. I believed the worst of everything then. After leaving Karl I think I lost my 'moral sense' too—as the old man said. I 'd saved up fifty pound in Scotland, and I spent the lot inside three weeks. I was as mad as Karl at losing the nine thousand quid, only in my most drunken moments I never lost sight of that point—my mother was straight. I stuck to it in my mind that my mother was straight. I just insisted on it, but I didn't attempt to prove it to myself till afterwards. When I got through my money I worked my way out to South America in a cargo steamer from Bristol. I was very ill on the way and I suffered hell. There was a Liverpool-Irish mate who was over us—"

Montague stared at the wall, and passed his hand over his brow, as though the memories of that voyage were too horrible to look back on.

"I did all sorts of job in Buenos Aires, on the wharf, in stores, looking after cattle, begging and touting in every way. I got locked up once. It was some business in connection with a faro club. I made my way to Mexico after that and lived for a long time on the ranch of a religious Scotchman who had married a Creole woman. They starved me and made me work fourteen hours a day, but there was something about the place I liked; it was—big—romantic, you know; old buildings and great open prairies. I left there because the Scotchman murdered the Creole woman, bashed 'er with the butt end of a gun—mad jealous 'e was. You couldn't believe it—she was one of the ugliest trolls you ever see. 'E managed to hush the matter up, but I cleared out. I hid on a train and made my way up to New Orleans. It was there that I met Tania."

Montague stopped and looked at his sister; then he leaned forward on his knees and kept his eyes fixed on the ground.

"I don't know now whether I 'm glad or sorry I met 'er. She was an American girl of Russian extraction—'er mother was Russian. She tended a bar there, and there was always a lot of fellers 'anging round 'er, I fell mad in love with 'er. I crawled after 'er, and tried to get 'er to run away with me. But she was like a lot of 'em, liked to mess about and lead you on, and play off one against another. There was a feller there, a big man, a foreman in an oil fuel works. 'E warned me off 'er, and shot at me one day with his gun, breaking my arm. I was in the 'orspital for some time. When I come out I goes back to 'er. I 'd 'ad a lot of time to think of 'er, and I was madder than ever. I told 'er a lot of lies and said I 'ad money and I 'd mate her rich. She fell to it at last, and said she 'd go off with me. I was desperit and did n't know what to do, and I stole four hundred dollars from a cigar merchant I knew in the town. But the oil foreman got wind of it some'ow and blew the gaff on me. I was shoved in quod again.

"When I comes out she was living with the oil man. I nearly went out of my mind and drowned myself. . . . One day I 'ears as 'e 's treating 'er cruelly and beatin' 'er. I lay in wait for 'im, and when 'e comes along I challenges 'im to fight. I knew 'e 'd kill me, but it seemed to me the only way. 'E scowls at me and says, 'Meet me to-morrer morning at eight o'clock at Scragg's Gully. ' I never slept that night, but I was there to time in the morning. 'E came alone and we each 'ad our gun. At thirty paces we started blazing. 'Is second shot clipped the top of my ear and then 'is machine jammed. I 'card 'im growl and rush at me. I could 'ave shot 'im like a dog. But I don't know 'ow it was I could n't bring myself to do it. I threw my gun down and went at 'im. 'E seemed surprised and knocked me clean over with his first blow. I was sort of unconscious. I saw 'im stoop and pick up my gun. I thought 'e was goin' to finish me. 'E came up and stared in my face. Then I saw 'im throw the gun away, and 'e threw some water over my face and sat down. After a time I got up and we both walked back to New Orleans without speakin'. When we got there Tania had gone! There was no trace of 'er. We both went rampaging around and on a clue I got I followed 'er to Charleston, Virginia. When I got there, she 'd left. I followed 'er around for four months. At last I got to Chicago. It was one day in the summer. I 'd fairly got on the track of 'er this time. She was a singer, you know, and could dance too like the best of 'em. I found 'er living in a brothel on Lake-side. That did me. I went raving mad. I bought neat spirit and raged like a maniac from morning to night. I made up my mind one night I 'd finish myself. I made straight down towards the lake in the darkness. Suddenly I feels a great 'and on my shoulder and I looks round. It was the oil foreman."

Montague wetted his lips nervously and pulled at his beard.

"I s'pose that 's the rummiest thing that could ever 'appen to any one. 'E says to me, "Ere, pard, don't put on that way; come with me.' I followed 'im to a room at the top of a building near a wharf. 'E 'ad a curious set expression on 'is face. 'E opened the winder and said, 'Listen!' I could 'ear in the distance the sound of music and dancin' and tambourines goin'. 'E comes close up to me and says, 'No one ain't got no darned monopoly in crucifixion,' e says. I could n 't catch the drift of 'im at first, but I did after a time. 'Why should yer burn yer soul out,' e says, 'when you can come 'ere and be comfortably crucified?' Comfortably crucified! My Gawd! I tried to fix that in my mind. D'you know 'ow it is, Olger? Somethin' seemed to come crashin' through my brain like a blaze of light. I think 'e was mad—the oil merchant—stark, raving mad. But 'e wasn't altogether mad when 'e said that. A comfortable crucifixion! Think of it! Don't you know, it was the idea of findin' a sort of sanctuary—is n't that the word?—in what you was suffering. 'E 'ired this room right above the place where she was carryin' on, and 'e come 'ere and 'comfortably crucified' himself. Did you ever 'ear anything like it? I come away then. I give 'im best. I 'd thought I 'd loved the girl, but I see that this big savage oilman left me guessing. I seemed to see lots of things I 'ad n 't seen before. It was as though all this vileness and wretchedness could be stood up against. There was us two—a couple of the choicest blackguards in the Middle West, who 'd tried to kill each other in our passion for this girl, looking at each other like a couple of lambs in that dark room, listenin' with beatin' 'earts to the tambourines and the sound of swishin' skirts, lookin' at each other with a sort of understandin', as though at any minute life might begin all over again. A comfortable crucifixion! My Gawd!"

"You may hear hor siphin',
You may hear her dyin'
On the ole plantation."

Montague wiped his brow. Suddenly he stood up and put out his hands:

"I 'ope you 'll be 'appy in the life you lead, Olger," he said.

She felt an overbearing contraction of her heart. She wanted to help Montague and at the same time to cry her eyes out. At last she managed to say:

"Montague, I 've been getting on quite well, and my husband is well off. Will you let me help you?"

"How could you help me?" he said quickly. He pondered for some moments, and then added, "I'm glad you're happy," and he shrugged his shoulders, as though, as far as he was concerned, the interview was at an end.

CHAPTER VIII

THE RETURN

There is surely nothing so green as the green of Devonshire on a morning in April. The boat train with its load of sleepy occupants crawled through the sea mists of Plymouth just after dawn and raced away towards London. How strange and penetrating is this nostalgia of familiar and endearing things to one who travels. Olga suddenly realized that during her three months' tour in America she had never seen anything really green. Gay hedges and precipitous slopes flashed by. The green was slashed here and there by red clay, and cattle of a very similar color struck a vivid note. She recalled the holiday she had spent there with Harry and the youngest child and the Streathams. She feared she had been a poor holiday companion that year, keeping too much to herself, pandering to those feelings that held her in abstraction. She must make up for that. They would go to Devonshire again this year. She would try and be more companionable. Soon the boys would be growing up. She would have the joy of educating them. She would make them ambitious—in the finest sense. Had she always been fair to Harry? It was very difficult. She had looked up to him so at first, relied on him. And then, when she had found—something missing—when she had, as it were, to take the lead, he had seemed to shrink from her. He had not argued with her. He had simply avoided every question on which they had differed, treating her with an aloofness not untouched with contempt. She made up her mind that she would develop a new intimacy. She would make him talk, even if they quarreled. Quarrels may be outlived, but suppression breeds alienation, indifference. . . . She would get down to what he really thought. She would try and understand his point of view, she would in any case sympathize with it if she did not agree. They must be more to each other. And she would fire him with new ambitions.

She had breakfast on the train, and talked to a nice American doctor and his wife. She felt garrulous and cheerful, more cheerful than she had felt for many years. As the train passed through Surrey, she remembered the morning when she had returned from her visit to Irene at "Lar-r-sham." It was just such a morning as this. She remembered how proud she had felt when the workman had asked her if she minded having the window up. And then the approach through the gray ponderous loveliness of London. There it was, looking just the same! supremely indifferent to whether she came or went. Would Harry be at the station? It was rather early for him. He would not know perhaps what time the train arrived. Perhaps he would have telephoned and found out, and driven down in a taxi? She would not allow herself to expect him. It was perhaps too much to expect. Nevertheless she would keep her eyes open. There was all the business of getting her things through the customs—not that he was much good at that, poor boy! Would he have altered? What would the children look like?

Signal boxes flashed by and great converging masses of rails on either side. The train was slowing down. Her heart beat quickly. There was a rumble and a few spasmodic jerks by the engine, and then they rolled alongside the big platform. Immediately all was confusion. She gripped a few belongings and with great difficulty secured a porter. There was a crowd waiting to meet people. For a second she thought she saw him—a young man in a felt hat—but it was not he, it was a boy waving to an elderly couple. She spent half an hour at the customs barrier. It was very cold, and she felt impatient. At last all her things were passed, and she was installed in a cab. She tipped the porter an unreasonable sum, and they glided off through the yard. Home! In half-an-hour she would indeed be home. She had not thought it possible that she would ever be so happy at the prospect of getting back to that home in Hampstead. How dear and familiar and slow-going the streets of London seemed! The cab darted across the river, skirted the Strand and went up Wellington Street. What was that occasion when she had felt so remarkably like she did at that moment? She remembered! It was when she returned from the visit to Miss Kenway, when she had kept on exclaiming, "Look! Look!" She yearned to say this to-day. She felt very young, as though she had never been in a cab before. She wanted to say "Look! Look!" when they passed the barrows in Camden Town, and she wanted to sing when the cab wound its way up Hampstead Hill. In five minutes she would be home! April! and the little green buds were already bursting forth in the Hampstead Gardens. Here was the road! How slowly the driver seemed to crawl along! She had to call out of the window:

"A little further along, on the right—Wildwood!"

They creaked into the drive and drew up. She sprang out of the cab and rang the bell. A strange maid opened the door and looked at her rather solemnly. "I didn't know Ellen had left," she thought. But she smiled gaily at the new maid and walked straight in. She looked into the dining-room and the drawing-room, but Harry was not there.

"The lazy darling!" she thought. "He's not up yet."

She ran up the stairs and darted into the bedroom. The bed was made up, but it had not been slept in. And then a strange and uncanny feeling came over her. She walked down the stairs more slowly. The new maid was carrying in some things. She said to her:

"Will you pay the cabman?" and she handed her some silver.

She went into the dining-room. It was all very neat and clean, almost as she had left it. A large fire was crackling. Her eye searched the room and alighted on the mantelpiece. There were two letters there. She went up on tiptoe and looked at them. They were both addressed to her and in writing that she recognized. She touched them with her hand, and then drew back, and suddenly looked at the door. For some unaccountable reason, she tiptoed across the room again and locked it. Then she stared across the room at the two notes. She felt physically sick, and had to lean on the table.

Then very slowly she went up to them. She picked them up with trembling hands and threw them on to the table. She could not account for the sense of guilty furtiveness that possessed her. She dreaded being seen. She went to the window and made sure that no one could see through the curtains. Then she went back and listened at the door. The maid had apparently dismissed the cabman—there was no sound of her. Then she took up the letters and sat in the easy chair by the fire, and opened them. Curiously enough she opened Mollie's first. She was in no fit state to read coherently; she saw the writing through a jangled vision. She tried to read the whole letter at a glance. She had the impression of a sequence of wild appeals.

Oh, my dear [it ran], how can I ever expect you to forgive me? You can't imagine what I have suffered and do suffer through you, dear. The thought of you is killing me. But oh, my dear, it is all so inexplicable, so frantically difficult. I somehow can't believe it is really wrong. God would not allow such a feeling. I feel sure, dear, you cannot love him as I love him. I have lain awake at night struggling with this thing. But it is no good. Oh, my dear Olga, you will be brave about this? I cannot believe that it can ever have been so much to you as it is to me—

There was more of this letter, but before she had got to these words she was reading Harry's, starting in the middle.

To say more would be madness. Please try and be charitable to me, Olga. You are so splendid. I know you will have the strength to live this down. I know that in your inmost heart you rather despise me, and for years your love for me has cooled as your ambitions have increased. Of course everything shall be done for you. You shall have the custody of the children, and half my income. I enclose the name and address of my lawyers, who will see that everything is arranged as you wish. To make excuses would be ridiculous. It simply seems to me—this is the best thing for the three of us. Life is a short business, and I do not believe in three people being unhappy because of the conventions. Since the birth of Richard we seemed to drift apart and to have little in common. I am willing to admit that this may have been as much my fault as yours. But I am sure you will be reasonable about it—

There was more of this letter also, but it blurred in her brain. She put a hand to her bosom, and the room became dark. But something inside her kept saying, "Don't give way." She went down on her knees and peered into the fire, as though she expected to find some fuller explanation there. Somehow this had never occurred to her. Her whole mental attitude would have to alter, everything would have to be on a different basis. But her immediate efforts were required to stem the flood of self-pity and the sense of outrage. She could not deny to herself that she had been yearning for her husband, for the touch of him and the sight of him. But now—she would never see him again, never, never, never! Even if she did see him he would be a stranger. All the little sacred intimacies of their connection came crowding upon her, the memory of his voice and of the moments when he had been kind and affectionate. It seemed so cruel, so terribly cruel and sudden. Had she been a fool to go away? and to ask Mollie to come and keep an eye on the children? She fought against this feeling. If it had got to happen, perhaps it were better to happen thus, rather than to linger over years, and for her to watch its gradual growth, to be conscious of its development, with all the secret meetings and heart burnings. Poor Mollie! would he be true to her and kind? Something told her that Mollie was a fitter mate than she. She remembered how it struck her when Mollie entered the room, her appropriateness in the setting of satinwood and tea-cups. She shivered, and the tears ran down her cheeks. His lawyers! She wished he hadn't mentioned them in that letter. The mention of them made her feel lonelier. She had come back to an empty world. The lawyers would look after her!

"Mummy! Mummy!"

She started up and dashed the tears from her eyes. In a second she had unlocked the door and her arms were around her eldest son. She buried her face in him, for she dared not let him see her eyes.

"My darling! my darling!" she kept murmuring. The nurse came down the stairs with the baby, and the same scene was repeated. It was a new nurse, an elderly person. They were all just going out.

"I 'll come with you," said Olga.

She spent the day with the children, afraid to leave them for a moment. She fondled them and played with them, and at seven o'clock helped the nurse to bathe them and put them to bed. Then the hours were approaching that she dreaded. She sat alone in the drawing-room after the children had gone to bed, on an upright chair under the reading-lamp, and knitted. She knitted hard—a woollen comforter for Richard—and blessed the memory of Mrs. Fittleworth who had taught her to knit. She knitted desperately till late at night, and her eyes ached. She tried to control the riot of emotions that pervaded her by concentrating on one or two clear issues: her duty, her children, her work.

She waited till long after all the servants had gone to bed. Then she turned out the light and crept upstairs. There were two bedrooms she might have used other than the one she had been in the habit of sharing with Harry, but by some instinct she chose the old room. It looked exactly the same as it did the night before she left England. Everything about it recalled him. She could almost see him moving about the room, laughing and talking and being impatient about his collar-stud. She could hear the melodious tones of his voice as he addressed her. She could see the boyish attitude of him as he sat up in bed and "ragged" her about the time it took to do her hair.

Curiously enough, in the corner of the room was a case of golf-clubs that had been packed ready to go. He had evidently forgotten them. The golf-clubs affected her strangely. She took them with trembling hands and put them under the bed out of sight. She struggled with herself and pushed back these visions that kept recurring. Very quietly she got into bed and turned out the light. She wished she weren't so tired. It made it so much more difficult. The moon was up and her pale light stole through the casement curtains. She knew she would not sleep, and yet she was so tired. She struggled to withstand the pressure of those memories. It was always when she was tired that she wanted him so much. She could at that moment almost feel his arms around her and his lips pressed against her eyes and hair. This would never, never, never occur to her again. Ah, God! she must not think of it. Was she not a woman? A woman! What did that mean? Did it not mean that she was entitled to her weakness, that she had the right to be loved and petted? A sudden wave of self-pity flooded her and in the still night she sobbed for her own wretchedness. She seemed to see her life in perspective, her sordid childhood, the even more sordid period when she was exploited by the Du Cassons, her brief years of happiness with Mrs. Fittleworth, her infatuation for Harry, her disillusionment, the stifling of her talents and her spiritual ambitions, and then—this! outrage! betrayal! She was alone, utterly alone, as she had always been, as she would always be. Her loves and affections had proved illusions. The man she had taken for a god had come, taken his need of her, and passed on to another woman. Could the children of such a passion be all in all to her? "Would they not, on the contrary'—, be a constant torment? Could happiness in any form ever come to her again?

Happiness! What was it Montague had said?—"the happier you are, the narrower the circle." Was that so? Was there a greater circle, something that stretched out and embraced the heavens? Strange! in that hour her mind kept recurring to Montague. She remembered the queer independent way he turned to her as she was going, and said, "How could you help me?" What did he mean by that? Could we not help each other? or were we all utterly alone, alone to follow these rings of light, to find our own place among the stars? Montague had suffered, he had been through every phase of sin and sorrow, and he had turned to her and with a certain buoyancy had said, "How could you help me?" It was as though out of the fires of the anguish he had endured he had discovered some secret. He had some quality that Karl had not, and that Irene had not. She wondered whether she could not find it in herself. . . .

Suddenly she got out of bed and took the case of golf -clubs from under it and put them on a chair by the window, so that she could see them by the light of the moon.

Her eyes were dry, and she smiled ironically. "This is what Montague would call my 'comfortable crucifixion,'" she said.

She lay there a long time looking at the golf-clubs, and after a while the bitterness passed from her and she slept. It was a fitful sleep, and half an hour later she was awake again and thinking, "It was not his fault. God made him like that. If he wanted her more than me it was—only natural." Then she sighed and muttered, "Poor Mollie!"

Near dawn she was becoming feverish. She had slept little and could not think coherently. She took some phenacetin and tried again.

"It 's got to be lived through," she thought.

At half-past seven a maid came in and pulled back the curtains and brought her a cup of tea. She was beginning to feel sleepy, but after drinking the tea she got up and went into the bathroom. The children were already up and singing about the house. She had a warm bath, and then a cold one, and as she rubbed herself down with the towel she made one definite decision. She committed Harry's lawyers "to the devil." She would have none of them. She had made a few hundred pounds in America. She would touch none of his money. She would keep the children herself. This thought stimulated her.

"There will be a lot to do," she kept thinking.

And in this surmise she was not incorrect. There followed days of strenuous toil, and in their friction her bruised heart found relief. She went to see her agents about engagements. She made efforts to get pupils. She took a much smaller house, and spent two hundred pounds furnishing it. She reduced her staff to a "cook-general" and a nurse. She moved and left the letters from Harry's lawyers unanswered. Neither did she write to him or Mollie. There seemed nothing to say, or rather, there seemed everything to say or nothing. She did not feel capable of writing, so she left it alone. She received a heart-broken letter from Emma in Scotland. Emma now had children of her own, and wanted Olga to go and live with her. The idea appeared to Olga to be preposterous, and she found it difficult to answer it. Then further letters came from Harry and the lawyers and Mollie, all urging her to be reasonable and to accept the money "for the sake of the children." The Guildeford girls called in a state of breathless emotionalism, and cried and kissed her. But she was unresponsive. Then one day a very important looking man forced his way in and interviewed her. He was Harry's lawyer. He talked incomprehensibly and at great length, and fluttered papers in her face. He was a terrifying person, so suave and clever and insincere. She came to the conclusion after he had gone that what he really wanted was that she should divorce Harry. She shivered at the idea, worked harder at her household affairs. The house and the children seemed to take up all her time. She very seldom got an opportunity of practising, and in spite of the success she had had, engagements seemed hard to get, and pupils even more so. She knew that her money would not last forever, and she would have to make desperate efforts to get more work.

The only person who seemed sympathetic to her in those days was Sir Philip Ballater. He called a few days after her return to England. He made no reference to her position, but was extremely gracious. He talked to her about abstract things, and listened attentively to her views on America. As he was leaving, he said in his quiet voice:

"You know, dear lady, I and my house and everything I have is always at your disposal. It may be that, as I have had more experience of the world, you may at some time find my services of some little value. Pray make me happy by making use of them. "

She thanked him sincerely, and did indeed go to him for advice when she took her new house, and, in fact, in all matters connected with business. She felt happy in the clear detachment of his views. He never made her feel self-conscious or restless, and on many occasions when the children were fractious or the demands of the household insupportable, she would walk over to Lugano—as his house was called—and practise in the music-room. After the lawyer had been, and hinted at the question of divorce, she called on Sir Philip to ask his advice, and to her surprise he strongly urged her to divorce her husband. He pointed out that it would not only make her freer, but it would be better for Harry and Mollie, as they would be able to marry. This had not occurred to her.

"Why couldn't the lawyer have said so?" she exclaimed, and Sir Philip smiled.

"It is a lawyer's prerogative to talk in parables," he answered.

It was perhaps more for Mollie's sake than any one's that she eventually set her teeth and determined to go through with the dreadful business. It was in effect rather less dreadful than she had anticipated. The suit, being undefended, did not entail a long trial, but the formalities seemed interminable. During those days she relied more and more upon Sir Philip, and he took a considerable amount of the unpleasant part of it out of her hands. Her agent also took advantage of the publicity that the case created and booked her for several engagements on the strength of it.

"This will be nice for the children when they grow up and understand, won't it?" she said to Sir Philip when it was all over.

The distinguished director looked at her through his pince-nez and sighed.

"Ah!" he murmured at last. "It will indeed be unpleasant knowledge, but it will be better than if—the circumstances had been reversed." Then he paused, and added:

"Perhaps one should not say it so soon, dear lady, but you are young yet, very, very young. It will perhaps be best for the children if their mother marries again before they have reached years of very great discretion."

Olga did not answer. The whole thing was so tragic that all her energies were devoted to avoiding thinking of it. She worked hard from morning to night, and would not let herself dwell too much upon it.

Through the influence of Sir Philip she got appointed as piano instructor at a very high-class girls' school in Buckinghamshire. She went there one day a week, and it became one of her principal means of support. She soon found that the musical profession without commercial backing was a grim and serious business. She gave another recital, and although it was a fair success, it cost her money and nothing came out of it.

"A prophet is not the only person without honor in his own country," the agent had said. "It would be much better if you called yourself Barjelski again."

But she would not do this, and she continued the struggle. She found that since the days when she had made a successful appearance, other girls and men had appeared on the field, and many of them with considerable talent, and many more with considerable influence.

"Given a certain technical proficiency," the agent, who was something of a cynic, had said, "and there is n't one person in five hundred who knows the difference between a great performance and a good performance. After that it 's all a question of push, luck, and influence."

At the same time he strongly advised her not to advertise for pupils.

"If you once do that, you 're labelled as a teacher. You go down the sink."

"Well, what shall I do?" she asked.

"Try another tour abroad—Germany, Holland or the States," he suggested.

But in these cases it meant another outlay of money she did not feel justified in speculating with. "You are a fool," some one said to her one day. "Why don 't you let the man pay for the keep and education of the children? They 're his. He 's responsible. He 's got the money, and he 's quite willing to." But against this idea she fought tooth and nail. Neither could she be reasonable about it even to herself. She felt that if she kept the children she would to an extent justify herself, it would be a sop to her pride. It was strange that, in spite of her sordid upbringing, this was the first time that she had been seriously up against material conditions. She hated and despised them, and would not acknowledge them her master.

"None of these things shall make a slave of me," she thought.

But the struggle was long and bitter. At the end of the year the eight hundred pounds that she possessed had been reduced to one hundred and fifty, and there were many bills owing. Yet she surprised many people with her youthfulness and virility and her eyes glowing with the light of battle.

One evening after she had returned from the school in Bucks, Sir Philip called on her. She was tired out with her day, but after she had washed and changed her frock she came into the drawing-room looking keen and well. He stepped forward and held her hand. After the usual greetings, he said:

"What is your secret, dear friend?"

She looked at him astonished. "Secret?" she asked.

"Yes," he answered. "Everything conspires to crush you, but you look younger every day. It is as though you had discovered the elixir of life's troubles. Please tell me the secret."

She smiled. "I 'm glad you don't think I look too bothered," she said. "I am, though. It 's a wretched world!" She stood by the piano, and her looks belied her words.

Sir Philip seemed curiously nervous and he fumbled with his beard.

"I am desperately ambitious," he said at last. "I hardly know how to express to you my thoughts. You are so young, so independent, so beautiful. But the time comes when these things are—how shall we say it?—less evocative of success. It may become more difficult. These two boys must go to school. They must go into the world and have careers. I am desirous to make this easier of accomplishment for you, and yet I would not for the world offend you."

"Ah!" Olga shuddered slightly. These ideas had occurred to her on many an occasion. Schools! Careers! How on earth was she going to provide schools and careers for her boys? And as she became older it would become increasingly difficult. She knew this, but she would not allow herself to think about it.

"How could you help me?" she said, and as she said it it flashed through her mind that it was the question Montague had put to her. And it occurred to her at the same moment that whereas her offer had been put to Montague in a material sense, he had accepted it in a spiritual sense. She was so concerned with the consideration of this strange fact that for the moment she hardly grasped what Sir Philip's reply was. When she did grasp it, she turned from him and gazed at the lamp. He had said:

"Perhaps I could help you more if you would consent to become my wife."

The proposal was so unexpected that it was some moments before she could grasp its significance. Then she turned and looked at him. Her first thought was, "I must not be cruel to him." He was so kind, so gentlemanly, so "safe." She liked him, she would not hurt him for the world. Tears came to her eyes and she said:

"Oh, please, Sir Philip, you are so kind. ... I have so few friends. I don't think I could marry you, but please forgive me. I don't want to lose you."

He jumped up and took her hand. "There! there!" he said. "It is I who must ask for forgiveness. I am old—"

"No, no, it 's not that," she said quickly. "You 're not old. I am tired to-night. I cannot think very clearly."

He drew his heels together like a fencer, then bowed and kissed her hands.

"I shall always remain your good servant and your friend," he said, and he smiled with the expression of a man who was accustomed to measure time and space in indefinite terms. "If not in this reincarnation, then in the next," a cold-blooded interpreter might have read it. But Olga suddenly ceased to consider his expression at all. Strange forces were at work within her. She was too moved to thank him for understanding and for treating her wayward refusal in the grand manner.

When he had departed, she went to her bedroom and looked at herself in the glass. "Why had he talked of a secret? Her eyes were flushed with excitement. It was true—she was still a young woman. She noticed the curves of her neck and shoulders and bosom. She drew a shawl round her shoulders and crept into the next room, and peeped at the two boys peacefully sleeping. Then she returned to her room and opened the window. It was February. In a few months the spring would be here. Had she a secret? Had n't every one a secret when they felt the warm night wind upon their temples? Was not Night, the mother of all secrets, already at work among the rustling foliage of the garden? She knew at that moment that from the hour when she had arrived home and found the two notes in the dining-room, that she had had a secret that had buoyed her up through those trying days. Perhaps it was sub-conscious, or it presented so dazzling a vision that she had not dared to give it substance in her thoughts. But to-night it laughed at her out of the whispering leaves. "You have been acting, playing a part," it seemed to say. "You are capricious, like all women—and men too, for that matter. Why not be honest with yourself?"

She got into bed and turned out the light. She had forgotten about the proposal of Sir Philip by this time, but before she went to sleep she made a definite resolution.

And as she turned restlessly upon her pillow, she muttered:

"To-morrow, to-morrow, to-morrow!"

CHAPTER IX

Nevertheless her resolution did not take effect on the morrow, for early in the morning the nurse came in to say that both the children were feverish. A doctor was called in, and pronounced the fact that they were suffering from measles. Immediately everything had to be reconsidered. Her work had to be given up, and she shared with the nurse the privilege of nursing them. The youngest boy was very ill, and caused a lot of anxiety. It was many days before he was considered safe; and then it was six weeks before they were both free, and at the end of that time she was very run down herself. The doctor said that a change for all of them was essential. Sir Philip wrote offering her the use of a house he owned near Broadstairs, and after a good deal of misgiving, she accepted it.

It was nearly the end of April when they returned to London, and Olga's mind was filled with resolutions of drastic economies. The nurse would have to go, and she and the "cook-general" would have to manage the household on their own. Expenses in every way would have to be cut down. The future was not roseate, and yet when she went out into the little garden on that first morning of the return her heart was singing.

"I will go to-morrow," she said to herself.

She passed a restless night, on the borderland of dreams which were so beautiful that in her waking moments she dare not contemplate them.

"It is madness," she thought as these recurring images kept passing before her.

In the morning she dressed herself with slow but deliberate cunning. She was conscious of looking her best when ultimately she kissed the children, and went forth to "do a little shopping in town."

It was a glorious day, clear and with light clouds high up in the heavens, and a warm wind. She took a bus to Portland Road and walked.

"No more taxis for me," she said to herself, and she enjoyed the rhythmic movement of swinging along the broad pavement of Portland Place. As she approached the turning where the studio was, she felt suddenly terribly nervous and self-conscious.

"What on earth am I doing?" she thought. "Why am I coming? What will he think of me?"

Her action seemed so blatant and importunate that for a moment she hesitated as to whether she had not better return. She arrived in front of the studio and stared at the wrought-iron hanging bell. She stood there for some moments looking up and down the street, her heart beating rapidly. Suddenly she thought:

"How ridiculous of me! Of course he won't be here now; he will have moved, gone away probably forever!"

She felt so convinced about this that her nerves were to some extent calmed, and she rang the bell. In a few moments a man opened the door.

"Can you tell me if Mr. John Braille is living here?" she asked quite calmly. She knew perfectly well that the man would shake his head and say, "No, madame," and so indeed he did.

"Do you happen to know where he lives?" she asked.

The man stared at her, and said, "I 'll ask Mr. Galrush, madame,"

He disappeared, and Olga stood trembling inside the entrance. Memories and associations were pulling at her heart-strings.

"What a fool I am! what a fool I am!" she kept thinking. Presently a dark Jewish-looking painter appeared. He looked her up and down rapidly, and said:

"Good morning. I 'm afraid I don't know where Mr. Braille went to. He left here about two years ago. I think he went to Rome, but I 'm not sure whether he 's there now."

"Oh!" said Olga. "I 'm sorry to have disturbed you. I presume you don't happen to know the address he went to in Rome?"

The dark painter looked at her closely, and then he said:

"Will you come in a moment? I 'll look in my bureau. I may have an address."

"It 's very kind of you," she answered, and stepped through into the studio. He showed her to a chair and rummaged among some papers. She looked round the room. It was the same dear room, and yet how different! All the glory and dignity seemed to have departed. When Braille lived there there seemed to be nothing in the studio but the picture he was working on, in any case nothing that caught the eye. But this little dark gentleman had packed the walls from floor to ceiling with his bright and meretricious paintings. They were mostly paintings of lovers in Napoleonic costumes posturing in sentimental attitudes in neat gardens.

When Olga beheld this display of redundant eroticism, she felt a wild and unreasonable dislike of the little painter. Braille's studio! Hallowed by the memory of him! What right had this prosperous-looking little picture merchant to profane the shades with his maudlin art? In the very spot where Braille had stood with his eye-shade on his temples gazing at her with fierce concentration, now reposed a large roll-top desk from the corner of which trailed a wreath of smoke from a half-smoked cigar! The fireplace against which she had so often seen the tall erect figure with the head thrown back and the eyes fixed upon her wistfully and boyishly, had been disfigured by a large new anthracite stove. There was the throne where she had sat, where a new world had awakened within her, now occupied by a lay figure in directoire dress. Mr. Galrush was talking to her. He seemed inclined to be garrulous and affable, perhaps a little too affable even for one who had the audacity to desecrate a high temple. She could not listen to him, for her heart was aching so. His face suddenly appeared before her, and his voice at last insisted:

"It is the only address I can find—the Villa Cordone, Rome."

"Ah! thank you; it is very kind."

"Is there nothing else I can do?" He was smiling, his fine teeth gleaming beneath his dark mustache. She could not answer. Her eye alighted on a certain corner of the throne. It was the spot where she had stooped to tie her shoe-lace, her silence did not seem to subdue the little man. He suddenly blinked at her and said:

"Are you interested in Art?" and he glanced comprehensively round the room. She suddenly felt that if he started showing her his pictures she would lose all control of herself. She would cry, or strike him, or do something equally as unreasonable. She gasped and looked at the card, and said in a desperate manner:

"No, I 'm afraid I 'm not," and she almost ran to the door. The little man followed her, and she kept saying, "Thank you so much! It's so kind!" She did not notice the hand he held out to her when she got there, and she ran up the street and hailed a cab. In the cab on the way home she became calmer.

"How ridiculous I am!" she thought. "I knew he would n 't be there! But he must be—somewhere. Perhaps here in London!" Nevertheless she wished she had n't gone. The memory of that throne disturbed her, and the jarring self-satisfaction of the little painter. In the meantime she must set to work. She had a great uphill task before her. The boys were growing up. Richard already should be at school, or should be getting better education than she could give him. She felt annoyed at having taken the cab.

"This sort of thing must stop," she said to herself.

On her return home she set to work once more to get her affairs under control. Her idea of mathematics was deplorable. She could not estimate her income or her expenditure. Bills accumulated, and she paid them when she could. The illness of the boys and the consequent loss of work and expenses in connection with the illness soon put her in a desperate position. But she did not realize it until two months later, when she discovered that her fees from the school where she taught did not amount to enough to pay the rent and the rates, and she had no more. Even then she would not acknowledge that it was a matter to cause serious heartburning. She did the obvious thing. She went to Sir Philip and borrowed fifty pounds from him. He lent it to her with alacrity and showed a nice sense of tact and thoughtfulness over the transaction. It did not occur to her to be in any way a compromising action. It was a natural thing to do. Sir Philip had plenty, and she had none. If the circumstances had been reversed, she would not have hesitated for a second to do likewise.

In coping with overpowering domestic difficulties two years passed away. At the end of that time she discovered, one morning, on looking through her accounts, that she owed Sir Philip eight hundred pounds! And Richard was now twelve and should be sent to a good school. She had passed through many vicissitudes. She occasionally got engagements, but the fees were small. She went on a tour in Germany, Holland, and Scandinavia, but after a great success in these countries, the agent disappeared with all her money, and she could not trace him. Her pupils were irregular and intermittent, but they were her chief means of support. And then one day the youngest boy, Cedric, became very ill and developed appendicitis, and an operation became necessary.

They were terrifying days, and the borrowing of fifty pounds from Sir Philip to pay for the operation was only the least of the evils.

In the meantime she had written two letters to John Braille and each of them had been returned "Gone away." Neither did the Guildefords seem to know of his whereabouts, though the boy McCartney announced one day that he believed that Braille was in Algeria, "painting sand." She felt convinced of one thing—Braille did not know. He had not heard of her tragic episode or he would have come to her. And every day youth and life were slipping away. Surely, surely one day she would see him standing there on the rug by the fire. He would say, "I did not know. Good heavens! how we have wasted these years!" That was her secret. She would sit alone in the evening and knit or read when the boys were in bed, and listen alertly. She had the idea that he would come in the evening or at some mad hour of the night, suddenly and dynamically, and cry out, "I did not know. Forgive me!" She could almost hear the sound of his voice. Ah, God! how her heart was bursting to tell him— everything—all that had happened since he went away, all that she had felt and thought, and the thousand things she dare not feel or think. Her dear secret! Without it she would have died.

One day at Sir Philip's she heard two men discussing Art, and one said:

"By the way, there 's a very good Braille at the Fine Arts—a new one I think—an Arab sheikh. One of the finest he 's done."

"Oh!" drawled the other man. "Is that so? Who was it told me that they thought they saw Braille in town the other day?"

The first man showed little interest in this query and changed the subject, but Olga's heart beat rapidly. On the following afternoon she hurried through two lessons she had to give, and went down to Bond Street. She had little difficulty in spotting the "Braille" in the gallery. It seemed to stand apart—a Triton among minnows—a virile, forceful painting of the Sheikh Raman al Elin. She looked at it breathlessly and felt irritated by the presence of half a dozen other people round the canvas discussing it in languid tones. Having drunk her fill of its convincing beauty, she went to the secretary's office and interviewed a young lady secretary.

"Excuse me," she said, "but do you happen to know whether Mr. Braille is in town, and what his address is?"

The young lady looked at her nonchalantly, and turned up a book. At that moment a large man in a silk hat, who had been standing by the telephone, came forward and smiled. He was evidently an official of some importance. He said:

"Yes, madam, I can tell you about Mr. Braille. He has been in town for a week, but he left last night for India—with his wife,"

Olga looked at him, and then turned her head quickly. She had a feeling that she was going to faint. She stumbled towards the door. She was conscious of the large man following her and saying:

"We can communicate with him, madam, if you wish. Cairns Hotel, Bombay—or we can telegraph to Marseilles or Alexandria."

She managed to say, "No, no, don't trouble, thank you," and got out into the passage. But when she arrived there, she did faint. It was a very momentary business, and two people and the manager came running up. She soon pulled herself together and they gave her smelling-salts and water. She kept repeating:

"How stupid of me! Thank you so much . . . please don't bother!"

The manager insisted on putting her in a cab, and she was grateful for the attention. It was a strange thing that on the way home her mind kept recurring to her husband. She felt weak and ill, and she yearned for his arms around her. There were very few moments when she had allowed herself to feel this, but at this hour the call was irresistible. It was as though something had snapped within her and she were alone, drifting helplessly through the miasma of a febrile world. She had fought hard all her life for something within her, something tremendous and worth fighting for, and then when the large man said, "He went off last night to India—with his wife,"it seemed as though the thing, whatever it was, had never been worth fighting for, as though it didn't matter. What was it she had been fighting for? "Nothing will ever matter again," she thought. People were drifting through the streets, the same people who had drifted on the night when she went down and met Irene and went to the cafe. The drone of London! How horrible it was! She felt a desire to drown herself in it. How splendid to be that third woman who was with Irene, who "loved everything too much!" She would like to get out and walk through the streets and speak to people like that. Perhaps they found some crude satisfaction in their sordid life. If only for a time—But for her, what was there? She knew that if she got out of the cab she would be too tired to walk. She would probably faint again. She noticed a bearded and wretched man crawling along the gutter, with his eyes on the ground; occasionally he stooped and picked up a cigarette end. His face and figure were wasted with disease. She cried softly to herself for pity of him. If there were a God, how cruel were His manifestations of power. Why did He not destroy these at once and forever? "Was this not better than the eternal drone of remorse and despair? All around her was ugliness, cruelty, and terror. And yet to that hour she had believed! Ah, God! she knew now it was all a single-minded, selfish love of hers, something as rank as the weeds around her. She was as bad as the vilest, as bad as Uncle Grubhofer had painted her. "One of Nathan's children," "fit for the prisons and brothels," he had said. She had yearned for her lover. She would have gone to him immediately and unreservedly at any moment that he had called her, either during her married life or after the divorce. She would have left everything—her husband, her children, her honor, her work. She would have flung them aside and have followed him barefoot through the world. This was her "secret"; this it was that through all the travail of those days had kept her foot light, her eye serene, her brow unclouded. And suddenly this dream was shattered and all around her were the sordid streets. Why did they go on living, all these people? Many were too old to hug the illusions that had buoyed her up, many were broken in their youth. Was there a spirit of the hive like bees had, something that drugged their personal desires and drove them irresistibly on to an unknown end?

As the cab was creeping up through the darkness of Haverstock Hill, she suddenly said, "Please God, help me to serve some purpose!" and then she cried again, and shivered in the corner of the cab. She felt calmer after that, and peered out into the dim streets.

Suddenly her mind wandered back to Prague, and she thought of the heavily built American boy—Irwin Cullum. What was it he had said to her? Something about ideas. Ah! yes. "Everything is illusion except ideas." She pondered on this. He had said that the thought was comforting. And he talked of his ambitions. He was going back to San Martino, "a bunch of wooden shacks nestling in a valley." And he had said, "Don't you think I can be ambitious there?"

It was nice to think of Irwin Cullum being ambitious in his obscure town. There must be thousands of people like that, working out their destiny in lonely places, sacrificing themselves for some purpose, living for "ideas."

When she entered the little house she heard the maid-of-all-work quarrelling with a charwoman in the kitchen. It was very dark. On the stairs she heard the laughter of the boys in a room they played in in the front of the house—fresh, gay, irresponsible laughter.

"I would have betrayed them," she thought. She crept into the bedroom quietly and locked the door. Then she lay on the bed in the darkness and wept. After a time she bathed her eyes and went down. The boys wanted their supper. The maid-of-all-work was full of complaints. Many household matters had been neglected and forgotten. On the mantelpiece were bills and a letter from a rich pupil saying that after this term she would not be able to continue her lessons. The boys squabbled at supper-time, and Richard pushed Cedric off his chair and he fell down and cut his temple. It was late before the turmoil of the little house subsided, and when at last the boys were put to bed and the maid pacified, she sat alone in the little sitting-room. On the piano she noticed a layer of dust. She got up with the idea of removing this disfigurement; then something impelled her to resume her seat. In front of her was a pile of bills and a letter from the master of the private school where Richard attended, saying that "he considered him a boy of considerable promise," and suggesting that he should take up certain subjects with the idea of entering for a scholarship at a well-known college. She heard the dreary voice of the maid humming in the kitchen, and all the time her eyes were fixed upon the dust of the piano. Suddenly she got up and made a mark with her thumb on the dust, as though she were doubting its reality. Then she sat there a long time thinking. After a while she lighted a candle and went up the stairs quietly, and went into the boys' room. They were sleeping peacefully, their petty squabbles forgotten, their red, healthy cheeks burrowing into the pillow. She listened to their regular breathing for some time, as though it meant much to her, and then with her eyes glistening she returned to the sitting-room. She sat for a moment on the edge of a chair, and looked into the grate.

"It is finished," she said at last, and started at the sound of her own voice. Then she turned out the light and went into the hall, where she had left her hat and cloak. A desire seemed to come to her to act quickly, as though she were in a terror of reaction. She put on her hat and cloak and clutched the latch-key and went out. She walked quickly through several streets and took a turning that led up to the heath. She found her way through the gorse and presently arrived at the door of Sir Philip's house. She rang the bell. It was now half-past ten. A man-servant opened the door. He knew her by sight and bowed her in.

"Is Sir Philip in?" she asked.

"Yes, madame," he answered.

"Alone?"

"Yes, madame."

She shuddered at this answer, as though she were half hoping it would be in the negative, but she fixed her eyes on the ground and followed him.

Sir Philip was sitting alone in the black and white marble hall. He had on some gold pince-nez and was examining some photogravures of Japanese porcelain. He rose as she entered and the man retired.

"This is indeed delightful of you," he said when they were alone. A powerful reading-lamp illumined the photogravures, but the rest of the room was dim, lighted only through the green shade on the lamp. He did not turn on more light, for he knew she liked it like this. He also knew at a glance that she came with some momentous purpose. She conveyed to him some telepathic excitement, stirring his pulses strangely. He pulled a chair into a more comfortable position facing the fire, and took her cloak from her. He then took a seat opposite to her and sat there looking at her like a large Newfoundland dog. She seemed to be trying to frame a sentence but she could not succeed. At last, to ease the situation, he remarked:

"It is a thousand pities that in this dear land of ours we have not acquired the habit which is so charming in Bohemia of making the petite visite after dinner. It is so much more sympathetic a time than in the raw hours of the afternoon. May I show you these excellent photogravures of some Kyoto ware?"

This speech seemed to release something in Olga, and she said rapidly:

"Sir Philip, I can't look at those to-night. I have something more urgent to say to you. I—"

She paused, and Sir Philip looked at her and slowly pulled his beard. Then he said:

"My dear lady, I do not want you to qualify your visit, that is all. For the rest, you know that I am ever tout a fait à votre service" and he shrugged his shoulders and waved his hands comprehensively. Then he smiled kindly and said:

"Tell me then, dear friend, in what way I may serve you?"

Olga looked at the fire, and then in a very low voice she answered:

"You may make me your wife."

There was a silence, broken only by the sound of the fountain playing in the adjoining courtyard. Olga continued gazing at the fire. She knew that his eyes were fixed on her and he was leaning forward as though unable to grasp the full significance of her statement. He started as though about to spring upon her, and then held himself back. He was trembling, but at last he said, in a voice that seemed almost charged with tears:

"Olga! is this true?" He stretched out and took her hand. She gave it, and tears streamed down her cheeks. Then she broke out and spoke in rapid, disjointed sentences.

"Don't misunderstand me, Sir Philip. You must think I 'm shameless. You have asked me, and I have come to you."

"My dear . . . my dear," he broke in.

"No, no," she cried excitedly. "We must understand each other first. You have asked me to be your wife, and I—accept. I will be your wife. I will—fulfil my part of the contract. You understand? In every way I will be your wife. But you know, you must know, it 's no question of love with me. I like you very much, you have been very kind, but I accept you because I 'm in great difficulty. I 'm thinking more of the boys than of myself. You will know what I mean. I mustn't be selfish, must I? . . . Will you accept me on these terms? I cannot do more. I cannot love you, but I will be your wife, I will be loyal to you. ... It seems dreadful to come to you like this. I am ashamed."

He gripped her hands as though in a vice, and said earnestly:

"Olga, I understand ... I understand, and I accept you. I will try and make you love me—"

She struggled in his hands, and said:

"Only, I want to make stipulations. Please forgive me ... I think you will understand. I don't want any honeymoon . . . nothing like that. Just to go on. I will come to you here, you see? I want to go on working, just doing things all the time. I will be your wife, only I 'm worried, do you understand? I don 't want to stop and think about things a lot. Perhaps one day we can travel, only not yet. I want to stop here and just go on. Perhaps we can send the boys to school, and then . . . Oh, my dear friend, I feel I 'm being mean to you, but—"

He pulled her to him and cried hoarsely:

"I understand ... I understand."

She allowed him to kiss her on the lips and she closed her eyes. Then she clutched the lapels of his coat and said:

"Oh, may I go now? Go away for a few days . . . Then I will come back. "We will perhaps be married in a registry office, and then go on just as though—as though we had been married a long time, as though it were quite a normal thing ..."

CHAPTER X

THE FURTIVE LOVERS

The wife of Cemray, the Academician, was giving a reception in honor of the visit of the famous French sculptor, Anton Vinas. The salons were crowded with luminaries from the artistic, social, and diplomatic world. Anton Vinas, a heavy, sensual-looking old man with a splendidly rugged head, was standing by the side of his hosts, and shaking hands with the guests as they were introduced to him. Sir Philip and Lady Ballater arrived rather late, and the room was very hot and crowded. Olga felt the pressure of the distinguished Frenchman's rather plump hand, and she was conscious of his approving glance that wandered from her face to her neck and shoulders. During these years she had indeed filled out, and though at that time only thirty-seven, she was beginning to develop that quality that people call "matronliness." Neither was this quality entirely a physical one. It was a satisfaction to her among the many acquaintances she met at the reception to talk about "her boys," and to inform them that Richard was leaving Harrow next term and going up to Oxford, and that Cedric played the violin "like an angel." And yet a close observer would have described Lady Ballater's normal expression as rather that of suppression than resignation. Her gray eyes were calm and serene, but strange lights still flashed in their unusual depths. The social life appealed to her even less than it did at the time when she was married to Harry Streatham, although she was at that time an undoubted social success. Women adored her, and men made love to her with tireless reiteration. The years had given her a certain savoir faire and an ability to cope with difficult situations with sympathy and understanding. She still worked at the piano, but she only played in public for charity; her view being that otherwise she would be taking the fees of professional musicians Who had to earn their own living. All her sympathies were with the people who worked, and she had started a society for registering and helping music teachers. A young under-secretary wrote to Emma in Scotland (on government official notepaper), and described her at that time in the following terms:

"I find your friend altogether adorable. She is the most beautiful person in the world. She moves with a curious and attractive grace. "When she looks at you you feel that nothing will ever matter again, and then when she speaks and smiles at you, you want it to matter ever so much. Her body is like a sounding-board of all the human emotions. She is charged with vivid intuitions and impulses. I have never met any one so unself-conscious, so quick to suffer and enjoy. Life is a tremendous business to her, torrential and overwhelming. How on earth did she happen to get married to that— Chinese mandarin? "

By which it may be observed that the young secretary's time and the government material should have been employed to more legitimate ends.

They wandered through the rooms, picking little scraps of conversation with people they knew. At last they worked their way back to the first room. It was very crowded, and she could not see the people near the door coming in, but she could hear the voice of the pompous butler announcing names with a sonorous dignity. For a moment she was alone and unattended. She stood against the wall and began to feel tired of the proceedings. She listened drowsily to the booming voice of the butler. Suddenly she started and almost cried out. Her agitation was caused solely by that voice. Could it be true? Amidst the drone of many names it had suddenly announced:

"Mr. John Braille."

Three large people in front of her were drawling in affected voices about futurism. Her husband had his back to her, and was laughing, an unusual act for him. She felt a sudden irritation, and a desire to push all these people rudely out of the way and go toward the door. It couldn't be true! It couldn't be true! It must be some mistake. The voice must have said some other name, or she was dreaming. She wished she could see. How abnormally large all these people seemed!

She stood there some moments—afraid, and trying to analyze her fear. If it were he? "What then? And why was he alone? She tried to lull her agitated feelings. Even if it were he, it would only be natural. Perhaps his wife had a headache—or a child? He would probably almost have forgotten her. They would meet and shake hands and pass on, and everything would be just the same as usual.

"You haven't been to see our new billiard-room yet, Lady Ballater."

A red-faced man with a head shaped like a horse was grinning at her. lie was the director of an insurance company and reputed to be enormously wealthy. His wife and three grown-up daughters were at the reception. She recollected having overheard some one say that "he was a cormorant with a penchant for married women." She muttered some excuse, and pushed her way into the background of an adjoining room that backed on to a conservatory. She still felt very frightened. Her eyes restlessly searched the room, and every one seemed intolerably platitudinous. Near the entrance to the conservatory a very old musical critic buttonholed her, and talked interminably about opera. He insisted on telling her the plot of a new German opera he had just heard in Leipzig, and describing the character of the music in detail. He was in the middle of the second act, and she remembered him saying:

"And then the fiddles have a very attractive theme, that is taken up by the wood wind. It is perhaps a little suggestive of the Meister singer, and equally redundant."

At that point she saw Braille. He was standing with his back to the wall, talking to a little man with curly hair and a monocle. His face was thinner than of yore but tanned by the sun, and the hair on his temples was quite gray. He looked straight at her, and his eyes glowed with the quiet light of understanding. She saw him apologizing to the little man and pushing his way through the crowd toward her. He had a stormy passage, buffeted and assailed by every one as he passed; but he kept his eyes fixed upon her, and came straight on. As he put out his hand to take hers, the musical critic was saying:

"The overture of the third act is a remarkable piece of scoring. The sense of climax is very skilfully managed, but I must say that in my opinion—"

Braille was holding her hand and looking into her eyes. She pulled him out of sound of the musical critic 's voice. The roar of conversation was so great that it was quite possible to hold an intimate conversation in the midst of it without the probability of being heard.

He said, "I came to-night because some one told me you would be here."

At the sound of his voice something seemed to contract within her, and for the moment she could not speak. She smiled at him, and her eyes were eloquent with amazement and delight. He continued:

"Yes, it is true. I know what you are thinking—I am a ghost! I died ten years ago. We are allowed sometimes to revisit the glimpses of the moon."

"Have you come back to finish the portrait?" she asked.

A boyish light came into his eyes and he tilted his head in a manner she knew so well, and looked at her keenly and shook his head.

"Ah! It was cruel of me to remember," she said, and added, "And next week my son goes to Oxford!"

"Your implication is a perverse one," he answered. "I have not come back to finish the portrait because my original reason for not being able to do so still holds good."

They looked at each other with shameless significance, and a gentleman with shiny cheeks standing by the door asked a friend "who the hatchet-faced man flirting with Lady Ballater was."

Suddenly they changed the timbre of their voices, and she whispered:

"Tell me about your wife."

Braille started, and she thought his lips became pale. He looked at her imploringly and answered:

"I 've never had a wife."

He thought for the moment she was going to faint, and he said:

"May I meet you, Olga? May I meet you and talk to you?"

The crowd seemed suddenly noisier and she was conscious of Sir Philip bringing up some one to introduce to her. She glanced round desperately and whispered:

"Meet me—by the flagstaff on Hampstead Heath tomorrow at seven o'clock in the evening."

He bowed and vanished. She impressed Lord Charles Wynsley, to whom her husband introduced her, as being "a perfect nincompoop. One of these damned women who say, 'Yes, yes,' and 'No, no.' Good Lord! why the hell did Sir Philip marry her? Not a bad-looking piece of stuff, in a way. Would be pleasant for a week-end trip on the river, but marriage! Pheugh! Never marry out of your class, dear boy!"

She feigned a headache after ten minutes' conversation with Lord Charles, and begged her husband to take her home. She passed a turbulent night, rocking with alternate hopes and fears. On the morrow the day took on the nature of a fantastic dream. It was a gray day in April, and a warm wind was blowing from the south-west. She had no recollection of how she got through the hours till seven o'clock; mostly by practising in fits and starts, and then going to the window and peering out.

It was nearly dark when she arrived under the flagstaff. She was conscious of the presence of furtive lovers. People strolled about in couples and became lost on the heath. For the moment she regretted the place of the appointment; it seemed sordid and unromantic.

"But after all," she thought, "why should I consider myself different from the others?"

He was standing there, erect and solemn like an Indian sentinel. She was conscious of him before she had seen him. He pressed both her hands and then walked a little way without speaking. She suddenly gripped his arm and said:

"I am in a fantastic mood, my friend. . . You must humor me. I told Sir Philip I was going out to dine with a girl friend. What shall we do?"

She could see his eyes glow in the dim light, and she felt the pressure of his hands.

"Let us walk," he said.

They went down into a hollow and up again and passed by some fir-trees. There were many people strolling about, and sitting very close to each other on seats and on the grass, which must have been damp. The constant meeting with these people made them both self-conscious, and they laughed about it uneasily after a while. Suddenly, as they were going round the bend of a sandy hillock, two people left a seat that was almost hidden against a fence.

"Let us sit here," said Olga, and she pulled him toward the seat. "You must remember that I was brought up in Canning Town," she added, by way of justification.

They sat side by side. Braille prodding the sand with his stick. He seemed unable to speak. At last she laughed and put her arm on his shoulder.

"Come," she said. "I have been so unhappy, so desolate . . . Humor my one fantastic night!"

"Ah!" he said with difficulty. "What must you think of me?"

She could see the drawn look on his face, and she whispered:

"What is it? Tell me."

"You asked about my wife." He looked at her, and she could not answer, but she nodded her head, and tried to convey the feeling that all was right with the world if only he would tell her.

"It would not be—you if you did not look at me like that, with forgiveness in your eyes, before you hear me," he said hoarsely.

"Oh, my dear!" she suddenly exclaimed, "the only thing the world has taught me is that there is never anything to forgive. Tell me—your experiences, your desires, if you like, only don't talk about forgiveness. Let me be more to you than that."

Braille started and seemed almost imperceptibly to hold himself back; then he leant forward on his knees and peering at the ground, he said:

"I want to tell you . . . everything exactly as it occurred to me. My father was a Puritan. He brought me up on a sort of Spartan system. I owe to him my strength and vigor of body and, I suppose, my moral bias. lie did not believe in beauty; at least, not as an integral part of one. The only beauty he believed in was the beauty of the sea at night when the wind raged . . . I believed in that too; I brought it to bear on my work. I sought truth in the most analytical manner, and tried to expose hypocrisies. I believed that the only issues worth fighting for were moral issues. I believed that one could lead one's life, if not divorced from all beauty, at least not in any way dependent upon it. One could take it in the way that one takes marmalade for breakfast. ... It is a curious thing that my meeting with you was not the cause of the sort of psychological upheaval that I went through at that time—you were rather the apotheosis of certain changes that had been started by something else. Do you know what it was that started them?—The Russian ballet at Covent Garden! I went in there one night quite casually, and before I came away I knew that life would never be the same to me again. I had never seen beauty expressed with such meaning and poignance. It was incredibly beautiful, and it went right through me. And it was neither moral nor unmoral, but it spoke to me of things greater than morality, the stuff that the fibers of life are made from. You asked me my desires. I tell you, my desire became at that time to have my life colored by beauty. And then you came."

Braille sighed, but he did not look at her, and he still prodded the ground with his stick.

"You were the most beautiful thing I had ever seen. You became to me the personification of the beauty of my dreams. Your image was always before me. Your eyes were between me and every action. I could not work. I could not think coherently. And I was afraid. It was not only that you were a married woman; it was something more than that. I desired you terribly. It was true that it was not only your body I desired, but I did desire your body. I was afraid of myself. If beauty were illusion! I went out alone into the country and wrestled with this thing. I thought of my father. I felt like a Japanese—what are those chaps called?—Samurai communing with the spirit of his ancestors. And at that hour my father spoke with no uncertain voice. I knew it was no good. I went back to the studio in Langham Place. There hung your unfinished portrait. This was going to be no chilling assertion of abstract truth. This was no 'Braille.' There was already about it something that frightened me. . . . You came again. And then—you remember the morning? Ah, God! I felt I was writing you that note with my own blood. I dashed away from you like a frightened animal, as so indeed I was. I went to Rome and Taormina, but I could not work. ... It was in Biskra, away out there in the desert, that the 'other thing' happened. I want to tell you about this, dear, all just exactly as it came about."

Olga leant forward, watching him intently through her half-closed eyes.

"I stayed out there in a small French hotel that had a roof garden from which one could see miles across the desert. I was very lonely there, and I could not work. The roof garden was my only joy. I used to sit there at night and watch the stars above the desert and breathe the warm air. It was amazingly beautiful. There were not more than half-a-dozen people in the hotel at that time. But there was a Spanish woman—at least, she was half Spanish and half French. She was tall and dark and had splendid e}es. I did not notice her at first. I noticed no one. I wanted to be alone, utterly alone in this ocean of sand. But I noticed after a time that she was always watching me and getting in my way. She tried to make conversation, and I believe I was rude to her. I really don't know. I was very distracted, and the sight of her irritated me. Then one night I was sitting on the roof. It was a wonderful night and the moon was up. The air was laden with the perfume of the oleanders. Some

Arabs were playing their tom-toms in the distance. It occurred to me that if I were in search of beauty I had at least discovered its setting. But my heart was aching for its central episode. Suddenly the girl came on to the roof. She had on a white frock. She passed close by me, and I saw her dark eyes looking at me furtively. She left a trail of some strange scent, and passed behind a clump of palms. I knew that she was beautiful, beautiful in a madly impersonal way, like the desert or the mango trees. She fitted in to the great scheme of things. I sat there a long time thinking. Beauty! . . . The strange Arab music penetrated me. A procession of heavily laden camels came hurrying across the desert. Something kept saying to me, 'The stars are fixed. For you—life and youth are slipping away.' On the morrow I felt more exhausted and sad. I wandered about and tried to paint. I passed the Spanish woman twice and on the second occasion I smiled at her. Three days and nights passed in this way. We said 'Good morning' and 'good night,' but nothing more. But I looked at her and gradually she moved me like a narcotic. On the third night there was no moon, but the air was warmer. I went up to the roof garden in a peculiar fever of excitement, and waited. It was very dark. I sat there a long time. In the distance a woman was singing some melancholy dirge. Then suddenly I saw the white dress appear and move slowly in my direction, pass by, and in the direction of the palms, leaving its trail of scent. I got up and followed her, and she turned. In the darkness I could just see her lazy eyes. We did not speak, not a word. I took her in my arms and kissed her silently on the lips. We went into the arbor enclosed by the palms . . .

"I hired a caravan the next day, and we went away together into the desert, attended by two Arabs. We lived there for three weeks. Ah, God! the desolation of those days and nights! Except for the mad hours when I clutched her in my arms I was more lonely than ever. The beauty that I sought was like a mirage that laughed at me across the sands. One cannot transubstantiate the central stuff of life. I felt like an outcast, a social leper. And always your eyes were before me, your eyes and the eyes of my father. But what could I do? I could not desert the woman after I had committed myself. She rallied me on my melancholy moods, and we went on to Algiers. From there we went to Nice and Bordighera, and then to Paris, and came over and spent a week in London. I fell into a state of moral apathy and just followed the woman about, doing as she bid me. For some reason we started out for India, but in Paris my immediate troubles were solved for me, for she left me to go and live with the son of a French deputy. She was quite frank about it. She said I had attracted her at first, but she had learnt to detest me. We parted quite good friends. . . .

"You may be surprised to know what I did next. I went to a town where I should not be likely to be known. I went to Lyons, and I lived in the poorest quarter of the town. I had suffered bitterly, and I felt an overwhelming desire to live among others who suffered. I gave up painting and I worked amongst the poorest of the poor. I lived in one room and did odd jobs for people. I found in the meanness and wretchedness of those streets something ennobling, and in the lives of the downtrodden something inspiring. I lived there nearly a year, and gradually my virility returned to me. My conception of beauty became mellowed. I found the salvation of suffering ..."

Olga leaned forward and touched his arm, and her eyes dilated.

"You have found that too!" she said in a low voice. They gazed at each other for some time, and then sat apart, looking up at the sky. At last she said: "Why did you go to the reception to see me?" "Partly caprice," he answered; "but I wanted one day to tell you everything."

"Where were you at the time of my divorce?"

"At Algiers. I did not hear about it till you were married to Ballater."

"And when you came to London, I missed you at the gallery by a few hours."

They sat silent; then Olga said bitterly: "The gods have not been very kind to you and me." There was another pause, during which she feasted her eyes on his drawn face. Suddenly she stood up in front of him and held out both her hands. He took them, and rose also. She went close up to him and spoke quickly:

"Listen, dear. I too am lonely. I don't know about all these things—morality and so on. I only know that in my life I have had the desire to do good, to help those that suffer, to be kind. I want to be of some service, but for the rest, I know nothing. I cannot understand that the world should talk of failure and success when there should only be 'understanding.' I had my wander-dream of passion, like you had. I too suffered bitterly. I too looked between the eyes of the poor and downcast."

Her face was very close to his and her cheeks were wet with tears. Suddenly she cried out:

"I cannot understand. I am sure of nothing. But I will tell you one thing."

"What is it?" he said hoarsely.

"If you would take me, I would come with you now—anywhere, to the ends of the earth!"

Braille started and his lips trembled.

"Olga!" he gasped. "I didn't come to tempt you."

"But I want you to tempt me. It is the only thing I understand, the only thing I am sure of—my love! I have been twice a wife, but I would come and be your mistress. Do you understand what I 'm saying? I say it 's the only thing I 'm sure of. I possess you already, I wear you in my heart day and night. What is the difference between that and what I ask? I care for nothing else. I gave my word of honor I would be loyal to my husband, but I have already broken that vow in my heart. I would sacrifice my honor for you, give you everything I possess, die for you! Oh, my dear, I know you understand me, and that is more to me than all the world."

They stood there held fast by the vibrant communion of their eyes. Suddenly he kissed her damp cheek, and then his arms were around her, and their lips met. She gave a little cry like a wounded animal, and hung limply in his arras, with her eyes closed. He kissed her again and again. A few paces away he heard people moving.

"Good God!" he muttered. "What are we doing!"

"We 're amidst the furtive lovers," she whispered, and she laughed weakly. He thought she was going to faint, and he helped her to a seat. Presently she said:

"This is madness! Oh, my dear, forgive me."

And Braille said:

"No, you are right. I should detest that more than anything—to be furtive. To carry on secret assignations, to always feel ashamed. You are right. Everything vital has already happened between us. Any other action would be a sham. My dear, I too wear you in my heart, and I shall claim you."

He kissed her again, and they moved away from the seat. She noticed that his coat was wet. And indeed a fine rain had been falling for nearly an hour. They stumbled across the heath in silence, he holding her arm.

"I believe I'm very hungry," she said suddenly. He laughed gaily, and looked at his watch by the light of a match. It was nine o'clock. They went to an hotel on the top of the heath, and caused considerable surprise by asking if it were possible to have dinner. The management was shocked and annoyed at this un-English request. After a lot of persuasion, however, they consented to give them some cold roast beef and pickles, with bread and cheese, in the coffee-room. They had the coffee-room to themselves, and they ate their beef and cheese, tremulously observant of each other. When the meal was finished, he said:

"When will you come to me?"

She thought for a moment, and answered:

"To-morrow."

She blushed and pushed her hair back with a rapid little motion of the back of the hand, and rose quickly. As they walked along the Spaniards Road, a regiment of boys passed with a drum-and-fife band. They were singing and waving their hats. Before they had passed Olga stopped suddenly and put her hand to her heart. Braille held her firmly and said:

"What is it, dear?"

She laughed uneasily, and answered:

"Oh, it's nothing! How silly of me! Only—some of those boys reminded me of my Richard."

The drum-and-fife band blared its gay and catching melody and the boys cheered as they passed the Whitestone pond. When the music had almost died away in the distance, Olga said:

"Will you put me into a cab, dear? "

They had to walk a little further before they found one, and they were both strangely silent. When the cab was discovered and she had been installed. Braille stood by the door and pressed her hand:

"To-morrow, then, at my rooms, at three o'clock."

"Yes, yes," she gasped in the faintest whisper. "Tomorrow!"

CHAPTER XI

THE LETTER

Braille stood for a long time at the spot where the cab had departed. He watched its scarlet rear-light flicker down the hill, and disappear.

"She has gone," he thought. "It is all over—the dream has vanished."

He walked a little way along the road and then dived down into the bracken. He walked rapidly through the rain, his jaw set with a grim determination. He tried to find the seat where they had sat before supper; but he missed it, and wandered on through the dark. "Tomorrow morning," he thought, "there will be a letter from her. She will have had time to see things clearer ... It will be all over."

It was getting late, and the furtive lovers had departed. He seemed to be alone on the heath. It was very cold. He looked toward the west where the drum-and-fife band had passed.

"The passing of youth!" he suddenly exclaimed to himself, and laughed bitterly. And then he thought, "If I did not know that she would write to-night, I should write myself. But she shall have the credit of— 'seeing clear'! It is all I have to give her." He strode on through the damp grass.

It was five o'clock in the morning when he let himself in at his rooms in Gyves Court. He was wet through. He had a bath and went to bed. But he did not sleep. He kept on visualizing the letter that would arrive at eight o'clock. At seven his man called him and brought a cup of tea. He drank it, and put on a dressing-gown, and sat up in bed waiting for the letter. It seemed an interminable time till the post came. At last he heard the click of the box and the sharp rat-tat. He nearly leapt out of bed and rushed for it, but some ingrained instinct kept him fixed to the bed. He smiled faintly when he heard the slow ponderous steps of Robeson coming along the passage to take the letter out of the box.

"The fool!" he thought. "If he only knew!"

Listening to the languid movements of Robeson taking the letters out of the box, and going slowly to the dining-room to fetch a silver tray, the story flashed through his mind of the man who was condemned to death, but the date and hour of his death were kept from him. He suffered unspeakable agonies of terror till suddenly one day, in a flash, he realized that after all his fate was only that of the rest of humanity!

"After all," thought Braille, "it will make no difference. I should have written if she hadn't."

Robeson tapped on the door with well-modulated restraint. He entered, and walked slowly towards the bed, holding out the tray. Braille's eyes were glued on the letter. There it was; the top one! He took it in his hand, and Robeson said in his pensive voice:

"Which suit will you wear to-day, sir? I 'm afraid you were caught in the rain last night."

Braille looked at him calmly and said, "My blue one, Robeson."

Robeson went with incredible deliberation to the wardrobe, lie sighed, and took down the suit from its stretcher. He spread it out with a lingering affection. Then he returned to the wardrobe, and routed with a superb dignity among the drawers for shirt, pants, and collar. He took all these things and placed each one separately and lovingly in a convenient place for Braille to get at. And at the same time, he told Braille of a calamity that had happened to the lift-boy's mother. It was an involved and unpleasant story, an affair of deception and alcoholic excess. Braille looked at him without listening. He was almost mesmerized by the man's amazing deliberation. He held the letter in his hand, and kept turning it over. "When Robeson had finished the story, Braille said:

"After all, Robeson, it won't make any difference, will it?"

"I beg your pardon, sir?" exclaimed the faithful attendant.

Braille looked at the letter and sighed. How adorably childish her writing was! large and straggling, and full of character. He said peremptorily:

"All right, Robeson, I can manage."

"Very good, sir!"

He was alone in the room, with the sheets of the letter trembling in his hand. He touched the sacred document with his lips, and read:

Oh, my dear, if I had been taught to pray I would pray tonight that I might have the power to tell you what is in my heart. I somehow feel that you will expect this letter, that you will know all the time what I am going to say, as I believe I know what you are feeling. Oh, it was madness this dream of ours!

I am a wanton, a thousand times worse than the Spanish woman at Biskra. I shall always hate myself that I tempted you. Nothing can alter that! I tempted you! I should have destroyed you! I know now that God never meant us to be lovers. We are more like two ships tossed on the great sea, and making for the same port. Oh, my dear, I want always to hold that memory of you as I saw you last night when you told me your story. I want to see those dear eyes of yours, and all that fine-drawn quality of your face that is just—you. I want to believe in you always as the one thing that has given life meaning to me. I want to think of you, strong, splendid, and triumphant. It has been a struggle of perversity; let us win out now to the end. If I may know that you are just there, somewhere in some great city, sometimes thinking of me, and always alive to suffering, expressing yourself, and fighting for what you represent—I somehow believe I can—go on. I did not know that love could reveal so much. All these people who have wandered through my life—I have seen them pass like a pageant—but you—I have found you in my heart revealing a world of infinite meaning. You have taught me to love—not merely you but all that you are. You have made me love myself, and the barbs and arrows that pierce me when I banish you. It is the supremest sacrifice that we can make, dear, isn't it? I feel strong to-night, and I think I can do this thing, but only if I may always hold the image of you in my heart when you said, "Olga, I did not come here to tempt you." Let us go on then, and perhaps one day, when we reach the great port, we may find each other side by side.

Olga.

Braille turned the letter over in his hand, and read it again and again. Then he continued staring at it, and turning it over without reading. At last he gripped it firmly but tenderly in his right hand, and buried his face in the pillow.

The marble room seemed strangely silent. The murmur of the fountain died away to a whisper. She sat there in the small Japanese recess, with some work upon her lap, listening. By her side was a large inlaid mahogany bird-cage with gilt wires. In the cage was a black Central-American macaw. He sat on his perch, with his small head hunched between his shoulders, and his little dark eyes were fixed upon her. He too seemed to be listening intently. Facing her was a mirror set in an ebony frame. It was set at such an angle that by leaning forward she could just see the reflection of her husband's profile behind the portiere. He had on his thick pince-nez, and his eyes were fixed in an ice-cold contemplation of three valuable Chinese pots upon the table in front of him. They had arrived that morning. His hands were resting on one of them, feeling the glaze. She did not move.

She knew that it was an hour when he did not like to be disturbed. She sometimes wondered whether his china was not more to him than—all the world. He seemed at times so much a part of it. And of late these periods of silence that had always been characteristic of him had become more pronounced and more prolonged. He would sit immobile by the hour, surrounded by the priceless pottery, appearing less like a man than like a frigid statement of humanity, a thing fixed and finished. On this afternoon his face had flushed at the arrival of the pots. He had seemed for the moment elated and gay. He had stroked them, and then carried them away to his lair like a jungle-cat. She remembered him saying, "The Chinese, my dear, are creators, the Japanese—imitators." He had looked at them long and earnestly, and then he had gradually settled down to his turgid contemplation. She knew by experience that to disturb him at such times was both dangerous and inexpedient. He would be strangely sulky and morose, and would look at her in a way that terrified her. His eyes would appear slightly bloodshot, and he would hardly seem to know her.

They had not been married three months before she discovered his secret. The flushed cheeks, and the bright eyes, the clear and brilliant conversation, and then the sudden mood of utter depression and apathy. She could not understand this till one day when he retired to his dressing-room, and slept from lunch-time till nearly half-past six, and she had become alarmed. She had gone in, and by the side of the couch she had found a little phial, and a glass with a strangely sweet and penetrating odor.

The affair had terrified her, and she had waited till he was normal. She was not the woman to leave a thing like that alone. She had gone down on her knees to him and begged him to think of her. She had conjured every form of persuasion she could contrive to save him. It had been terrible. Even now she could see the ghastly, hunted look on his face, and hear the weak laugh. He had tried to be candid with her, was a man for a few moments. He had suddenly clutched her hands, and said, "Ah, God! if I had met you fifteen years ago!"

Fifteen years! Then she too felt self-conscious and ashamed. He made her feel that she had been loyal to nothing, not even an idea. She had helped no one, saved no one, been no one's companion. She had compromised with opportunity, followed her impulses, and lived for herself. Inside she had always yearned for something finer and greater, some chance of expressing what was best in herself, but always she seemed the slave of compromise, unable to cope with the unpitying conditions that social life imposed on her. Fifteen years! This man, who was now her husband, must have had similar experiences. lie was cleverer than she, more intellectual, and yet he found life insupportable, so insupportable that he found escape in what the Easterners had called "the little window of the night." He was destroying himself, and she could not save him. He had said, "If I had met you fifteen years ago!"

But she knew that if she had met him fifteen years ago, she would not have saved him. She did not love him, and she could never have loved him. Under the stress of various emotions, and a very definite social difficulty, she had compromised again with herself. She had said, "It is finished." He had deceived her by not telling her about the drugs. And she had deceived him by pretending to herself that "it was finished," when she knew in her heart of hearts that she was yearning for the love of another man. They had drifted together like two straws in the maelstrom of social life, having only in common a certain kindred appreciation of esthetic values; admiring in each other the other's sensibilities. He was always kind to her, considerate, and courteous—except in the lapses when he did not remember his own behavior, and even then he was never brusk; only sullen and obtuse . . .

The macaw shuffled a little nearer to her on his perch, and turned his dark eyes obliquely toward her.

"What is it, Jacky?" she said quietly. "What is the matter?"

And so it would go on. The day would pass, and other days; and then she would become old. She did not care to think of this, and she fumbled with a letter on the work-table. It was from Richard at Oxford. It enclosed a press-cutting, with a sentence underlined in ink:

Young Streatham at three-quarters also played a good game, tackling low, and having a very safe pair of hands.

She smiled with pleasure as she read this. It was nice to think that perhaps on this gray afternoon "Young Streatham" was distinguishing himself. She could see his eager young face, his bright eyes, his muddy clothes, and those swift young legs racing across a damp field, hugging a ball.

Richard was growing up. He was n 't exactly clever, but he was a very lovable boy. Everybody adored him. He had a certain rugged philosophy too. She remembered during the last vacation she had been talking to him in a tentative manner about—what one owes to one's neighbor, and he had suddenly laughed and said:

"Oh, life isn't a thing that requires justifying. Mother. It 's an experience to be lived!"

She liked the way he said that, and she often wondered whether it were true. He would grow up and go out into the world. He would probably leave her, but it would all have been very wonderful. "An experience to be lived!"

"What is it, Jacky?"

The bird suddenly behaved in a strange manner. It fluttered all over its body and cowered into the corner of the cage. Its small head seemed to be trembling and craning forward. She followed the line of the eye. It was fixed upon the mirror opposite. Automatically she looked into the mirror. She could still just see Sir Philip's profile. It appeared more rigid than ever, like the face of a porcelain god. The room was getting darker. She thought she would go up to her room, but she became aware of the bird behaving in an even more remarkable manner. It gave a little cry and looked at her, and huddled itself together and trembled violently.

She said, "Jacky, Jacky, what is it?"

But the bird continued trembling. Suddenly a curious feeling of concern came over her. She thought she had never felt that room to be so utterly silent. She could not hear the fountain. Everything seemed incredibly still. She peered forward into the mirror. Sir Philip had not moved. She could not account for the feeling of terror that suddenly came over her. She stood up and called out in a low voice:

"Philip!"

There was no answer, and she moved silently and quickly through the marble room. She knew that she was trembling violently herself, and was conscious that she raised her voice to a louder pitch:

"Philip! Philip!"

And the silence seemed more terrifying than before.

THE ROOF OF PURBECK STONE

The pallid stars had given up their vigil of the incomprehensible city, and had slunk back into the sky. The dawn was heralded in by fitful gusts of rain that beat against the window. Braille caught hold of the hasp and peered out into Gyves Court. His face was pale, but lighted by an exultant gladness.

"If you were to ask me what are the seven wonders of the world," he said, "to be candid, I could not tell you. But if you were to ask me what is the greatest wonder in the world, I should say—the laughter of children! Nobody but a Frenchman could have coined that ridiculous paraphrase, 'Man proposes, woman disposes.' We all know in our hearts that men and women can propose what they like;—all the 'disposing' is done by children. They are the masters of the world. There is nothing to prevent men and women playing ducks-and-drakes with the whole cosmic equation, except that when they meet together, in some dim chamber, and mumble the conspiracy of their turgid desires, suddenly above their heads they hear the patter of little feet, and the crash of that free and splendid laughter. Strange, is n't it? how seldom one hears a man or woman really laugh—freely, frankly, splendidly! And when we do hear such a one, we know that he or she has retained some vision of the 'trailing clouds' that makes us envious."

He drummed on the panes, and then turned suddenly to me, and said:

"I think you will like my place at Rading. It is in rather a jolly position on a bend of the downs, just eight and a half miles from the sea. I had some fun with it. I bought some old Purbeck stone from a builder at Lewes. It came from a monastery that had been destroyed. I used it for roofing, and the fact was—there was much too much of it. I added a wing to the farmhouse, and built an absurdly large studio. It is true I abolished the pigs, but I extended the stables, and built a ridiculous sort of archaeological museum—stuff picked up on the downs. I really did it all to use up this Purbeck stone. It will amuse you to see what a 'roofy' place it is. It looks very jolly, though, especially looking down on it coming by the road from Lewes. Posterity will probably write me down as a great archaeologist and authority on Sussex history, whereas I simply did it to use up the stone, and also to help a young chap I know who really is an authority. It was just caprice!

"Do you ever allow your mind to dwell upon the vagaries of Caprice? It is the flicker of the eyelid that controls the balance when the irresistible force meets the immovable mass. By caprice the king turns aside on some unusual path, and meets the beggar-maid. He looks into her eyes, and lo! a new aristocracy is born! and people call it—evolution! By caprice this Uncle Grubhofer went one day to a concert in Liverpool—you should know the result better than I! Do you remember, Tony, that mad night two years ago when in a capricious mood you left some unholy function and ran into me at the corner of Jermyn Street? and we sat here—the slaves of some whimsical good—and we talked of some one and of her life, and you told me of your desire to 'set it down'? I got the better of you over that, you wretched quill-driver! I warned you how it would be! When you start trying to see a life in pattern form you soon realize that no life is a complete thing in itself. You are marooned! But come! It will be grand up on the downs to-day, it 's always at its best when the sea is beaten up like churned milk, and the rain is driving in your face, and the sea-cats go shrieking before the wind. When you see my Purbeck roof and all that it covers, you will have a moment of revelation, you will understand what my old friend Paes meant by 'apotheosis,' perhaps you will even know why I painted 'The Mother' . . . All these things will be good for you to see, they will emphasize how much superior a painter is to a mug who 'sets things down.' What else shall I tell you? What more of my foolishness and horror? . . . When the hair of the world turned gray in a night, mine was already gray. The horror of it! When Europe picked up sides and decided to destroy itself, I visited a gentleman in Whitehall. Ye Gods! You talk of my 'little visions,' Tony, I have none more vivid than that! That little gray-faced man with a receding beard who glanced at me and said 'You 're too old for the sea!' Too old for the sea! The lying, bleary-eyed huckster! Then may the edifices of Humanity crumble in the dust! Look at my torso! feel my forearm, Tony! Too old for the sea! . . .

"I was at Maggis Square when the boy went. You remember it was the house she moved to after Sir Philip's death. I hovered in the background like a specter. I felt at moments I had no right to be there, and at other moments that I had every right, that I possessed the whole show, as it were; that I was the only real person in it. You know how sometimes when things are happening of tremendous moment to oneself, they are apt to take on a fantastic appearance, as though they were the actions of other people who had lived long ago, and were being reflected on a screen. . . .

"One thing was very clear, an unstated fact that we all knew, and shared, and said nothing about. You see, the boy was only just over seventeen. He had lied to the authorities, and made out he was nineteen. He looked ridiculously young—a mere baby. No one could have been deceived. Olga had only to go down to the War Office and denounce him, and he would have been restored to her. I had hinted at this very vaguely one day, and I saw her troubled expression. She had said nothing. On this day while he was up-stairs, I looked at her again, with this suggestion on my lips, but somehow I had not the heart to express it. I knew that she knew of what I was thinking. She put her hand on my arm, and shook her head very slowly. Somewhere in the distance a cornet struck a bizarre note. The boy came down the stairs. He was ready. He looked fresh, gay, and excited. He was splendidly handsome, with his father's eyes and bearing, but with that determined chin of his mother's, and something of her atmosphere. His clothes fitted him perfectly, and he looked taller and broader than he really was.

"The Minotaur of War likes them like that, brilliant, joyous, and bewilderingly young, with that glad, virginal, elevated expression of the eyes. Tempting morsels! My heart almost stopped as I saw him standing there in the hall, and his mother gazing at him, afraid to go and throw her arms around him . . .

"I think of all the emotions of humanity there is none quite so—what shall I call it?—distinguished? —as the love of a mother for a grown-up son. It has lost something of its primitiveness and has become tempered with a finely-wrought quality of mysticism, as though she had looked between the eyes of a god, and assisted at so profound a miracle that the world should ever after remain a place for the contemplation of her act. The boy, of course, was blustering, and 'bucking his mother up ' when he kissed her good-by. I had not the courage to tear myself away. I tell you, Anthony, I felt ashamed. The love that I held in my two hands seemed to crumble, to be a poor thing, unworthy to flash in the presence of this virile sorrow. The dreary note of the cornet in some far-away street seemed to jeer at me, and say:

"'You have no place in this. It is the sweet breath of Youth that the gods demand.'

"I turned and looked out into the street. I heard her kiss him, and murmur:

"'My dear . . . my dear!'

"She did not cry, and her eyes had that splendid, impassioned look that filled them at great moments.

She held him from her, and looked at his eyes and hair lingeringly, as though she were impressing on her mind an eternal picture. Then she looked down. The boy was brave enough, and he said—I 've forgotten what, but it seemed the right thing, and he swung out into the street. She stood by the door, and watched him go. As he turned the corner of the street, and waved for the last time, one might almost have thought from her expression that she was welcoming him home, her smile was so radiant, and her face so young and flushed with pride. When he had gone at last, she shut the door, and stood for some moments looking at the peg where his hat had hung. Then she swayed slightly, and walked along the hall into the back of the house.

"You know how the houses are built in that square. There are three rooms, and a kitchen, on the ground floor, and a yard at the back. As women will in such moments, she immediately busied herself with her hands. I didn't exactly notice what she did, but I followed her into the kitchen. None of the maids were there. She walked across the kitchen, and picked up a—teapot, I think it was. She shook it, and stood indecisively in the middle of the kitchen for a second. And then a very remarkable thing happened. I hardly know how to tell you about it, Anthony, it may seem to you trivial and inconsequential, but to me it was the most poignant moment I have ever experienced. As she stood there at that moment, a starling fluttered through the yard at the back, and gave forth three long deep notes. She started, and tiptoed to the table flap in front of the window, and looked up at the starling with an expression of amazed delight. She leant forward, and her lips were parted. The starling continued his song. I cannot tell you how that moment affected me.

"Think of it! At that poignant hour crystallizing the wayward sorrows of her life, she turned aside and listened to the song of a bird! With her heart crushed by the perversities of fate, she gazed dumbly, reverently, like a child looking up at an apple-tree on a morning in spring. Everything from the moment of her birth had conspired to crush that quality in her, but it had triumphed! and I thanked God that I was there to see.

"Neither heredity, environment, nor the tyranny of saints or sinners, the material calls of artificial fame, or superficial love, neither despair, disappointment, outrage, death, or sorrow had by one hair 's-breadth disturbed the serenity of that great soul; nay! it meant more than that, for I knew that as she turned and looked at me, out of her great love of me that came burning from her eyes there arose the breath of something greater, more impersonal, divine. Greater than love, greater than honor, greater than death, the power of a soul to renew itself, to look at life 'like a child.' They could not crush this in her, for they had not the power. I could not crush it in her if I had wished, for I had not the power. I could only see her at a distance, intangible and eternal like a star . . .

"Then she came to me, and I went down on my knees. I don't know what I said—something in the nature of what I have been telling you. I tried to express to her how I felt, but she still seemed far away. My head was against her bosom, and her lips were upon my brow, those lips of which I had dreamt for twenty years and more—they were mine, given to me, and my arms were around her, and yet she seemed so far away, as though it had all happened long ago. I tell you, I do not know what I said, but suddenly some phrase of mine gripped her, and she clung to it, as though it were the sanctuary of all her sorrows. Across the years she seemed to come back to me, and we stood there side by side, listening to the notes of the starling...."

STACY AUMONIER – A SHORT BIOGRAPHY

Stacy Aumonier was born at Hampstead Road near Regent's Park, London on 31st March 1877.

He came from a family with a strong and sustained tradition in the visual arts; sculptors and painters.

In 1890 the teenage Aumonier attended Cranleigh School in Surrey. Although he would later write critically about English public schools (with articles for the London Evening Standard and New York Times) in how they tried to impose conformity on students, records indicate that he integrated well into Cranleigh. Aumonier was a passionate cricket player, belonged to the Literary and Debating Society, and, in his final year, became a prefect.

On leaving school it seemed the family tradition of the visual arts would be his career path. In particular his early talents were that of a landscape painter. He exhibited paintings at the Royal Academy in 1902 and 1903, and 1908. An exhibition of his work would later be held at the Goupil Gallery in London in 1911.

In 1907 he married the international concert pianist, Gertrude Peppercorn, at West Horsley in Surrey. She herself was the daughter of a landscape painter (Arthur Douglas Peppercorn, occasionally cited as 'the English Corot'.) A son, Timothy, was born in 1921.

A year after his marriage, Aumonier began a brief career in a second branch of the arts at which he enjoyed outstanding success—as a stage performer writing and performing his own sketches.

The Observer newspaper commented that "...the stage lost in him a real and rare genius, he could walk out alone before any audience, from the simplest to the most sophisticated, and make it laugh or cry at will."

In 1915, Aumonier published a short story 'The Friends' which was well received (and voted one of the best short stories of 1915 by the Boston Magazine, Transcript).

Despite his age being 40 in 1917 he was called up for service in World War I. He began as a private in the Army Pay Corps, and then transferred as a draughtsman in the Ministry of National Service.

By now he had four books published—two novels and two books of short stories—and his occupation is recorded with the Army Medical Board as 'author.'

In the mid-1920s, Aumonier received the shattering diagnosis that he had contracted tuberculosis. In the last few years of his life, he would spend long spells in various sanatoria, some better than others. In a letter to his friend, Rebecca West, written shortly before his death, he described the debilitating conditions in a sanatorium in Norfolk during the winter of 1927, where the dampness was so severe that a newspaper left beside the bed would feel "sodden to the touch in the morning."

Shortly before his death, Stacy Aumonier sought treatment in Switzerland, but died of the disease in Clinique La Prairie at Clarens beside Lake Geneva on 21st December 1928. He was 55.

Whilst Aumonier's works are now slowly coming back into circulation at the time of his death his works were extremely popular and his loss was a profound tragedy for literary society.

The chief fiction critic of The Observer, Gerald Gould wrote: "His gifts were almost fantastically various; they embraced all the arts; but it was the charm and generosity of his personality which made him—what he unquestionably was—one of the most popular men of his generation." It went on: "The things he wrote will be remembered when the company of his friends (no man had more friends, or more devoted and admiring) are with him in the grave; but just now, to those who knew him, the thing most vividly present is the charm and wisdom of the man they knew."

Of his general appearance and manner Gerald Cumberland gives us this interesting set of observations: "A distinguished man, this—distinguished both in mind and appearance. Self-conscious. Perhaps. Why not? His hair is worn a trifle long, and it is arranged so that his fine forehead, broad and high, may be fully revealed. Round his neck is a very high collar and a modern stock. When in repose, his face has a look of shy eagerness; his quick eyes glance here and there gathering a thousand impressions to be stored up in his brain. It is the face of a man extremely sensitive to external stimulus; one feels that his brain works not only rapidly, but with great accuracy. And at heart, he takes himself and his work seriously, though he likes on occasion to pretend that he is only a philanderer."

In literary terms Aumonier was amongst the best short story writers these shores have produced.

The Nobel Prize winning author John Galsworthy called him "A real master of the short story. The first essential in a short-story writer is the power of interesting sentence by sentence. Aumonier had this power in prime degree. You do not have to 'get into' his stories. He is especially notable for investing his figures with the breadth of life within a few sentences." Galsworthy asserted that Aumonier "is never heavy, never boring, never really trivial; interested himself, he keeps us interested. At the back of his tales, there is belief in life and a philosophy of life, and of how many short story writers can that be said? ...He follows no fashion and no school. He is always himself. And can't he write? Ah! Far better than far more pretentious writers. Nothing escapes his eye, but he describes without affectation or redundancy, and you sense in him a feeling for beauty that is never obtruded. He gets values right, and that is to say nearly everything. The easeful fidelity of his style has militated against his reputation in these somewhat posturing times. But his shade may rest in peace, for in this volume, at least he will outlive nearly all the writers of his day." In summing his up Galsworthy suggested that, through his stories, he would "outlive all the writers of his day."

James Hilton (author of Goodbye, Mr Chips and Lost Horizon) said "I think his very best works ought to be included in any anthology of the best short stories ever written." He cited 'The Octave of Jealously' as his favourite short story for the March 1939 edition of Good Housekeeping saying it was a "bitterly brilliant tale."

Rebecca West said of his writing in 1922 that his ability to blend reality with the imaginary was "the envy of all artists."

STACY AUMONIER – A CONCISE BIBLIOGRAPHY

More than 87 short stories in more than 25 magazines, and in 6 volumes published during Aumonier's lifetime.

Among more than 20 other magazines, his work appeared in Argosy Magazine, John O' London's Weekly, The Strand Magazine and The Saturday Evening Post, as well as being anthologized, and adapted for film and television.

Short Story Collections

The Golden Windmill & Other Stories (1921)
The Friends & Other Stories (1917)
Miss Bracegirdle & Other Stories (1923)

Novels

Olga Bardel (1916)
Three Bars Interval (1917)
Just Outside (1917)
The Querrils (1919)
One After Another (1920)
Heartbeat (1922)

Other Works

A volume of 14 Character Studies: Odd Fish (1923)

A volume of 15 Essays: Essays of Today and Yesterday (1926)

www.ingramcontent.com/pod-product-compliance
Lightning Source LLC
Chambersburg PA
CBHW060119260626
47160CB00005B/1941